Plain Seeing

Also by Sandra Scofield

A Chance to See Egypt
Opal on Dry Ground
More Than Allies
Walking Dunes
Beyond Deserving
Gringa

Plain Seeing

A NOVEL

Sandra Scofield

Cliff Street Books
An Imprint of HarperPerennial
A Division of HarperCollins*Publishers*

Grateful acknowledgment is made to the following for permission to quote from copyrighted material:

"Separation," from *The Moving Target* copyright © 1960, 1961, 1962, 1963 by W. S. Merwin. Reprinted by permission.
"After Your Death," from *Waving from Shore*, by Lisel Mueller. Copyright © 1989 by Lisel Mueller. Reprinted by permission of Louisiana State University Press.

A hardcover edition of this book was published in 1997 by Cliff Street Books, an imprint of HarperCollins Publishers.

HarperCollins books may be purchased for educational, business, or sales promotional use. For information please write: Special Markets Department, HarperCollins Publishers, Inc., 10 East 53rd Street, New York, NY 10022.

First HarperPerennial edition published 1998.

Designed by Joseph Rutt

The Library of Congress has catalogued the hardcover edition as follows:

Scofield, Sandra Jean, 1943–
   Plain seeing : a novel / Sandra Scofield. — 1st ed.
     p. cm.
   ISBN 0-06-017342-4
   I. Title.
  PS3569.C584P58   1997
  813'.54—dc21   97-5848

ISBN 0-06-092945-6 (pbk.)

98 99 00 01 02 ❖/RRD 10 9 8 7 6 5 4 3 2 1

In memory
of my mother and grandmother

And for my daughter

*Not to see more than is there, we learn from photographs, is to see
more than enough.*

WRIGHT MORRIS

Your absence has gone through me
Like thread through a needle.
Everything I do is stitched with its color.

W. S. MERWIN, "SEPARATION"

ACKNOWLEDGMENTS

I am deeply grateful to Aunt Mae (since Day One) and Mary Economidy for ideas that were crucial to my story. I thank Jack Fuhs (lost and found) and Jennifer Carr for valuable information and suggestions, and my new sister, Sherry, for the Gallup High School oral history journals. Thanks to Bonnie Comfort for writerly empathy, and to Meaghan Dowling for her steady, sure management of the manuscript. I thank both Oregon Literary Arts and the Oregon Arts Commission for travel grants.

I am especially grateful to Jessica for so many late-night consultations. I am indebted to my patient and perspicacious editor, Diane Reverand, to my husband, Bill Ferguson (like breathing). And always, I thank my agent and friend, Emma Sweeney.

CONTENTS

EMMA LAURA'S BOOK
1938–1943

"The dream started when she understood that she was beautiful."
DORIS GRUMBACH, *The Missing Person*

The photograph was taken on a Sunday in May 1938, in the small farming community of Aileen, Texas, east of Lubbock. There were actually two photographs, but only one was given to the family. The one I have in mind was unremarkable, although the quality of its print was good. It was taken on an uneventful occasion, the work of a boy learning his craft.

The photograph has no real edges; it bleeds off the page, arbitrarily bound by its oval frame, which seems to be, as much as anything, a reminder that what is inside the frame has been severed from everything that existed outside. It is plain, and something about its tones—it is black and white, of course—gives it a feeling of candor, as if it was taken by someone completely honest, with nothing to prove except that the camera saw what it saw. As if the arrangement—and the gift—of the photograph was reciprocal. We think of these things now, if we think of them at all, as commonplace, and amateur. Point-and-shoot, we call it. The camera can do it all. We only have to be present, to grasp the opportunity. We simply try to get everyone in the frame, to avoid red eyes and shadows. Our children will decide if we took enough care. All our photographs will be in color.

I saw the one photograph—the "successful" one—hundreds of times in my childhood. It hung in my grandmother's homes, always on what passed for the hallway in those overcrowded dollhouses. I don't

3

remember ever asking about it, nor did I ever hear anyone comment on it, though once I saw my grandmother standing in front of it, one finger touching the glass. I couldn't see who it was she reached out to; I don't suppose it occurred to me to wonder. If I thought anything at all, it was how curious and simple they all were, how old-fashioned and outgrown, how forgotten. I thought they looked stunned and limp. I was a child with an inclination toward contempt. I thought the world in books was so much superior to our own. I was often accused of sullenness, but more often I was coaxed into my family's fellowship. My unhappiness, unlike my mother's, was viewed as innocent and curable. Over the years, this part of my disposition faded; it became mere distance. I filled the space with yearning. I couldn't pretend that I disdained the dreams of others. I could only try to hold my own close, where pity would not reach me. At forty-five years of age, I was still being asked, "Why the long face?" but at least I couldn't be ridiculed for reaching too high. All that I longed for was secret. It took me a long time to learn that my buffer of privacy and pride was easily read as that same childish contempt. I was always to be the child in the hall, impatient and solitary and ever misunderstood.

Fifty-odd years later, paired with its peculiar twin, the photograph has taken on a certain melancholy significance, as plain words and plain pictures sometimes do. Everyone in the photograph is dead, except the younger of the girls. I remember thinking, a few moments after the surprise of its discovery, that the moment captured in the photograph—the second one, with the shut eyes and whipped-away cap—was a perished moment, and yet it belonged, somehow, to that little town of Aileen, to the history of the region, and of course to me. Until I saw the second photograph, I did not know the moment existed. Until then, I believe, none of the people in it were real to me. For all my education and training, for all my "sense of history," I figured on a world that began with me. Before that was chaos and myth, and stories I had not been told or did not bother to hear.

I was born on August 5, 1943, in Wichita Falls, Texas. There were no snapshots that day. The first time a camera was available to record my presence, I was five months old. A good-looking corporal from Chicago, based at Shepard Air Force Base, had come with his Kodak to spend the day with my mother. (No one remembers how they met, but not long before she died, my grandmother lamented my mother's refusal to marry the young man, saying, "He adored her. He had fine manners." In fact, his mother wrote my mother a letter and warned her, "Dub is a selfish boy." Somehow, the letter was saved through all the years, when hardly anything that mattered was. I'm certain it had nothing to do with my mother's choices.)

Anyway, on that day my grandmother made silly faces to make me laugh, then took a photo of me with my mother and the visitor, and after, another of me with my young uncle, Amos, who was an astonishingly handsome boy.

None of which really matters to what I wish to do here. I only mean to say: I exist. More, I *survive*. I have chosen to tell this story now, and so it is *this* story, and not the one I might have written at twenty, or thirty, or sixty. Until I do this, my own life makes no sense to me, as if, without the history before me—my mother's history—I cannot begin my own. What follows is a story about the time between that windy day in West Texas—the day of the photograph— and the day I was born. The story isn't really mine to tell, but who else is there to tell it? The key people are dead, and those who might know something—might know any of the "truth"—have forgotten as much as they remember. Just let's say this is about a woman who lost one voice and image and took on, or accepted, another. The least she should have is a story.

AILEEN, TEXAS

The Good Faith Church of God was something like a white clapboard garage—boxy and long, with pews instead of cars. It had a peaked roof, two double-width doors, and steps that ran the width of the front. It was not the church either Ira or Frieda Clarehope would have chosen, given first preference. Frieda was raised Lutheran, but the nearest Lutheran church was nine miles away, and they no longer had a car or a team of horses. Ira's father was a Methodist minister in Chickasha, Oklahoma, and Ira had grown up singing hymns and praises, the only time he lifted his voice. In Aileen, though, there were hard-shell Baptists, the kind to turn their backs on a sinner, when anyone, Ira's father had often said, could slide from God and need a prayerful community to bring him back. So the Clarehopes belonged to this independent fellowship, and found it good enough for the sharing of these Sunday mornings, respite from hard labor and distress, and reason enough for a scalding scrub and their best clothes.

Emma Laura Clarehope, who would turn thirteen in June, craved the society of Sundays, and prayed as if she meant it, earnest to be

6

seen. She liked this time best, when the congregation spilled out onto the packed-dirt yard, and they all paused to visit for a few minutes before going home to midday dinner. The young children ran about, tagging one another and shouting, letting out their capped energy. The older girls posed a little, in case someone took the trouble to look. They wore sandals or low-heeled pumps and socks with their Sunday dresses. The boys, in overalls or blue jeans with stiff clean shirts, stood in closed clusters like football players in a huddle.

It was an unusually pleasant spring day, neither hot nor cold, and though people, by habit, looked both north and south for signs of weather, and though there was the faint odor of dust in the air, the sky was a calm rinsed blue color, with long fingers of white clouds. A month ago, two days of summer heat had been followed by a sand-storm, then a norther—four inches of snow! Last week there had been heavy rain, when what they needed was planting weather. No one had long out of mind the memory of a hundred storms, the worst on a Sunday in 1935, when the eerie silence had been broken by the wild chatter of birds on the ground, and then a black boiling blizzard had rolled over and turned day to night. Everyone on the plains remembered where they were that day. Frieda Clarehope and her children had been in Oklahoma, living in the old settler's cabin, a sod house, on Frieda's stepfather's farm. Ira had been working for the Santa Fe railroad, somewhere out in Arizona. He had had his family with him for a short while before, living in a boxcar, follow-ing the section gang working the tracks, but then the baby, Amos, had fallen from their boxcar onto the tracks, snatched to safety no more than a minute before a train passed by. After that he'd sent them home until he could earn a stable station, or find a way to work in Oklahoma. He hadn't farmed since 1930, when it became clear he couldn't feed his family as a tenant, and his brother-in-law was able to help him get a job on the railroad.

He hadn't thought they'd end up in Aileen. None of them had ever seen Aileen before the day they arrived, just in time to pick cotton with all the schoolchildren, let out until the crop was in.

These things were much in Frieda's mind. Always a kind of

recounting of their narrative: the minor accident that hurt Ira's back and sent him home at the worst of times, when tenants were being put off the land, and there was no work in towns. The year in Ira's parents' home, all of them in one back room, drunk with shame and gratitude, then back on the farm again, until Frieda's mother found them a new situation in Aileen. The long ride in a tied-together jalopy, as surely awful as any tin-can tourists headed west, and even that they'd since lost and sorely missed. She had thought more than once they'd have done better to keep going, but she knew that was only the allure of the unknown tempting her, and she was not romantic. Her father had died when she was just Opal's age; a broken hame had driven through one lung. She was not romantic.

Emma didn't think about these things. Although she never for a moment expected to spend her adult life on farms, she had a plains farmer's optimism—a drought couldn't last forever—and a child's faith in wishing. And wish she did. "You'll wish your life away, child," her relatives had said to her a thousand times. She talked about books (she read any she could find, lots of them turn-of-the-century romances tossed aside in nickel sales). She talked about movies (she had seen Jean Harlow and Myrna Loy in *Libeled Lady*, and Katharine Hepburn in *Little Women*, and cowboy movies with John Wayne—his were silly, awful movies, but sometimes she liked the women—all in Chickasha), and about cities (she'd seen none), and countries, as if everything *out there* waited for her. Twice she'd had a fever that took her close to dying. Her grandmother, Mama Sophie, who adored her, often said the fevers had been bouts of dreaming; they all worried that she had never become completely well.

She listened to the church folks greeting one another—"Nice day," they all said now. She listened to one man say, "I could stand to do some work on my chicken roost, if God'd understand a Sabbath chore." Another said they might get up a game of softball after dinner, on the back of the school lot. She wondered if her mother would let them go watch. Maybe so, for Amos's sake. Most of the time, he played alone, at school or on the farm.

She saw a boy she recognized from school, and because he was looking her way, she raised her hand to her chin, so that her fingers brushed her lips, then gave him a small wave she thought was entirely proper. He grinned and waved back, with a much bigger gesture.

The boy leaned over to his mother to say he knew the girls. "The older one is the best speller in school," he said.

"Pretty girls," his mother said.

The boy approached the family as they stepped out onto the cobblestones. He spoke to the father, Ira.

"Good day, sir," he said politely, holding his cap in his hands. He told him what he wanted. "You would have a nice family portrait for your trouble." His voice, which was not yet firmly adult, cracked. "You understand, sir, it wouldn't be like my mama took it, but she will do the print."

"And it won't cost us a thing?" The girls' mother put her arm around her husband's elbow.

Emma said coyly, "A portrait, for free?" She had a fragile beauty, her hair a rare, almost white, color, and the boy, at fifteen almost a man in a farming town, admired her. She had a serious demeanor, a clear-eyed and straightforward gaze, and, of course, she was smart.

She stepped forward to take the hand of her little brother, who scuffed his foot in the dirt and whined that he was like to starving.

The boy's mother stepped forward, too. She owned the photography studio, where there was little business, nor had there been for a long time, and the drugstore, where much of the business was on credit, and where, in these hard times, she had stopped stocking sedatives. Her father had been a county clerk, then justice of the peace, and, briefly, a state legislator, and she was known to everyone. (He had also been a photographer, with an admiration for cowboys, whose way of life he had seen diminished in his lifetime.)

She said, "It won't take too long, if you're willing, and we would be mighty pleased to offer you chicken sandwiches and lemonade after." She glanced at the sky. "It's a nice day for a visit."

The man said, "I don't know," his brow furrowed. He was used to worrying. "What do you think, Mama?" he asked Frieda.

Before her mother could answer, Emma spoke up. "You're telling us *you'd* be taking it?" Her chin was up, her head at an impudent angle. In the last spelling bee, she had bested kids older than she by two and three years. She could draw a face you'd recognize, and write a poem with beats like Edna St. Vincent Millay. Her handwriting was so fine she had been asked to write out the eighth grade certificates, and she had a voice more like a lady than an ordinary farm girl.

"I've done photographs of objects and buildings and individual persons, ma'am," the boy said. "I took a picture of a black blizzard when I was twelve that like to swept us off the earth." He spoke directly to the mother, as if she had been the one asking the challenging question. "This is a new step for me in my apprenticeship." He stole a quick look at his own mother, for encouragement. She was smiling ever so slightly. So was Emma.

He said, "I think I can offer you a good trade for a little of your time."

"Oh Sunday—" Frieda said, a bit doubtful.

"We're already dressed up as it is, for church," the younger girl, Opal Mae, said, smoothing her skirt. It was the first thing she'd had to say all day.

"We haven't had so clear a day in quite a while," the boy reminded them. "I like a fine sky, don't you?"

"Oh, Mama, let's," Opal pleaded. She was dark-haired and wide-eyed, sturdy, and already taller than her sister. Though she wasn't a plain girl, she would never be a beauty. She didn't have the feel for it.

"I don't see why not," their father said. He reached up to adjust the cap on his head. "It's just a surprise, you know, something for nothing, like it is."

The boy smiled happily. "This way, then," he said, and he and his mother turned and led the parading family across the square, past the pool hall, the general mercantile store, the drugstore, and the Rose Rock Cafe and thence to the studio, where, with a polite explanation and a promise to hurry, he went inside to fetch his equipment.

Outside, his mother shook hands with the family and made their acquaintance. The Perkinses, the Clarehopes. "He's so excited," she said, offering mild apology for the lack of proper introductions. She couldn't help taking note of the mother's weathered skin, her tired eyes and thinness. She thought there might be enough buttermilk pie to go around, if she cut the pieces small. She thought the older girl, pretty as she was, looked puny.

The boy set up his equipment in his own yard, where it sloped gently down toward the street. He could remember, vaguely, when the yard had been green and he had played in the grass while his parents sat close together on a soft wool blanket. For a long time now there had been only the two of them, he and his mother. There was a photograph of his father on the table by his mother's bed. In the photograph, his father was wearing a big-brimmed, high-crowned hat.

The ground was hard, broken through here and there with scratchy tufts of bleached grass. He and his mother spread a dark green cloth down; it was the size of a large dining table.

"Please," he said, gesturing toward the cloth. "Arrange yourself however you like. No need to be stiff or shy." He had heard his mother say these words a hundred times. She always gave her subjects all the time they needed to relax. She taught her son that it was up to them to decide what a picture was about.

They were in the shade of a Chinese elm, the leaves so scant, he had heard his mother say, *That's not much more than an idea for a tree, now is it?* but it cast lacy shadows and cut the glare, and the curve of it was graceful.

The family sat down, looking at one another and then, shyly, at the boy. He gave his attention to his camera, steadying the tripod. He put his head under the black hood and looked through the glass, then pulled his head out again to say they were fine, just fine, he'd tell them when to be still.

The father was a small, handsome man, with high cheekbones and smooth, hairless skin, like an Indian. He wore his hat at a jaunty angle. It was a checked wool newsboy's cap, as the style was called. His white shirt was worn, but so clean it had to have been boiled. He wore ironed khaki trousers and suspenders. He sat with his legs pulled up and apart so that his young son, Amos, who was already his spitting image, could sit between his heels with his father's hands on his shoulders.

The mother sat beside her husband, her legs turned and tucked under the skirt of her flower-print dress, which was old but of a nice crepe fabric. Her hair was cut in bangs and a bob, ragged in the back, since she cut it herself. On her other side sat her older daughter, wearing a pale blue checked cotton dress with puffed sleeves and a full skirt and petticoat and covered belt. The younger girl sat below her mother, almost out of the family cluster. If the boy had not just told them to sit as they liked, he would have asked the girl to scoot closer. She wore a dress that had been cut down from an old one of her mother's, and it did not fit well across the chest. She fiddled with the collar until it lay flat to suit her. Just as the boy was about to say, "Hold that," the mother touched her fair daughter's neck, and the girl reached up to clasp her hand and pull it against her cheek. That was when he did say, "Don't move!" and so caught the tender gesture.

He said, "We'll take one more," and then a low dry wind gust came up, gritty and gray as powdered gravel. "Oh, look!" the man said, pointing to the southwest as his cap blew right off his head. A fierce small dust devil, whirling like a baby twister, roared over them. The older girl bent forward and pulled her skirt up to cover her face, but at the last moment, she covered only her mouth, leaving her eyes visible and as exotic as a harem girl's. Her sister threw both hands over her eyes, and twisted her mouth in a terrific grimace. The mother held one hand up like a shade against her forehead, the other along her cheek on the side the wind hit. The little boy turned and buried his face in the crook of his father's knee. The man watched his hat bounce and blow away; then he stuck out his arm in the same direction, as if the wind might back up and return the hat to him.

Under the black hood, the boy held his head and the camera motionless. He snapped this second picture, too focused to worry whether he had caught it at the exact moment their movements ceased. Sometimes, his mother had taught him, you took a picture and did not know what you had done until it came up in the chemical bath. You acted on instinct, before you lost your opportunity. People would not sit still for long.

In no time at all the dust devil was gone and they were all exclaiming and laughing and brushing their hair back into place.

"Yoo hoo!" his mother called from the wide porch with its shiny gray boards, painted like the verandah of a house by the sea. "Y'all come on in the parlor now, where you won't blow away," she said.

She looked toward her son. Mr. Clarehope was helping his wife to her feet. The two younger children were running toward the house.

Her boy was standing with his hands resting lightly on top of the camera, looking at the fair girl. She was left standing alone on the green cloth, her hands half-hidden in the folds of her skirt. She had turned a little, so that one shoulder led her body, and she had raised her chin. Her wind-whipped hair was tangled, the front held off her brow by a clip.

She's a little girl playing grown-up, the boy's mother thought. "Come now," she said gaily. Her son turned, and she gave him a big wave, as if he were just coming home from a day away. He lifted the camera from the tripod. The girl folded the green cloth.

Wesley caught up with Emma Laura after school. It was the last day of the school year, a couple of weeks after the family portrait was taken. There had been recreation and celebration all day: poetry reading and declamations, some fiddle playing and a couple of kids on horns, softball games and a big pie fest. Wesley's mother had been there with the viewfinder and tripod, to take unofficial class pictures that would appear in a special edition of the town weekly.

"You were great," he said, coming within one last stride of her. She didn't turn around. She wasn't walking fast, anyway.

She had recited Coventry Patmore's "The Toys": "I struck him, and dismissed/With hard words and unkissed,/His mother, who was patient, being dead," and A. E. Housman's "To an Athlete Dying Young." She had breathed deeply from her diaphragm, and rounded her vowels and clipped her t's, sharp as a nail on glass, the way Miss McClurkan had taught her. (All the other kids thought elocution practice silly.)

She didn't mind his flattery, but she didn't return it, either. He had caught a couple of fly balls.

"My ma's printed up your family's portrait." He was beside her now, slowing down to her pace. "It's nice. You're looking right at me in it."

She gave him the merest glance. "I was looking at the camera."

"Same thing."

"You say."

"I could bring it out to you. I know your place. Ulmer Praeger built it for his son Thomas. He had my ma take a portrait of them all, lined up in front."

"No need. I expect Papa will want to pick it up," she said. "I'll tell him what you said."

They had come to the end of the paved street. Wesley was past where he needed to be, and Emma had to cut across a lot and go north up a dirt road to the Praeger place. She kept walking.

"See you!" he called. She glanced back over her shoulder and waved.

The little house where the Clarehopes were living sat behind the main house, barn, and other outbuildings, past the windmill, on the edge of pasture. It was a "weaning house," built by the family for a grown son so he could stay on the family land but be independent. He could get married. There were a lot of them on farms in those days, when a young man couldn't find the cash to rent land on his own. The Praeger boy hadn't lived in it long, though. He liked to dress in his Sunday best and go to town on trading days, Saturdays. He didn't think of Aileen as town. He didn't much like Lubbock. He drove his father's Model A all the way to Snyder. A pretty girl served him ice cream from behind her daddy's counter in the drugstore on the square. The photo Wesley mentioned was followed less than a year later with a wedding portrait. The Snyder girl didn't think much of the tiny house, even if it did have a linoleum rug in the kitchen, and wallpaper with tiny flowers. It didn't have a bathroom, or running water at all. It didn't have electricity. The couple sat Ben's parents down one night and said they needed a little cash from them, to match what her parents had given. The Praegers puffed up in pride. They thought there was a grandson on the way. What the kids wanted, though, was to leave. They headed west on the train, then north, all the way to Oregon. Thomas found work in a mill on the coast. He wrote home about rain when his folks were eating dust. He said they had seen whales.

Ulmer Praeger wrote his sister Sophie in Oklahoma to say he was looking for help. His wife wasn't strong and he needed a hand, too. Good German that he was, he had a lot of interests besides cotton: cows (he sold cream in neighboring Barrettville), a few hogs, some turkeys. He thought he ought to ask relations first, in case there was someone needing work. Frieda was dying to leave the farm. She didn't like Ira working for her stepfather, or her half-sister Josephine—they called her Tootie—living in the house, going to school like a princess, driven in a car, while Frieda's kids walked! Ira wrote Ulmer to say they would come for a year, then he figured to get on again with the Santa Fe, once a doctor certified his back. Ulmer must have wondered about a man with a bad back coming out to labor, but he didn't say. People didn't coddle themselves in those days. Work was work. Only employment had compensation.

Frieda's brother Lou—they were as close as twins—gave them gas money for the trip to Aileen. Their mother packed two huge hampers with food. Lou worked for the railroad, and he told Ira he'd see to it he was reinstated, anything he could do. He'd have given them a little more money, too, but there'd have been hell to pay from his wife.

By the time they got there, Ulmer had hired a neighbor's son, but he hadn't given away the house. His wife, Ruby Lynn, wanted

Frieda's help; she was "feeling poorly" a lot of the time. Inside a week they all fell into routines. It was Opal Mae who helped Ruby every day after school, with the house and the little kids. Frieda took over the turkeys (how the girls hated them!) and wired in a small section of yard for chickens of her own. She took enough Praeger cream to sell butter to the cafe in town, and on Saturdays she relieved the cafe cook, going in before dawn to make dozens of her famous buttermilk biscuits. (A FARMER'S BREAKFAST AT DEPRESSION PRICES the Saturday sign in the window said.) She made a dozen custard pies a week for them, too, usually walking them in, sometimes taking a horse and wagon. And she took in laundry. Emma tried to help after school, too, but as often as not her mother shooed her away. She didn't think Emma had any business wringing laundry, though she'd let her take it off the line. Emma had never been strong; Frieda didn't want to push their luck.

Ira helped Ulmer however he asked. He hired out anywhere he could, and then in April good luck came at last. He got a job with the state. They were grading roads and paving a highway. Frieda's brother Lou said when that job was up, he ought to go out to Phoenix to see the railroad doc. There would be work again; Ira had been a dependable employee, a switchman. People said the Depression was playing itself out. They didn't know much about all the folks who'd given up and gone out west. The ones who had held on had had something to hold onto. Well, now there were some fields of crops coming up green, and hummocks yellow with tallow weed. There seemed to be more birds than ever this spring: mockingbirds, scissortails, orioles, all kinds of brown birds. Ira especially loved birds. He could do a dozen whistles; Amos could do two or three pretty well, too.

Frieda didn't think of herself as a religious woman. She never asked God for anything except to keep her family together. When they were parted, she took it as part of life's burden, and waited for better times. She wrote in her Bible, little notes to mark the events: babies born, moves they made. She saved the letters Ira wrote her when he was in Arizona. "I'm talking to you in my heart, sweet girl.

You know the things I say." She worked hard. There wasn't time to think too much. Her children had good manners and clean clothes, and were smart as whips, all three of them. Emma Laura was as pretty as a movie star. In a town like this, there wasn't all that much difference, family to family. Some had more, and that meant they worried less, but if they looked down on everybody else, who would they have for company? Some of the women had friendship circles, for sewing, baking, prayer groups, even a small literary society, but Frieda didn't have time for that, and if nobody asked her to join, it could just as well have been consideration, to keep her from a necessary refusal.

Ira and Frieda talked once in a while about having a house of their own someday. They wanted to live in Oklahoma if they could, because they loved their families, but they wanted to be on their own. Frieda had once thought she'd take a secretary's course. In a town like Chickasha, she still could; the kids were getting big. If they settled in a real city, there'd be more opportunity, but they hoped it wouldn't come to that. They never used words like "optimistic" and "pessimistic." They believed there was reward for hard work, but they believed in bad luck, too. They'd seen a lot of people pack it up and leave home behind forever. They didn't think of themselves ever doing that.

It was morning. Opal Mae was in Ruby's kitchen, setting bread. Amos was doing what he could at the chore his papa set him to, repairing loose boards on the chicken house. Frieda and Ira were cleaning cream cans, a terrible task with wretched smells. Only Emma was free.

She set off on a leisurely stroll down a hard-beaten wagon path across a pasture. Eccentric Uncle Ulmer had left half a dozen mesquite trees in place, most of them older than he was. Twisted branches were visible from every direction across the table-flat ground, it seemed miles away. Nobody called them trees, always "m'skeets," but birds didn't mind the distorted limbs. And in one of them there was still an old swing. Emma headed there and sat in it gingerly, testing the wood slat seat in case this was the day it gave way at last. She liked to dally there, her eyes half-closed, her head back, feeling the last of the cool morning air on her face. She liked to dream all awake, and sometimes she sang songs she'd learned in school, old songs like "I Come from Alabama," and "Love Like a Wreath, a Song of Flowers." She saw her life from far away in that dream time. In dreams, it got better and better.

She dragged her feet in the dirt to stop, and saw something coming across the little pasture toward her. It was someone on a bicycle. She stepped back behind the huge trunk of the mesquite and watched. Wesley Perkins laid his bicycle against the rotted post of an old barbed wire fence. He was dressed like a town boy in a striped polo shirt and snappy khakis with a shiny leather belt, and he was wearing a pouch like a sling over his shoulder. Out of it he took a small camera; then he knelt to look through it at one wheel of the bike. From that he moved to peer at the post itself, then at a tumbleweed caught at the bottom of the wire. He got down on his knees and lined up with the camera at the ground in one spot, then turned to look up at the grand old tree where Emma was standing.

She stepped out slowly, letting one leg lead her. There was a moment when Wes didn't know what he was seeing, then he looked up in surprise. She struck a pose, leaning one arm back on a gnarled limb. She was wearing boxy shorts and a white blouse. Her legs were pale and skinny, a child's legs. He came closer, twirled something on the front of the little box, then pushed a button to make a click.

She came toward him, her arms stretched up over her head toward the sky, the picture of exuberance, only to shift her mood abruptly, one arm thrown across her chest, her hand wrapping her arm above the other. "Hold that," he said. And, "Be still now." He said, "I like it." He was bending forward. His voice had a slight gruffness. Not looking at her, he said, "A camera like this, you can take a picture without much fuss." She walked over quickly to his bicycle, lifted it from the fence post, and straddled it. She leaned her elbows on the handlebars. He came closer and closer, snapping pictures, until she began to laugh. Even then, he moved, shifting his angle, close, then back, then close again. Sometimes he looked like he might fall right over.

"Are you going to give me some of those?" she finally said. Suddenly it wasn't cool anymore. On top of her head she'd pulled a hank of hair up and twisted it into a coil and secured it with pins like she'd seen in a tattered old movie magazine she kept under her bed.

"Oh, sure," he said, but he didn't sound so sure.

"Your mama's going to print them?"

He put a cover on the camera lens and tucked it back in his pouch. He was blushing beet red. Emma moved so close to him she might have sent her hot breath on his face if she'd tried.

"I can't," he said.

"Can't what? Print?"

"I can't make any up for you this time."

"I made all those poses for you, and I don't get a single one!"

He ducked his head so she couldn't see his eyes. "I don't have any film in the camera," he said. "I was just practicing focusing, you see. It's all new to me."

She laughed and clapped her hands and said he was a hoot.

"You're not mad?" he asked.

"Shoot, I wouldn't want your *practice* photos anyway," she said. She pointed at his pouch. "Show me how you do it."

He took the camera back out. She reached for it.

"Careful!" he half-shouted. "It came all the way from Germany! There's not another one in the whole county, I bet."

She already had the lens cap off. She held it up. "You look through here?"

He came around the back of her and put his arms over her shoulder, to show her how to hold it. She smelled clean and sweet. She'd just finished eighth grade. He said she was a swell subject for a photograph. Next time, he'd have film.

Frieda knew all about the Leica, because of the German. His relatives had been out to ask if she would talk to him! She told them no; she hadn't uttered a word since a bunch of hoodlums beat up her

Uncle Albert and little brother Ernst in 1917. "Fritzes," they called them. Said they ought to go back to Germany. And they'd been born in Indian Territory, as much as the rest of them! Daddy Pa didn't speak German, so after that, Mama Sophie didn't have anyone to talk to in the old language. For a long time, she was lost in between German and English, but after a while, she only said her prayers, under her breath, in German. And sometimes she said, *Gott im Himmel.*

"I don't care where he comes from," she said. "I don't have time to babysit somebody's relative." The Aileen family had lost their German back in childhood, then here they were with a cousin from the old country in their laps. The German gave his relatives the camera as part payment for taking him in, and Sue Adele Perkins bought it on first sight. Nobody knew just why the German had come so far, or who was left behind. Ira said, Wasn't there going to be a war any day now?

"What's the boy doing with it, anyway?" Ira wondered. A good German camera had to be valuable. Then Wesley showed up. His mother had found an oval frame for their portrait, and made a gift of it.

"It's not brand new," he told them, "but she said she's got no use for it, if you'd want it anyway."

They would have liked to decline the frame, it being secondhand and charity, but here it was on their table, a moment in their lives behind glass, amazing as a miracle, even if it was commonplace enough. What to gain with false pride? In a frame, it could be saved, and hung, and gazed upon.

"You did a fine job," Ira said.

Frieda said thank you.

They had just been clearing supper. Corn bread, beans and fried potatoes. It embarrassed Frieda not to have pie. She had molasses, though. She poured some on a saucer for Ira and Wesley, and set the leftover corn bread between them, then made coffee. The cloth on the table was threadbare, but it had been clean that evening.

Opal sat in the rocker with Amos on her lap. His long legs draped over the side of the chair. He was sleepy, but Opal didn't want to pack him off to bed just yet. Wesley was their first real company. Uncle Ulmer didn't count; he'd never sat down once. He liked to stand in the doorway and cast his shadow on them. The people who came about their German cousin talked to Frieda in the yard while she ran overalls through the wringer.

The two men, one proud to be treated like so, talked about the weather and the likelihood of good crops. Wesley knew about Farm Security Administration help with debt. He'd heard his mother say some people were too proud for their own good, then others too darned needy. He had wondered aloud what she thought was in the middle, and made her mad. Ira laughed, hearing him tell it. He said he didn't know, his people were town folk, and he'd never had his own land, but there was such a thing as too much government, and there had to be too little, and you were never going to find agreement with three people in a room.

Frieda asked Wesley if he played 42, and he said his papa had loved dominoes, but he wasn't even half good. Nobody had asked about his father, but he threw in the news that they'd got a letter from him, out in L.A., where he was a cameraman on a movie with Deanna Durbin. It was awkward. Who could ask him why his pa was way out there and he was here? Ira nodded slightly. He had ideas about how such things happened. Besides, it was getting dark, and Wesley's ma would be wondering what trouble he was making somebody. He said, with a sly glance at Emma, that he should have driven the Model A.

Emma sat at one end of the table, opposite her father, and never said a word. The light through the window was already dim, and Frieda had lit a lamp. She looked pale and ghostly at the edge of its circle of light. Emma, too, was washed out by the light. Her hair around her face shone yellow.

"I'd like to bring the little camera," Wesley told them. "It's so fast and easy, nothing to cart around and set up. I'm going to try to take photographs of lots of the farm families around here, but I'd like to do a bunch of photographs of one family. More than the one. A study, you could say. My ma showed me in a book how some photographers have done. I wouldn't get in the way, and you don't have to stop what you're doing. It'll be like a story in pictures. The Clarehopes of Aileen, Texas. I'd rather it be you than anybody I know. And there'd be lots of photos for you, too. Swell your album quite a lot."

Frieda lifted her hand, put the back of it against her mouth. You couldn't see if she was laughing or what. "Nothing here to want to save," she said, but her voice wavered.

"Maybe one afternoon," Ira said. "When Mama doesn't mind."

Opal and Emma exchanged a look. Then Frieda struck the table with her domino and announced the game was done. Wesley shook Ira's hand, then took off down the road toward town, into the dark.

"I hope he knows where he's going," Emma said. The way she spoke, half the time you could take more than one meaning from her words. Opal was the one who noticed.

Frieda said, when he was gone, "I wouldn't call us Aileen folk, would you, Papa?"

Later, Opal whispered to Emma, "You hope he knows his way back." Emma held still a moment, then giggled, so Opal could as well. They were just girls, but they could see a lot of what lay ahead. Opal was already more resigned, more realistic. She had hopes set on high school, then training to do more than knead bread. Emma thought she was somehow set apart from the rest. Both of them longed for caught moments; they were in need of treasures. They saw themselves as older. They felt worthy of preservation. They believed in the magic of a camera's eye.

Wesley was a boy anyone could grow to like. He had manners, but he was never mumbly with them. He had a natural enthusiasm that rubbed off on other people. He was interested in how things worked, and where people had come from. He talked the kids into getting in with the turkeys, and took some photographs that he knew would be fun. Those birds were so dumb. Opal recalled aloud that on the Oklahoma farm when it rained, it was her job, little girl that she was, to race around beating at them with a long stick, to get them back into the shed. Otherwise, in a hard rain, they'd drown, standing looking up at the sky. Once there was such a flash of rain, she and Daddy Pa, her mother's stepfather, had to rescue some of them. They'd crowded together on little hillocks of soil, surrounded by rising water. Wesley said that was great, as if he hadn't grown up hearing stories about farm life. He said Opal ought to write it all down, to go with the pictures. He said maybe they would make a book together. He was excited at the notion. There were photographers taking pictures all over Texas, for the WPA, he said, and writers interviewing old-timers, but he wondered if they saw the good times. The humor. His mother had copies of photographs Dorothea Lange had taken in Hardeman County, too, and Oklahoma, but they were downright sad. He didn't say how it made his heart clutch to see how good she was.

Emma said she wondered if the people in the photographs thought anything was funny. Her mother worked so hard, at night she turned in her bed with a held-back sigh, turned like a person with a cracked back, too much pained to sleep. Ira never made a sound, but he'd lost a job over pain, hadn't he? Emma said she thought farm life was short on humor and short on good times, but she didn't want to make Wes feel too bad and not come back. He did bring his ma's car once, and took her and Opal for a ride down the road along Uncle Ulmer's pasture. Ira wouldn't let them go any farther than that, with a boy in the driver's seat, but Emma could see her father liked Wes well enough.

First he came out when Frieda said it was okay, and then he showed up as if it was all agreed upon. He was so cheery, nobody could have run him off. He said, "Go on about your business," and made it out to be so *interesting*. He took a few photos of Frieda doing her laundry, and Amos with the chickens, and then he told Frieda he was uncomfortable working like that. He didn't think it was right to catch a person off guard. After that, he took photographs they'd all agreed on; the family looked at the camera's eye, solemn and proud and ready.

He took Amos and Emma down to a little creek—it actually had some water in it again!—and brought a pole for Amos to try fishing, not that there were likely to be any fish. There were baby frogs, though, and that was plenty of distraction for a boy. Wes and Emma sat on the bank and talked about going to a city someday. Wes said he thought they'd end up in L.A. with his pa, but his ma had to get used to the idea first. He told Emma the most romantic story, about how his parents met.

Mickey Perkins was a cameraman from Boston. (He had an accent.) He'd come out with a crew to make a Dodge commercial on the Double Y Ranch in 1921. Sue Adele's daddy had taken her out there—she was seventeen, a little bitty girl with a braid that went down past her waist.

"Love at first sight, I guess," Emma said. She was willing to abet a romantic story. She'd love to go to L.A. someday, too.

Wesley nodded sadly. He missed his father.

Emma said she didn't think of her parents as romantic. She saw them every day, it wasn't like that. She hadn't heard any stories about how they met, except Frieda had gone to Chickasha to start a secretary's course, working in the laundry at the girls' college across the street from her boardinghouse. She met Ira before she learned shorthand. But she remembered seeing her mother take out the packet of letters from Ira and read them all over again, night after night, when he was gone on the railroad.

Wes's mother had made fudge for him to bring, and the three of them ate it fast before it melted. They saved a small sludgy bit of it for Opal, who gave Emma a hateful look, but thanked Wesley anyway.

He took photographs of Opal straight on, the way you would of a grown woman. She looked right at the camera, unsmiling. As if she saw far down the years. She was ten years old.

Emma he liked to catch in less formal poses, out of doors. She wasn't a bit shy. Once he did photograph her in the studio, with his mother's permission. His mother lent her a long pale green dress she'd worn when she was fifteen or so. It was gathered under the bosom, then it flowed to the ankle. She helped Emma with her hair.

Emma was dying to see how it turned out. Wesley's mother said she'd get to it right away. She told Wes that they might send it away to be hand-tinted, as a gift. The family had been so nice to Wesley.

By then he had rolls of negatives from the Leica. Frieda suggested maybe he had what he needed and it would be nice to fix them up, and he said he would. It was time for that part of it. But could he come visit anyway? Frieda smiled; she'd come to like him. He was a lucky, foolish kid, he didn't know what it was to eat beans day after day, but he was sweet and good-natured and polite. He had his mother's long nose, dipped down at the tip.

He came back one more time. He said the ones he'd done of Frieda with her laundry weren't right. Something about the light. He came at the perfect time. Frieda was hanging sheets on the line behind the house. Opal and Emma were there to help, while Amos played with a slingshot off to one side. Ira was still away with the road crew, not due back until supper. Frieda said, "Smells like rain," turning to speak to him. Behind her, across the fields, he could see long streaks of rain.

Wesley was crouching down behind Frieda, looking up into the flapping sheets, when the truck with the crew came up too fast and two men jumped out and ran toward Frieda. They stopped short of her, took their hats off and held them tight in their hands. "Mrs. Clarehope," one of them said. His voice was coarse and dark and shaky. The other one said, "It's real bad, ma'am." He was crying. A grown man! Frieda's hand went up to her mouth. She was holding onto a sheet with the other, one she had just hung on the line. Emma and Opal pushed in close beside her, not looking one bit grown-up just then.

"Tell me," Frieda said. She knew, she knew, she'd always known.

"An awful accident," they said. They looked off at the sky, then back. It was a dusty, hot day, with those streaks five or six miles away. The air was still. There had been no warning.

There had been two of them riding on the back of the pickup. The men were on their way home from the last work of the day. They quit because the sky looked bad, and there had been a short, sharp burst of rain. Ira had pulled a tarp over his head. Across an open pasture a dust devil came straight at them. They hadn't seen it coming. It picked Ira up off that truck and threw him right into the air, all wrapped up in his tarp. The other man scrambled in the bed and crouched in the corner below the cab. He howled and banged the metal above his head. The driver slammed on his brakes. They jumped down in time to see Ira smashed against the highway, his face into pavement, his body broken like someone hit by a plow. He didn't live five minutes. They had him in town; they had come for Mrs. Clarehope.

"You God!" Frieda screamed. Her arms went up stiff to the sky, her hands bolted into fists. The girls cowered, as if the twister was over them right then. Wesley was kneeling in the dirt. He had his camera at his eye. He snapped photographs of the men with their hats in their hands, and the girls with their arms up around their heads. He snapped a photograph of Frieda as her arms came down and grasped the sheets on the line, as she screamed and fell, pulling white laundered cloth down around her in a cloud of anguish. There was a smell of soap and ozone in the air.

Amos came around the corner wailing, and landed on his mother like so much more laundry. Wesley fell back in the dirt, the camera something hot. He scurried away like an insect, out of sight. It was unholy to see a man's wife hearing news like that. He sat in the dirt and no one paid him any mind, while Frieda herded her children into the cab of the truck. The second man jumped in the back— imagine, after the news he'd brought!—and the truck pulled out, slow and careful as if it was the body in the back. Wesley sprang to life and ran after them, but it was too late to shoot. There wasn't any way for him to help.

Frieda's brother Lou came for her and the children, and took them back to Mama Sophie and Daddy Pa. ("Worst news," Daddy said in that rough quiet voice of his. Mama looked at her daughter with an old grief and anger and said, "You might as well be strong.") They shipped the body on the railroad back to Chickasha, and buried it in the lot where his parents would someday go. His sisters crowded closest to the casket, everywhere they took it. In the cemetery there was a space for her, too, but she said, standing at the grave, to no one in particular, "I want to lie beside my mother," and it was Opal who said, "Yes, Mama."

Back at the farm, she took to bed for a day, then rose and washed her face. She came into the kitchen and helped with supper. After the dishes were washed, everyone always sat a while in the kitchen. They would play dominoes, or read the paper. They might listen to news on the radio. Now, of course, they were sitting quietly, waiting for life to be ordinary again.

Frieda sat at the kitchen table across from her mother. Her children were scattered around the room. She said, "I cannot bear to hear my name spoken aloud from any mouth but my sweet husband's. And he will never speak it again." She had been named in the German way: Frieda Greta Katherine Hannah Harms. Then Clarehope. She said, "You must all call me Greta. I won't answer to Frieda anymore." They all saw that she had pulled her bangs to the sides with bobby pins, that her unrouged lips had grown smaller.

Her mother's eyes were wide. She opened her mouth to speak, but Daddy Pa had already reached out from his rocker to touch her arm, and that silenced her.

Frieda, now Greta, said she would like to change all their names. She would like to be called Harms again. Her maiden name, as if she realized that grieving would turn her heart to stone.

"I want my daddy's name!" Emma cried. "Clarehope! Clarehope!" She began to weep. Amos wailed, "Daddy! Daddy!" and ran to Daddy Pa.

"Here we are, in harm's way," Greta went on. "What better acknowledgment? When was the name any other thing?" It was her father's name. She looked at her mother harshly, as if the silent woman had denied their history. Her daddy had lain in the farmhouse, lingering for days, then rasped something they couldn't understand, and died. Now history repeated itself.

"Frieda," Mama Sophie said.

Her daughter's eyes were cold.

"Greta," Mama Sophie said more gently. Already her daughter

had grown bitter, swallowing her memory. But Sophie said, "It's not right for the children not to carry their father's name. Do you want to pretend they had no father? That you were never married? You, with three young ones? You'll invite judgment where there should be understanding." She did not say *pity*.

Of course that was what Greta did want. Already memory had moved into a new geography. Already Ira was a man who had left her precipitously, left a wife and three children in the depths of the Depression, left nothing behind but a gift ham from the road crew.

"All right," she said, after they waited for long moments. Emma rushed to her and threw her arms around her from behind. Greta reached up to hold her daughter's hand.

She had buried Ira in sorrow, and laid with him her name, but sorrow turned to bile in the grim business of survival. They remained Clarehope, at least there was that. The Harmses now were only her brothers' families. Her mother was a Stone by marriage, her sister Tootie a Stone by birth.

Lou rescued her the best he could. He said he'd talked to them on the Santa Fe, and she could have a job as cook for a road gang. She would live in a boxcar again. They were expecting her in Gallup, New Mexico, within the week.

"Not with the children," she said. No one was surprised by that. Opal and Amos began to cry loudly when they heard. Emma didn't make a sound. She knew her mother wouldn't leave her.

Lou picked them up to take to the railroad station. Everyone was lined up on the farmhouse porch. The children were crying and waving. Mama Sophie stood behind them, plump as bread dough, but rigid with sorrow and responsibility. Greta cried, too, and turned in the car for one last look. Only Emma was dry-eyed. She had adored her Papa, but he was gone. She took her mother's lessons right to heart. They would have to have each other.

Wesley was ashamed. There was no one he could tell. He lay in bed at night and remembered the scene. He saw Frieda in the sheets, he saw the children crying, the men with the hats, and he saw himself crouched in the dirt with a camera at his eye. And there were photographs to prove it.

He put the negatives in jackets and slid them in envelopes in his mother's studio drawer. He couldn't bring himself to destroy the prints, but he couldn't show them, either, so he put them in the drawer as well.

There were many fine pictures from the rolls he had taken on the farm. He and his mother worked to print them; there was really nothing to it. He put them together in a strong envelope with a clasp, and he walked out to the Praeger property to give them to the Clarehopes. He didn't think they would remember anything about him on the day that Ira died. They would have these photographs, to remember Ira by.

They would have had time to compose themselves.

He walked past the Praeger house to the weaning house. There was no sign of life. He pushed open the door. There was the kitchen table, a few chairs, the cold stove. He put his hand flat on the stove surface. He went out into the yard. The washing tub was in its place, with a scrub board stuck in it. There were wooden clothespins in a sack on the line.

He backed away, then turned and ran until his chest hurt. He walked the rest of the way, every few minutes wiping the tears from his face with the back of his hand.

His mother was on the porch when he reached home.

"They're gone," he said.

She shook her head. "You didn't know?"

He had heard they were gone. He'd heard Ulmer Praeger was looking for help. That wasn't the same as an empty house.

"Maybe I could send them the photographs," he said.

His mother took them out of his hands. "Maybe later," she said. "Come inside. We've got a letter from your father. He wants us to come to L.A. He wants us to be a family again."

Grand Canyon, Arizona
October 4, 1934

Sweetheart,

You are a dear I think the world of you an those sweet baby's. It sure is hard to stay here, but as hard as times are an no money makes one do it.

The more I see of the wemon an Girls here runing around the more I Love you dear. I know you are true and some day I am going to be back with you an be happy.

Honey you may not mean so much to them but you are the world to me. I wish I could put my arm's around you an try to sooth your heartacks , but as I cant I send my Love an kisses in this letter to the dearist little mother in the world.

Your Ira

GALLUP, NEW MEXICO

Emma said there was nothing she needed to know that she couldn't get from a book, but it worried Greta to see her out of school. In September 1941, she packed her up to send her to her grandmother in Oklahoma to attend high school. Emma, furious, protested that that wouldn't be any better than no school, and for the first time since Papa died, they quarreled. After all, Greta had graduated from the high school in Devol—she had been on a basketball team that went all the way to state—and it had been good enough for *her*, so Emma could just climb down off her high horse and rejoin the human race, where people didn't always get what they wanted. They had never been in one place long enough for Emma to go to school. Say they were with a crew working between Gallup and Belen. It might take a month to get from one place to the other. And before you knew it they could be in Arizona. It broke Greta's heart to send Emma away, but there was no life in a boxcar with windows, cots, and a coal stove. The winters had been cruel. In Devol, she could have friends. She could have her sister and brother and all her other kin. She could go to parties. Have a good time, like young girls should.

31

"But I won't have my mama!" Emma cried. When the time came, she climbed on the train with swollen eyes. The first thing she said at the other end was to Opal: "What did you do to your hair?" There could have been no sorer point. Mama Sophie made Opal get permanents at the beauty parlor in Grandfield, where they wound her up in curlers attached to long cords out of a machine that plugged into electricity and almost burned her scalp black. Opal was crying before they had even hugged hello. Sure enough, the boys were thrilled to have Emma back, all grown up in her little black skirt above the knee—Sophie ran it up on her machine exactly as Emma drew it on the back of an envelope. But it was a hard time for Emma, who was placed in algebra with baby freshmen, and with seniors in history and English and government. And the boys in their coveralls and long johns never got past goggling, and that was as far as Emma wished for.

Back in New Mexico, Greta took up with a railroad man famous for his daring. He loved to walk the tops of the cars, especially at night, when they had to count on strings stretched across the tracks to warn the workers before they came into a tunnel. *Whack!* went the strings, and *whoosh!* went the wind in the tunnel. The railroad man, Ed Dailies, had almost lost a hand once when he went to close a hatch on a refrigerated car and the train went into emergency and knocked him off. Greta enjoyed his pride, his high spirits. He took her mind off her troubles. You might say, he swept her off her feet. Here she was, up in the middle of the night starting on biscuits, and a good-enough-looking man was flirting with her at breakfast!

He could help her bring her kids out to live with her. He knew that was what mattered most. More than a little sneaky love under the covers. They got married in a clerk's office with no to-do.

He helped her move into Gallup and find a house with two tiny bedrooms. It didn't take her until noon to find a job. It was the week after Pearl Harbor, and everyone was sitting up. The town was hopping. She went to work for a Greek called Patty, for Patsoureas, at a cafe up the street from the Harvey House restaurant, which cost more and had white tablecloths. Of course that didn't last long, with the volume of train travel up five times over, overnight. So much for the famous Harvey standards, Patty said. Cafes were all raking it in. Patty was stingy, but he paid Greta more than the railroad had, and he let her take home leftovers after every shift.

Ed Dailies gave her money to bring her kids out. He couldn't have done anything that meant more. (What else had she had in mind?) The kids arrived by bus the week before Christmas, exhausted from sitting up squeezed together in a packed bus, three to a two-person seat. Gallup was slushy after a light snow, but Amos and Opal wanted to see where it was they lived. They went outside and sat down on a cold, wet rock, to survey the place. They were in a neighborhood of tiny stucco houses, up a hill and across the river from town. Emma went about the house daintily peering into each room, each closet, even the cupboard in the kitchen, scantily stocked with cans and sacks. There was running water, electricity, a bathroom. She and Opal had a bed; Amos would sleep on a cot at the foot of it. There was no sign of Ed Dailies just then.

Greta called the children together and served them canned soup, which they considered a treat, with soda crackers and chocolate milk. When they were full and sleepy, she broke the news about Ed Dailies. They were all flabbergasted, but only Emma had the nerve to speak. "How could you?" she asked. When Greta didn't answer, sitting up with her spine stiff and her face a mask of privacy, the kids went to bed. When Ed finally showed up, there were heads bobbing all around, but none of them ever exchanged a word with him. He came and went like a boarder. Whatever he did with Greta, he didn't do it with the children in the house.

Amos and Opal signed up for school their second day in town, but Emma dug in her heels. There was *no* way she was going to go to school in a town that had a swinging bridge, called its river the Perky, and was practically the Old West. She had no *business* in school when she could get a job and earn hard dollars.

Her argument was sealed when Ed Dailies sat Greta down one night soon after and said he'd joined the navy and was leaving in the morning. "How could I not?" was his argument, and Greta didn't object. It wasn't just that she'd already had enough of being married again. It wasn't just that it wouldn't do any good; she thought there would be an income from the Navy. There wasn't. There wasn't, in fact, a word, ever, from Ed Dailies, good or bad, as if the ocean had swallowed him in one gulp. Eventually she got around to divorcing him. All she cared was, she was in town, in one place, with her children under the same roof, and even if the Greek did pat her fanny now and then, and even if the cafe stank of grease and olives and oregano, and even if Emma wouldn't go to school, this was bearable. Besides, Tootie was watching the papers in Wichita Falls, where she was living now, newly married and teaching algebra to ninth graders. She wrote Greta to say they weren't hiring women in the factories yet, but everyone knew they would any day now. Greta's dream was to have a union job. She had had enough of women's work, she had had enough of men. It was like the war came along to save her. All she had to do was keep food on the table until the mills put out the word and they could move. The war was going to change their lives for the better. After all, Amos was too young for it, the kids' daddy was already gone (she never said, or thought, "dead"), her brothers were too old, and she had no intention of ever being attached to anybody else as long as she lived. (She wasn't thinking, yet, of her children's babies.)

They had Christmas in the little house. Greta was able to give each child a dollar to shop, and they came back with trinkets, lipstick, toys for Amos, a special shampoo for Greta. They strung popcorn and cut out colored paper decorations for a tree that was nothing more than a sprig of sagebrush on the table. They didn't care. They turned on all their electric lights, in every room, just for a while, and sang.

They were about to go to bed when they heard noises in the yard, then hard knocks on the door. Opal swung it open and they heard her gasp. An Indian was standing there, in front of two or three more, behind. There was a light snow falling, and the Indians were wearing blankets over their shoulders. The one in front said, "Kish ma, kish ma," and Opal cried, "I will not!" It was Emma who had the mind to go over and say, "Merry Christmas." She said, "They want us to give them something." Greta took a string of popcorn off the little bush, and an apple from the bowl on the counter—there were exactly four, and she would do without—and she handed them to the Indian without a word, then shut the door firmly.

"Turn off the lights," she said. "Go to bed."

When they were tucked in, she kissed each of them and said, "This is the best Christmas." They knew what she meant. It wasn't the same as being happy, but it was better than it had been for a long time.

In the morning they were at the tiny metal table, eating oatmeal. Greta poured coffee for herself and sat down and said, "I'll tell you about the time your Papa danced with the Indians." They set their spoons down with a clatter. It was the first time she had mentioned their papa. And Indians! They leaned toward her eagerly.

"It was in 1932. Amos was just a baby. We were in Gallup for a couple months. It was a rough place, but the boxcar was parked in place all that time, it made it more like home. Emma Laura was in school. Your Uncle Lou was working here, too, and one day he showed up in his Model T and he said he'd heard they were dancing up on the reservation. Papa always wanted to see it so bad.

"I said, 'Isn't that their secret business?' I'd seen postcards from the twenties—even the rain dance—but nobody was allowed around anymore. 'Oh, I know just where to go to watch,' Uncle Lou said. I told Papa, 'I don't want you out there.' He had work the next day. It'd take hours to get up to Shiprock and back.

There was no stopping them. They'd just got paid, they had their pay in their pockets. Papa said, 'Make us some sandwiches, why don't you?' and I said, 'If I'm making sandwiches, I'm coming along to eat them.' So we all squeezed into that tiny car, all on top of one another, and drove up onto the reservation.

"Lou had a spot all picked out. There was an outcrop of rocks. He could park there, and the Indians were below. They couldn't see the car, and we were far enough away, they didn't hear it, either. I had a bottle for Amos, and then all three of you kids fell asleep. The men said they were just going to look down over the rocks. I could wait in the car. I watched them sneaking along this little ridge, like they were some kind of army scouts, and I thought, they're looking for trouble, sure as anything. They looked funny out there, wearing suits, like they were going to town. They looked like those old pictures of outlaws, except they didn't have guns. I wanted to holler at them to come back, but I was afraid the Indians would hear me.

"Sure enough, they had to get a little closer, and that went okay, so they sneaked down the other side of the rocks where they could get a real good view, and then here came two Indians, stocky like those Navajos can be, like you couldn't push them over with a railroad car. I'd got out of the car and I could see it all, my husband and brother half pushed along right down to the circle of those dancing Indians, and the next thing you know, there were drums and *whaa! whaa! whaa!* and they were right in the middle, dancing."

Amos was wide-eyed. "With the Injuns!"

"Oh, yes, with the Indians," Greta said, "but it wasn't no party. Those Indians were making them dance, like for their lives. I had my heart in my throat, thinking should I drive for help, but it was hours to anybody. Then I saw Papa and Uncle Lou come running back up that ridge to the car, all out of breath and dusty and laughing and shaky."

"They were okay, though," Opal said matter-of-factly. The story was exciting, but the best part was hearing how the men got back safe.

"Okay?" Greta said. Her voice had turned hard and surprised her children. Their oatmeal was cold in the bowls. "They were okay. But those Indians had taken their wallets, with two weeks' pay! What do you think we did for the next two weeks? How much can you cook from an empty bean sack? No flour? I had some little money set back, I spent on milk for you kids."

The girls hung their heads. Amos kept looking at his mother, waiting for something else. The cords in her neck were rigid.

She stood up. "Finish up that porridge now. We haven't got it to waste." She was muttering as she took her empty coffee cup to the sink. Looking at her back, the kids could see how anger stiffened her spine. She didn't tell any more stories after that.

She didn't even mention Ira. The girls tried to tell Amos things they remembered about their father, but they had to do it when their mother wasn't around, and after a while they had used up what they knew, and it was tiresome to tell the same old things. They didn't even know if they truly remembered anything. What was lost was gone.

Under a gloomy wet winter sky, Emma Laura went to town dressed in her black wool pleated skirt, a white blouse with a tiny crossed ribbon at the neck, white leather shoes and dark blue socks. She had a long wool coat Mama Sophie had given her, and she liked to wear it open, swinging as she walked. She had pulled her hair up on one side in a roll. She wore dark red lipstick, and pencil on her pale eyebrows. She took the first job she found, in a bakery on the other side of the bridge near the courthouse. It was near the library, too.

The problem was, work started early, and she was always late to bed. She took books from the library, two or three a week. She read *Ramona* and *The Grapes of Wrath, Mrs. Miniver* and *To Have and Have Not.* Now the librarian saw her coming; she had Katherine Anne Porter and Graham Greene set aside. "I wondered why I'd ordered them," the librarian said. "Folks here like their Zane Grey." She loved to talk. Her name was Twyla Dandee. Her parents had come to Gallup in a covered wagon. Her husband's folks had been traders. She had a sister who lived in New York City. "Keep on reading," she told Emma, "and you'll read yourself out of Gallup." Of course there she was, Mrs. Dandee, dispensing culture out of a tiny two-room library. How had her sister made it to New York? She had to ask. It was marriage to an army recruiter. A man. Of course.

Many mornings, it was bitter cold and snowing. Emma had to be at the bakery by a quarter to seven (they would have liked her earlier), to help set out the rolls and donuts for the morning crowd.

Greta was long gone to the cafe by then, but Amos and Opal Mae were still shuffling around with sleep in their eyes when she left. She stood behind the counter and slid donuts onto small squares of paper for men in coveralls, blue jeans, work pants, and, quite in the minority, suits. The workmen greeted one another laconically. The lawyers, accountants, and so on stepped up briskly. They shook hands with one another. Women didn't show up until later in the morning, to fetch snacks for their office staffs, or for their families. Clad in a crisp white apron over her skirt and blouse, Emma smiled and wished everyone a good day. The bakery was owned by a Slavic woman, Mrs. Brlyvich, who could be very nice at times, but was mostly busy and nosy and bossy. If Emma said too much to customers, Mrs. B. complained that she was making others wait. If she worked quickly, Mrs. B. said she was rude. And she didn't understand why a girl in need of a job couldn't arrive at six-thirty. "You uppa too late with your boyfriend?"

"It's dark," Emma said. It was dark at seven, too. Sometimes, though, Mrs. B. would light up when she saw Emma in the morning. "Aren't you sucha ray of sunshine?" she'd say. She'd put down a saucer of donut holes on the counter. "Eat, eat," she'd say. "Who'll marry sucha skinny girl?" And away she'd go, with her talk about the old country, and recipes, the good old days, until Emma could have screamed. "We're notta rich, notta poor, we're justa medium," Mrs. Brlyvich said. Emma wondered why she hadn't stayed behind in the old country.

She left work at two and went up the block to Patty's cafe to have a bite to eat. She sat at the end of the counter near the kitchen. Usually Greta took a break and had a cup of coffee with her. She was finishing up the pies for the next day, and then she'd be off work and walk home with Emma. She always gave Emma more than she could eat. What Emma really liked was the coffee, which was getting scarcer and would soon be rationed. Already it was too expensive for them to have at home. While Emma pushed food around on her plate and nibbled at the potatoes, she caught glances of Uno, the Jap dishwasher. His back was to her; he was bent over a huge sink, enveloped in steam. When he turned around, he never looked at her directly, but she couldn't believe he didn't see her. She smiled at him. A few times she called out a hello, but Greta scowled. Later she said, "He's a good worker, but if anybody sees him talking to a pretty girl, it'll just make it worse for him."

"Worse how?" Emma wanted to know. "Worse why?" She had a good idea, but she wanted her mother to say it. Somebody should say it.

It was being Japanese that made Uno's life a problem. His country had bombed hell out of our navy, and people acted like he'd flown one of the planes. Customers would say to Patty, "Help that hard to find?" and "If I's you, I'd wash dishes my own self." Greta was surprised Patty didn't let him go, but the Greek was stubborn. Uno had never missed a day of work in six years, he never complained, and the dishes were clean. He didn't seem to have any people, but Patty wasn't the nosy sort. Lately, though, the FBI had been around asking questions. How much did Uno get paid? Where did he get his mail? Who were his friends? "How the hell would I know?" Patty roared. "I'm running a cafe here."

One afternoon a railroad man sat down on the stool next to Emma. He was maybe five years older than her. He wore his trousers baggy and his shirt tight. "There's a movie with Claudette Colbert on," he said, "and I bet you just love her."

"I like her, but I don't love her. I love Bette Davis."

"We can see Bette Davis next time she's here," the railroad man said, and just then Greta seemed to be on top of them. A steak knife came down hard enough, it stuck in the counter, right in front of the railroad man's hand. He didn't flinch. He grinned.

"We're going home now, Emma," Greta said. "Get your coat." Emma didn't protest. She got up with a little flick of her head. The railroad man winked.

Patty yelled something as they went out the door, but with the tinkle of the bell on the door and the roar of a truck going by just then, Emma didn't hear what he said. Her mother was stiff with anger. She was mad a lot these days.

"He was just asking me out on a date," Emma ventured as they turned the corner and started toward their house on Terrace.

"If you were in school where you belong, you'd be meeting boys your own age," Greta said.

"Boys is right."

Greta stopped walking and looked Emma in the eye. "You will not date those railroad men," she said, and Emma didn't even bother to argue. Greta wouldn't say another word about it, she knew, so she wouldn't know if it was the man's age or occupation that made him undesirable. All Emma would have asked was what he liked to read.

As for movies, Emma preferred to go alone. She gave her checks to her mother, who always gave her money back, enough for lipstick and copies of *Silver Screen*, and a movie every week. Usually Opal Mae went with her, sometimes Amos. What Emma liked, though, was to sit in a seat on the aisle, two-thirds of the way down, right at the point where she had to crane her neck a little to look up. She liked to let the images come over her like clouds of light and music, like dreams. Ginger Rogers, quicksilver on her feet. Ingrid Bergman, more beautiful than anybody. Haughty Katharine Hepburn and Bette Davis, tender Olivia de Havilland. Veronica Lake, with that wonderful dip of hair on her cheek. It didn't matter what the movies were. They were all good. The lively clip of the women's talk, the wonderful clothes, and the men running around being tough and bossy and finding out the women were the ones who knew. Or maybe the men didn't know, but Emma did. The audience did. Those were the best stories. But she was willing to watch anything. She'd take Amos to double feature westerns; there were lots of those. She talked her mother into going to see Bing Crosby and Bob Hope. It was good to hear Greta laugh. Movies weren't really luxuries. They were like air, like water. She had to have them. She had to make up for all the movies she'd missed. She thought they were telling her something important about being a woman. If you were beautiful, it was worth something. If you were smart, and tough, it was worth everything. There were certain things you had to do, if you were a woman, but you could make them work for you. Marriage was for love, sure, but in movies there were a hundred roads in and out of marriage. There was danger. Passion. Temptation. Terrible errors of judgment back in your face. There were mistakes that sent women to prison, into insane asylums, onto the streets, but there was always a way home, to love, to redemption.

Movies were nothing, nothing, nothing like Emma's life. That was why they were sheer joy. That, and their beauty, and their seductive, wicked siren's call: *You could do this.*

One afternoon, coming out of the bakery—she smelled of yeast and cinnamon, and she'd never eat another raisin as long as she lived—Emma saw a sign in the window of the dry goods store across the street. She went inside, brushing at her hair with her hands. She smelled candles and cologne. The woman in charge said they needed a young lady for the back, where the sewing notions and the fabrics were. Could she cut fabric? Emma almost laughed out loud; she had grown up wearing clothes made from feed sacks, or farmer's britches. But how hard could it be to measure cloth?

The hard part, she learned, was staying all smiles to the women who came in fussing over their choices, this print or that one, these buttons or those. They turned a rack of buttons into a despairing task; at the end of the day, the yard goods all had to be rolled up neatly and stacked. It made her arms ache. She hated them for having the money to treat her like a servant.

She showed Opal Mae at home. They were in the kitchen, laying out bread and butter and plates, wondering why Greta was late coming home from the cafe.

Emma was imitating one Mrs. Larsen, who had come looking for the "perfect worsted" to make a skirt for her daughter. She had told Emma, "She's about your size, dear, but she has such a tiny waist." Emma had had to gargle to keep from mocking her. Emma's waist was sixteen inches! Was this Larsen girl five years old? Was she sick?

The woman had said, "I suppose I'll have to cut down my suits for my Vicky, what with this horrid war." Emma was scandalized. As if the war were a mere inconvenience!

Opal had to sit down, she was laughing so hard at Emma's little scene. Mrs. Larsen, it turned out, was a secretary at the high school, and her darling Vicki was skinny, all right, with a nose like—

She didn't get to finish her description. Greta came in the room with a pinched face, and plopped right down in a chair at the table. She wasn't carrying her usual leftovers (dry pork chops, but they heated them in a little water; biscuits left from morning; and the noon vegetable).

The government men had been at the cafe again that day, pushing the little dishwasher against the wall with their questions. After they left, he finished up the load he was doing, then went into the bathroom, sat down on the toilet, and slit his throat.

"Don't tell Amos," she said, and then she went to wash up and put on her pajamas. Opal heated up their last can of soup and thinned it with water. Greta didn't feel like eating. Amos nearly fell asleep in his bowl.

Emma and Opal lay close together in their bed and whispered about the Japanese suicide.

Opal asked, "Do you think Mama had to help clean it up?"

It was too awful to think of. Something like this—wouldn't there be official people? It wasn't a cook's job to mop up. And there wasn't any blood on Greta's clothes. They never asked.

Emma said, "I heard it's what they do when their honor's at stake, kill themselves."

"What honor?" Opal said. "What was he accused of?"

"They're our enemy," Emma said. "They're so easy to spot, why didn't the navy see them coming?"

Opal never heard irony in Emma's bitter remarks. She was full of them, her observations on Indians, the war, the poor and the rich. (You didn't actually see anybody rich in Gallup, except maybe the Indian traders, and they didn't flaunt it, except with bracelets and rings, and those you saw everywhere anyway. To Emma's way of thinking, though, the division was between those *serving* and those *served*. She didn't like where she was in that equation.)

"It was a sneaky, dirty attack," Opal said.

"I *know that*," Emma said. "But *Uno* was in *New Mexico, washing dishes,* wasn't he?"

"You just don't see any of it coming, do you?" Opal whispered. She felt scared, as if she might be next. Or her mother.

"Oh, I see it," Emma said. Even when Opal said, "What?" over and over, at least five times, she wouldn't answer.

The next day Opal came home and said she'd heard the Harvey House restaurant was hiring nearly anyone who was neat and nice and at least sixteen. She figured she looked that old. (She had just turned fourteen.) The rule had always been you had to be eighteen. Besides, in Gallup, they had always used the Navajo girls from the mission school. But the war was changing everything.

School was out. Greta wanted Opal to watch Amos, but Amos was big enough to watch himself; they could use Opal's wages. She wanted to be out there like Emma was. Emma said she would go with her to apply. Buttons seemed damned trivial. She would rather feed the troops. She would rather make some tips. She would have died if Opal got a better job.

Opal was right about the Harvey House restaurant. They wanted girls especially to serve the troop trains. In fact, it was a little like joining the army. The girls lived in dormitories and were on call day and night. The manager, an older waitress, gave Opal a close look and asked her a second time, "Sixteen, are you?" Of course Opal said she was. She went to work the next day. She had to stay in the dormitory, except for her days off. (At first there were three free days. By August she had only two, but she had some time in the evenings to see her mother, who often came to her instead of the other way around.) She napped dressed in all her clothes except her shoes and her skirt and apron. Other girls played cards and read. One had a flute. All Opal wanted was sleep.

Emma was offered a better job, in Winslow, Arizona, a hundred miles away. Winslow was one of the main stops for troop trains; they had so many boys to feed, local women had formed a patriotic group to provide extra help when the hired waitresses couldn't do it all. She lived in a dormitory there, too, set aside from the regular waitresses. Mostly, the girls in her group were young, eighteen to twenty-two or twenty-three. They were from New Mexico and Arizona, Colorado and Texas. A few were from farther away than that. They were a convivial group, housed in two-person bedrooms,

44

nicely furnished. Downstairs there was a parlor with a piano and a record player. They had a housemother, Dorothy Abbott, who had come out of retirement in Albuquerque as a contribution to the war effort. She was seventy years old, with white hair pulled up in a beautiful, fashionable roll. She regaled them with tales of her early days with the railroad. "When I came out here, it was all miners and cowboys, a rough place, but full of promise for a poor girl. And I was protected, because of where I worked."

"Shoot, Dorothy," some girl would say. "It's still a rough place out here. I saw a bull snake day before yesterday a stone's throw away."

Then there'd be a motherly lecture about paths and boots and curfews and half a dozen other topics, including gentlemen who came around looking for sweethearts and all that implied.

Emma came home on the train once a week for a day. Greta worried about her, with such a schedule, but Emma said it was fun, for all the work—they made hundreds of box lunches every day, served the boys, then went upstairs to do their hair and talk more before bed. She had a swell roommate, Margaret Lily, from Texarkana. Margaret could sing, dance, play the piano, talk with accents (Mexican, Italian, French, and Yankee), fix hair and sew. She had them all dancing to Glenn Miller's "Chattanooga Choo-Choo." Only with Emma, though, did she pour her heart out. Those other girls wanted to get married and have babies. (There was one who wanted to be a teacher.) She wanted to be a movie star.

"Star, heck," she said, "I'd be happy in a chorus. I could be the girl behind the perfume counter that waits on Barbara Stanwyck or the hat girl that takes the coat from Marlene Dietrich. I just want to be out there, where everything is. California." She had stacks of magazines; she and Emma lay on their beds, stretched out on their stomachs, their legs bent, their feet up over them, dancing in the air while they read.

"Come on, I'll show you a great dance," she said. She could see something in a movie, and go home and know how to do it, she said. It was a special kind of memory. And she was strong. She practiced with Emma until she could throw Emma under her legs like a man, then swing her back up to her feet and not miss a beat. They showed Dorothy and all the girls, and the girls said the soldiers would love to see that. "Okay, time for the whistle to blow," Dorothy said. They weren't showgirls. They were waitresses. But she didn't mean to dampen their fun. "In here, dance to your heart's content," she said. She meant the parlor. "Out there"—she pointed with her thumb toward the restaurant—"you're Harvey Girls."

Late in August, Emma woke up with a fever and a stomachache. Dorothy said it was some kind of flu. She spent a lot of time in Emma's room, and when she wasn't better at the end of a day, she got a doctor to come and look. It took days to feel well enough to get up and move around, and they sent her home for a week. Margaret was busy in the dining room when the train came. All Emma managed was a wave across the room.

Her mother said it was this awful heat. She kept cool water in a basin by Emma's bed, to dip a cloth in for her face. She spent hard-earned money for a fan. When it was Opal's day off, Greta moved her into bed with her, to leave Emma alone in the other room. Emma wasn't too sick anymore. It was good, having both girls home for a few days. Greta made lemon pie, and bought a piece of beef she could cook slowly with onions, to make a good gravy. Emma stayed home a week, then another. Her mother went down to the Gallup restaurant and had them wire Winslow to say she'd be back but not right away.

Emma wrote Margaret and said sometimes she thought what was wrong with her was what was wrong with the world. She felt pockets of terrible emptiness. She had never expressed herself like that in words, on paper, not to anyone. (Who had there ever been?) She said she missed the dorm, missed Margaret, missed the dancing, and the talks. Margaret wrote back and said they'd packed her things into a corner of the room, and moved a new girl in. The new girl had a nice soprano voice, to Margaret's alto. They were practicing some duets. Emma told herself she didn't care. She began to have terrible headaches, throbbing in her eyes. Her cheeks were sunken. Greta brought her magazines and ginger ale, cool glasses of tea, her homemade bread and butter. She was forever putting the back of her hand to Emma's forehead. "You don't have to get up until you're ready," she'd say, and then turn around and tell her, "At least you should walk outside in the evening when it cools down. You've got to move around. You've got to eat, Emma Laura."

When she felt better she went downtown. She heard they had made a movie during the summer, out at the Canyon de Chelly. They'd used a hundred Navajo horsemen. She walked to the El Rancho Hotel, a beautiful place, its hallways hung with photographs of all the movie stars who had stayed there, working on films, or passing through by train and stopping over.

She went back to work in Winslow, but she didn't like it so much this time. It was hard work, long hours of it. She felt lonely, not for her mother, exactly, but for something, for someone, she didn't know. She felt like a boat anchored where there's no water. She tried to tell Margaret, and discovered she didn't have to. Margaret felt the same way. She said so now, though she never referred to Emma's heartfelt letter. "I've put in my name to work in L.A.," Margaret said. "No telling when it'll go through, I'm junior as hell—" She cocked a brow, to show she knew she was being vulgar. "And I'm saving my money anyway, half to my mother, half in my sock. My L.A. sock."

Emma felt her throat swell with love and solidarity. She almost felt she *was* Margaret. They were that close, that much alike, even if they weren't in a room together anymore. Emma would have liked to embrace Margaret for a moment. A hug, like her mother gave her when she came home from Winslow. Something full of love, and, with Margaret, friendship. But Margaret was always in movement, elusive as a hummingbird.

It was hot. It didn't cool off the way it usually did. Emma felt headachy and bad-tempered. The sound of the sewing machine and the record player, the chatter of the other girls, it all made her want to scream. She washed her face clean of makeup and brushed her hair out onto her shoulders, then went downstairs and slipped out onto the porch. There was a slight breeze coming up, and a sky full of brilliant stars. She looked to the west and watched a train coming in. It pulled up, some of the cars right in front of her. Through the windows she could see soldiers sleeping, sitting in their seats, their heads turned this way and that to find support. She thought: *If I could, I'd go in that train car, and I'd take each one of those boys in my arms. One by one. I'd kiss him and put my palm on his brow. I'd unbutton my blouse so he could see my breasts. I'd say, I'll miss you. I'd say, take care.*

Her eyes were full of tears. She heard heavy footsteps on the porch, at the other end, where it led into the station office. In a few moments there were steps again, slower this time, and she realized the steps had come toward her.

A young officer leaned against a post nearby. He struck a match on the post and lit a cigarette. He was looking out over her head, in the direction he had come, from the west.

She tried not to make any sound at all, but he could see her. He touched his cap with his finger. "Evening, ma'am," he said.

"Good evening, Officer," she said. "Don't you get to sleep, too?"

"Oh, yes, ma'am, I do so, shortly. Not that I feel much like it."

"You think too much?"

"I think a lot."

"Of the war, I suppose. Are you on your way somewhere far?"

"I suppose I am," he said. "They don't tell us, you know. And if I knew, I couldn't say."

"Maybe Europe," she said. "You're going the wrong way for the Pacific."

"Likely so."

"Your mother must be very worried."

"Like other mothers," he said.

"And your girl."

There was a long silence while he drew on his cigarette. He was careful to blow the smoke away from her, though he wasn't standing too close. She had almost forgotten her comment—she meant nothing in particular by it, except to express her sympathy—when he finally replied.

"I don't have a girl," he said. "I haven't had time."

She was sitting on a bench. She had kicked off her shoes and tucked her legs to the side. Her skirt hiked up a little; she was too self-conscious to pull it down now.

The officer said, "I'd like to have a girl to think of, over there, to think she cares."

There was nothing to be said to that.

An older officer came out and walked by. The younger one stubbed out his cigarette with his shoe. He spoke so quietly now, she could hardly hear him. "Would you mind—"

"Pardon?"

He stepped closer and put his hands out to pull her to her feet. He was taller than she. There was a shadow on his cheeks. A lock of dark hair fell on his forehead. Did only the privates wear their hair cut to the skin? She hadn't really ever noticed.

They held hands, their arms outstretched between them.

"I'll think about you," he said. "I'll keep this picture of you with me in my mind."

He let go of her, touched his cap again, and was gone.

She went upstairs to tell Margaret what had happened, but Margaret and all the other girls had gone to bed.

The housemother peeked out of her room. She was in her robe, and her white hair fell down her back. "You're not out past curfew, are you, Emma?"

"Only on the porch, ma'am. It's barely ten o'clock."

"We all got tired," the housemother said, and shut her door quietly.

It was deflating, not to tell about the officer. He had chosen Emma as his memory.

The next day, Emma went back to Gallup to stay.

Emma did date a railroad man. She met him in the library, and so thought he couldn't be too bad, but he was a grown man, and pushy when he shouldn't be. She wasn't ready for that. He might have married her, to get what he craved, but she wasn't ready for that, either. She couldn't even imagine being ready for marriage. She could imagine making love—she did imagine it—but the face in the dream wasn't anywhere in sight, and the railroad man was too crude, too old, too impatient—everything Greta might have warned her about, if she had spoken. When she told him she couldn't see him anymore, he wouldn't go with grace. He had to push until she said she didn't like his ways. "But your ways," he said, "now those are something else, aren't they, little lady?" Then the man who had tried to run his rough hands through her hair, along her arms, told her she was high and mighty, too good for her britches, and riding for a fall. She hated him just for the clichés.

Sometimes Emma helped out during lunch at Patty's, working for tips. Greta didn't like that much, either, but she simply set her lips in a straight tight line and kept her opinion to herself, trusting God to look out for her children when she couldn't do it all herself. Emma was like a child who insists on going in deep water, until she finds out how cold it is. It's better not to argue too much, and keep a close eye and a long stick to offer from the bank. One good thing about Emma coming around the cafe was that Greta could ply her with food, and put a few pounds back on her. After a while, she was better, but they didn't mention Winslow. It was just as well, they tacitly agreed; Emma should take it easy.

In October Margaret wrote Emma from Winslow to say she missed her. She could take a few days and come over, she said. Was there an invite at the Gallup end? Emma was so excited she seemed to fly to the telegraph station. She scrubbed the house from top to bottom and moved Amos's cot into Greta's room. Opal would sleep with Greta so that Emma and Margaret could have the other room.

Emma and Opal went to meet the train. Opal, back in school, was through working in the restaurant, except on Saturday, when she went in to pack box lunches. She told Emma, "Doesn't it seem funny to meet someone? I'm so used to racing into the dining room when the whistle blows."

"I've forgotten every bit of it," Emma said. "Except Margaret Lily."

Margaret got off the train wearing a red suit she had sewn herself in Winslow. It clashed wonderfully with her auburn hair. Opal, beside Emma, gasped. Emma got her hug from Margaret. Both of them started talking a mile a minute. Margaret wanted to go to the movies that very night, if that was all right. Opal said, "Mama's planned a special dinner," and Emma was quick to say, "After that we can go, if you want," which they did. Margaret politely asked Opal if she would like to come along, but Greta said, "It's a school night for some people." She still wondered what Emma thought she could do without a high school education.

Opal stayed home to write an essay for American History on the cotton gin and the Southern economy. She heard the girls come in after the movie. They made hot chocolate and sat in the kitchen talking for a long time. Then they brushed their hair and tried to make it look like Veronica Lake's. Even after they went to bed they talked, but in a whisper. When Greta got up in the morning, and then a little later, Amos and Opal, they were fast asleep, side by side, looking like angelic sisters from *Little Women.* Greta looked in on them. "Peas in a pod," she said to no one, shutting the door again.

In the middle of the morning, Emma and Margaret went downtown for coffee at Patty's cafe, then walked up to the El Rancho Hotel. They had taken great care dressing. Margaret wore her red suit skirt and a soft, close-fitting black sweater. Emma wore a pleated skirt and white blouse with a navy cardigan, like a schoolgirl, but she had a pretty red print rayon scarf she draped around her shoulders. Margaret had styled Emma's hair. On each side, she brought the hair up into a roll, the two sides meeting in the center. "It shows off your widow's peak, you lucky duck," she said.

They climbed the big hotel staircase slowly, holding onto the polished banister, gawking about at the lavish decor. When they reached the top, they turned to the right and made their way along the corridor, looking at photographs, trying to match the faces with movies. Margaret gave Emma a little punch in the side with her elbow and said, in her thickest French accent, "Oh, cheree, I love ze peectures. Ze 'otel ees tray elegant." And Emma, suppressing her giggles, replied with broad British strokes, "Of course, my dear, for the West, it is quite adequate, but nothing at all like home."

"Excuse me, ladies," they heard from behind, and almost jumped out of their skin. A man was there with his fedora in his hand, pressed against his chest in a courtly gesture. "Are you guests, too? I haven't had the pleasure."

"*Ah, non,*" Margaret said. She was squeezing her pocketbook so hard her knuckles were white. "We are only—how you say—passing through."

Emma couldn't keep it up. She blushed violently and, feeling her face so hot, turned and buried it in Margaret's shoulder. Then both of them burst into girlish laughter.

"So!" the man said. Peeking, Emma saw that he, too, was laughing. "You were inspired by the photos, I presume?"

The girls nodded, trying to compose themselves. The nice man, who appeared to be at least several years older than they were, but certainly not old, was handsome, in a subdued way. He wore a suit and a shirt open at the collar, with no tie. He was tall and thin, with long sandy hair combed straight back. He patted his chest with his hat. "Hollis Berry," he said. "And I am a guest, I'm happy to say, so I can be your guide and host and mentor."

"Mentor?" Emma echoed shyly.

"We could start with lunch," he suggested.

"I don't know," Emma said.

"We'd love to, Mr. Berry," Margaret said. She stuck her hand out for shaking. "I'm Margaret Lily, of Texarkana, Arkansas, currently of the Winslow Harvey House restaurant. This is my friend and hostess, Emma Laura Clarehope, who lives right here in Gallup."

He stepped between them and took their elbows, guiding them down the wide stairs and into the dining room, where they were shown a nice table near a window, and served a pleasant meal with a Mexican theme, though not too spicy. "Good afternoon, Mr. Berry," the Mexican waitress said.

"Call me Hollis, if you will," Hollis Berry said to the girls. "I live in Los Angeles now, and we're not so hot on these old formalities, Mr.

This and Miss That. You don't mind, do you, Margaret, and Emma Laura, modern ladies that you are?"

Margaret spoke seriously, if not sharply. "Not so modern as you might be thinking most erroneously, Hollis Berry."

He laughed. "I've nothing tawdry in mind, I assure you. Only I was thinking you might like to visit the set, not far from the edge of town. They're shooting this afternoon. I have a car, and I've completed my own business."

"We could do that?" Emma said. Oh, she did want to go.

"We could."

"And have them run us off?" Margaret asked.

"I know the director. I'm a scriptwriter, and I came to visit my mother in Albuquerque, then stopped off to visit the set for a few days. Not that westerns are my thing. I like the modern movie, with women in smart clothes. In my business, though, it's best to show a wide range of interests. You don't know where they'll put you.

"But here's lunch," he observed. "And I want to hear about Winslow, and Gallup, and those wonderful accents—"

"Please," Emma said. "Don't remind me one more time, I'm so embarrassed."

"Don't be," he said. "There's nowhere to go if you don't risk your dignity. That's not the same as self-respect and honesty and other virtues. I mean you have to try new things to get to new places."

"Why, Hollis," Margaret said. "How did you know we wanted to go?"

The set turned out to be a chaotic jumble of cars and chairs and covered wagons and horses, people running about shouting at people across the heads of other people, and actors standing around in Old West costumes, smoking cigarettes and chatting, or sometimes sitting in chairs and dozing. Truth to tell, hardly anything seemed to be going on.

Hollis led the girls past other bystanders, greeting a few workers on the way. They stood near the back of a truck piled with boxes and equipment. "Wait here a minute," he told them. When he came back he said they could use one of them as a stand-in for one of the actresses. He pointed toward a woman in a pioneer dress. At that very moment, she turned and strode away.

"For what?" Emma asked.

"To check lighting, position, stuff like that. It's good enough weather, or I wouldn't suggest it. Sometimes, when it's hot, a person can stand out there until she just keels over."

"Only one?" Margaret said.

"Only one."

"We'll flip a coin," she suggested. Hollis dug into his pocket, and Emma called heads. The nickel came up tails.

"I'm just as glad," Hollis said when he came back from leading Margaret over. "We can visit while she stands around." He gave Emma a lift onto the back of the truck, and climbed up beside her.

"They should call it a 'stand-around,'" Emma said, hoping she wasn't making too stupid a joke.

"How old are you, Emma?"

"I'm seventeen." June had been her birthday.

"You're not in school?"

"I'm—out."

"And what now?"

She looked at him closely, wondering if he meant to mock her, if his questions were idle, if he had other things in mind. Already he had grown on her. She liked his lanky posture, his nice voice. And a writer was a clever person. An intelligent person.

"Something far away from here," she said.

"Did you always live here?"

"No. But always in small places. Places where the world is awfully far away." She sighed.

"Tell me about it."

She couldn't imagine what he wanted to know. "Where I lived?"

"Your life. I like life stories."

"We were poor, and then my Papa died, and we were even poorer."

He didn't say anything.

"See? It's not much of a story. How about this? My father was an explorer, lost at the South Pole. My mother married again, to make a home for her children. She married—a doctor. It turned out he had abandoned a rich cruel wife in another town, and she found him. Her powerful father said he would send him to prison for bigamy if we didn't leave. He knew someone in Gallup who could give my mother a job—"

"Say, you could take my job. You made all that up?"

"Nobody wants to hear about poor girls who keep on being poor."

"But you're just a kid. All sorts of opportunities will come your way."

She spoke bitterly. "You went to college, didn't you?"

"Two years. Then I worked for a newspaper, and then went west."

"Well, if you want ideas for a romantic story, you better pack up and get out of here. You'll have to write about Indians, and Mexicans, and look what's happened to them."

He took her hands. "I'm sorry. I didn't mean to upset you. Listen to me, Emma Clarehope. You're too beautiful to be poor."

"Margaret's beautiful. She's the one over there." Bitterly.

"She's over there because you called heads and it came up tails. My good luck. She's a pretty girl, but girls like her, they're a dime a dozen in Hollywood."

"And girls like me?"

"I've never seen anybody like you. You can't be just seventeen. I think you're the reincarnation of an ancient queen."

She laughed. "You're seducing me, Hollis Berry!"

"It'll always be the other way around with men for you," he said. He didn't look happy about it. It didn't seem to be good news.

There was a boy in Opal's English class, Nick Perry, who, it turned out, lived just up the street from the Clarehopes. They figured it out that afternoon when they hit the same corner at the same time, just across the bridge. "I see you all the time," Nick said. That was when they sorted out addresses.

Nick said he was from Abilene, Texas, but his mother had TB and was in a sanitorium in Colorado, and he was living this year with his aunt and cousin here in Gallup. He didn't say what had happened to his father, and Opal didn't ask. Sometimes fathers died, sometimes they went away, sometimes they didn't know what to do with kids without a wife. It was a lot worse, having your mother sick. She felt sorry for him.

They stopped in front of a house, one street over, one block down from the Clarehopes. "Maybe we could go to a movie sometime," Nick said. He must have been the same age as Opal, but he was skinny and an inch shorter, with a big Adam's apple, and the first thought she had was, *I'd never let him kiss me.*

"Maybe sometime," she said. They were standing in the street. There was a Model A parked there, and she was leaning against it. Just then someone came out of the house—they heard the door slam—and Nick called out, "Hi, Perk!" and then said to Opal, "It's my cousin. Here, you could meet him."

Opal and Nick's cousin stared at one another so hard Nick said, "What's the matter? What's the matter? What'd I say?"

Opal couldn't believe it. "Wesley Perkins!" she finally said. "It's me, Opal Clarehope."

"It is you," Wes said. "So grown up."

"You're here!" Opal said. She pointed up the street. "We just live up there." His house was less shabby, but it wasn't anything like the Aileen house. It wasn't an *inheritance.*

"Here, hop in," he said, and opened the door to his car. "Hey Nick," he said, "when Ma gets home, tell her I'll be late, okay?"

Nick looked like someone doused with water. He watched Wes get in and start the car, then walked dolefully toward the house.

Opal showed Wes where she lived. He walked her to the door. They were still so surprised, they hadn't done any explaining. Suddenly they started to talk, both of them at once.

"My father's working on a movie here—" Wes began.

"My mother came out here to work on the railroad—" Opal began.

They laughed. "We've been here since Christmas," Opal said.

"What about you?"

"Since June, when they started shooting another movie. I've got a job in a service station. My ma is working for the photography studio downtown."

"I don't believe it," Opal said. "Wesley Perkins."

Wes's dark hair fell over his brow. He leaned against the porch post and crossed one foot in front of the other. He'd turned out to be a handsome boy. Young man. How old was he? Older than Emma. "I don't believe it," Opal said again.

"I finished high school in L.A.," he said. "Once we were in Las Vegas while Dad was on a movie."

"Wow," Opal said.

"I wouldn't have recognized you. I'm surprised you knew me."

"Oh yeah, you look—well, the same, but older. Grown up."

"Yeah? So do you, Miss Opal."

She blushed.

"You want to see a movie?"

"Sure, I guess." How could her mother say no? Wesley Perkins, from Aileen! "A movie would be nice. When?"

"How about tonight? First show. I'll pick you up. You tell Mrs. Clarehope we won't stay out late. But it's Friday, no school tomorrow."

"I work."

"See you later," he said.

She went straight into the house and threw herself down on her back on her mother's bed, her arms straight out from her sides.

Amos came in from the kitchen and stared at her. "You look like a scarecrow all fell-over, Opal Mae," he said.

She chased him through the house and to the yard, caught him and gave him a big wet kiss on the back of his neck. "Yech!" he said, and squirmed away. She went back in the house and put her hair in bobby pins, and patted it with water. Then she got out the ironing board and her favorite skirt.

Hollis took Margaret and Emma home and said he'd be back in a little while. He needed to get gas for the car before the station closed. He was going to take them to a movie. They didn't tell him they had gone last night.

Opal had on her best skirt and was combing her hair in the bathroom with the door open. She had laid the table for supper. "We're out of milk. Could you run to the store and get a bottle?" she asked Emma.

"Send Amos."

"He's playing over at Carl's house."

"I can't," Emma said, and slammed the door to the bedroom. So Opal hurried with her dressing, then ran down the street to the bottom of the hill. Emma and Margaret changed into slacks and put on fresh lipstick and mascara, winked at one another, and went by the door to wait for Hollis.

Wesley Perkins and Hollis Berry arrived simultaneously at the Clarehope house. Wes pulled his Model A in behind Hollis's Ford coupe. They introduced themselves, then strolled up to the house.

Emma opened the door and greeted Hollis. Behind him, Wes was partly obscured. As Hollis stepped inside, Wes grinned.

"Remember me?"

Emma couldn't believe her eyes. "Margaret!" she cried, her hand stuck out as if she needed protection. "It's somebody I used to know," she said stupidly when Margaret was beside her.

They stood around for a minute. Then Emma said, "I left Mama a note on the kitchen table so she won't worry. We can go now."

"Where to?" Wes said. His childhood exuberance had turned cocky. He would never need an invitation anywhere.

"We had made plans to go to the movies," Hollis said pointedly, and saw that his point was lost. Besides, four was a nicer number than three.

"Shoot, it's Friday night," Wes said. "We could find something more fun than that."

"A movie's fun," Hollis said. He was looking at Emma.

"Actually, we saw it last night," she told him.

"What did you have in mind?" Hollis asked Wes.

"We could take the girls for a bite to eat, somewhere with music."

Margaret's face almost split with the big grin that suggestion brought on. "I love to dance," she said. "I'm good at it, too." In the time of a breath, she added, "So's Emma."

"You know a place?" Hollis asked Wes. "Someplace decent for these girls?"

"You want to come with me?" Wes asked Emma. "And you follow?" he said to Hollis.

"My car's big enough for all of us." Hollis opened the door and motioned for the exit to begin.

They passed Opal trudging up the street with her bottle of milk. Hollis had his hands on the wheel, but the other three waved and called her name. She stopped long enough to figure out she had just been stood up for her first date, and started to cry.

Hollis suggested they go to the El Rancho, but Wesley said they would have more fun in a less ritzy bar. There were dozens of them, from one end of town to the other. The fellows asked the girls what they thought, and Margaret said, "Take us where the music's hot."

They went to a roadhouse across from the El Rancho. "Fine," Hollis said. "If we don't like the bar, we can go across the street." They settled right in, though. It was Friday night, and people were out to have some fun. They took a booth beneath a long mirror, and ordered food. Margaret went with the fellows' choices and ate a hamburger, but Emma ordered a plain cheese sandwich. She didn't want to get grease on her pretty blouse. She nibbled on it, then pushed it to one side. She watched Margaret a little enviously; Margaret could eat, drink, talk and laugh all at the same time, it seemed.

Emma sipped at the same beer for an hour, until Wesley insisted she take a fresh one. By eight, a western band was warming up, and when it started playing—guitar, fiddle, harmonica and accordion—they wore western shirts with bolo ties, but they were Slavs—couples began to dance. Hollis, who reminded them he was "a tad gimpy," had a routine all worked out. He almost stood in place, with a shuffle, stomp stomp, shuffle stomp stomp, but was easy to dance with because he was so good with his arms. He nudged and tugged, and sent a girl flying out, to be reeled in. Wesley was less accomplished than Hollis, but more energetic; he liked to get around the floor. There were young couples and old couples, and a kind of cheering squad of men alone, along the bar. One of them asked Margaret to dance, and she obliged, managing to get in a little of her jitterbug steps, her hair flying. When she came back, she said to Emma, "Why don't we show them how it's done?" Emma was, for just a moment, completely unsure, and then she said, "Heck, why not?" They went off to the girls' room and put on fresh lipstick, and combed their blown hair.

When the band came back from intermission, they hopped onto the floor with the first song of the new set. Margaret led, of course, twirling Emma in and out like a lariat. They were both laughing, and soon the crowd moved back to give them plenty of room. Everyone started clapping, and the band, knowing a crowd-pleaser when they saw it, went on and on with the same song, until Margaret threw her arms up and cried, "Reel us in, boys!" and the band played down with a flourish. Emma fell into Margaret's arms, and they stumbled back to their booth, flushed with pleasure.

"Boy, you're something," Wesley said. "You're the stars of this show!"

Hollis said, "I'd like to write a movie for you girls! I can see you now, in low-cut bar dresses, your hair piled on your heads. *Two Whores of the Old West*." He grinned. "John Wayne would get one of you, and the other one would run away with the gambler."

Margaret laughed, but Emma's face went white. She raised up in her seat, leaned across the table and slapped Hollis soundly on the cheek. Then, mortified, she sank back into the corner of the booth.

There was silent surprise, and then Margaret said, "Who'd have thought you were such a *lay-dee*?" and made Emma's cheeks burn.

Hollis, rubbing his cheek, said gently, "I meant no insult, Emma Laura. I was being a studio writer, a kind of Hollywood rat you don't have any reason to recognize. Always on the lookout for characters. I was just thinking screenplay, you see. I was thinking heroines. I was thinking—you didn't really belong in the bar, don't you see? You were trapped by misfortune."

She bit her lip, then murmured an apology.

"Nothing for you to apologize for," Hollis said. He reached across and squeezed her hand. "Nobody would ever think of you for a role like that."

Margaret tried to lighten the mood with a joke, and Wesley acted as if he never did see what the problem was. Hollis and Emma, though, looked at one another almost slyly, never quite eye to eye. It was Hollis who said maybe it was time to go. When they went out into the now-dark night, cold on their faces, they felt better right away. "It's too early to go home," Wesley said, and even Emma agreed.

"We could go back to the hotel," Hollis said. "I've got whiskey in my room."

"I wouldn't want to drink hard liquor," Emma said. "My mama would know it before I hit the bottom step."

"We could take a drive," Margaret said. "I love being out after ten." She winked at Emma. "Just like a grown-up."

Wesley directed Hollis to drive into the low hills above town, through one small mining company town, where the bars were full and more bands were playing, to the next, shabbier encampment of shanties, where the Mexicans lived. Hollis slowed down to a crawl as they drove along.

"Oh, look!" Emma said. Ahead of them there was a small fire in the street, and around it a group of Mexicans with their guitars, playing and singing. "Could we stop and listen? Do you think they'd mind?"

"Why would they mind?" Margaret asked gaily.

The miners greeted them politely, some of them standing as the girls came near. The musicians held their instruments still. "No, don't stop," Emma said. Someone made space on an overturned fruit crate for her to sit. Hollis stood behind her, his hand on her shoulder.

One of the Mexicans had a plaintive voice that climbed to a mournful high and brought tears to Emma's eyes. He sang with his hands in front of him as if praying. Then several of the men sang livelier tunes with the easy beat of the Western music they'd been listening to all night. Wesley went into a bar and came out with bottles of beer for the four of them. Hollis knew a little Spanish and traded pleasantries with some of the men, then turned to his friends and said, "They say we're welcome, though I think they're surprised." The men did seem terribly shy, Emma thought. She tried to smile nicely when she caught the eye of one of them, but he looked away.

She scooted over on the box to make room for Margaret. The music and the light of the fire and the stars overhead were intoxicating. In a little while, Margaret draped one arm over her and leaned her head on her shoulder. "It's so beautiful up here," she said softly, "I don't think I'll ever forget it."

Later, when Wesley came back with more beer, Margaret stood over by him to drink. The man with the mournful voice began to sing a beautiful song, and Emma, without really thinking about it, rose from the fruit crate and took a step into the circle toward the fire. The singer was looking at her, as if she were the only woman in the world, she thought; she felt herself hypnotized, drawn closer and closer to the center of the song. She didn't really decide to dance; she found herself swaying, then taking small steps, then moving closer to the fire. The men stared at her. Emma danced. She felt comfortable in the space; she moved around in a circle, her arms sweeping above her head, then out from her sides as she twirled. Her eyes were half closed. She could feel the warmth of the little jumble fire on her legs, and the light on her hair. The singer's voice grew full and throaty and tragic, and she poured herself into the dance, as if no one were there; no, as if the whole world were watching.

Suddenly she stopped, and in a few phrases, the song was over. She blinked. Some of the men called out soft phrases she did not understand. She stumbled back to her friends. Margaret put her arms out for her. Wes said, "Aren't you something?"

Margaret said—was there a tinge of jealousy in her voice?— "Won't your mother be worrying, you out so late?"

They all climbed in the car and started home. Emma sat next to Hollis. As they came down into the town, he leaned over to say, "I presume you've read *The Day of the Locust*? The scene with the dance?"

"No. Should I?" Emma said. She was still warm from her dance, warm in the flesh of her arms and shoulders, and inside, too, in a way she couldn't have described. Hollis laughed, tousled her hair, and leaned over to give her a quick kiss on the cheek. She scooted a tiny bit closer to his thigh, and where their legs touched through their clothes, her skin burned.

It didn't seem possible that they had just met that afternoon. He hadn't said how long he would remain in Gallup. He hadn't said he would see her again. Yet. He was so unlike any man she had ever known, more sophisticated. She thought, *I'd never be bored with Hollis.*

At her house, they stood in the yard a moment, saying how much fun they had had, how cold it was all of a sudden, how tired they were. Emma was wondering how to get a moment with Hollis alone when he announced that he was leaving for Los Angeles in the morning. Margaret jumped on the information and asked for a ride to Winslow. Emma's heart sank. The whole day would amount to nothing more than a movie. See it, and it's gone.

When Emma and Margaret went into the house, tiptoeing and suppressing their whispers, their fingers at their lips—*shhh*—they were startled by the sight of Greta standing in the door of her bedroom, clutching her housecoat at the neck. She didn't take time to say a word, just turned and closed her door with a firm click. Emma's cheeks burned. She wanted to go in to see her mother, she wanted to tell her that she'd had a good time and everything was fine, but she didn't want to seem so young, so much a girl.

"Weren't they a couple of sweethearts, though?" Margaret said, as if she hadn't seen Greta at all. She yawned. "It was lots more fun than I was counting on." Emma bit her lip; she hadn't thought it mattered, that Margaret had come to see *her.* Margaret went on talking. "That Wesley, he thinks he's Clark Gable, what a joke." She was unbuttoning her blouse and walking to the other bedroom. "He's cute as they come, I give him that. But Hollis, he's the one with city written all over him. Even with his one lousy leg, he's the better dancer. It's like honey, isn't it? That look that says, 'I've been where you want to be.' God, it makes a man sexy." She sat on the edge of the bed and tugged off her trousers and let them drop in a heap on the floor. She climbed under the covers in her panties and bra, and then undid the bra and threw it over Emma's head to the floor, too. "I'm too tired to put on my pajamas," she said. "I'm too happy and warm and eager to dream. In my dream, there'll be a big band with a pretty singer, and not that old cowboy stuff." She giggled. "And men in suits, and women in high heels, and champagne in tall glasses. And we won't have to dance with each other. Oh, Emma, don't you wish? Don't you just wish?"

Emma was burning with resentment—Margaret would have the whole morning with Hollis, and she acted like it was nothing, like she had it coming to her—but she was exhausted, too, and the bed was suddenly the most inviting place in the world to be. In bed, she could dream any dream she wanted, just like Margaret said. She could sleep right beyond the boredom and dust of New Mexico. She stripped to her panties and bra, too, then crawled into bed and touched Margaret's leg with her cold toes.

"Yikes!" Margaret said, but when Emma pulled away, Margaret threw one leg over Emma's leg, and her arm across her waist. Her thumb lay under the curve of Emma's breast. "We've got to get out of New Mexico," she whispered.

"I know," Emma said, but she didn't know how. She didn't move a muscle. She almost didn't breathe, to keep Margaret's warmth against her until she slept.

In the morning, the girls had barely managed to get up and drink some tea before Hollis showed up. Emma had heard Opal and Greta earlier, then had fallen back asleep. Now she was in her slacks and a sweater, her hair barely brushed and pulled back in a ponytail.

Margaret was still in the bathroom. "Tell him I'm not quite ready!" she yelled through the door. "I'm not through packing. God, why does he have to leave so early?"

It was a little after eight. Amos was sprawled on the lumpy divan in the living room, his long legs sticking out from under the rumpled quilt. Emma rushed Hollis into the kitchen and offered him tea. "Sorry there's no coffee."

"I just ate a breakfast big enough for a cowpoke. Anyway, I'm glad to have a few minutes with you alone. Here, I want you to take this." He reached into his coat pocket, then handed her a card.

"Twentieth Century–Fox," she read. "Hollis Berry, Scriptwriter." She looked at him, perplexed.

"See," he said, "it's got my office number printed on it, and below that, I've written my home number. Listen to me, Emma, and look right at me so you know I'm serious." He tucked one finger under her chin. "You call me collect when you're ready to come. I'll wire you money for a train ticket. I'm not rolling in dough, but I've got enough to do a beautiful girl a favor, and myself one, too, because I know we'd be great pals if you came—I don't mean anything crummy, either. I'm a good guy and I know you're a sweet girl. You have to come, it's inevitable. It's like they say, written in the stars. Emma, you could be in the movies. I know you could. You wouldn't be a whore, either. God, I could slice my nose off for saying that. You'll be a princess. You'll be the girl of every man's dream. There's a war on, every kid overseas wants to come home to a girl like you. You have to come, say you will."

She couldn't get her breath to answer.

Just then Margaret made her appearance, and before Emma could think what to say, her friends were gone. She stood at the edge of the street, still clutching the card Hollis had given her, and waved until they were out of sight. Not an hour later, Wesley showed up. Emma had barely had time to fix breakfast for Amos and put the kitchen to rights. She told Wesley she was going back to bed.

"I have to go to the station," he said, "but I didn't want you to make any plans for tonight. I'll be by after work."

"I suppose you will," she sighed, then smiled. "I'm as worn out as an old dishrag, Wesley. We better see a movie."

Then she crawled back into bed, hoping it would still be warm, but it wasn't. She slept all day, until her mother came home.

Greta sat on the edge of the bed. Emma turned over and opened her eyes. "Hi, Mama," she said. "You didn't worry, did you? We had a real good time."

"You go out with that Wesley Perkins, you take Opal with you," Greta said.

"I can't do that, Mama, what'll he think?"

"He'll think you're a nice girl."

It was Opal who made a fuss about the idea. "Like a *dog*," she said. "Like a little old pet *dog*." But she always did what her mother said.

Wesley didn't even blink. He came in and saw two girls dressed up and waiting, and he held out both arms and said, "It'll be a squeeze."

Emma talked about going back to work, but neither Greta nor Opal commented. Instead of looking for work, she slept a lot, and read. She had more of those sharp headaches that cut into her eyes and took the breath out of her. She kept the house tidy and made supper. Most evenings, Wesley came by. Opal wouldn't go out on a school night, so Emma got in the habit of taking a ride with him, not gone long enough to upset Greta. One night he took Amos with them to bowl. The bowling alley was a makeshift affair, with four lanes, and no one to set pins most of the time. Wes told Amos he'd give him a quarter to do it, and Amos got the idea to go back after supper sometimes and work for tips.

On the weekend, Wesley took both girls to the movies, or on longer rides. He drove them onto the Navajo reservation, all the way to Shiprock, stopping at a trader's store for sandwiches and a pack of cards. Off-road, in view of nothing but rocks and dust and sky, he taught Emma to play gin rummy while Opal slept curled up behind the seat. Once he arrived as Emma was dishing up supper, and Greta asked him to stay, although unenthusiastically. That was all it took for him to pull up a chair and help himself to a plate of potatoes and applesauce. "Maybe you could get your own place," he advised Greta. "Everybody who wants to go east or west has to come through here. Food is good business."

Greta excused herself and left the table.

The movie they had been filming out at the canyon had wrapped, and Wesley mentioned that his father had gone back to L.A. for the time being. He offered no explanation. If you were a cameraman, you went where the movies were.

He suggested yet another ride. "I bet Nick would like to get out, too," he said, with a sly glance at Opal, but she was scraping plates and running dishwater, and she said she had algebra to do, and no inclination to stay up one minute later than she needed to. At fifteen, she was already five feet eight inches tall; Greta said her growing was hard work. All Opal knew was, she was hungry and sleepy most all the time, and she had to stay awake to make straight A's.

"I'll go," Emma said. It was twilight, a lovely time of day when the harsh landscape was muted and sweetened by falling light. Wes started up the road toward the mining towns.

"My mother never drives," he said. "Lucky for us, we can use her gas."

Emma shrugged. Gas had never crossed her mind. In her experience, when there was something to worry about, there was always someone to do the worrying.

Before they reached Chihuita, it had started to snow. In the time it took Wes to find a good place to turn around, they couldn't see anything but the whiteness. Wes got out and stomped around awhile, then climbed back into the car and said they were in a good spot to wait it out. He had blankets in the car, and a bag of caramel candy. They wrapped up close together.

They were there a couple of hours. "Don't be scared," Wesley told Emma. "It's not blowing. We'll get out of here before long. And I'm prepared, though this is early for snow." He sounded downright proud of himself. She wasn't scared. It was cold, though. She leaned against his chest, with his arms wrapped around her. When she shivered once, he rubbed her shoulders. "I could take a nap," she said, already half dozing.

"I don't think that's a good idea. Let's talk. My ma always told me, If you're ever cold, stay awake. Move around."

Emma laughed, and wiggled her shoulders. "Like this?"

He laughed, too, and kissed her. "You're beautiful," he said, and melted her doubts. She had never been kissed, except by the railroad man, and he had scared her, and then made her angry. Wesley was warm and familiar and he whispered things to her. It was easy to fold into his endearments. He said he was crazy about her. There they were, like two characters lost in a fairy tale, with all the time in the world. He wore an aftershave lotion, something pleasantly spicy. He touched her so gently she hardly stirred. He warmed his hands inside her coat, then slid them under her skirt. He wrapped himself around her. She didn't know if she was awake or dreaming. She was beautiful, and her life lay ahead of her. She fell into a happiness, toward Wesley, and then away again, into herself.

"Emma, baby, you better wake up."

She heard Wesley's voice, then felt the scratchiness of his jacket. She pulled away, blinking. Outside, everything was white.

"You're okay, aren't you?" He sounded worried.

"Yes," she said irritably. "Why wouldn't I be?"

He kissed her cheek. She pulled away. "Let's talk," she said. For a moment, she was scared. She could have slept forever, a maiden in a fairy tale, lost in the snow, but Wes was beside her—so close she smelled his male smell—and she was in her real life.

"What?" Wes said.

"You," she said. "You talk."

"Okay." He told her about L.A. How when he arrived, as a way to learn the city, he spent days and days riding the trolley car to the ends of the line. He told her about the palm trees and orange trees and climbing flowers, and the ocean an hour away. There was a brand new Pasadena highway, slick as a whistle, he said. You could drive for miles and miles and never have to make a stop. He had got a job in the railroad yard the first summer, until they found out he wasn't eighteen, and fired him. Then there was school to finish, and all kinds of odd jobs. He wanted his father to get him some kind of work in the movies—he could move things, hold things, run errands—but his mother was adamant. One member of the family in that business was enough. She blamed the movies for his father's undependability.

On and on he went.

"I bet I'd love it in California," Emma said, in the middle of one of his sentences. "I'd love to wear sundresses and eat oranges—" She felt cozy and coddled. She thought she smelled cinnamon on their breath, from the supper's applesauce. "Give me a piece of candy, please," she said.

He handed her a chunk of caramel, and then, as if she hadn't said anything about California, he veered onto another subject. The war. "I've been thinking about it constantly, and I don't want to go into the army. Crawl around in mud, get shot at in trenches? Not me. I'm going to join the navy. My ma won't hear of it, but she's got a job, and Pop sends a little money. I can send her my pay. Nick can take my job at the station." He had it all figured out.

Emma's mind was still on palm trees and the smell of oranges in balmy air. She nibbled at a corner of the candy.

"I was thinking," he said, "about whether we should get married before I go. I could send you some of my pay, but I don't know what my ma would say. And you'd be with your mother still."

"I could go to L.A. now," Emma said. "We could go together." It seemed a grand offer. "I could get a job there. Maybe I could be a waitress in a fancy restaurant. There are always clerk jobs. You don't have to join the navy yet. You could do it out there, later, after I'm settled. I don't want to spend the war with my mother. I don't want to stay here." She didn't say the thought uppermost in her mind, that Hollis could help her, that he thought she was beautiful, too, and he had professional experience, in a Hollywood studio. After all, Wesley was the one right here beside her, talking love, talking future.

"Why would I want to go to L.A., where every hick from every stick state in the nation has already landed?" he asked. "I been there. It's not the place for me."

How could she answer that? Here, the dreary landscape looked stunted to her. Everything was squat and grubby. What would become of her in a place like this? And if they went back to Texas, like her mother talked about? It wouldn't be any different. In

California, though, there was everything beautiful. There was the sea.

Why couldn't it be Hollis Berry sitting beside her in this car, talking about the future? Somebody who understood what it was like to yearn for beauty, for smart people, for cities? Oh, why couldn't it be Hollis Berry who said those things, did those things, in the long snowy night?

"What do you think, sweetheart? Would you wait for me? Would you write me?" He clasped her hand so hard it hurt. "Don't you know I love you? I think I loved you back in Aileen, but I didn't know that's what it was. Now I sure do. After tonight, don't you know it, too?"

The snow had stopped and the sky was clearing. They were sitting on a big white cake of land, the middle of nowhere. "Wait here?" she asked incredulously. "Instead of L.A.? Weren't you listening?"

"Weren't *you* listening?" he asked. "I'm not going back to L.A. I like it here in Gallup, and my ma is sick of moving. I don't know what my pa will do, but I'm a grown man now, and I'm going to make things happen on my own. Gallup is up and coming. This is where the opportunity is. Don't you realize? We're a buckle on the belt right across the Southwest. We're the town that serves the Navajo Nation. This town needs filling stations and stores and houses, and after the war, it's going to be a building bonanza. I'm going to stay right here, Emma. I'm going to be a rich man." He kissed her, and didn't notice that she gave nothing back. "I'm going to have a whole mess of kids and run for mayor someday."

Suddenly something occurred to her. "What about your pictures, Wes? Don't you take them anymore?"

He laughed and started the car and edged gingerly onto the road. "Who needs photographers anymore? You'll see, five years from now everybody will own a camera. There's no future in photographs, Emma. Photographs are for amateurs now."

She scooted over to the door and rolled down the window. The air was crisp and cold, but not bitterly so. It was dry and still.

As they climbed the hill to her house, Wes said, "It was a beautiful night. Thank you. I'll never forget it." Already he was nostalgic.

*   *   *

As they went up the steps of the house, Greta threw the door open and screamed, "What do you think I've been thinking? What kind of idiot are you? Stay away from here!" She jerked Emma inside. They heard Wes say, "Sorry, ma'am!" and then the sound of his car in the street.

"Mama, for heaven's sake!" Emma cried. "We had a damned blizzard!"

The living room was piled with clothes and kitchen goods. "What's going on?" she asked.

"We're getting out of here," Greta said furiously. She put her hands on Emma's shoulders and dug her fingers in hard. "Don't think I've forgotten that boy, coming around our place in Aileen, snooping, taking pictures, bringing us bad luck."

"Mama, you can't mean that. It's silly."

"Is it? Is it?"

Wesley's portrait of the family was hanging in Greta's bedroom. Emma didn't mention it.

Opal, in her pajamas, stumbled in sleepily. "It's so late," she complained.

"You're not going to school tomorrow," Greta said. "We're packing."

"Where are we going?" Emma and Opal said at the same time.

"Tootie's coming for us," Greta said. She pushed them away. "Go on, go on to bed. Leave it all for me."

Emma was crying. "I don't know what you're so mad about, Mama."

"I'm not mad! I'm happy as a bedbug!" Greta almost shrieked. Then she sat down hard on the divan and stared at them. "Everything depends on me," she said quietly. She shook her head slowly, as if it were too much to believe. Suddenly she was calm. "It's just hard to hope too much."

Opal went to bed, but Emma sat beside her mother, with her arms around her, until Greta told her the plan, and they went to bed.

Tootie had mailed Greta posters from Wichita Falls, taken from bulletin boards around town. DON'T BE A SLACKER! one said. And FIND

THE FACTORY THAT NEEDS YOU! They had cartoon pictures of women with their heads wrapped in cloths to protect their hair from machinery. In Wichita Falls, they would be near Mama Sophie's farm, across the Red River. Tootie would be in the same town. There would be better schools, and most of all, a good job for Greta.

Wesley didn't come to the house the day after the snow. All day Opal and Emma packed. That afternoon, Emma went downtown to the station. They told her Wes had gone to Dallas to buy used tires. He wouldn't be back for a couple of days.

On the way home, she stopped at the Perkinses' house. Nobody was home yet. When she got home herself, she sat down and wrote a short note to Wes, and tucked it in her shirt pocket to take over later.

It wasn't that she forgot to deliver it. Not really. It was more that she postponed it. Whatever she had written wasn't really what she wanted to say. And it wasn't what he wanted to read. There wasn't any point in leaving it. Maybe he would come back before Tootie came for them. Maybe there would be time for a goodbye.

In Wichita Falls, the family piled into the back bedroom in Tootie and Taylor's house. In a few days, Greta took a job packing flour for General Mills. She rented another tiny stucco house, just inside the city limits at the far north side of the town. Opal and Amos enrolled in school. Opal came home the second day all excited. She had learned about the vocational program. After Christmas, when the new semester started, she could start a program that would send her, afternoons, into the hospital to learn lab work. She and Greta would both learn about buses—and patience—taking two or three each way every day. Greta worked rotating shifts, changing every two weeks. The midnight shift paid eight cents an hour more. Her regular pay was sixty-five cents an hour. On the railroad, she had worked for a dollar a day. She worked five and a half days a week. In six months, she'd get a raise. It was a union job. For the first time in her life, she could see the possibility of something beyond survival. The little house she had rented was for sale.

Emma wasn't taking to the move as well as the others. She was lethargic and nauseated and withdrawn, but there just wasn't time for Greta to attend to her. She put food in their little icebox and she got extra quilts from the farm. She bought copies of *Life* and *Silver Screen* for Emma to read. She kissed her before she left for work, and checked on her when she got back, covered in a silty coating of white flour.

When Emma left, it was a blow to bring a mother to the ground, but Greta told herself that there was a balance in her fortune. Emma would come to her senses. California was a heathen place. Here, there was family to love her.

"Come home soon," she prayed. She faced west to say it.

June 16, 1943
Miss Emma Clarehope
207 East Terrace
Gallup, New Mexico

Dear Emma,

I hope you will forgive my familiar address. I found letters from you in my daughter Margaret's belongings, and I felt some closeness to someone who loved her. I am sorry it has taken me so long to write, but I have not been well enough to manage same for quite a while.

Margaret was killed in Los Angeles last March, in an accident. She had just stepped off the trolley car, and was struck by an automobile that had veered to miss a dog in the street. She had been working for a movie studio. She was a "stand-in" for a movie actress. I'm sorry, but the actress's name just doesn't come to my mind right now, and I don't have the heart to read my darling Margaret's letters yet, to look for it. I take comfort from knowing that she was very happy to be out there, and to be doing a job she loved. I remember she wrote me to say that the actress was very nice to her, and even gave her some dresses, and that it was wonderful to have a job in the movies that was steddy work and didn't put her under too much preshure. I tell you all that because you are young, and I think you will understand it better than I did, or her father. Margaret was always diferent from our other children, allthough we loved them all the same.

The last letter from you in Margaret's things was addressed to her in Winslow, Arizona in October, so I don't know if there was more letters after that. I just hope this one reaches you, and that you will pray to the Lord as we do, that He will keep her close and make her truely happy, for the good girl she always was.

Yours,
Mrs. Charles (Edna) Lily

Los Angeles, California

Hollis lived in Hollywood in a neighborhood that, although it could not be called fashionable, had its own special dash. For several blocks, most residents of the modest apartments were studio personnel from MGM, Twentieth Century-Fox, and Warner Brothers. Tucked back behind a high fence, there was a women's residence packed with girls hoping for a break, while they worked in offices and shops, and took acting and voice lessons when they could manage. The scriptwriters clustered together, generally a hard-drinking, poker-playing, late-night crowd, as if they had themselves been cast in that particular role. Hollis's apartment building, two lots down from the Christian Ladies Residence, was a pearly pink stucco with a high wall on which large crimson flowers rambled. He took Emma's photograph there soon after she arrived. She stood leaning one arm against the building, looking at that very wall, and asked herself if she could be merely dreaming. The yucca plants a few feet in front of her could have been back in Gallup, but the smells in the air were all new to her, all wide-awake California.

75

From the moment she stepped off the train, walked into the main room of the station, and stared up at the brilliantly tiled Moorish dome, she doubted the reality of her presence in this fanciful kingdom. In the tiny dressing area off the toilet on the train, she had changed from her slacks and shirt into a fresh white blouse, pleated skirt, and, because it was cold in the early morning, a navy cardigan sweater Margaret had given her back in Winslow. At the moment she spotted Hollis, who was making an arc of greeting with his arm, she was worried that she had made a mistake, turning into a schoolgirl at the very moment she ought to be trying for sophistication, but he was delighted to see her attire.

"Aren't you the sweetheart? What an absolutely perfect outfit!" He held her at arm's length and twirled her like a dancer back to him, and put his arm around her shoulders. He was delighted, too, that she was wide awake after a long night on the train. "I made up a bed for you," he said, "but I'd rather take you to breakfast. I want to look at you, be sure you're here."

"How could I be tired?" she asked, though her lower back ached terribly, and her legs were half-numb, and she had felt nauseated all night on the crowded train. "I've arrived where I want to be. I'll pay you back, I promise, I'll pay you back with interest, but there'll never be a way to thank you enough."

She threw her arms around his neck and put her face up to his. He kissed her on her forehead, and patted her shoulder. "Don't you worry about it," he said. He picked up her small striped cardboard suitcase and led her to his car.

They went to a diner and ate eggs and bacon, toast and coffee. Her appetite amazed her. It was the best meal she could remember in the longest time. Then he drove her around Hollywood, promising a long tour of greater Los Angeles on the weekend. She was dying to see the ocean, but she didn't say it. The ocean wasn't going anywhere, and she wasn't either. He took her back to his building, and took pictures of her, then led her up to the second floor apartment. The front room was small but adequately furnished with a couch and low table, a small desk and chair, and two lamps. There were books everywhere. She couldn't help staring; it was like Christmas. She saw books by Fitzgerald, Steinbeck, and Camus. She saw *The Song of Bernadette* and *Darkness at Noon*. He saw her looking at the books. "Anything you want," he said. He swept the room with his gesture. "But excuse the mess." In fact, the apartment was quite clean, the desktop shining with polish. She loved the room. She loved the books, the light, her sense of freedom. To be what? she thought. She smiled and walked over to the window.

She pulled back a gauzy strip of curtain to look down on the courtyard. "It's so pretty here," she said. She turned to smile at him. "Just like I knew it would be." She was careful to hold her head high, to show him the long white line of her neck.

"I wish my Kodak would work in here," he said. "You look lovely in the light there. Hell, let's try it, anyway." He got his camera and snapped several pictures. "I'm going to run these out to the studio and see if I can get a buddy to print us a couple right away. I've got an idea—no, I don't want to tell you yet—and while I'm gone you can rest. There are lots of magazines on the floor in the bedroom."

He showed her the little kitchenette, behind folding doors, and the bathroom. He opened the door to the bedroom. "See, I've put fresh sheets on and everything, it's all yours." A towel and washcloth were folded neatly at the end of the bed.

"I couldn't," she said. "I thought—" She pointed to the couch. "I'll sleep in here."

"I won't have it," he said grandly. "Hell, I can sleep anywhere, the floor's fine as far as that goes." The bed did look soft and inviting, with a blue chenille spread. "Say, if you're too uncomfortable with this, I could bunk with my buddy Teddy downstairs, he's got a pull-out couch, too—"

"Oh, no, I'm happy here with you. I'd be scared to be here alone. And I'm sure I'll get a job right away, and I'll find a place—"

"Now look here, Emma. I asked you to come. And I've got ideas about what you can do. You don't have to think about that yet. You just got here. Take a nap and go down to the patio and get a little sun. There are umbrellas down there, too, if it's too bright for you.

There's soda pop in the icebox, and some cheese and crackers. I want you to feel like this is home. You've come a long way. There's a lot to see, a lot to do. Don't you know this is swell for me, too?"

All of a sudden she was so tired she felt she might swoon. She put her hand to her forehead.

He pulled the spread back. "Here, lie down." The sheets were bright, clean. He fluffed a pillow, then reached down and brought up a couple of magazines and put them on the bed. "There are some scripts under here, too—" He pointed to the shelf under the bedside table. "Might be a kick for you, see how a movie looks when it's just an idea on paper. I'll be back in a few hours. We'll go for Chinese tonight with some pals of mine."

She sat on the bed. He lifted her feet, pulled off her shoes, and tenderly put her feet on the bed. She sank back against the pillow and smiled at him. "I've never eaten Chinese food," she said. "You'll have to order for me."

In the morning, she felt all the tiredness she had managed to ignore the day before. She stumbled to the bathroom and was sick. She felt better after she washed and made herself a cup of tea. She dressed carefully in a pair of slacks she had paid too much for. She'd bought them with the last of her small savings from the days in Winslow. The pants had a high wide waist, pleats in the front, and wide legs. She wore them with a red sweater with shoulder pads, and she put her hair up in a French roll. When Hollis came in, late in the morning, he let out a long whistle and turned her around admiringly, but then he said he couldn't explain, but he wanted her to change back into her outfit with the pleated skirt.

She stood like a chided child, with her mouth turned down, but he cheered her up with some lines from the smart comedy he was writing for an actor and actress the studio was hoping to promote as something of a sparring couple onscreen. She laughed obligingly, then went off to change, still a little dismayed. Her hair looked all wrong with the old outfit, so she took it down and brushed it out, simple as if for bedtime. Once again he pronounced her "perfect," gave her a kiss on her forehead and escorted her to his car cheerily.

In the studio commissary they ate tunafish sandwiches served on big white plates, seated at a table under a huge, zany mural. Several times someone called out Hollis's name and waved from across the room. Once it was an actor dressed in a toga, who ate his lunch with half his chest bare. Another time, a man in a suit and hat like Hollis came to the table and was introduced as "my fellow slave, works up the hall from me." She felt dizzy from all she had seen. Walking across the lot from the car, she saw Indians and sheiks, showgirls and cowboys. A backdrop, as big as the side of a house, was being hauled along by men in jumpsuits.

She had eaten half her sandwich—all she could manage—and was wondering if she should wrap it in her napkin and carry it out. She could hear her mother saying, *Waste not, want not,* right in her ear. There she was, staring at that silly sandwich, her brow all furrowed as she puzzled over it, when Hollis said, "Come on, Emma, stand up, will you?"

She slid out from the table and did as he asked. A woman wearing a smart green suit, with the worst hairdo Emma had ever seen—her rolls had rolls, and a piece of metal underneath the hair was showing at one end—looked her over. She took hold of Emma's hair on the sides and pulled it straight out. "Hmmm," she said, and nodded her head.

"Didn't I tell you, Stella?" Hollis said. He had Emma's hand and was squeezing it.

"I showed the photos to Buster, and he says if I say so, she can come up." She lifted Emma's chin with her fingers. "Now honey, you don't sound like one of those Okies, do you? Didn't Hollis tell me you were from Oklahoma?"

"I'm from Texas," Emma said, since it was more or less the truth. One thing she knew for sure was she didn't sound like an Okie. It bothered everybody in her family, the fact that she was so "highfalutin" sounding. "I've had lessons, and I'm sure I talk just fine."

"Well, well, indeed you do." Stella's laugh was mostly a bark. "Not that it makes a diddly damn difference. You aren't likely to have one word to speak!" She seemed to find that especially funny; she struck Hollis's arm with the flat of her hand, laughing.

"Around three," she said to Emma. "Wipe your makeup off, and put your hair in pigtails, honey. You're gonna be fifteen and scared to death." Across the room, she scooted into a booth with a couple of other women.

Emma had forgotten all about her sandwich. In fact, her stomach was turning upside down. She had an idea what was going on, but it was the sort of thing you don't want to hope for and misunderstand, in case you are working yourself up to some big disappointment.

Hollis was too happy for it to be anything but good. "I knew it back in Gallup, and I knew it when you stepped off that train." He marched her out of the commissary and toward his office, which she had yet to see. It wasn't until they were inside and seated that he explained. "They've put out a call for girls for a production of *Jane Eyre*, and I could just see you in it. You've read *Jane Eyre*? Good. Remember at the beginning, that awful charity school? They need girls for it. It's perfect. All you have to do is stand there and look piti- ful. *You just have to be seen*, Emma, that's how it all starts."

"It can't be that easy," she said.

"Stella's in casting. Her boss has to okay it, but this isn't Cleopatra on the Nile here, it's just a poor girl in a one- or two-minute scene. Buddy will say yes. He'll act like it's a big favor, because it's so easy for him to do. He likes pretty girls, and you're a wispy one, besides. And then, well, we'll see, Emma. They'll see."

"I do hope so," she said brightly. She thought she sounded just like Deanna Durbin in *It's a Date*, discovered in her college play. She wanted so much to kiss Hollis, or maybe just to sit in his lap and feel safe, but there was a big desk between them, and he had his legs up on it, and she was practically tucked into her chair against the wall.

She patted her mussed hair into place and lowered her head demurely. "I could fall in love with you, Hollis Berry," she whispered. She was that happy, already. He grinned and rubbed his eyebrows.

"The whole country's going to fall in love with you," he said back. "I wonder what they'll call you."

* * *

Who was going to notice her? There were dozens of extras playing the poor girls in Mr. Brocklehurst's charity school. They were all dressed up in smocks with white aprons, their hair pulled into braids so tight their scalps stung. Emma's pale hair stood out, though. (Later, when she saw the scene in which little Jane is standing punished on a chair while the girls are lined up like soldiers in formation, and the black-garbed teachers along the back are stiff as dead trees, she wanted to shout, "That's me! Look, it's me!" She was visible just off the left shoulder of Jane, but of course by then everything had changed, and it didn't matter anymore, and truth told, you couldn't tell it was her.)

But now, now it was exciting, even if she was just one more body in a line. In crazy production logic, before they filmed the scenes with the girls, they filmed a later one, opening on Jane all alone and fretting on her chair. Little curly-haired Helen brings her a crust of bread and the glimmer of friendship and love in a terrible place. Jane was played by a bright-eyed little child star, darling and lively and completely professional—Emma felt she ought to be taking notes—but the child who played Helen was something else altogether. Emma found her stunningly beautiful and serene, as if a wise woman's soul was housed in her child's chest. When she said, "It's wrong to hate people," it *was* wrong. And when, dying, she said, "I'm not afraid," Emma's eyes smarted with tears. Right then and there she thought, I'm going to be like her. Like a girl eleven or twelve years old! I'm going to be as brave and good and serene as little Elizabeth Taylor. She loved her always. Years later, this was the moment she would remember best, the one moment she savored. Not her own appearances, but Elizabeth's.

Hollis wormed his way in to see the rushes. He only spotted Emma twice, once ever so quickly, washing up in the dormitory, and then, noticeable if you were looking, lined up for one of the evil master's tirades. "Isn't she a sweetheart?" he asked one of the director's assistants, and an editor, and of course he mentioned it in casting. Luckily, he had never asked anyone for anything at the studio, and when starlets were a dime a dozen, why couldn't one of them be his dime's worth? He had his photographs, too, and the truth was, this Emma was a very pretty girl. She had a fresh, sweet look to her, no hard edges.

"Oh, hell, bring her in for a test, who can tell anything in a lousy Brit film?" they told him. This time she didn't go in in pigtails. In fact, Hollis took her downtown and bought her a terrific dress, a navy silk nipped in at her tiny waist, with a modest neckline. He bought her new high-heeled shoes, and she had her nails done for the first time in her life. One of Hollis's friends lent her a string of proper pearls to fill in the throat of the dress, and a sweet comb for her hair.

"I won't know what to say. I won't know how to act," she said in a panic as they got to the studio. "This is a mistake. I've never had lessons. I don't know anything about acting."

He took her hand and stroked the top of it. "Shh, you just go in there and be the little lady. Now, listen to me, Emma, you're not a bimbo, you know? Don't try to throw it around. You be this beautiful girl, a real lady, and let the beauty speak for itself. They'll tell you everything to do. You don't have to worry about acting. Hell, you can act, anybody can see that. What counts is how you look on the screen. Nobody can teach you that. You can't put it on. You just have it. And I'm sure of it, I'm sure of you."

She tried to hear his words in her head, going in to meet men whose names flew over her and were lost. They told her to go onto a set where there was a couch and a pretty coffee table with a tea service on it. "Walk over to the couch, honey, and sit down." She could do that. She didn't know whether to cross her legs, though. She sat turned to the side, so she could pull her legs back in what she hoped was a pretty pose, not crossed. Then a voice said, "He isn't coming, honey, look over at the door, but you don't care."

She did exactly as he said. He wasn't coming. Was he hurt? Was something wrong? She bent forward, inclined toward the door. She decided not. He couldn't meet her demands, he wasn't good enough for her. He resented her pride. Her head went higher, her back arched a little. She settled back into the couch, and she crossed her legs. To hell with him.

She heard muttered voices out there. She didn't know what else she was supposed to do. She put her fingers to her throat, to the string of pearls there. She let her fingers slide inside her dress, down onto her flesh.

"That's dandy. Now we've got some questions," a voice said. "Emily, isn't it?"

"Emma Laura Clarehope," she said, herself again. Her voice was clear enough; she didn't think she sounded scared.

"Emma, you've got a family back in Oklahoma, have you?"

She scooted up on the edge of the couch. She wanted to look perched and eager now. She wanted them to know she would answer their questions, just ask. "Oh yes sir, I do. My mother and brother and sister." Nobody said anything, so she went on, filling the silence. She was hot as hell. "My mother works in a factory, there aren't men to do the job now, with a war on. My sister is in nurse's training; they'll need her if they don't get this awful war won soon, and she'll be ready. My brother is too little for war, but he does his part. He collects scrap metal after school." The studios were out there pumping up patriotism; they sent their stars around to sell war bonds. She could tell them she knew whose side was the right side. She believed every word of it. Here she was in her screen test, and already she had learned what acting was. She was proud of her little family, and it showed.

"And you, Emma Hope. What's your part? What do you do for the war?"

She took her time. "I just want to make people happy, sir. Make their hearts soar, you know, the way the movies can do when nothing else can. I'm not a big girl, I wouldn't be much use in a factory, but—" She clasped her hands at her breast. "I can make people forget for a little while, and go home smiling." And she lifted her chin high. She smiled her most radiant smile. She had done just fine. Her beauty filled the screen.

*   *   *

Her contract said she would be paid thirty-five dollars a week, except when she was on studio furlough, when her pay dropped to twenty. She had to promise to meet standards of public decency, not to insult the public or the studio. She signed.

She made Hollis take her to a grocery store so she could cook supper for him. They went out a lot to eat, and the rest of the time they ate takeout from delis and Chinese restaurants. It felt good to put an apron on—he had an apron!—and act like the little woman. She was so happy to do something for him.

There was hardly room in his little kitchen, but she managed fried chicken and mashed potatoes, and sliced tomatoes. She was starving, and as the chicken fried and the delicious smells filled the apartment, she realized she was starved for exactly this, home cooking, her mother's cooking. Hollis had bought a bottle of red wine. They ate sitting on the couch with plates on their laps, and licked their fingers and sucked the chicken bones and laughed about it.

"I'll go out when I get my first paycheck and find an apartment," she promised. "And I'll start sending money home."

"Wait—" Hollis said. "Don't be in a hurry. First you'll need makeup. Some clothes. Then why don't you see if there's a room up the street, in the ladies' place? An apartment, heck, that's too lonesome, and you couldn't afford too much on thirty bucks a week." She already knew it wasn't as much as some of the starlets got, but it was a lot to her. She bet it was more than her mother made packing flour.

"Thirty-five," she would have him know.

He nodded.

Hollis was right. The money disappeared as fast as it came in. And it was hard, getting to the studio every morning, rushing to classes and casting calls and meetings. They put her in a Gene Tierney film right away. She wore an extravagant turn-of-the-century costume—New York City—and sat on a park bench for all of five seconds. Then she was a secretary, but she got to say, "I'll see if he's in, Mr. Benton." After that she was a chorus girl in a Western saloon, and she teased Hollis, saying he had planned it all along. She wasn't much of a dancer, but none of them were, except the girls in the front. The next movie, she had another walk-on part, but the girl cast as a friend who comes to lunch and spills a little gossip to set things in motion got sick with the mumps, and with the snap of a finger, Emma had a script in her hand, a coach, a part.

She came home exhausted and thrilled and told her roommate Cecelia all about it. Cecelia was a singer, working as a waitress, and Emma wasn't sure what kind of singer she would ever be, she was so religious. Half the time she was reading about virgin martyrs, or books of spiritual reflections. Emma borrowed *The Song of Bernadette* from Hollis for her to read, and she was thrilled. Everyone knew that Jennifer Jones was going to play Bernadette, and envied her. All those scenes, looking up to heaven, or at the Virgin, whatever it was that made her pretty and holy.

"I don't think holy girls have an easy time," Cecelia said solemnly. "Nobody ever believes a girl is all that good." She looked like she knew what she was talking about.

"The studios want us to be as good as saints," Emma said. She laughed and made a face. "I heard about a girl who got fired for going out to nightclubs. She had a boyfriend the studio didn't like."

Cecelia shrugged. "I bet she got married."

"I think I did hear that."

"She's better off," was Cecelia's judgment.

Emma ran off to the bathroom to wash her hair and didn't bring up the subject of behavior again. She and Cecelia got along fine, but it wasn't because Cecelia was a laugh a minute or anything. And Emma didn't like dwelling on a subject as boring as goodness. She was doing the best she could.

Hollis read her script and pronounced it "quite satisfactory." He pointed out that he had not worked on it. "So it's not fabulous, you understand—"

She took it back from him. "It doesn't have to be fabulous, Hollis. It just has to have lines for me." She sighed. "Emma Hope. They didn't even ask me. It was on the contract. Emma Hope."

"What'll your mother say?"

"I don't know. I don't think she'll believe any of it. I sent her ten dollars late for her January birthday, and she wrote back as if I'd gone off to visit a distant cousin. 'I guess the weather is nice out there. When do you think you'll be home?' I told her I have a contract to work in the movies, and she wants to know when I'll be home!"

"My mother asks me that twice a year, Christmas and Mother's Day," Hollis said. "It's what mothers say. What I say is, let's go out and celebrate your part. Saturday night. I'll take you to Santa Monica, to a restaurant that looks out on the ocean. I could get Buddy and Susan to come—"

"Just us," she said. "Is that okay? This time?" A shiver of fear passed through her, just like a wind picking up on the prairie. She had felt it before, but she never allowed herself to feel it. She never thought about it.

He said of course they would go alone, and yawned so big it seemed put on. He was always watching the hour when they were together. He said she couldn't afford to get a reputation. What reputation? She never did anything except work and spend time with Hollis, and he persisted in being her big brother. All those weeks they lived together in his apartment, she used to curl up in his bed and wish him to come to her, but she slept alone. He sat up and read, or sometimes he went out with one of his pals, or played poker. He was like a relative, when you thought about it. He was tall and good looking and kind and intelligent, and he told her all the time that she was beautiful and clever, and he never made any attempt at all to touch her. Even when she made it easy, he wasn't looking for it. Yet she was absolutely sure that his friends thought they were lovers. They were never nasty about it—you couldn't be nasty around Hollis, he wouldn't have put up with it, and maybe he didn't have those kinds of friends—but they treated the two of them like a couple. They took them for granted. When you really thought about it, the result was to take her out of circulation when she had never been put in. Sooner or later, she was going to have to talk to him about it, but the last thing she wanted was to make him angry or unhappy. If she didn't have Hollis, she would be a lonely lost soul, job or not. And she wasn't interested in meeting new guys. In a boyfriend.

They walked down the block to her residence. At the front steps, she asked him, "Do you still think I'm pretty?"

"More than ever," he said. Really, she looked just the same, except that she wore pencil on her pale eyebrows every day now, and she dressed better.

"Kiss me?"

She thought he was going to say something. She could see his mind working, his eyes boring into her, his hesitance. It hurt her feelings, and she took a step back, but he reached out for her. Gently, he bent to kiss her, then he put his arms around her and held her close. "You can count on me," he said.

The April night was so inky the sky was a curtain of black a few steps into the ocean. Emma had eaten little of her fine grilled fish and asparagus, and she had said almost nothing. She drank a lot of champagne. She rubbed the glass between her palms, and held herself in such a way that the candlelight flattered her. Her silence could be interpreted as mystery, but when bitterness knotted her chest, she was restless, shifting in her chair, clasping and unclasping her hands. She had bitten her thumbnails to the quick, and she kept rubbing them as if to will their regrowth. Once she caught herself squeezing the wine glass dangerously hard.

"Tell me what's wrong," Hollis said for the third time.

"Nothing. Things have happened so quickly, more quickly than I ever dreamed, and now I'm wondering, who will I be in a year? Emma Hope, with half her name. What's to become of me?"

"Don't worry. Talent will carry you."

"What talent? What have I done, except dress up and stand around? What talent does that require?"

"You've this wonderful quality, a kind of concentration, like a child has, listening to a seashell. It's the very quality every director wants in an actress, and no one can teach you. It's what makes you luminous on the screen. A stillness. One of these times, you'll have a part that lets you show it, and you'll never have to worry after that."

"You see that? Do you really?"

"I watch you sometimes. When you're reading. When you're gazing out at something, transported—"

"But that doesn't sound concentrated at all! It sounds distracted. That's what I am, really. Distracted." She realized she had slumped into her chair, and she sat up.

"Dreaming is another form of concentration, Emma. You look at things in a way other people don't. As if every object had a soul, and you could speak to it. It's a way of pushing against what's ordinary. An aliveness. Hell, it's drama!"

She laughed at that, sounding herself again. She thought he was in love with her. Didn't he know? Hadn't he said, You can count on me? "I've been writing poetry," she said. "Not that I know anything about it."

"Will you show me sometime?"

"I'll tell you." She took a deep breath.

"We don't know what comes tomorrow.
Will we laugh or will we sorrow?
Time is a mystery, the fate of man
Hidden behind Lady Future's fan.

But when the trouble seems
To be the worst, we have dreams.
And whether we laugh or weep,
We forget everything in blessed sleep."

Suddenly shy, she drained her glass. "Can I have more wine?"

He was looking at her so intently, a rouge of embarrassment spread from her face down onto her chest. She was wearing a black silk blouse sprinkled with tiny white dots, like faraway stars, and she could feel it on her flesh all the length of her torso, cool, soothing silk.

He reached across the table and took her hand. His long, tapered fingers covered hers. "It is frightening to get what you think you want. You're still so young." What was he?

She fought tears. She thought of Elizabeth: *I'm not afraid.* She bent, and pulled her hand up, so that her cheek lay against the backs of his fingers. "Darling Hollis. I ask too much of you." It was as if someone whispered the lines into her ear. She pulled her hand free and smoothed her hair. He was staring at her, something working at the corner of his mouth. Amusement? Was she funny, then? A fool, with her pathetic rhymes, her neediness? She stood up abruptly, knocking over her chair. Blood rushed to her face and she felt dizzy. She grabbed the back of the chair.

Across from her, Hollis got up slowly. It seemed she clung to the chair for many minutes, while he peeled bills onto the table and slid his chair into a tidy place under the table. As he moved toward her at last, she walked unsteadily to the oceanside door. A long wooden staircase led down to the beach.

"Wait, Emma, don't hurry."

There was a breeze off the ocean. She smelled salt. She made her way to the first landing, and sat down.

"Are you all right?"

"It's so beautiful," she said. All evening, she had been thinking, *I'm seventeen years old.*

They left their shoes at the bottom of the stairs and walked for a long while along the sand. The breeze off the water was cool. He put his arm around her. She felt heavy, each step an effort. She thought, *He won't love me anymore, and then I'll have nothing at all. Seventeen.* She didn't know if she thought that was young or old. It seemed so strange, to be her, to be seventeen, to be where she was. She couldn't remember if he had ever asked her age.

She missed her mother.

She pulled away from him and ran a little way down the sand. She faced the black horizon and waded into the surf.

She turned back and kicked her feet and splashed, watching him on the beach. He was wearing a suit and a hat. He had rolled his pant legs up onto his calves. She walked backwards a few steps, and waved at him. He waved back. She wasn't far, it was like a small joke between them.

She turned and walked into the surf. As a small wave struck her knees, she almost lost her balance.

"Emma, don't go any farther!" she heard behind her. She trudged on, swaying to keep on her feet. The waves weren't all the same. She hadn't remembered this. A large one came in; she sensed it when it was still far away, like a rumble inside her belly. She planted her feet apart and dug into the sand, so that when it rolled over her, across her chest, she would not be knocked down.

"Emma, for God's sake!" she heard, but his voice was fainter now.

She thought of how Elizabeth would walk. Not looking back, not afraid. She took another step, and was swept backwards. She came up again, coughing, her eyes stinging. The air was cold now. She could see nothing at all in front of her. There was only the sound of the water, that seashell sound grown huge. She wasn't afraid.

Hollis grabbed her from behind and pulled her into the shallow surf. "What are you doing!" he shouted angrily. "What the hell are you doing?"

"Let me go! Oh, God, Hollis, you don't know!"

He enclosed her in his arms and held her tightly against him. "Don't know what? What is it? For God's sake, tell me!"

They stumbled onto the sand. She pulled away from him. She didn't want to whisper this news. She didn't want to tell him up close. She wanted him to look at her. She wanted the whole screen.

"It's all over, Hollis. My big career. My life in California. It's all over." She ran her hands down the front of her, and held them on the tiny mound of her belly, where the sopping cloth of her skirt clung. "I see you every day and you haven't noticed. My roommate knows. She stares at me when she thinks I don't know, she says the rosary for me. I'm pregnant! I'm pregnant!" She fell to her knees, crying.

He knelt in front of her. "Oh Emma, darling Emma." He lifted her face.

"This isn't a movie," she said. "This is my life."

"Emma, Emma."

"Emma, what?" Her voice was barely a whimper. "You should have let me go."

"But a baby—"

"I don't want a baby. What about my career? What about the movies? Don't you think a baby might *break my concentration*?"

"There are things to do, sweetheart. This is Hollywood."

"It's way too late. I'm a small woman. I've starved myself, and I've pretended—it's too late for that, Hollis. I couldn't do that, anyway."

"Come on." He pulled her to her feet. "We can't talk about it here. We've got to get dry." He took off his dripping jacket and wrung it out and draped it over one arm. He tugged her along on the sand. "Hell, Emma, why didn't you tell me back in Hollywood? We've got such a long way to go and we're so damned wet!"

He sounded amused. A scene in a comedy. He had lost his hat.

In the car, dripping onto his seat, it didn't seem funny. Neither of them said anything all the long way home. She wrapped her arms around herself. Her teeth chattered.

He took her clothes off and washed her face with a hot cloth, dried her hair with a towel, and put her into bed in one of his undershirts. Then he crawled in beside her, and both of them slept until late the next morning.

When she woke, he was already dressed and moving around the apartment. She pulled herself up on the pillows. "Hollis?"

He came in and lifted the shade on the small window across the room. It didn't matter that her life was ruined; it was spring in Hollywood, and it was a beautiful day. He went out of the room and returned with coffee. He gave it to her and sat on the bed.

"What am I going to do?" she asked.

"You're sure you don't want this baby?"

"I don't, I don't." She wished they had never spoken the word. *Baby*. She thought, *I don't want it.*

"You don't want to tell the father?"

"*I don't want the baby.*"

"You know, I don't think of myself as an unobservant person, but you're right, I had no idea. You're very small, still."

"I know. But I can feel the baby."

"Can you do this new part you've got?"

"I have to! Yes. If they shoot my scenes early on, it'll be okay. Fifteen minutes into the movie, I disappear." She wouldn't eat. Coffee, oranges, crackers. Anything else, she would not eat.

"Listen to me. I love you, Emma. Maybe I'm not everything you need. But I think we should get married. We can sort it all out later. Right now, well, you need to be married. Marry me."

She turned her head away and fought her tears.

"Maybe you should call in sick on Monday. Just a day. And then again another day a little later. They'll be mad at you, but you haven't missed a day so far. Then in a while we can say you're sick, you need a furlough."

"They'll figure it out in a minute," she said bitterly. "They'll know in wardrobe. They'll talk."

"Maybe. But I'm betting they won't make anything of it. People talk to each other, not to the ones upstairs. Once, some of us bailed out a contract actor and paid off the reporter at the station. Nobody ever knew about his disorderly charge. You'll be sick, and then you'll be well, and you'll be back at work. It could work out. It's possible."

"You don't really believe that. How are we going to explain a baby? Take care of a baby? It's the end of everything, that's what it is." She put her fist against her teeth and pushed hard. Then, her knuckles smarting, she looked at him and she said, "I don't deserve this, you know. It's not fair at all."

"There's something else. An idea I have." He got up and paced around the room. "I know a producer at Warner. He's an important man. He's married to a beautiful woman, been married for years, and they've never been able to have a family."

"Yes?"

"Let me go talk to him. What would you think of that? Of adoption? If you could have the baby, and go back to work after, if your life could go on just as if this never happened—"

"Yes! That's exactly what I want."

"Afterwards, you'd have to forget—"

"I wish I could forget right now."

He sat back down and took her hands in his. "We can work something out, Emma. You're foolish to think you need to throw your life away."

She couldn't keep the tears from spilling.

"You poor kid," he said. "You are just a kid."

"Thank you, Hollis," she whispered. She tucked her head and looked up at him like a penitent.

"You think about this the rest of the day, Emma, and tomorrow, call in sick. I'm going to go over to Warner in the morning. But think about it. They're fine people, but you'd be giving up your flesh and blood. You have to be sure. We could get married. I mean that. I'd be glad to marry you."

"Go see your important producer. I don't want to marry you, Hollis. When I get married, it's going to be because I'm in love with someone who can't stand to live without me."

"I'm sorry—I know I'm clumsy—"

"No. Don't say it. You can't help it if you don't feel that way about me."

"I want to explain, but I don't know how. Does it help to say I love you as much as I could love a sister? More? That I always want to be around you?"

She sat up straighter and smiled prettily. She tried to think of something cheery to say, like Ginger Rogers would. "Explaining won't make it any different. You're my best friend. There. How many girls have a friend like you? I wouldn't want to make you hate me. I'd rather keep things like they are. If you forgive me, for all the trouble I've caused."

"Say, why don't you get up and get dressed. I've got this really great idea for a Sunday afternoon. Let's go see a movie."

She wore a pair of his trousers rolled up, with a tie through the belt loops, and a big white shirt, and walked into her residence with her head high. Nobody said a word. Upstairs, she did her hair and face carefully. She sat at her mirror and pursed her lips and blew herself a big kiss. This was a mess, but Hollis would make it go away. She would have to be patient. She would have to believe.

"If you ever need to talk, you know I'm your friend," twitty Cecelia had said a few days ago. Cecelia with the holy soul.

Emma kicked Cecelia's mattress on the way out.

Her face burning, Emma stood in her slip as the costumer's assistant took her measurements again. "Relax it, sweetie, it'll make it easier." She almost died. *Relax it.* Of course they knew, they all knew, but Hollis was right, they didn't tell. "I'll put a little dart here," the costumer said nonchalantly. "I like the way it lays better." So they could let it out if the filming took too long. So it wasn't flat and snug on her belly. They put her in a smart suit with a jacket cropped at the hips instead of fitted at the waist. They gave her a pretty hat, to draw the eye upward.

She did fine with the filming. She was the green-eyed friend, Betty, looking innocent as an angel while she bore news of her girlfriend's fiancé's dastardly betrayal with another woman. Of course Betty was exaggerating—or misinterpreting—and the man was innocent of all he was accused. And the scheming friend, if that was what she was, lost out in the end, though there was this one touching moment when—in the star's most generous, sympathetic scene—the girlfriend said something that promised a little bit of hope. At least forgave her. "Someday you'll love someone like I love Roger, and you'll understand what real happiness is. I hope you will. Really I do."

They filmed that scene before they filmed the first one, which made Emma uneasy, but they were through with her entirely in a

95

little over a week. The director told her Betty was a bitch. "Just read those lines with that in mind," he said, that was the extent of his interpretation.

She did what he said, but after a couple of takes, she said, "Could I try something—?" There were all kinds of people standing around, she never knew what they were all there for. She felt their impatience with her, talking out of turn. But she had a different idea about her character. She thought Betty did love her friend, but she was so grieved at the thought of losing her to marriage, so bereft at the notion of herself shut out, that the news she brought—a funny little story about Roger and that tacky girl Ann, the one they all met at the Carlsons' cocktail party—turned dark in her mouth and came out mean, when all she really meant to say was, I'll miss you.

There were layers in that. She could think one thing and then think another, mean to say something and end up saying something else. She could be morally confused, and be made interesting. She thought acting was about hiding the truth, then letting it find a way out where the audience could see it.

The director said, "Cut! Print! Fabulous! You're a princess, Miss Hope!" Even the starring actress, who had hardly given her the time of day before, said, "You really gave me something to play against in that scene, Emmy. Good job." Then—Emma was certain of this—she gave Emma's belly a wink. And when Emma came in the next day, they told her they were done with her. Her scenes were fine. She went to the costume shop and thanked everybody. They wished her luck. *They knew*.

Hollis rubbed her feet and fed her a cheese sandwich. She was too tired to go out. She was sleepy just about all the time. She was so tired of fighting the burping mound in her belly, of holding it in, of pretending to be gay when she was worried sick and her back hurt and her feet hurt.

"Tom Parrish wants to meet you," Hollis said. Her heart thumped. "He says this is what Mrs. Parrish has been praying for so long. His wife is very religious. You don't mind, do you?"

They met in a posh bar in a hotel. Hollis introduced them, then quietly went to the bar. She took a seat facing the corner; she could see no one except him.

She had dressed very carefully, modestly but with as much style as she could manage. She had borrowed the pearls again. She didn't want Mr. Parrish to think she was ashamed.

"You're a beautiful young woman, Miss Hope," he said.

She didn't think he expected her to say anything.

"What would you like to drink?"

She thought that it was a kind of test. Everything was bound to be. She ordered a virgin Bloody Mary and sat with an attentive expression, exactly as she might do in a job interview. Tom Parrish was an attractive man, in a disturbing way. He would never be cast as a hero. He was balding slightly, but his hair was lustrous and dark and of course it was perfectly cut. His clothes were conservative, very expensive. There was nothing about his appearance to criticize. Yet his gaze—his dark eyes were almost blazing—had about it a kind of smugness, or perhaps a smirk—she couldn't put her finger on it, but she knew she was not comfortable with him. Then, why should she be? She was the bad girl, seeking his help.

"My wife and I have wanted a child for a long time."

At that exact moment, the waitress arrived with her tomato juice and his club soda. The pause, brief as it was, gave her time to remember that they were there to talk about her child. Her body. She was the one who had something he wanted, not the other way around.

She sipped her drink. She said nothing, and she sensed that he was growing uncomfortable.

"You may wonder why we haven't adopted already."

She hadn't thought about it.

"We have been talking about doing so. But we would like—we would like to know something about the unborn child. Something about its—" He stumbled, and she could see that he minded terribly that he did so.

"Its breeding?"

His nostrils flared. "I would not have put it that way."

"It's all right," she said. She was trying to guess his age. Thirty-five? Older? She hoped his wife was not too old. A baby should have someone to play with her. Him. Someone who wouldn't mind when the baby cried. Someone who would hang its tiny shirts on the line proudly. Who would tell her friends when the baby smiled. Spoke. Walked.

She drank more juice, determined not to cry.

"Of course you are quite lovely. And intelligent."

"Hollis told you that?"

"Yes, yes he did. And there's something else—" Parrish paused for effect. "I saw you on the set the other day. You are quite a good actress. It's all instinct, I imagine. You're not trained."

"I haven't studied acting."

"Yet you made a lot more of that little part than anybody had seen in it. It was good for the scene, and the movie, and it was certainly good for you."

"And you were there to see it."

"I mentioned that I was looking for a certain type. Someone had told me about you, I said. I could—borrow you, you see. Sometimes a studio does that."

That amused her. "Rents out one of the contract players. I've heard that. The actress makes her salary, the studio makes a profit. Only I thought it was usually the stars."

"This would be an unusual arrangement. But the studio does, as you say, stand to gain." Now he had her. "And so do you, Miss Hope."

"Actually, my name is Clarehope. Emma Clarehope."

"An elegant name."

"Tell me how it would work." She was growing impatient.

"I would buy your contract. I would pay you your salary, and all your medical expenses, of course. When you are ready to go back to work, I'll find something for you at my studio. It's that simple. You won't lose anything."

"Except my baby."

He shrugged. Now he was growing impatient. She was wasting his time. It was like a game, where she pushed against something that resisted, and it inspired her to push harder. She wanted to push. She wanted him to resist.

"As I understand it, you don't want this child. We do." He drained his glass. "It's as simple as that."

"Well." She wasn't going to jump through his hoop on a moment's notice. She didn't know, for one thing, if what he offered was good enough. She didn't know what a baby was worth. She would have to talk to Hollis. Maybe she should talk to a lawyer. Nobody had thought of that.

"There is something else," he said. "I would like to ask you about the father."

"I don't want to talk about him. He isn't here. He won't ever show up, if that's what you're worried about. He knows nothing about it."

"That's not what I want to know."

"He has your coloring. He's not as tall as you, but he has nice dark eyes like you." She smiled. Perhaps that would flatter and please him.

But he was quite earnest now. "Nor that. What I want to ask—it's difficult, Miss Clarehope. I want to ask—" At least he didn't look away. He looked right at her as he dared to ask, "Was this child conceived in a rape? Is that why you don't want the child? You see, I don't think I could take a child from violence. I think—I wouldn't be able to forget. I would be watching for it to show up."

"How dare you," she said so quietly she wasn't sure he heard her. She slid from behind the table. "It's none of your business how I *made* this baby. How about you? How about your wife? Don't you think I wonder about the two of you? Maybe one of you is sick." She was shaking. Hollis had turned and noticed her. She waved to him. He came toward them slowly.

"Mr. Parrish, so nice to meet you," she said when Hollis was there. She put out her hand for him to shake. He was standing by now, too. He didn't take her hand.

"I'll hear from you, then?" he said coolly. He gave her a card, which she took.

"I do need to think about it," she answered.

*   *   *

She called in sick, but they had beat her to it. They were putting her on furlough. Twenty dollars a week. She was lucky not to be fired yet. She knew it was coming.

Hollis helped her move her few things back into his apartment. She couldn't stop weeping. She couldn't explain to him why she didn't want to give her baby to the Parrishes, and he didn't seem to care. "This is all up to you, sweetheart," he said soothingly. "If you don't feel right about it, forget it. We'll figure something else out. Get settled in here. We'll put our heads together and come up with an answer. I don't think you really know what you want yet." He hugged her. "Remember, I'm on your side. I'm not going anywhere."

She thanked him and she tried to cheer up, but she kept crying. She chewed all her nails down. All day while Hollis was gone, she slept in his bed. At night, she read.

Hollis, though, wasn't letting the days slide by as casually as he seemed. He came home the week following the meeting and said the Parrishes had asked to meet with her again.

"I don't know," she said miserably.

"Mrs. Parrish wants to talk to you. She's awfully nice, Emma. Maybe you'd like her better. Don't you think it must be hard for a man to talk about this sort of thing?"

She tried not to be offended. *This sort of thing*? "You don't seem to find it so hard to talk to me about it."

"But I love you, sweetheart," he said. She felt sullen, but she agreed to the meeting when Hollis said it would be in a judge's chambers. "The bar was a mistake," he said. "Parrish feels bad about it. It's where so much business is done in Hollywood, people forget it's not always the right place."

She did feel better at the judge's office. There was no judge in sight, but there was a secretary, and a big office with a leather couch and chairs to match, a big oak desk, and a huge window looking out on the hills. There was a brass plaque on the desk: JUDGE WILBUR D. ADAMS.

She had asked Hollis to stay with her. He helped her sit down on the couch, then sat on a chair nearby. In a few minutes, there was a light knock on the door, the door opened, and a pretty woman came in.

Hollis said, "I could wait outside." He looked to Emma for approval. She nodded.

"I'm Pilar Parrish." Mrs. Parrish sat beside Emma on the couch. "Thomas told me how lovely you are. He didn't tell me you are so young."

"I don't think he realized," Emma said.

Mrs. Parrish laughed lightly. "In his business, he thinks he sees everything in a person, but if he is not looking—" She raised her hands. "Then he sees nothing."

"He thought my child might not be good enough."

"Oh no, dear. He came home and said all good things. Only he was worried he had not been kind enough. He had not known what to say. I told him from the beginning, it should be between women. Between mothers."

"You are a mother?"

Mrs. Parrish touched herself. "Here, in my heart. When I heard—"

"What did you hear?"

"That you are a young actress, that good things have begun for you, that this is not the right time for a child."

"I suppose all that is true."

"That you are a friend of Mr. Berry."

"Have you met Hollis? Before today?"

"Several times. He has been in my home."

Emma was relaxing. Mrs. Parrish was a gentle person.

"Emma—I've been thinking. Do you want to give this child away, and forget it forever? Although we have met, seal the adoption for all time?"

Emma started to cry immediately. Mrs. Parrish took her hands in her own.

"I thought so. It is sometimes cruel, adoption. Or so it seems at the time. I thought, if you knew something more about us. If you knew how much we could give a baby."

"More than I could," Emma said, and it hurt to say it.

Mrs. Parrish did not press her advantage. Instead she said, "I thought that, once a year, I could write you a letter, and tell you about the child. If you did not want to read it, you could throw it away. If you never wanted to receive it again, you could send it back: *Return to Sender*."

Emma fumbled for a handkerchief in her purse. She blew her nose. "I hadn't thought of such an arrangement," she said. "I've never heard of it being done that way. The truth is, I don't know much of anything about adoptions. One of my mother's cousins adopted a boy, he is much older than I am. I've hardly ever seen him." She knew that she was babbling.

"Please, dear, will you consider this? We can meet again soon, with Judge Adams, and make things legal, so that you are protected. So that you feel safe in the arrangement."

Emma stiffened. "There's nothing to make legal yet, Mrs. Parrish. Not until the baby is born."

"I see." Mrs. Parrish's hands were folded now, as if in prayer. "Would you wait just a moment? My husband is outside, and he would like to speak to you, too."

"It's not necessary. I just need—to think—"

Mrs. Parrish went to the door and opened it a crack. Then the door opened wider, and Mr. Parrish came in, followed by Hollis.

Parrish was holding a thick script. Mrs. Parrish went back to sit beside Emma, close enough to take her hand. Emma wanted to pull back, to refuse to be enlisted so easily, but the warmth of the woman's hand was comforting.

"Look here, Miss Clarehope," Parrish said. He waved the script in front of her. "I have come across the most wonderful screenplay. It's as if it were written for you. A young college student, married to a German, is caught in Germany in the early war. She becomes a spy for America. You're perfect. Sweet, vulnerable, young—and underneath, tough and smart—"

Emma looked from Parrish to Hollis. Hollis was the very picture of neutrality. He wouldn't meet her eyes.

"You have to be clearer, sir," she said to Parrish. "What, exactly, are you telling me?"

He knelt in front of her. Oh, such a clever negotiator. He knelt, and he said, "I'm telling you you can play the lead in a swell movie, Emma."

"But I'll look like a kangaroo."

He laughed. "I'm not making this movie for—oh, at least six months. Say early next year. You'll be your old self by then. You'll have time for lessons, if you want. Perfect timing. Emma, I'm going to make you a star."

She got up and ran from the room. Shortly after, Hollis followed. "Is he serious?" she asked, falling against his chest. "Can he do this?"

"Oh yes, he can do it. And he made this promise in front of his very Catholic wife, and in front of me. You're talented, Emma. It's not even a gift, really. It's a deal."

"I guess I should shake his hand, then," she said.

One day, a few weeks later, Pilar came to take Emma shopping. She bought her everything, "ground up," as she said, and then she took her to lunch at a restaurant where they served food Emma had never even seen before. "Seafood is so full of minerals, darling," she told her, reaching across to spear a morsel of scallop and lift it to Emma's mouth. It was as if Pilar were her rich older sister, as if Emma were a pet. "Oh, you're an angel in that," she cried when Emma tried on a velvety smooth smock. And "See how soft they are," when they were in the lingerie department. "Aren't you just like a little pixie?" when Emma tried on comfortable flat shoes. They sat in the restaurant for two hours talking. Emma told her about her papa, and about the years she lived in a boxcar. She told her about the night the Indians came for Christmas, and the story about her papa dancing on the reservation. She didn't say anything about later years, after she began to work. Pilar asked nothing.

Pilar told her, in turn, about growing up the daughter of a wealthy Mexican rancher and his Anglo wife in Arizona, with homes in Los

Angeles and Mexico City. She met her husband—she called him Thomas—in Mexico, actually, on a movie set. As a lark, she had taken a small role. "I'm no actress, but I was very young, and I was pretty enough." She came from a large family, many brothers and sisters, and now nieces and nephews too numerous to name. She shrugged—a sad, fleeting expression—and then a wonderful happy smile. "Won't they love a blond cousin?"

Emma found she didn't mind talking about the baby so much with Pilar. "I can't promise that," she said. "I'm the only blonde in my whole family. I don't know where it came from." She blushed.

On the way home, Pilar stopped at a small church. "Would you like to come in while I light a candle? It's a favorite spot of mine, so peaceful."

It was peaceful. They knelt in an alcove with a bank of candles in front of a beautiful Madonna in a blue coat, with a gold halo. "She looks so young," Emma whispered to Pilar, and Pilar bent close to speak in her ear.

"She looks like you, dear."

Another afternoon, she took Emma to see "her" church, the Church of the Good Shepherd, in Beverly Hills. She said that their home wasn't far away. "Would you like to see our house?" she asked, but Emma shook her head. What would it be like later, to think of her baby, and to see the very house in which she—or he—took first steps, said first words?

A one-room apartment came open in Hollis's building, and Hollis and a friend cleaned it up and moved Emma in. She saw Hollis every day, but more and more often, he came by to kiss her good night and then went out at night with his friends, while she went to bed early. She was exhausted, and she fell into deep dreamless sleep which her body craved, which she craved. Pilar brought her groceries—a lot of milk, and fruit, cereal, and wonderful breads unlike any Emma had ever eaten. Several times a week, Pilar took her to lunch somewhere, and they made an afternoon of it. They took drives to the beach, and once all the way to Santa Barbara. There, they walked on the grounds of the Old Mission, a Franciscan monastery, and afterwards had lunch in a luxurious hotel. From their table they looked out on such a profusion of flowering bushes and beds of blossoms, Emma thought to herself it couldn't be real. That day, driving back to Los Angeles, Pilar said, quite casually, "This is the life people in the movie business live, darling. This is what your life will be like, when you are a star." Emma, startled, realized she had not been thinking about the promised script. The resumed, improved career. The deal. *She had stopped thinking.* As Pilar drove along then, humming, Emma drifted away into the dream. Pilar must have thought she was asleep; she didn't speak again until they were at the apartment.

That night, Emma stayed awake a long time. She wrote a new poem:

Will the stars shine like this
when I am empty again?
Will the flowers bloom
when you call another Mother?

She read over the page again and again, and though she noted that she had not rhymed, and she wondered if that meant what she wrote was not poetic, she found that the words soothed her, took away her hurt, as a balm soothes a stinging cut. And when she slept, she dreamed of the American girl hiding in Berlin, knowing that the dream was on a huge screen in a darkened theatre, and that she was sitting in a row cordoned off just for her, and for her friends.

One day, a month after the night on the beach, Hollis came home in the middle of the day and told Emma he was leaving California. He was anguished, but she could see that there was, beneath his sincere sorrow at leaving her, an excitement born of a man's fever to join a war. He had of course been unable to enter any of the service branches, with his mildly crippled leg. Even when he asked to work on Army newspapers, he was turned down. Now, he had been asked to join the Office of War Information. He would be working in New

York and Washington, D.C. Another screenwriter—one who was much more successful, an important, politically active Democrat—was an important man in the OWI now, and he had arranged for Hollis to be invited, too. Hollis's competency in Spanish was a real plus, he said. The first thing that would happen was they would send him to D.C. for a crash course in Spanish.

"But we're not fighting in Spanish!" Emma cried. She felt as if her ceiling had crashed down on her. She felt hollow. She felt abandoned and panicky.

"I know. But we're doing a lot of propaganda in South America. It's important work. And maybe I'll go on to other projects, too. We have to stop Fascism, Emma. The good of the world depends on this war, besides our country's safety. Don't you see? It's bigger than we are."

She crumpled into his arms, sobbing, and soon he was crying, too, and out of that, a wonderful thing happened. In the still dark center of the night, Hollis loved her at last.

Hollis said he didn't want her to do a thing. Her job, he said, was to stay well. To eat and sleep. He didn't want her to do anything to strain herself.

"I'm hardly showing!" she said, though she was wearing the sweet maternity dresses Pilar had bought for her. She wasn't at all clumsy. She thought she could have worn her old clothes, if she opened them at the waist and wore something on top. It was a point of pride with her; she packed her own suitcase, the old yellow striped cardboard one she had come with, and carried it down to Hollis's car. It had taken Hollis and Pilar two days to talk her into the move. "I'll tell them I can't come," Hollis said, counting on her not to call his bluff. The foolish risk of it touched her. She let him rattle on. He said, "I can't leave you here alone. It's not right. I'll take you home on the train on my way. Whatever you say, but I won't leave you alone."

He had already given her his sweetest gift. She said she would move to the Parrishes' house. The night before he left, he sat with her in the Parrish driveway for hours, in his car. They talked about everything they had ever done together, from the moment they met in the El Rancho back in Gallup. It didn't seem possible; they had only known each other since October. There was one last thing she wanted him to do. At first he refused, but she begged and begged. She tried to make light of it, but at the same time, she begged. Finally, he relented; it wasn't really so bad so much as childish. He took out his pocketknife and quickly made tiny incisions in his finger and hers, and they sucked one another's blood.

"Come back," she said. "The Parrishes will be through with me and I'll be all by myself. Please come back to Hollywood."

He said, "Where else would I have a life? Don't you understand? There aren't very many places for people like me. I love America, but artists—they're freaks, Emma. I'm a freak. And you. You'll be everybody's sweetheart. Wait and see. Parrish isn't going to do you a favor. He knows a star when he sees one. He's going to make himself a hero, by making you a star. I'll be lucky I know you."

She was unprepared for the luxury, the splendor, the beauty of the Parrish house. She was given the guest cottage behind the gardens and the swimming pool. It was larger than Hollis's apartment, and of course it was much nicer. Pilar made it clear that nobody expected her to prepare food, or do anything except what she wanted. "The sun will do you good, but be careful of midday. If you would like to lie out nude, tell Elena, and she will keep the gardener away from that part of the house."

Emma could only giggle at the idea.

Hollis had given her a box of books, and Pilar brought her magazines she had never even heard of before. There were even magazines in Spanish and Italian and French. Usually she ate breakfast with Pilar on the patio. Often they ate dinner in the house, because Thomas was gone so much. Pilar seldom accompanied him, although when she did, she went out to Emma's cottage to show her her dress, to twirl and hear Emma's approval.

Slowly it dawned on Emma that Pilar had been very lonely before she came. She seldom had friends over, and when she did, they kept to themselves, away from the cottage. Emma sensed that Pilar was protecting her, Emma, from people who might judge her. That Pilar preferred Emma's company, but there were some things she had to do. At least, it was nice to believe that.

One morning she went into the house looking for Pilar. She knocked on the door of Pilar's suite of rooms—Thomas had a separate bedroom and bath, an arrangement Emma found peculiar and yet oddly comforting. Pilar called for her to enter, and when she did, she discovered Pilar seated on a low cushion in front of a beautifully decorated altar with a statue of Mary on it. The altar was draped in exquisite lace, and bedecked with candles in extravagant holders, and small gold-framed pictures of saints. In her hand, Pilar held a long chained necklace of beads.

"Do you know the rosary?" she asked Emma.

"No."

Pilar patted the bed behind her. "Sit down. I'll explain it to you."

That day, Emma learned the Hail Mary. . . . *Blessed art thou among women* . . .

A week later, Pilar gave her a beautiful rosary of pearls, and a pamphlet to remind her of what she had taught her. Emma was embarrassed—for Pilar, she thought, who was so pious that she didn't recognize a heathen when she saw one. Emma knew nothing of the wiles of missionaries.

In her cottage, she slid the rosary through her fingers without prayer, for the comfort of the cool hard beads against her skin, and the distraction from her growing sadness. She took to carrying it around. Naked, she draped it over her belly, positioning the crucifix precisely over her protruding navel. Sometimes she wore it around her neck. One night, she said the Hail Mary all the way through. It came easily from her lips, a whispered prayer. One prayer led to another.

It was June, a hot night, and Emma was swollen and agitated. She could not concentrate enough to read a page all the way through. She did not like the music on the radio. The Parrishes had gone out for the evening; she was alone, except for the maid in the far corner of the house, who was probably asleep. Emma missed Hollis terribly. She had talked to him several times, but there was no way to reach across the distance. California to New York. It might as well have been an ocean between them. The phone line crackled. And she had nothing to say. Yes, she was well. Yes, everything was fine, she was comfortable. And he was well, too, doing things he wasn't allowed to talk about. He sounded happy, and remote. He sent her a card every week or so, but it was only another way to feel the distance. She would have liked to talk to him about certain practical things. That Thomas gave her money instead of studio checks. The uncomfortable feeling of the bills in her palm. The growing sense that Pilar not only loved her, but owned her.

The blankness that came across her mind when she tried to think of life after the baby.

The gnawing pain of the distance from her mother, to whom she had written nothing since the birthday card.

Her fear of the pain of childbirth, about which no one had spoken to her. The scalding embarrassment and hatred she felt when Pilar took her to the doctor, and the doctor said, "You are a lucky little gal, Miss Smith." A certain intonation when he said *Smith*. "A lot of girls in your predicament would be at the Salvation Army home."

She had only Pilar.

Pilar had bought her a black maternity swimsuit. It had a skirt that was more like an apron, starting above the line of what had once been a waist. She was embarrassed to be seen in it, and had only gone in the pool perhaps half a dozen times, when she was alone during the day. This night, though, she lay stretched out on a chaise longue beside the pool. The lights in the pool gave it an otherworldly flavor; it was a rich blue color. The blue water seemed to beckon her. Why sit there in hot misery? Why wallow in your doubts? She went to put on her suit.

She sat on the edge of the pool and put her feet in. She was holding her hands over her belly. Suddenly there was a ridge of movement across the entire front of her abdomen, a tiny knot of *baby* traveling under her outer flesh. A foot, or an elbow? She felt it again, and cried out in delight and astonishment. Then it stopped. Her pulse was racing.

She slid into the water with her eyes closed. The water was a perfect temperature; it was as if she had entered her own amniotic fluid. She and the baby and the pregnancy and the pool were all one thing, one miraculous, mysterious, wonderful thing.

She went from one end of the pool to the other and back, in slow, easy strokes, interspersed with floating. It was not a very large pool, but at her pace, it took her five minutes to make the lap. Then she sat on the second step, half-immersed in the water, and leaned back against the first step. She felt almost happy. Content, at least, for the moment.

He had entered the pool so quietly she didn't know he was there until he put his hands on her stomach. She was so startled, she shrieked.

"Shh," he said. "It's your baby's father, silly girl."

Ire shot up her back like a dye in the spine. In that instant she knew she despised Thomas Parrish. She had despised him the moment she met him. She pushed at his hands, but he held fast. She squirmed to get away, but he was pushing on her abdomen so hard it hurt to move.

"Stop," she said. "You're hurting me. What do you think you're doing?"

He bent his head into the water, to put his cheek against her belly. His hands held her on each side.

"This is rape!" she screamed. She beat on his head with her fists. She scratched his face, though her nails were so short, the flesh of her fingertips dug into his skin without hurting him. He brought his head up out of the water, his eyes gleaming. "Do you hear me?" she shouted. "Here's your goddamned rape!"

He put his hand over her mouth. "Stop it, Emma," he said. His voice was quiet, even, frightening. "I only want to feel the baby. Don't you think that's what a loving parent does, waiting for a child? Don't you think I love this baby? I love you, too, Emma, mother of my baby. I'll take care of you, didn't I promise? Aren't we good to you? Are you hungry? Are you cold? Are you alone? No? No?" He took his hand away, made a big show of demonstrating that she was free to speak.

She couldn't speak. She looked at him as at an insane person. He *was* insane, and she was afraid of him. He lowered his hand onto her body again.

"Please," she said, trying to be calm and quiet and compliant. "Please take your hands away. I'm tired. I want to go to my room now. Please, Mr. Parrish."

He laughed. "Mr. Parrish! You are so intimate with my wife, and you call me Mr. Parrish? Thomas, Emma. Don't you see how close we are? How joined we are, by this child?" But he did take his hands off of her. He held them in front of him, his palms flat toward her, as she crept up the steps backwards, then turned and fled to the cottage. At the door, she turned back and saw he was out of the pool. Pilar stood on the other side, in a flowing white robe. She was holding her arms out to him.

She threw herself on her bed and wept until there were no more tears left. She slept fitfully for a while. When she woke, she clasped the rosary in her fingers. She tried to pray. *Hail Mary, Hail Mary*, she began again and again. She laid the lower end of the crucifix against her wrist. It was a lacy metal, thin and sharp and cold. Lightly, she wiped it across her wrist. Then again, harder. And harder. Again and again she scraped her wrist, until thin lines of blood appeared and trickled off her arm onto the sheet. Then she switched hands and scratched the other arm. She slept again, but she awoke wretched, nauseated, and afraid.

She looked at the clock. It was only a quarter past two in the morning. She switched on her light and sat up. She picked up a magazine. The blood on her wrists had dried. There were a few crusts, and brown streaks. She turned the pages of a magazine in another language. Opulent country homes were featured on the glossy thick pages. She stared at each page for a long time.

"Emma, darling, Emma, Emma." She heard Pilar's voice from the door. She froze in place, but she said nothing. She had forgotten to lock the door. Maybe Pilar would give up, think her asleep. But of course the light was on.

Pilar let herself in. "Emma, darling."

Sometime in the night Emma had changed into a nightgown. She clutched it at the neck. "Go away," she said.

Pilar approached her slowly, on tiptoe. She looked quite silly. "It's all a misunderstanding," she said.

"My foot," Emma said.

"He's so sorry he frightened you. It was a gesture of affection. You misunderstood."

"It was a violation," Emma said. "And you heard me, didn't you? You heard me call out, rape, rape, and you did nothing."

"I came out to see. I was frightened. Then I saw you were with Thomas. I knew you were safe with him. I saw that he was kneeling before you in the water, as if—as if you were the Virgin Madonna, Emma. That's how we look at you. As if this baby—God, Emma, don't you know how we feel? I've wanted a baby so long, it's a gift from God—"

"You're crazy. You're both crazy."

Pilar almost sprang on her. She was on the bed, trying to put her arms around Emma. Emma scrambled away, to the far edge of the bed. "Don't touch me. I don't know what I'll do if you touch me."

Pilar began crying. "Emma, you're like a daughter to me. I've come to love you so much. You're family to us."

"You're not my mother! I don't want you to be my mother. *I want my own mother.*"

"*Mijita.*"

"I want my mother. I want my baby. Get out, Pilar. Get out now."

As soon as Pilar shut the door, Emma sprang from the bed. She dressed hurriedly, and she took out her little cardboard suitcase. Into it she threw a few of Hollis's cards, and the photograph he had taken the day she arrived. She threw in a few pieces of underwear, a sweater, her hairbrush. From under her mattress, she took the four hundred dollars she had hidden there.

She turned off the lights, except for a night light near her bed. She sat on the bed and she made herself wait half an hour. She watched the clock agonizingly, counting each minute off aloud. When exactly thirty minutes had passed since she had closed her suitcase, she crept out of the cottage and across the gardens and down the driveway. Pebbles crunched beneath her step; she stopped to let silence break the noises into unintelligible sounds.

It took her several minutes to figure out how to let herself out of the gate. She would have climbed it if her fingers had not found the latch. Then she was out on a street in Beverly Hills at three-thirty in the morning. She went to the very middle of the street and walked in the direction that sloped down. She walked past beautiful huge homes surrounded by gates and fences and walls. She woke several dogs that barked furiously from behind those walls. She kept walking. She walked until she came to a corner and did not know which direction to take, and when she had a decision to make, she always took the way she thought was down, until, at last, she saw the lights of a boulevard ahead of her.

She hailed a cab, swallowing her fear, and went to the train station. There would not be a train to Texas until ten the next night. She went to buy a ticket. She asked for a sleeping car, but there was none available. She tried everything. "Look at me," she said. She was shameless. She stepped back so the agent could see that she was pregnant. She pulled her dress taut over her belly. He shook his head. He wasn't unkind, but there was nothing he could do. He had no berths. In truth, he said, he shouldn't sell her a ticket. He had only a few, and they were reserved in a block for soldiers. He did sell her one, though, and he advised her to get a good night's sleep, and to eat well the next day. "It's a long way, ma'am. I hope you're up to it."

She spent the long day in the station. There were beautiful seats, high-backed and shiny, like church pews, though they weren't especially comfortable. She took out her nightgown and made a sort of pillow of it, and leaned into the corner of her seat and tried to get a little sleep. She did eat, twice, though she wasn't able to finish what she bought. She was terribly hot, and she drank bottles of water, and tea, and juice. Twice, older women asked her if she was well, and could they do anything? She said she was fine, only tired and eager to go home. She said her husband had shipped out and she was going to her mother. They patted her arm and wished her well, then went off to take their own trains to their own destinations.

Vendors came around selling wares. She bought a thin gold ring with tiny, tiny diamond chips for her finger, and a fake pearl drop necklace for her sister. She sent a telegram to her mother: *Coming home, need you*, and the time of arrival. She signed it *Laura*. Not long before she boarded the train, a nicely dressed woman sat down beside her and said she didn't mean to intrude, but she had been noticing her, and she was concerned. They learned that they were taking the same train. The woman was traveling to Oklahoma City, and she would change trains in Wichita Falls. It was more than a coincidence, the woman said, it was an act of God.

Emma Laura thought that was an exaggeration, but by the time they reached Texas, she understood that it was true, and she was grateful.

Los Angeles Reporter
September 8, 1943

THE NORA WARREN WATCH

. . . Did you see Virginia Turner in her latest, lied to and put upon by her vixen friend? Those dark lashes are made for blinking when they hear from a new actress, E. H., in a role good enough to catch this reporter's eye.

Don't bother noticing the minor lassie, though, she won't be around. Word is she's gone back to Kansas, like a hundred other gals a year. They come out starry-eyed and can't wait to earn their stripes the way decent girls do.

When will those country girls learn, a movie mogul's bed is a slick sled straight to hell? Or back to Kansas.

E. H., wherever you are—and the rest of you, too—a "lucky" break turns out to be a bad one. It's a hard way to learn a lesson. We'll say a prayer for you, and hope you do the same.

This is Nora, watching out for stars and stars-to-come, and watching out for you.

Years later, after Laura is dead, her daughter, Lucy, hears the story about the train trip. She is idly turning the pages of the fall issue of *Mademoiselle*, the college issue of the magazine, with all the rich girls in their beautiful clothes. In one of the layouts they are getting off the train in Boston. In the background, admiring Harvard boys lean against their cars.

Across the room, her grandmother is mending white cotton panties.

"Did you ever travel by train?" Lucy asks. She is sixteen, dreaming of a life far away. New York, Boston. She thinks that in the East life is richer because the intellect is more respected than in Texas. She thinks that if she could go to a college there, she would lead an unimaginably wonderful life among very special people. Her mother used to tell her, Get away, Lucy. Study hard, go to college, and get away. There wasn't time to discuss how Lucy would manage it, though of course Texas colleges are quite cheap, and already Lucy, about to begin her senior year in high school, knows she can work her way through.

"Well sure I did," Greta says. "In the thirties, we got around that way a lot. Your grandfather worked for the Santa Fe line. Why, we even lived in a boxcar once when the children were small, and again later, when their Papa was gone."

116

She always uses euphemisms for death. Her loved ones have passed on, or away, or are gone. For much of her childhood, Lucy thought people Greta knew were inclined to disappear. She thought Ira had gotten on a train one day and didn't come back.

"Emma Laura took the long trip, though," Greta says. This is followed by a huge sigh. Maybe it is the effort of speaking her daughter's name, though Lucy notes that Greta has given her child back her girlhood name.

"Really?" Lucy says, closing her magazine. "Where did she go?"

"All the way to L.A., before you were born."

"When? When was that? She never told me that." Lucy knows that her mother was young when Lucy was born, and it occurs to her at once that Laura must have struck out on her own when she was not much older than Lucy is now. A small thrill runs through her, as if she has discovered a heretofore unknown talent in herself, or a vein of gold under her bed. The story of a mother brave in her youth is a kind of gift to her child, especially when the mother is gone.

Because Greta doesn't answer right away, Lucy asks, "You don't mean that time when I was little?" She was six or seven when her mother went away, and eventually Lucy learned that that trip was to California. All she remembers is that her mother came home on an airplane, that they all went out to meet her, that she wore a beautiful hat.

This is new information, and Lucy, who is dismayed that she knows so little about her mother, except for her ardent Catholicism—altars, novenas, rosaries, once a priest who came to dinner—and her mother's illnesses—a string of them, a sort of rosary of another kind, culminating in her death at thirty-three, like Christ—leaps to the hint of a story. Her mother young. Before Lucy!

Greta folds her panties and lays them on the couch. She tucks her needle and her thimble into a wooden box she keeps on a nearby shelf. She takes her time, and then she tells only a little: the young Laura, gone without a word for months, and then coming home, sick, to her mama.

"What was she sick with?" Lucy asks, her heart sinking at this disappointing turn in the story. In her mind's eye, she was already seeing Laura as she was in one of her teenage photographs, slim and blonde and radiant. It seems more important now than ever to believe that Laura had once been well. Happy, even. "What did she have?"

"A fever, child," Greta says impatiently, as if Lucy has been hounding her. Lucy, who is given to quick sulks, opens her magazine again.

Greta says, gently, "And she was pregnant with you, of course."

Of course? Of course! So that is where Lucy's own life begins, with her mother stepping off a train. Lucy had thought maybe her father was an airman in Wichita Falls, and now she hears that her mother came home pregnant *from California*. There's no chance that her grandmother will tell her more. Once not long ago she asked her about her father, and Greta said, "There's nothing I can say," as elusive and sly and ungiving, as wicked as she could be with her held-back information, but Lucy has forgiven her her silence. Silence, in this family, is nothing new, and she is certain that Greta refers to the vast silence that lay between her and Laura all the years of Lucy's childhood, a silence marked by sudden storms of anger and long empty weeks of separation. Maybe there is something Greta thinks too terrible for Lucy to know. Lucy knows that whatever her grandmother knows is bedded deep in pain, and covered over with promises and history, and the truth is, fathers don't seem to matter much anyway. It's her mother she misses.

So she says now, moving to the couch beside her grandmother, "So then you could take care of both of us," and both of them are crying then, caught again in the surprise of their grief. After a year of mourning, they know they will not die of it, but neither expects it to go away. Maybe neither of them would want it to go, because then what would be left of Laura?

Later she asks Opal about her mother's train ride home, and Opal is happy to give all the details. Afterwards, Lucy tries to tell it to herself, so that she won't forget. When she sees her aunt again, she asks for the story again. She discovers that she craves the story, as a child craves a certain tale or a pop-up book. It seems to amuse Opal. She always pulls herself together very seriously for the telling. She always tells it something like this:

"Now I was awfully busy, you understand. I was working hard in school, and then working every afternoon at the hospital. I came home at six and made supper and cleaned up and did my clothes and studied, and then I just fell into bed. But this one day, Mommy said, We've got to be at the train station tonight. She had to take off work—I think she traded a shift. She made me get dressed up, like I was going to church, and Amos, too. She wore a suit and a hat, and our neighbor, the greengrocer's wife, Dotty Purves, gave us a ride and came into the station with us. Your mama was coming home from Hollywood. Nobody told me anything. When she got off the train, she was sick as a dog and clutching her poochy little stomach. This wonderful woman, Mrs. Hurst, got off with her. She said she had a short layover and she wanted to be sure that Laura was safe in her mother's arms.

"'Laura?' we all said. She'd been Emma Laura to us. Mrs. Hurst said your mama had been sick the whole way, and Mrs. Hurst had nursed her, wiping her fevered face and neck and arms with her handkerchief dampened with whiskey. She had fed her bottled water and crackers, and she only slept when your mother slept. Your mother was leaning on her when she got off the train, but she went straight to her own mother's arms.

"This is what your mother said. 'I married Hollis Berry, but he had to ship out the very next day, so here I am.' She had her chin on Mommy's shoulder, so over it she was staring at me, sort of daring me, you know? She said, 'I'm so sorry, Mama.' Of course Mommy just shushed her. It's all right, you're home, you're home, that sort of thing. It was such a big relief to have her home!

"Then your mother said, 'Please, I want everybody to call me Laura. My name is Laura Berry now.' Of course Mommy said, 'Now why is that, Emma Laura?' and your mother said, 'Emma died in Hollywood, Mama. I'm sorry.'

"Amos said, 'Welcome home, Laura.' He thought it was a cool thing to change your name. In the army later, everybody would call him Chief, because he never had to shave his smooth cheeks. There was a little bit of Indian in us, from our Papa's side.

"And Mommy said, 'I'll call you whatever you say. You don't ever need to tell me anything about it, sugar.'

"And that's everything I remember."

When Opal says, "That's everything I remember," Lucy's heart always sinks.

And though Opal always says the same thing, Lucy doesn't think she ever minds telling it. And though she always says the same thing, Lucy still wants to hear it. Sometimes she has thought, *It's a sad thing, to put your mother's whole life into such a small story.* She has thought, *I wish there was more to the story. More to know. More to tell.*

LUCY'S BOOK
1965–1989

. . . As long as we live, we keep you
from dying your real death,
which is being forgotten. We say,
we don't want to abandon you,
when we mean, *we can't let you go.*

LISEL MUELLER, "AFTER YOUR DEATH"

Lucy was sixteen when she graduated from high school. She turned seventeen that next August. Her grandmother said she was precocious, like her mother. Lucy thought she meant because she was through with school so young. Greta wasn't thinking about age and precocity the way Lucy was.

The summer before that, she had gone to a debate camp at the University of Texas in Austin. It was the highlight of her life so far. The students stayed in dorm rooms, ate dorm food, and spent the mornings in the library. In the afternoons they met in seminars and critiqued their cases and evidence. In the last week, they debated in a mock tournament. They had "mentors" and "coaches" instead of teachers. Some were graduate students, some were high school teachers. The director was in the university speech department. Every one of them treated the youngsters like smart young adults.

One of the high school teachers was a redheaded, freckly high school social studies teacher named Max Litinger. By the second of the three weeks, Lucy was madly in love with him, head over, as they say. It must have been written all over her face. The other students teased her good-naturedly—they were an amicable group, so happy to be in the company of other geeky debaters, where they

123

could act as smart as they felt they were. Once, Max and Lucy were bent over some papers at a small desk, alone in the room, when four other students came bursting into the room, hooting and shouting. They stopped dead when they saw Lucy and Max. One of them said, in a singsong chant, "Shoulda locked the door you know—" Lucy was so embarrassed she didn't look up until they were gone, and then when she did look up, she saw that Max's face was crimson. They gathered up their papers, shoved them into briefcases, started to say things and then didn't, and walked out together. They came down out of the old speech building onto the walk, and suddenly Max said, "Come here, I want to tell you something." He pulled her over onto the grass, under a big tree, and they sat down.

"You can't imagine what a pleasure it is for a teacher like me to do this in the summer," he said. "To work with good minds, with kids who lap up everything you have to teach them. Not to be resented. And you're the best, you know. You're like a chipped gem, raw and beautiful and not yet set.

"If you were a college student, if you were older—listen, I'm thirty-one years old. Nearly twice your age? I shouldn't say this, except that I've seen you look at me. You're grown up and you're a little girl and I have to ignore the grown-up part because it's what nobody else can see. It's trouble."

Lucy thought she would die of embarrassment, but she wouldn't have made this not happen for anything in the world. He saw inside her! He liked her! Whatever garbage he was raking up to explain why he wouldn't kiss her, the truth was out. He liked her.

She grinned at him. She couldn't stop grinning. "I know, I know," she said, and then she was laughing so hard she was bending over. It was a kind of hysteria. It made him laugh, too. They must have looked like idiots. After that, they were perfectly comfortable together. Nobody ever said anything to them again, not even a hint. They ate lunch together every day. He told her all about his marriage—he was in the middle of a divorce, "not too bad," he said—and his little girl— two years old—and about how much he loved school. He had studied the American West, had dreamed of becoming a professor, but he had gotten his girlfriend pregnant the first year he was in graduate school, had married her, dropped out, and started teaching.

Lucy wanted Max to go back to school. She was filled with longing for him to have everything he wanted. It was, she thought, as if they were angels, flitting around, waiting to get into heaven, not quite human, not quite celestial. They didn't belong, but they knew they were special. They recognized it in one another. When they said goodbye, he finally kissed her. It was chaste, there wasn't a speck of spittle in it, but he did kiss her. She had never had a boyfriend. She had had some dates. Once there was a Jewish boy—his father was an optometrist, and for some reason she couldn't get that out of her mind even when he was kissing her. She had let him run his fingers up the inside of her thighs, then hook them in the elastic of her panties. She let him touch her inside, and she loved it. That was the sum total of her romantic experience.

Max kissed her so lightly, and she remembered all the feelings the Jewish boy had raised in her. *Someday soon*, she thought.

So when she graduated, and she thought, *Now I am an adult*, she asked her grandmother if she could take the bus down to Austin and look for her housing for fall alone. Not that Greta would have forbidden her; she didn't ever tell her what to do. But Lucy wanted her approval. "I want to get the feel of the campus," she said. "I want to walk around like a student, like I'll be in a little while." She knew that would win her over; Greta was so proud of her. "So I won't be afraid in September."

Greta let her take her car, a little white Nash Rambler. All alone, Lucy drove to Austin. At a filling station, she stopped and looked up Max's phone number. When she saw it was listed, with his address, she didn't call. She wrote down the address, got directions, and drove directly there. It was a Wednesday afternoon, a little after six. It was blazing hot. He lived in an apartment house a couple of miles away from the university. There were a few people out by the pool, though it seemed far too hot to be sitting in the sun. A little kid was in the wading pool, splashing. He was calling out, something that sounded like "Turtle ice! Turtle ice!"

Max answered the door. Behind him the room was icy cold; the delicious air hit Lucy's face. His television was on; she could hear the news blaring. There were books and magazines and newspapers all over his table and on the floor in front of the couch. There was a case of beer bottles by the kitchen counter.

Max smiled a sly, provocative, knowing smile, this fully adult-to-adult, thrilling, amazed and delighted smile, and he gestured for her to come right in.

She drank one of his beers while he watched the rest of the news. He patted the couch and she sat down beside him. He was wearing boxer shorts and a white T-shirt, the very picture of a slob. She didn't care. He drained the last of his beer and belched, so she did the same. Then he clicked off the television, stood up, and beckoned her to follow. In his bedroom, he kissed her and undressed her and took her to his bed, and she didn't think about anything until they were done, lying side by side.

"You okay?" he asked.

"My mother was this age when she conceived me," she announced.

"Hey, kiddo," he said. "You'll notice I used a rubber. I'm not into making babies."

She laughed. "Me either. But I was thinking, maybe this is how it happened. Maybe it was some really nice guy she liked, and they did this, because it was fun and it felt good, and then they went their separate ways, not knowing what they had made. Me. They had made me."

She thought: *I could never have understood, before this.*

Max found a robe for her and called for pizza to be delivered. "This was an honor," he said, rather formally. "You don't forget that, Lucy. I was honored."

They ate pizza and she spent the night. In the morning, she left and went to the campus housing department to get the names of off-campus houses with rooms for the fall. She looked at a couple of them, nice big old houses with pleasant rooms, good beds, big-drawered dressers. She wondered if she would finally make some friends there.

Before she left town, she called Max. He said she should call him when she came down to start school. "It's all up to you," he said.

She stayed home with her grandmother for the first year, though. It made sense, financially. There was a college there. She could have stayed all the way through, but they didn't discuss that; it was understood that she had to get out of the house. When she moved to Austin the second year, she had nearly two years of credits already earned, with the two summers added in.

She called Max around ten o'clock one night, and he said sleepily, "It's you, I wondered about you all last year. Why didn't you ever call?"

She said, "I didn't come then, but I'm here now." Her mouth was dry and metallic with loneliness, already.

"Well, listen, kiddo," he said. "I got married last month." She was a Mexican girl he had met in a bar. "She's my Nahuatl princess," he said. Then he said something in Spanish, and a woman giggled. Lucy realized he was lying in bed with her. Why wouldn't he be? Lucy assumed she was pregnant.

She wouldn't have minded if she had learned that that was how she was made. A man as nice as Max, and as strange. Someone who maybe didn't fully love Laura, didn't want to be married to her—at least not yet—or maybe she didn't want to be married—but someone who thought she was terrific. Someone who thought she was really smart, which she was.

Of course, she didn't know. It could have been anybody. It could have been something Laura didn't want, pressed on her in the dark where no one would hear if she cried out.

Texas

The first time Lucy slept with Gordon, she cried. It was surprising and embarrassing and wonderful to discover so much feeling. She had thought there was only pain, that it lasted forever, that she couldn't give in, or show it to anyone. Sex and lacrimation had never occurred together before. She had thought of herself as brave and sporty, picking partners who thought they had picked her. Her tears had been childhood tears, hot and sullen and secretive. She had cried out of resentment and impatience, but never for joy. Then she lay beneath him and tears washed out of her eyes, down her temples into her hair and onto the pillow. Her chest heaved. There were things she wanted to tell him—to tell someone—but she swallowed the words, to be the woman he might love. She was twenty-one years old. She thought she was very grown up. She had put herself through college. This was in 1964, in Austin, Texas. Jackie was a widow. (At least those children had a mother!) Lyndon was President. She was in her first semester of graduate school, not looking very far ahead.

He smoothed her hair back and shushed her again and again. He

128

thought it was something he had done. "I'm sorry, I'm sorry," he said. She put her fingers to his lips. She couldn't stop crying. There were so many tears inside, capped, like a well. He had opened a valve in her with his courtly, gentle manner, his sweet shyness that turned ardent, then encompassing. She knew nothing of the manners of his class. She had never been with a man before who didn't forget all about her at his climax. Gordon was a scholar. By day, he was all decorum. She believed that something about her had ignited him, and the thought thrilled her, then made her cry.

When she could talk, she whispered, "I come with nothing, a motherless child." She assumed fatherless was implied. She knew as soon as she said it that she was breaking his heart—he carried photographs of his parents in his wallet—that he would marry her, that she would never have to be alone again. Her sorrow, her burden, her empty heart were suddenly of value, the coin of a new kingdom. She needed him, and her need was her gift to him, her dowry. She felt powerful, as if she were beautiful. She understood, for the moment, the pleasure of power and beauty. She felt like her mother, only luckier.

The music then was wonderful. Think Willie Nelson. Ike and Tina, if you went to colored town. All her friends loved to dance. He thought she was lively and robust in a way she had never really been; her energy was manic, moving toward desperation, in the way of a flailing swimmer too far out from shore. He was bookish and reserved, though in no way awkward. On the contrary, he had that easy kind of adaptability rich people always do. (It was years before she realized he had been trained by his mother to be at ease in all company. And where had he ever been out of place?) He had been studying hard for a long time, and he had monkish habits. He looked to her to draw him out. She introduced him to her friends, all of them tardy and extended graduate students, common in Austin in those days of cheap housing and student grants. Like a good tourist, he took to everything without much comment.

They liked to go to bars out on the lake and dance until they were drunk and exhausted and could hardly imagine the way home. He was always the driver; he saw quickly that someone had to stay sober. He wasn't an especially good dancer himself, but he didn't mind the easy way they all partnered, and he was game to try anything she showed him.

He was from Massachusetts, though he had spent most of his childhood in Manhattan. His father was a professor, his mother an artist. His great-grandfathers had been in textiles; his parents' parents had gone public, diversified, withdrawn to summer houses. It took ten years to learn the details, mostly from his sister.

She teased him about his accent. He would say, "You oughta talk," the way Texans said it, only from him it was droll and winning. Other times he would say to her, "Will you look at that," with that same drawl. She wore short skirts, t-shirts without bras, her hair long and loose. She caught him watching her with a frankly curious, avid stare. He thought she was wild and passionate, but then so did she. She had no idea how marriage would change her. She had grown up surrounded by bitter women and weak men. With his serious eyes, his preppie haircut, his earnest love of academic life, he was as rare, as exotic to her as she was to him. What he knew of passion was almost entirely literary. Someone might have whispered to him: *It's all false, beware.* Not her, though. She was what she was because it was what she thought herself to be. She was self-conscious, but she meant to be honest. If ever she pretended anything, it was to be good, for goodness and accomplishment had been her shield throughout adolescence. It was only in college, when there was no one watching her who mattered, that she felt free to shed the burden of virtue.

He was in his first teaching job after finishing his dissertation in history at Chicago. She had just started a program in American studies. She met him at a party in a house near the university. She was living with a dramatically handsome teaching assistant who had goaded her into grad school. Willie. She thought Willie was looking for a nice way to dump her—he was fiercely ambitious, digging in for the hard business of a thesis, and she was a distraction—but he was fond of her.

"See the blond man over by that lava lamp?" She knew exactly who Willie meant. "He's the bright young thing in History this year."

She had had the feeling the man was watching her, something she was conscious of because she was watching him. In a room full of chinos and jeans, he was wearing a cashmere polo shirt the color of toast, and creamy pants of a lighter color, so soft they draped with the fluidity of a skirt. He had the look of someone thinking, which was not at all like the other young men, who were looking for some kind of action, or else working on getting drunk.

Willie nudged her. "Talk to him, Luce," he said. "See if he's dull as well as smart." Willie developed a small plot, then set it in motion. Hadn't he said he had to go home early to study? She should take her time? They weren't deeply attached, except in some basic practical way on her part; she had had other lovers in the year they had shared an apartment. There was little to worry about, then, if your heart wasn't in it.

She more or less fell in Gordon's direction. He had come alone. He was attractive, and it was true, he was watching her. She was flattered. She simply marched up to him and introduced herself. "No, you don't know me," she said. "I saw you were wondering." Which wasn't true, and they both knew it. "Chicago, right?" she said, after they had exchanged names. He nodded.

"Civil War," he said, neatly slicing away unnecessary questions. She smiled and said, "I read a lot of Civil War letters my senior year. I think I fell in love with the cadence."

He brushed his lank blond hair back and said, "I know more about Yankee munitions." Years later she remembered the exchange exactly, a clear sign of their differences, a warning, if she had been half-awake, but of course they weren't having a conversation.

She danced with him and nibbled on his ear. He said, "Are you free to leave with me?" It was a polite question, more seductive than a hand under her blouse would have been. She left his apartment at six in the morning; it was still cold and dark outside.

She saw him around now and then in the next weeks. She suggested he come along to hear a band in from Nashville. He met them at their apartment. She and Willie were getting along fine; they had already passed into a state of nostalgia. She went to her grandmother's house in Wichita Falls at Christmas, and never mentioned either man. But she was thinking about Gordon. She went back to Austin a few days early, and called him. He was away. Willie was away, too. She spent the time packing and cleaning all signs of her messes. She walked over to his building, a newer complex, nothing like the cut-up old houses everyone she knew lived in. She couldn't figure out which windows might be his. She wrote him a note on the back of a library call slip she had in her wallet, folded it in accordion pleats, and stuck it in his mailbox. It said, "I'm packing."

Either he would come or he wouldn't, and if he didn't, well, she'd ignore him ever after.

Of course he came. He said they should wait for Willie to come back.

"Why? I'm a free agent," she said.

They waited. Gordon and Willie went out on the porch to talk. Willie and she went in the bathroom to talk. Willie cried a little. He said he'd seen it coming. Then he went out somewhere while Gordon moved her.

Gordon was six years older, with family money. He was on his way up. It was easy to fall in love with him. Years passed before he said, "You'll never get over your mother, Lucy." He meant no criticism. It was simply the sad truth, baldly stated. The central truth of her life.

She had long kept calendars, rather than diaries. The kind with fat blank squares and no messages except for holidays. She wrote on the calendar every day, just a phrase to remind her, if she wanted to remember, what it had been like. She wrote things like *Muggy, bathed twice*. Sometimes a progress note, a paper completed, that sort of thing. She made a note whenever she had sex, put the initials, though in a few months she would forget the names. She did that all through college, until she lived with Willie. Later she looked back at the initials and she wondered, what had she thought she was doing? There was something a little sick about it. Of course she was, in some small way, a historian.

Willie was an amateur photographer. He had all the stuff he needed to set up a makeshift darkroom in the bathroom when he wanted to develop film. He let her stand out of the way and watch. He liked to take candid shots of people who didn't know he was looking at them. It took some doing. He could study someone out of the corner of his eye, while he was turned—and his camera was pointed—in another direction entirely, then turn the camera quickly for the shot. He said he'd learned the trick from a photographer he had met in Oaxaca, where you could get stoned for pointing at the wrong people.

He turned his camera on her the summer before she met Gordon.

They knew a place with a small waterfall and pool and creek, not far out of town, past Barton Springs, where everybody went. It was on private property. They had to get through a barbed wire fence, then make their way through dense brush, and there it was, as beautiful a setting as you could imagine. The pool was neither deep nor large enough to swim in, but it was always cold and fresh, and on torpid summer days they took off all their clothes and splashed in it.

One impossibly hot day in August, they were out there with a couple of six-packs of beer and some sandwiches. By the time they went in the water they were threatening to expire from the heat. They immersed themselves and came up sputtering happily. Her bathing suit, a rather old-fashioned one-piece, tied around her neck, and she had done a careless job of fastening it. With the sudden dunk and pull up again from the water, it came undone, and as water cascaded off of her, it fell down and bared her breasts. She laughed and reached to fix it. Willie said, "No, wait, let me get my camera."

"I don't know—" She crossed her arms, her hands over her breasts. As if Willie were a stranger! It wasn't that she was embarrassed by nudity, not with him, but a photograph was something else entirely. She was a slim girl, and she didn't feel she had breasts worth recording. Once, in her second year of college, a boy she had been seeing awhile teased her about her padded bra. He wanted to know if it was something from her hope chest. She wouldn't go out with him after that, even though he apologized and said he'd only been teasing, that he thought she was beautiful, she was neat, he adored her.

"Please," Willie said. "If you don't like the pictures, we'll tear them up. I promise."

So that was the first of several times out by the water. The second time she was completely nude, but self-conscious and awkward. By the third, she was comfortable enough to pose, to flirt with the lens, to toss her hair. Willie had her jump from a low rock into the water, over and over, while he tried different angles. He shot from up close and from the other side of the pool. She lay down and brushed her hand through the water. He cooed and soothed and praised her; he talked so steadily, she never heard the camera clicking.

The photographs were amazing to her. She stood behind him in the dark bathroom under the colored light and watched as her image came up in the solution. None of them seemed sexy to her in a way she minded at all. She saw herself away from herself for the first time; she was more than the sum of her feelings. She was the woman in the photograph. Her body was sleek and supple. Her breasts seemed just right. Willie kept saying how "fresh" she looked. The surprise to her was her confidence, her ease, in the later pictures. She would always be that person, the woman who could smile into the camera's eye. "I thought I knew you," he said, "but look—you're you and someone else, too." She said she didn't know what he meant, but she was pleased, because she knew it was a compliment.

"It's that mystery thing women have," he said. "Like, look at me, jay naked, and you don't know a thing about me." He shrugged. "I honestly don't know how to explain it, but I see it."

"In every woman?"

"No. You look for it in every woman who interests you, but they don't all have it. They don't all photograph well."

"You've lots of experience?"

"Not with nudes, no," he said. He kissed her cheek. "I loved photographing you. I want to do more."

"You just want to know my mystery," she teased.

He said, "I don't think that's possible. The more I learn about you—the more the camera learns—the more mysterious you are. You become her—" He touched the image. "And how can I ever know who she really is?"

"But you're the one who has created her, Willie," she said.

"If I found what I was looking for, it was only because I knew it was there."

She liked that. He was seductive. So on another afternoon, when it seemed too hot to go out, he made gin rickeys for them, and then she took off her clothes and posed. The apartment had been made out of half of the first floor of a large house. It had a small kitchen and bathroom, but other than that, it was really just the open parlor and dining room, so the bed was where people had probably once sat to socialize, near the large bay window, jutting out toward the center of the room. There were three windows to make the bay, each with six panes of glass. There were sheer white curtains on the windows, and shades. She stood by the window nearest the bed and reached over to pull up the shade on the middle window. Then she pushed the curtain away from her slightly, to let the light in to fall on her. It was five in the afternoon, a Sunday. No one seemed to be out on the street. Somewhere a few houses away, an Edith Piaf record was playing. Still holding the curtain, she turned back to him, looking slightly over her shoulder, and she said, "Something makes me so sad just now." She could feel tears welling.

"Sundays are lonely," he said softly. He was on one knee, then up again, shooting. "Beautiful, beautiful!" he exclaimed.

She dropped the curtain. He asked her to lean against it, against the light. She would look like someone stepping out of a halo, her image dark against light.

As soon as she saw the photographs in the pan, the ones with the curtain pulled back, she knew what the sadness had been about. Watching her naked self appear on the paper, she felt the sadness turn to grief, and turned away. Willie was too absorbed to notice. By the time she was free to leave the bathroom, her tears were dried. They sat at their table and drank beers in glasses cold from the freezer, and she told him about her mother's last pictures. A children's photographer had lived next door. He had done all the kids—Lucy, her sister, her cousins—for a reduced price. He was round-faced and cheerful, about her mother's age, thirtyish, with a wife and baby of his own. Lucy had babysat for them a couple of times, but she didn't like doing it at all, and after she refused awhile, they stopped asking.

She found she had to tell Willie all these things, before she could get to the part about her mother.

"I had a terrible migraine in biology. We were cutting earthworms. I went home in the middle of the day, and I walked in on them. He was up on her bed, kneeling, to get the right shot. She was standing by her window—not so nice a window as ours, just an ordinary, frame-house window—with the curtain pulled aside, and she was naked." Willie's expression was perfectly bland. Was he listening? "This was 1959, Willie! In Odessa, Texas, not New York or someplace! She'd put on makeup—she didn't have any eyebrows, she'd lost them after surgery, something about the anesthesia—and arranged her short hair carefully. She had lovely, translucent skin, pale as porcelain, but I thought she looked puffy and ugly, and I was shocked and ashamed. She gave a little wave when I opened the door, she didn't even say anything. The neighbor turned and saw me and went right back to looking through his camera. I asked my mother if I could have a pain pill, and she told me where they were—I already knew—and I went off to lie down. We never exchanged a word about it, except that, some weeks later, she gave me a large manila envelope, and she said I should have them, the photographs from that day—she called it 'that day.' I knew which photos she meant, and she knew I knew, so we didn't have to discuss them. In fact, I think I said, 'Thank you, Mother,' as if they were gloves or something. I put them in my bottom dresser drawer. Later that dresser went into storage, and then to my grandmother's house. It was a long time before I actually saw the pictures."

Willie had put his free hand over hers on the table. They finished the beers. Then he said, "Do you have them here?"

"What?"

"Could I see them? I'd love to see them."

"They're pictures of my mother—naked!" she said. She was furious with him.

"She must have wanted someone to see them," he said most reasonably. "Was she pretty?"

"She had been very pretty," she said stiffly. "But she was sick. She was dying."

"Maybe she wanted the photographs, then, before all the beauty was gone. She didn't want you to forget."

She glared at Willie. She said, "They were for me."

*   *   *

In Gordon's study, three handsomely framed photographs hung above his desk. In the first, an Irish setter was calmly posed on a couch. Paws crossed, head raised, it looked straight at the camera. A very fair boy of eight or nine years sat beside the dog, one arm draped over its back. He was wearing a white shirt and white shorts. He had the self-possessed gaze of someone noble. In the second photo, the same boy, in jeans, a year or so older and more recognizably Gordon, stood against a fence holding his bicycle. The bicycle had a basket. The sea grass behind the fence was higher than the boy, and beyond the grass a dark blue strip of water was visible. In the third photograph, a family was seated on the step of a gray, slightly shabby porch, except for an elderly woman who was seated on a chair on the spotty grass in front of the step. She was wearing an ivory blouse and dark blue skirt. Everyone else was wearing some combination of white and faded red. There were two boys and two girls, ranging from six or so to a teenager. Everyone was tan. All of the children were blond except for the oldest boy, who was dark and handsome. The mother—her arm around the shoulders of the youngest boy—was beautiful. The man—her husband?—was much older.

"Siasconset," Gordon said, standing behind Lucy. "Our place on Nantucket. We say 'Sconset.' Every good thing I remember about my childhood happened there." He pointed to the people in the group photograph. "Father, Mother, Peter—he's a Jesuit priest now—and Lynnie, then Bliss—she lives in California—and me. I'm the squirt. And that"—he pointed to the dog in the first picture—"is Rhodes." He squeezed her shoulder. "Now you know all of us."

"The old woman. You didn't say who she is. A grandmother?"

"She was my mother's nanny. Miss Polly. She lived to be ninety-nine."

That made her smile. "It's like looking into one of those turn-of-the-century novels. My mother had a box of them. I read them as a little girl. Nannies and picnics and children peeking over banisters to watch the elegant visitors below."

Gordon said, with a little laugh, "My childhood exactly."

Yet his apartment was nothing special. It wasn't at all well furnished. It had a temporary feeling, as if he might have begun moving out. He had a good bed and a boxy, generic dresser in his bedroom. His desk was made of a plywood door across two metal file cabinets. In the living room, he had a comfortable old club chair which he said he had bought at a yard sale, a standard dinette set, and several good lamps. On a stiff, rented couch, he piled papers, a jacket, his mail.

He saw her looking around. "I don't know what's going to happen," he explained. "I'd never settle into an apartment like this. I would want a house. But I don't know if I'll stay. If this is the place to build a career, you know. I'm not ready to think about rugs and sofas. None of it seemed to matter, with just me."

She shrugged. "Maybe it will seem more like home with two of us in it." She was relieved when that prompted him to embrace her.

It did feel more like home when both of them were studying. Gordon worked at his desk or in his sagging chair. He had a concentration that was almost ferocious; it was difficult to get his attention if he was reading. Lucy worked at the table. He bought another floor lamp so that she could read in bed if she wished, so sometimes she did, while he marked papers or prepared his lectures. They listened to classical records, or to the college radio station, where they picked up jazz and blues and bluegrass. Once a week they made spaghetti. More exactly, Gordon made spaghetti sauce and she prepared the rest of the meal, slathering butter and garlic juice on french bread to toast in the oven. She couldn't understand why he went to so much trouble, when the sauce you could make from a packet was good, but he liked to pull out his spices and make an evening of it. He explained plum tomatoes to her. He had linen napkins. Mostly they ate in beer gardens or one of the college hamburger houses. Sometimes they went out for Mexican food. On the weekend, they saw a movie, and afterwards they might go somewhere to listen to a band. Sometimes they met up with her old friends, but they didn't make plans for it. No one called her. Gordon seemed to have no friends of his own. She asked him about the department, and he said that, as a single man, he was in a social limbo. "It's all very rigid, Lucy," he said. She wondered if that meant he was ashamed of her, but when they ran into someone, he always introduced her. His friend, Lucy Widemar. She didn't know what people thought, what Gordon wanted them to think. She was sure it was best not to ask. She hadn't wondered such things with Willie, why complicate life now? She was content, less lost in the universe. She admired him. And, if she had still been keeping a calendar, there would have been many nights that deserved stars to mark the joy of their lovemaking. That closeness—it was love. It had to be. Once, lying beside her in the dark, he said, "I'm so glad you're Catholic." What could that mean, if not that it was a reason they were compatible? Something to balance other differences in their backgrounds?

Every Sunday morning, he called his mother. He stood by the couch and talked to her—Bell was her name—about the strangest things. He paced three steps one way, three steps back. He discussed refinishing a straight-back chair in the Manhattan apartment. Setting out bulbs at the country house. So many domestic details. He offered the advice she sought, or, alternatively, professed bafflement. How could he know if the rose or the mauve would be better, without seeing the chair, the room, the rug? Of course she should not try to save money by using a new upholsterer. It might take Mr. Paskowitz longer, but his work was dependable. It was as Lucy imagined a man might speak with a wife with whom he no longer cared to live, but about whom he still felt concern and attachment. What of the girls, Bliss, Lynnie? Did Bell ask them all the same questions, or were they women with no such interests? Like her, now that she thought about it. Her grandmother had had a vegetable garden and roses for all of Lucy's life, but Lucy could not remember that she had ever shown the slightest interest.

Gordon always finished his conversation by saying, "Hugs, Mother." The way he said to her each night, "Dreams, Lucy." He was a man of habits. He liked ritual. He always chose the same cup for his coffee. She had never seen the slightest sign of anger in him.

After he had talked with his mother, they went to Mass. He took communion, apparently not bothered by guilt—their cohabitation—and he never asked her why she did not. She would have liked to tell him, but never felt an opportunity to do so. She had decided, standing at her mother's open grave, that she did not have the faith to go on without her mother. She had been cheated—by years of her mother's illnesses, by separations, by her mother's preoccupations and withdrawals and then, of course, by death. She stood by her sister, Faith, who was four years younger, and she didn't think to reach for her hand. She thought all the pain belonged to her. Her grandmother was so grieved she was mad, temporarily. She had lost a child. Lucy knew her grandmother would look out for her, but the range of Greta's power was as small as her house. If, at fifteen, Lucy was to be on her own, it would be in a chaotic, false world from which her grandmother could not protect her. She would be smart, and good, and she would survive, but she would not believe. Now she found the service pleasant and sociable, and she liked sitting beside Gordon on the pew, but she did not believe in sacraments anymore. Perhaps she did not believe in God.

On Valentine's Day, Gordon brought home flowers for her, a bouquet of pale yellow roses. She thought that they seemed a reflection of his fair beauty, and thus slightly narcissistic. She was pleased, of course, surprised. She had bought a humorous card for him, but in light of the flowers, didn't present it. They drank a bottle of champagne and ate cheese, and went to bed with no more supper than that. She felt wildly happy—drunkenly euphoric, of course, but it felt like happy. She thought it was as if they had been together a long time. It felt right.

One day in March she came home and discovered he had moved the apartment around. He had moved his desk and bookcase into the living room and he had brought in a bed for her in the second bedroom. He had moved the new floor lamp in beside it. She was shocked. What did it mean? And why was she always wondering *what does it mean?* He looked at her expectantly, and she took a step back. He was expelling her, within the confines of the apartment. It didn't make any sense. Their lovemaking was fine. Better than fine. And it was frequent, almost every day.

What did this mean?

He saw the look on her face, and his own face fell. "I'm a clod," he said. "I should have talked it over with you first." He took her hand and led her over to the table and pulled out a chair. She sat mute, as if someone had just died. He made tea for them, Earl Grey, which she preferred. When they were drinking it, he explained.

"My parents always had separate rooms. All my friends' parents did, too. At least as far as I could tell. My parents had different schedules. Mother has always liked to stay up late, reading. Father is an early riser. He says he goes to bed and gets up with the birds. His passion, birds. It doesn't mean—it doesn't mean things aren't okay. Honestly, I meant to be thoughtful. Sometimes I work so late. Sometimes I'm restless."

That was the first time she realized she had entered a new country. Sleep was a kind of privacy for him. It was part of his upbringing. He would come to her bed, then sleep alone, but it was not rejection. It was a habit of the line, acquired, like a blood type, at birth. She would have other things to learn, but she would try not to be so surprised each time. "It's all right," she said. She got up and brought the kettle to the table to pour more water in the pot. She had never had a double bed of her own. It had its appeal.

On Saturday she went downtown to the best department store and bought herself a set of expensive pima cotton sheets, a fine, soft wool blanket, and two more pillows. It was more money than she had ever spent on herself, but she had been saving most of her small stipend checks since the first of the year. Living with Gordon, she had no expenses, except for her few personal items, and lunch on campus. She paid nothing for food or laundry, paid no rent. Gordon said he wouldn't hear of it. He had money, it was his apartment; what the hell, she thought.

* * *

She had a menial assistantship. She was a grader for two of the advanced doctoral students who taught American Government, a required course for undergraduates. A classic example of rote learning, it was not a course with room for a mind to work. The tests were uniform, controlled by the department, mind-numbing. She sat up on the uncomfortable kitchen chair to keep her attention on the work. For all the sameness of the work, she could see the differences in students at each end of the curve. There were those who wrote clearly, precisely, even elegantly, though they were merely paraphrasing from a text they had bothered to memorize, and there were those who, no matter how simple the response, managed to turn it on its head, sometimes, even, to make the answer mean the opposite of what it should have meant.

She was bored with the assistantship, as mostly she was bored with her classes. The good student veneer she had had as a girl had finally worn thin. She thought she would fit somewhere in the middle, neither brilliant nor mediocre. In the face of Gordon's ambitions, she recognized the absence of her own. Her ambitions had always been about oblivion and solace, and now she found those things in bed. Scholarship was a discarded beau. She began each course with enthusiasm, then faltered under the load of reading and writing. She was too slow for the load, four classes this semester alone. She never felt she had time to think about anything. If she had studied harder, she wouldn't have had to worry, she knew that, but she wanted to understand the work if she did it, the why of it, and she wanted to understand herself, her life. School wasn't helping.

In her seminar, "The Proletarian Novel," she was having a difficult time following the line of thought. They were reading critics of the thirties, all men: Granville Hicks, Dwight Macdonald, and others. They were reading two trilogies of the period: Dos Passos's *U.S.A.* and Farrell's *Studs Lonigan*. She didn't mind the novels, but she was exasperated by the criticism. She didn't "get it." Then the other woman in the seminar—the only other woman in the program just then, and one who was writing her dissertation that year—challenged the professor's choice of readings.

"We're not hearing anything from women critics," she said. Her name was Suzanne Berger. She had a strident New York accent, curly black hair, long scarves, boots.

"Women wrote reviews, certainly," the professor, Dr. Cantwell, said. "But you must realize, Miss Berger, that men wrote the criticism." He stressed the word *criticism*, with a sarcastic tone.

"Of course," Suzanne said. "And we could spend some time discussing just why that was so. It would be more productive, though, to concede the point, and turn to the literature produced by women as the source of our theory."

"Our?" Dr. Cantwell said. "As in, *female* theory?"

"I had in mind *our* as in this seminar's analysis, Professor. I had in mind that we might work a little. So far we have ignored the female body as a site of conflict in society—" There were soft hoots from some of the male students. "But the women who recognized that sexual and gender conflict were part of class struggle and then wrote about it—they repositioned working-class women—"

"Dare I interrupt?" The professor was a man known for his brittle intellect, his lacerating sarcasm. No one chose him for a dissertation committee unless he was the chairman, unless the candidate was his darling. Lucy was terrified of him, and had taken his seminar only because her advisor did everything but tie her up and toss her into the room.

Suzanne Berger gestured politely, yielding the floor, but her expression remained challenging.

Professor Cantwell said, "I believe you will find a sympathetic ear in Professor Helen Slesinger, over in English. She has a special passion for Mary McCarthy, I hear. I also believe that her peculiarly slanted courses—in English—would be a better place for you to plow the field of female subjectivity, *Miss* Berger."

"I was thinking I would plow it in my seminar paper, Professor Cantwell."

"At your own peril, ma'am," he said, smiling. Lucy thought he was counting on it.

*   *   *

Lucy ran up to Suzanne after class. "I'm totally ignorant," she said. "I don't know any of the women writers. Josephine Herbst. I saw her name somewhere. I don't know what her book was."

"Books," Suzanne said. "I'd start with *Rope of Gold*. At least you can probably get a library copy. Most of the writers are not just out of print, they're unavailable, excised from the culture, like a carbuncle. You want to get a cup of coffee? I love a convert."

They spent almost three hours in the student union. Suzanne talked most of that time, although Lucy, prodded by something Suzanne asked, told about her grandmother working for the railroad, about the move to factory work, and how that had helped the family out of poverty.

What really interested her, though, and she found herself telling Suzanne this, was the idea—put forth by Suzanne about three cups of coffee and half a tunafish sandwich into the discussion—that some women writers were transgressive. They overstepped the boundaries of discourse. They were radical, not because of their politics— although Suzanne was talking about politically conscious, working-class writers—but because of their female subjectivity. It was exciting. It was like discovering that you were walking around with part of your clothes unbuttoned. You looked down, and you said, look at that, will you? And then, for the first time, you looked at your Self.

Suzanne scribbled down names for her—Meridel LeSueur, Tillie Olsen, and a few others she said Lucy could find in the library. Then, in the same moment, they looked up at the big clock on the wall and squealed in amazement.

She rushed to meet Gordon for supper. She apologized for being late, though he had only just been served a mug of beer. She was excited about Suzanne's challenge in class that day. When she tried to explain it to Gordon, wanting to go on and talk about the long conversation they had had after class, he interrupted her.

"I'd be careful of Cantwell, Luce. He's a devourer. He doesn't like women in the doctoral program, for starters."

"I think he was only half-awake until Suzanne Berger stirred up things," she replied. "She's the only real intellectual in the class except for maybe Burt Fincher, and he doesn't have anything to say if it isn't about the Wagner Act. The rest of the class could be in high school, studying civics with the coach." She laughed. "I bet they didn't have classes like that at prep school, huh?"

Gordon was aghast. "Do you hear yourself talking? What about you? You're in that class."

She couldn't admit the truth in what she had said. "You don't talk about yourself when you're criticizing," she said.

"Oh, you better, if you want to survive in academe," he said. "You better be ready to talk plenty, and sharply, about your very pretty, competent little self. She's right, you know, you've got a hill with a sharper incline, being a woman. You knew that. So you bend in to it. You work hard enough."

"Mmm," she said, and then took a sip of his beer. The awful truth of it seemed to have crashed down on her. She wasn't about to tell him.

Suzanne Berger gave a brilliant paper. It was brilliant not just for the analytical skill it demonstrated, but for its political acuity. She managed to do what she wanted—introduce an alternative view of literary culture, a female view—and still maintain respect for Professor Cantwell's intellectual stance. She argued that Josephine Herbst's Trexler trilogy perfectly complemented the other two great trilogies of the period—those already under discussion by Cantwell's design—by layering history and displaying the fractures in the decaying middle class. The few comments by the male students in the class were juvenile, tedious, and envious, and they were deflected without mercy by Professor Cantwell's scathing rejection of their intellectual content. Or non-content, as he called it. He was critical of Suzanne, too, but it was a lively, amiable, almost collegial critique. Lucy wanted to applaud. Later, when she thought back on it, she wondered if Suzanne or Professor Cantwell knew anything about the working class or decaying middle class either one. She wondered what they would have thought if she'd told them about putting checks in the wrong envelopes in a vain effort to fool the utility companies. Telling collectors her mother was out of the house when they called. Putting clothes on layaway and losing the deposit, time and time again. None of that would be intellectual enough for graduate school.

She read *The Rope of Gold* so that one day after class she could tell Suzanne that she had done so. She didn't say that reading it had meant that she didn't finish the last of the Farrell trilogy. She didn't say that she had gotten something entirely different out of the Herbst book. She had been moved by the thread of family history running through it, by the way the protagonist, Victoria, is shaped by her mother's stories. She didn't say that she didn't really care about all the politics, the solidarity, the failure of the collective spirit, all that. As she read, she missed her own mother, and she really thought about having a child of her own. She couldn't bring back the lost generation, but she could make a new one. She could go from being a daughter without a mother to a mother with a child. She didn't think her body was a site of political action, but it had its possibilities for changing her own existence. She could use it to try for happiness.

She wondered if she ought to be able to talk to Gordon about these things; she couldn't imagine quite how she would bring them up. When they were together—as bodies—they weren't thinking politically. They weren't thinking at all; wasn't that what sex was about?

She and Suzanne didn't have much time to talk. Suzanne said, "Are you presenting next week?" and Lucy said, "I've asked Cantwell for an Incomplete. I just couldn't settle on a topic soon enough."

"Good," Suzanne said. "You'll have time to do what you want." Lucy felt the warmth of the other woman's good wishes, but when they parted, and Lucy was walking across campus toward the apartment, she realized that Suzanne had only been kind. Suzanne was the sort of student—the sort of woman—who went from one task to the next with dispatch. She would already be on to something else. She would not understand how Lucy could have failed to find a subject. Hadn't she just shown Lucy how all of cultural history was ripe for reinterpretation?

Lucy's advisor understood, though. He spoke to her a couple of weeks before the term was over. He said he didn't think the department could offer her an assistantship for the next year.

"Has my work been unsatisfactory?" she asked. She expected him to say yes. People in this business didn't muck around in sensitivity.

He said, "I don't think you have the spirit for it, Lucy. The track you are on is competitive and incredibly draining. It requires a single-mindedness I don't see in you. You have to want it, the way Parry wanted the Pole. I think you should take a year off and do something else. Anything else, away from university life. I'm not kicking you out. You've got a good mind. Let's just say it's time out. A leave. Finish your Incomplete, and I think we can arrange for you to get your M.A. Then, if you get focused, if you want to come back, get in touch with me after the first of the year so I can get you back in the assistantship pool."

It was all so unsurprising, so relieving, so silly. Parry at the Pole. She would have to remember that for Gordon. She must have had an absentminded expression on her face. Her advisor asked her what she was thinking. If she was okay.

"Oh yes, Professor. It's all right, really it is. I'm going to marry Gordon Hambleton. In History." She laughed. "I'm going to get him out of social limbo."

"I beg your pardon?" her advisor said. She saw his confusion. The comment about limbo.

"Thank you," she said, gathering up her things.

They both stood. Her advisor stuck out his hand. She took it.

"Congratulations," he said. As if felicitations were in order, when she had just been sent home from camp. Someone always was, every year.

"On your coming marriage," her advisor added.

"We aren't quite ready to announce it," she said, but she shook his hand.

By the next day, everyone in History, in American Studies, in the whole damned college, had heard. Gordon came home and told her.

"Fortunately, my mother taught me that when you don't know what to say, a bland expression will suffice." He certainly was giving her one, standing above her as she sat.

"Like this?" she said, pulling her mouth down.

"That's much too serious." He lifted the corners of her mouth with his fingers and smiled weakly. She turned her head quickly and caught his finger between her teeth. Slowly, he scraped free. She was sitting in his comfortable chair, and it embarrassed her. Another way she had gone too far.

He knelt on the floor in front of her, a parody of proposal. He said, "I don't much like this department. I don't much like Austin weather. Don't you see? I must sort out my professional life before I can make a personal commitment. That sounds so cold, spoken aloud, but I want you to understand. I don't want to be divided. It would hurt both tracks of my life. You do mean so much to me."

"I'm so humiliated, Gordon. I don't know what came over me."

"I'm the top candidate for two positions, but there's been a delay in hiring because of funding— Damn, I should have talked to you about all this, but it's been so frustrating."

"All along, you've been planning to leave?" If someone had asked her how she would react to this news, she would have said, I'd roll over, punched in the belly, but it wasn't like that at all. The hurt was a small, precise, terrible pain in her breastbone. She had gone about her business, while he was campaigning to leave her.

She should have known.

She and Willie met for lunch. They both had huge messy chiliburgers. It felt so good to see him again. He had brought her photographs to her in a special envelope with corrugated thick paper to protect them. He had a job for the fall, teaching history at a private college in Salem, Oregon. He was pleased.

"I thought I wanted a major university, but this is Texas, not Harvard, and I'm Willie, not a hotshot. At the last minute I decided I honestly wanted to teach. I wanted to live somewhere nice and teach smart kids. Does that sound so bad?"

"They'll all have terrific crushes on you. I bet you anything you marry a student. Maybe when she's just graduating. A really pretty girl with long blonde hair. A smart girl, of course. You like smart girls."

"Sounds okay!" he said.

She wiped chili from her chin with a wadded-up napkin. "I wish it were me. I wish I were going to Salem with you, that it was all decided."

She could see his Adam's apple bob at that. She grinned at him over the top of her burger. "I'm not asking."

So she had to tell him about Gordon. Her terrible blurted lie.

"Oh, that," Willie said. "I heard. Nobody thinks anything of it. I

150

mean, everyone believes it's true. Maybe a summer wedding? I heard someone ask. Isn't it true? Even if you said it first?"

"I don't think so. I don't think I'm his type."

"I remember he thought so soon enough. He didn't come to Texas to look for an Old Line or Old Main or whatever they call the Eastern women, now, did he?"

"You're my type," she said plaintively.

"Hey, come with me. Really."

"It's a crazy thing, Willie. I love you. I'd love to live across the street from you forever. Maybe even with you. I can imagine it, living with you. But here's the thing: I can imagine living without you, too. Gordon, I can't imagine, after this. I can't imagine him leaving me."

"And he's going to?"

"He says no. He's exactly the way he was before I told the world I was marrying him. He cleared the air, and now we're the way we were all along. But I don't know what he thinks. And there are no plans. The plan is, I'm going home to Wichita Falls to live with my grandmother this summer, while I figure out what I'm going to do next. That part—figuring things out—that's my agenda. He's just putting me on ice." She laughed. "In a Texas summer, he's really a Yankee."

"He must have something to say about you going."

"He says he'll drive me."

Willie took the rest of Lucy's hamburger off her plate and ate it while she watched. When he was done, he said, "When you remember me, Lucy, will you think all nice things?"

"I'll probably kick myself, you greedy bastard," she answered. "You want to split a milkshake? Will you drop me cards? I'll give you my grandmother's address."

"Chocolate," he said, and he slid a small pad across to her, and a pen.

The week school was out, she packed up everything, from her little portable typewriter to the silky new sheets she had bought.

Gordon said, "It looks like an abandoned hotel in here," standing in the middle of the living room, looking surprised and sad.

They drove up 281. The countryside was pretty. There were still bluebonnets along the highway. They saw a series of signs, YARD SALE: HANDYCRAFS, and followed them off the main road to a small dilapidated farmhouse. She tried on a bonnet from a pile of them on a white painted table in the yard, then put it back carefully. On a clothesline, there were half a dozen quilts flapping in the soft breeze, beautiful things. The lady selling them—she was the quilter, she said—was so pleased that they'd stopped, she brought them iced tea in Mason jars, with sprigs of mint floating on top. Gordon paid eighty dollars for one of the quilts, then presented it to Lucy. The woman sighed happily. "I knew you were a couple."

Lucy got in the car, the quilt on her lap. She looked down at it and said, "Gordon, you don't understand, my grandmother's house is stuffed with quilts and boxes and photos and books and dishes. What'll I do with this?"

He laid it carefully on the back seat. "I'll take it back to the apartment and keep it for you," he said. "You won't be cold all summer anyway." He spoke in his dry, even way.

In Hico they stopped for coffee at a cafe. There were six booths, half of them occupied by men in jeans and boots and hats, smoking and telling jokes. The waitress served Gordon and Lucy their coffee, then went back to flirt with the guys. The bell on the door chimed and a boy came in, high school age. He had a high pomaded hairdo, and he wore a starched white shirt with his jeans, and a bolo tie. The waitress called out hello and said, "You're gonna play for us, ain't you, Marvin?" That was the first time Lucy noticed that just around the corner from her there was an upright piano, shiny as glass, a big doily drooping over the front. The boy sat down and began to play. He played "Try to Remember," from *The Fantastiks*, and "Fly Me to the Moon," then "Days of Wine and Roses." The guys in the booth called out encouragement, urging Marvin to play louder, to sing, to play "Fly Me to the Moon" again, and this time he did sing, in a strong, dramatic voice. On the high notes, he warbled.

Lucy bent forward, touched and embarrassed and giddy. Across the table, Gordon raised himself to reach her, and kissed her forehead. "Ready?" he said. She slid out from the seat. There were tears in her eyes.

Outside, he opened the door of the car for her and as she bent to scoot inside, he bent after her and said, "This is temporary, Lucy. You need to spend some time with your grandmother before we make plans. We might live far away."

Her heart pounded. He had whispered to her sometimes, in the dark, *I love you*, but nothing was settled between them. She hadn't even asked him which colleges wanted him. When he got in the car, she turned and threw her arms around him and kissed him. He said, "You'll see."

When they reached Wichita Falls, Greta had a cold supper laid for them. Sliced ham and tomatoes, home-baked bread, potato salad, pickled beets and green onion stalks. The food was spread out over the kitchen table, covered by white cheesecloth. She had set up a card table in the living room. With three folding chairs around it, there was hardly room to squeeze in, but they arranged themselves, and ate well. Gordon was lavish with his praise. Greta liked that. She ate small bites and dabbed at her lips with her paper napkin, prissy and sitting tall. He said he liked the glaze on the ham, how had she done it? When she told him she cooked the ham in Coca-Cola, Lucy winced, but he took it in his same bland, polite manner. He said he had never heard of that, but it made a good glaze. Then he said he had to leave first thing in the morning.

He had a reservation at a motel. Greta protested. She had made the bed for him fresh; Lucy could see it from where she sat, through the doors, in the second bedroom. Greta had put on a beautiful star quilt she only took out for special occasions, and she had turned back the sheets. The air conditioner was in that bedroom, making it frigid there, then cool in the living room and Greta's bedroom. Between the bed and the far wall boxes were stacked four feet high.

Lucy would have to sleep with Greta, but that was fine. She might anyway, the first night home.

Gordon couldn't be talked into staying. "I wouldn't dream of it," he said. He must have seen that there was no shower, only a tub scrubbed for so many years the enamel was scored. Maybe it was too cold—he had been complaining about the Texas air conditioning, as if you could live without it! He made his way to the door. "You've already been so hospitable, Mrs. Clarehope." He shook her hand. Couldn't he see how stiffly she held her arm, how she pursed her lips? No matter what he did in the future—if there were a future—he would ever be the uppity Yankee, too good to sleep in her house.

Lucy went out with him to the car, and when he kissed her, she started to cry. "Will I ever see you again? Will I really?" She hated herself for it. She had felt safe with him, unsettled, perhaps, but safe, and now she felt adrift again. You didn't go home after a year of graduate school, you moved on, made your life.

He said, "Could you come with me for a little while? I'll bring you back. Will that be all right with your grandmother?"

She ran to tell Greta. "We're going to take a ride, Mommy, you go on to bed if you want." Greta nodded, not saying a word.

At the motel, Gordon bought 7-Ups from a machine for them, and poured them into glasses Lucy unwrapped. She sat on the bed and sipped her drink while he went back to the car. He brought in his small bag, and the quilt from the back seat. He put the bag on the table and the quilt on the chair. Then he turned down the bed and made love to Lucy the way he had at the very beginning, hungry and exploratory and surprised. "I love you," he said. "I'll call you every Sunday. I'll know what I'm going to do soon, and I'll tell you as soon as I do. I give you my word."

"Before you tell your mother?" she asked. When he didn't answer, she said, "Call me whenever you want."

When she got home, her grandmother was watching Johnny Carson. It had cooled down outside, and she had turned off the air conditioner and opened the bedroom windows. Lucy watched the rest of the program with her, and then they ate bowls of ice cream, and Greta went to bed. Lucy took a bath and then peeked in to tell Greta good night.

"Nice of that boy to bring you home," Greta said dryly.

From Austin? From the motel? She didn't say, and Lucy didn't ask. She grinned, though, and went to bed thinking, *I'll make her happy while I'm here. I'll be thoughtful and grown up and neat and I'll watch Johnny Carson with her every night.* Just the sort of resolution she had made dozens of times in high school after a siege of hurt feelings and cold silence, never resolved but soon forgotten.

And when she had crawled into bed, hugging the side near the window, her back to the stacked boxes, she felt like the girl she had been in this house. She remembered all the nights of loneliness and hopelessness, the black hurt she wanted Gordon to wash away with his fair love.

Her grandmother's house was home. It should have been soothing, an extension of years of the same routines. Her grandmother winding her way around the clock as the mill's shifts shifted. Meals of beans and fried potatoes and vegetables from the garden, biscuits in the morning. The news, the late talk show. Maybe, for Lucy, a part-time job at the nearby shopping center.

It wasn't like that at all. Her grandmother was brittle with anger. She closed the door too loudly, coming and going. She spent hours at her card table, going over bills and figures. Lucy tiptoed around her. She started to worry it was something she had done, then recognized her guilty uneasiness with her grandmother's dark mood for the habit it was.

She completed her paper for Cantwell. She knew as she put it in the mail that it was at best a C, but she didn't care. If she received the credit, she would receive her master's degree, something to keep her from complete shamefacedness. The paper was about the girl Lucy in *Studs Lonigan*, or more accurately, about Studs loving her. He couldn't bring himself to tell her. He couldn't even be nice to her. It wasn't manly to express feelings. The street held up an irresistible model for him, and tenderness, emotion, they weren't in it.

The paper was without scholarship—no critics quoted, no references to history. She tried to keep it formal and properly unemotional. It was risky, submitting her personal analysis to Cantwell. The course hadn't been about the novel, really; it had been about radical politics. Well, what were Studs and his sexual aggression but politics? A novel could be about large and small things at the same time, and to Lucy, that terrible failure of Studs to show his heart was a large thing. Whatever Suzanne might say, it moved Lucy.

She walked to the post office in searing heat and put the envelope in with a prayer. She could hear Cantwell's derision: take it over to English! She hoped she could squeeze by with a B.

Her grandmother came home from the mill covered with flour, like soot. She stood in the bathroom and unwound the rag from her head, then stripped from her pedal pushers and sleeveless blouse. Her socks were caked with sweat and flour. It was over a hundred degrees, day in, day out, at the mill. Greta was on fifty-pound sacks. She weighed about the same as Lucy, around one-five.

Lucy ran a bath for her, sat on the edge of the tub and washed her hair, then scrubbed her back. Her grandmother made soft moaning sounds. Lucy could remember when her grandmother was shop steward. The mill put her on seventy-five-pound sacks; she wore a wrestler's wide belt around the outside of her clothes. She never missed a day. Now she was crying. It wasn't like her.

"They're closing the damned place," she said, her voice thick. "They're giving us a farewell luncheon. We received *invitations* in our boxes. I want you to come." She turned to look up at Lucy. "It'd make me proud to have you there, my smart baby." Her face was still streaked with white flour mud, along the jawline. After she was dry and dressed, she sat down with Lucy and ate the supper Lucy had put together. It was so hot, they didn't want anything cooked, just chilled vegetables, sliced bread, a dish of rice pudding Lucy made early in the day.

"I'm one of three senior employees. We've all got twenty-two years, minus five to eight weeks. They're shutting down now so we won't be vested. We won't get full pensions. They're giving me eighteen hundred dollars severance, and sixty dollars a month at sixty-two. I've got to find another job. A career." She stabbed a cucumber with her fork. She was fifty-nine years old.

Lucy drove her grandmother to work on Tuesday. She ironed a skirt and blouse, pulled her hair back neatly, and went back for lunch. Her grandmother took her around to all the girls. They called themselves the girls; they were close as sisters.

In high school, in the summer, Lucy had often taken supper up to Greta, then sat in the workers' lounge while the girls ate and gossiped. (The men huddled at one end of the room, or went outside to smoke and talk rough.) It had always been excruciating—the noise, heat, smell, and boredom—but she had done her best to show off for her grandmother's friends, with fancy sandwiches, fresh brownies, jars of lemonade and tea.

Now those women wanted to hear what good things Lucy was up to. Their daughters were married, with babies, no college for them. They were proud of her, for Greta's sake. She stammered something about graduate school, about working toward her teaching certificate. Who knew? Maybe she would take courses at the college in the fall. She couldn't look at her grandmother, who hadn't asked one question about Lucy's plans for work or love or domicile. If every member of the family had shown up needy on the same night, Greta would have found blankets. And for nobody more than for Lucy, who, if you thought about it, had been a sort of refugee from the very beginning.

Lunch was laid out on long tables. There were six kinds of pies, and barbecue. Everyone piled their plates high, then sat around and cursed General Mills. One of the floor supervisors came by where Lucy was sitting with her grandmother, and there was a subtle shifting, heads turned in. He stopped—a man of forty, perhaps—and put his hands on his hips. "Hey, folks," he said loudly. "I'm out of a job, too, you know." Nobody answered. He passed the group. Greta's friend Jamesy (they called each other versions of their last names) said, "What's his severance, you figger?"

Greta threw herself into cleaning the house. It wasn't easy, it was so crowded. There were boxes of Laura's things, the closets crammed with Laura's clothes, Lucy's high school clothes, old coats and shoes. There were towels that went back to Lucy's childhood. Greta had kept Laura's dresser with the big round mirror crammed against the wall in her bedroom, leaving so little room that to make the bed she had to lean over and work the sheets in from the top of the bed. Lucy helped her pull stuff out from under the beds and move furniture around so they could vacuum. There were two refrigerators in the kitchen, and Lucy cleaned them both. One had been Laura's, new the year before she died, a gift from Greta.

"Olson's tearing down a chicken coop," Greta told her, pulling her head out from the oven. The room stank of oven cleaner. "Maybe we could build a storage shed with the lumber."

Lucy didn't think she understood. "Oh, who?" she asked.

Her grandmother snorted. "Me and the King of Siam," she said.

"Us?" Lucy had never driven a nail.

"You think I haven't built coops, sheds, fences? We can do it."

First, though, Greta went over to the farm, across the Red River, to look after her mother. Mama Sophie had had a couple of small strokes but she didn't want to leave the farm. Her brother Albert was dead, and the other brother, Ulmer, was in a Lubbock rest home, but Daddy Pa, older than both of them, was still farming. Aunt Tootie's daughter Jenny, recently divorced, was living over there with her bratty kids, cooking and looking after Mama Sophie—emptying her chamberpot!—but Greta didn't like it. Jenny was unreliable and scatterbrained and lazy, and a bad cook besides, and Sophie was worse off than anyone wanted to admit. Greta thought she was malnourished. She had been going over there every day off she had.

"We'll move this stuff into storage, then some of Mama's things," Greta said, just before she took off for the farm. "I'm bound to have Mama soon enough, we'll need more space." She was unhappy that Lucy wasn't going, but Lucy lied and said she had her paper to finish. She said she would water the garden. She knew the farm would depress her, and who wanted to use an outhouse, in this day and age? Mostly, though, she was waiting to hear from Gordon. Sunday had come and gone twice, and he hadn't called. She wasn't surprised. What reason did she have to believe that love brought order and stability? Her Aunt Opal always said, Men make depressions in the cushions and you don't even remember seeing them sit there.

She thought of Charlie in a rented room up the block from them, banished by Laura's whim. She thought of her mother at the end, crying, crying, when her doctor-lover was late. Would he come? Would he make her well? *Would he still love her?*

She didn't know how much had been her mother, how much had been the men, but love had not been reliable. She thought she had chosen better—a man from a fine family, an educated man—but it was possible she had not chosen at all. It was possible she had been—what was that old expression?—a passing fancy. Gordon's passing fancy.

She wasn't going to lie around and weep for him. He would become part of her history, *and she would learn from history.*

She got a phone call from an old school friend, Doris McGaffey. They had gone to Mary Immaculate together, and now her friend was Sister Boniface, about to commence teaching biology and chemistry at their old school.

"I heard you were in town," Sister said. "Mechtilde saw you at Mass Sunday. Why didn't you come over? Everybody would love it."

"I never thought of it," Lucy said. "I'm so preoccupied with my grandmother."

"Is she sick?"

"They closed the mill."

"I heard. Ouch. Listen, why not after eleven o'clock Mass this Sunday? You can eat lunch with us."

"Actually, Mommy's in Oklahoma. I don't have any transportation."

"I'll pick you up."

"You will?"

Sister laughed. "We do drive, you know. Hey, Lucy, you can call me Bonnie, you know. The younger sisters, we all have nicknames."

Lunch was fun, though it was strange to sit at the long polished table in the basement, with nuns who had been her teachers. Old Sister Thecla had slapped her hand with a ruler once, in fifth grade, for something she hadn't done. The funny thing was, Lucy could remember the injustice but not the terms of the accusation. Sister Thecla was blind with glaucoma now, and mostly deaf. She sat next to Lucy and asked her half a dozen times which girl she was. There was a nun just back from Africa, too. She was thin and pale—how did you stay pale in Africa?—and didn't say anything.

They were eating BLTs and Jell-O. To make conversation, Lucy asked the mission nun what she had eaten in Africa. Sister shrugged and said, "Whatever we had," then looked down at her plate, picking at the melting lumps of red Jell-O. Lucy's face burned. She felt scolded. She helped clear the table, and she and Sister Boniface did the dishes, then she said she needed to go home.

On the way, Sister Boniface said they could use her in the fall, if she stayed. "If you told us soon, we'd quit looking." The old history teacher was retiring. She was seventy-three. Her health wasn't good, and she was going to the order's home in Fort Worth.

"I don't know for sure," Lucy said. She wondered if she was wearing a sign on her forehead: NO FUTURE. "I'll think about it."

The minute she was in the house, she called Gordon. She let the phone ring and ring, but he wasn't there. She threw herself on her bed and wept until her nose was running and her eyes burned. When she got up to wash her face and saw how swollen and ugly she was, she pulled herself together. It was a terrible mark against Gordon, this silence. Just what you might expect, but she wouldn't forgive him. She wasn't ready to stop caring altogether, but she would care a lot less. He would have to work hard to make it up to her.

Monday, though, there was a note from him. He'd lost the number, couldn't remember Greta's last name, wanted her to call. She didn't believe him, but she paced the little house all day, waiting for night, and tried him again. She burned with shame, dialing the number.

"Clarehope," she said, as soon as he answered. "I know your family's names. Bell, Howard, Peter—"

"I miss you," he said, instead of apologizing.

She started crying right away, and she could hear it in her voice, but he didn't ask. She sure didn't ask, either, not anything. They talked about weather. She told him about seeing Bonnie and the nuns. He said he was flying home for a few days for a cousin's wedding. Bells went off in her head, but she stayed nonchalant. "A big wedding?" she asked smoothly. He said, "Is there any other kind?" *As if it was a subject that didn't matter at all!* Then he said the wedding would be in the country, at their summer parish. He would get to see his old dog Rhodes.

"That dog in the photo is still alive?"

"His son. I thought about bringing him to Texas, but he's such a comfort to my father."

A comfort how? Why did Mr. Hambleton need comfort? Wasn't that what a wife was for? Gordon spoke in maddening ellipses. She thought to attach herself to this conversation.

"My mother had a little Scottie once. She took it out one day and it darted in front of a car. I remember the family kept telling her she had to get over it." The memory of the dog, and her mother's grieving, was a grief in itself. She would have told Gordon that—how images of her mother welled up, uninvited, and filled the whole canvas of her mind—but he didn't leave her time.

"I have to go, Lucy. I have a committee meeting at seven-thirty in the morning."

She hung up furious, but he didn't know that.

She read magazines and watched terrible daytime TV. She went over to the shopping center and filled out an application at the drugstore for part-time counter work. She opened two of the boxes in her room. One was packed with white dishes trimmed with green tendrils. The other was all *stuff*, the sort of thing her grandmother would die before she'd throw away. Some baby clothes, old birthday cards, clippings from Lucy's high school achievements, a shoebox full of baby pictures of her, a couple of albums. Laura's prayerbook, *Moments with God.*

She opened the oldest album. It had been put together by Laura and captioned in her pretty handwriting, with white ink on black pages. There was a studio portrait of Greta with her brothers. She was a child in button shoes, her hair in tight ringlets. She looked scared to death. On the back it said 1911. There was one of her at thirteen, another at fourteen. In both, her hair was pulled so tight it looked cruel, and she wore a dark sailor-blouse–style dress. There were pictures of her with Ira; in all of them she was wearing a white cloche hat. Another was of Ira in overalls, behind a team of scrawny horses. 1929. There was a page of tiny square pictures of the children, Laura, Opal, Amos. Amos on a pony. Lucy loved the picture of a Model T Ford with ten kids, including Tootie at thirteen or so. A 1939 photograph showed Greta in white, leaning against a Chevy with Opal. They both looked so sad. Why wouldn't they? Ira was dead. And there she was outside a railroad car, arms folded, *laughing.* "You can't imagine," she had written. Did she dare ask her about it? Probably not. Altogether, there were only four album pages.

Lucy picked up a fat envelope with more photographs. These were of her mother, taken, Lucy guessed, right around the time Lucy was a baby. Laura in a two-piece black bathing suit, posing movie-star style, ankles crossed, on the cracked wooden porch of Greta's house in the old section of town. There were other photos of her around the same age, and one of her with Lucy, both of them in fur coats. Lucy was four years old; they were living in Indiana, where Charlie had taken them for a while. *Why, we were beautiful!* Lucy thought. Then, shockingly different, there was a photograph of Laura near the end of her life. Her hair was thin and short, her shoulders bare. She had carefully painted on eyebrows.

It was more than Lucy could bear. She shoved everything into the box, threw back the covers on her bed, lay down, curled up, and cried until she fell asleep. She dreamed that her mother was at the door of the old stucco house, banging to be let in, but no one heard her.

She woke in a little while with a start and pulled out the box again. She took out the photograph of her mother taken just before she died. Of course her shoulders were bare! The picture had been cut from one of the nudes. Disembodied, she was only a head floating free. Frantically Lucy ruffled through the box looking for the manila envelope with the rest of the photos. It wasn't there.

She went through the dresser drawers, one by one. She found the envelope in one of her grandmother's drawers, under clothing. She took it back to the bed and held it against her chest. She remembered exactly what she had said to her mother. *How did you pay for them?* There hadn't been time, or a way, to apologize. She had been so angry, so mean—and her mother so sad. She had known her mother was dying for a long time—she had gone in the bathroom and *rehearsed* her sorrow—yet Laura had died with Lucy's insult between them. It was too much to bear, it could not be forgotten, or forgiven. Her mother had had the last word.

She put the envelope in her own drawer. They were hers. The pictures belonged to her.

As soon as her grandmother was back from the farm, she took Lucy over to get the lumber. Her old co-worker and his son had taken off the roof. He suggested they separate the walls and move them intact; he and his son had a pickup and would help. Disassembly went quickly, but they would never have been able to manage moving the walls without the men, even with a truck. At the end of the day, the walls were laid out in Greta's yard, like fabric yardage, except that the walls were caked with chicken manure. Greta walked the rectangle where she planned to put the structure. The ground would have to be leveled. She said they would make a foundation out of used bricks. She was paying someone's son for them, delivered. Both of them sighed, then Greta handed Lucy a putty knife and gloves and a scarf for her hair. Lucy thought a bad attack of flu would be welcome at that moment, but she went to work, swallowing her sour protest. In the morning, she heard her grandmother out there banging around, but she turned over and pulled a pillow over her head. In the middle of the day, it was too hot to work. Greta took a long nap. They were back at it after an early supper. Lucy's arms burned with fatigue. At one point she groaned aloud, then caught her grandmother's eye and grinned.

"I didn't think you'd last," Greta said. She grinned, too. It was the first time Lucy had seen her happy since she came home.

By Sunday they had the land leveled and most of the bricks in place for a foundation. Lucy went to nine-thirty Mass, and then over to the church hall for a pancake breakfast. There was a long line curling from the door to the front of the room and the serving tables. Lucy looked around the room, dismayed to see no one as young as she. Then she spotted two young men sitting at the end of a long table. They had cups but no plates. Further down, the table was filling up, but no one sat near them. They were airmen from the base, in uniform. One was a tall, handsome Negro man. Next to him was a white man, his hair buzzed against his skull. He was cute, Lucy thought. She got a cup of coffee and went to sit across from the men. They looked up, surprised, and introduced themselves. Airmen First Class Roosevelt Cullins and Dustin Mackey. Dustin had a delighted, boyish expression at her appearance.

"Did you do something I don't know about?" she asked, turning to scan the room.

"Believe they don't like soldiers," Dustin said.

"Or black boys?" Roosevelt suggested.

"I can't believe either," Lucy said, believing both. She had them follow her in Dustin's little red MG back to the house. Greta was in the yard, and Lucy took them around there to meet her. She was on her hands and knees putting bricks in place, and looked up, her hand at her forehead, clearly surprised. Roosevelt, who was standing closest to her, put his hand out to help her up, and with the merest hesitation, she took it.

She came inside. There was a pot of coffee on the stove. While the men drank a cup, the women prepared a breakfast of biscuits, bacon, tomatoes and scrambled eggs. The men obviously loved it.

Lucy asked a few questions, and they answered as well as they could, in between bites. They were both mechanics out at the base. Dustin was Catholic, Roosevelt was Baptist, but he liked to visit other houses of worship. The two of them were friends, you could see that. They had that easy way of giving each other room to talk.

Greta wouldn't sit down. She leaned against the counter, over near the back door. They asked her what she was building. When they had finished eating, they went outside again to look the whole thing over, and before Greta could stop them, they had stripped off their shirts, taken up tools, and decided how to split up the work of finishing the shed.

While the men were working, they began talking about fishing. "I'd rather catch 'em than eat 'em," Dustin said. He was from Arkansas. He stopped to cast a phantom line and reel it in.

"You sure don't know about catfish," Roosevelt said, shaking his hammer for emphasis. "Heck, eating is the point of catching, boy." They both grinned; Lucy wondered, was it for the fish talk, or the easy way Roosevelt called Dustin *boy*?

Greta finally couldn't ignore the banter. "I love to fish for catfish," she said, "and I love to eat them, too."

It turned out Dustin hadn't had any experience with catfish. Before long, Greta was telling them they ought to go to Possum Kingdom with her for a little fishing. They'd have to use rod and reel. She explained that her favorite spot was on a little river where she could string line and come back the next day, but nobody had the time for that just now.

Lucy couldn't stop herself; she went over and gave her grandmother a hug. Greta's bare arms had burned in the past week. The upper part, where you would think they would be hard from labor, was fleshy. The two of them had always been affectionate with one another. Touching was easy. It was talking that hung up Greta and made everyone wonder what she was so mad about.

By the end of the day they had the roof on. There was a little work left on the roof, and Greta was wondering how to make the shed more snug. Roosevelt said he'd line it with tarpaper, if it was up to him, then he laughed and said, "Inside, for a change." He had a soft East Texas drawl, and though he was polite, it wasn't all head-ducking and uncomfortable; he didn't act sorry he was black. Dustin said he would come back one evening later in the week and help them finish up the roof, and cut shelves, if they could wait. Greta had stopped protesting hours ago; she was grateful for their assistance. Lucy's role had degenerated to fetcher of ice water, which suited her fine. And as the day wore on, Greta took her aside and told her to go buy beer. "Believe I could drink one myself," she said, raising her head, as if someone were challenging the idea. They sat around on the living room floor—Greta was on a kitchen chair—and told more fishing stories. When Lucy admitted that she had never caught a fish in her life, the men were astonished. "With a granny like Mrs. Greta?" Roosevelt said. "It don't seem right." Greta, amused, put on a smug look and said, "Some things you can't tell a girl who's so *smart*."

Dustin and Lucy took his MG over to the White Kitchen, a tiny hamburger hut half a dozen blocks away. On the way he told her he had salvaged the car from a wreck. He'd rebuilt it himself. He had even done most of the body work.

"How'd you learn to do that sort of work?" she wanted to know.

"My pop's a mechanic. He can make anything run. He says, why buy something new when you can fix the old part? Course, in the air force, I've learned a lot." He was proud of working on planes. He said they were getting ready for "out and out conflict" in Southeast Asia. "Can't do it without planes," he said. Lucy didn't know anything about it.

They were back in the car with sacks of hamburgers on Lucy's lap. He asked her, "Have you ever driven a sports car?"

"Never even been in one before," she said, although in college she had once dated a bigheaded fraternity boy who had an expensive foreign car. She couldn't remember the name of the car —or the boy, for that matter. She thought Dustin would like being first at something.

"I'll take you out and let you drive this one, if you want," Dustin said. He glanced over at her shyly. Lucy could tell the idea was about more than the car.

The hamburgers were hot on her thighs. She bent to suck in their aroma.

"Would you want to?" he said. "My pleasure."

"Sure," she said. "I'd love that."

First they took out the big dresser. They wrapped it in sheets and old blankets. They had to take it out the front door, then carry it around to the back of the house. Lucy said that if they waited, the guys could do it. Greta went on fussing with the blankets. Lucy said, "We could wait for Dustin" again, and her grandmother gave her a blistering look. They managed the move a few torturous steps at a time; Lucy didn't dare complain of the strain. They took their time arranging the boxes. It was a mournful job. Each box had to be opened and pawed through so that Greta could label it for stacking. She tucked folds of brown paper on top of the contents before closing and taping the flaps. She took an oversized envelope out of one box and tapped it against Lucy's forearm. "Your hospital birth certificate," she said. "With the little footprints." Lucy just nodded. Greta added, "And the other one." Lucy's heart pounded, but she didn't say anything. Greta laid the envelope on Lucy's bed.

They stood in the doorway of the little structure. It looked raw but sturdy. Before they put on the roof, the men had laid a thick layer of plastic. The biggest danger wouldn't be to the contents, but to anyone coming inside later, if they weren't cautious. This area was known for black widow spiders.

"And there's room for Mama's things," Greta said. Lucy hoped Mama Sophie didn't have a lot to bring with her. What was the use of it all, anyway? Her grandmother had saved an old hand mirror of Laura's. It wasn't even in perfect condition. But chipped or not, it had held her precious daughter's image.

Lucy was surprised to realize her eyes had filled with tears. She wiped them angrily. Greta closed the shed door and said, "I hope you're going to have a home of your own and come get all this. I'm saving it for you, you know that, don't you?" She snapped the padlock. "It's nothing to me, any of it. Everything's gone, for me."

Lucy's heart sank. She didn't want her mother's dishes. Every time she picked one up, her heart would break. And she didn't want to feed her grandmother's fantasy; some cruel impulse made her want to say it was junk, worth nothing; throw the damned stuff away! Instead, she nodded mutely, and then, seeing her grandmother's anguished expression, she embraced her for a long awkward moment. She should have said something. She should have said anything, but the rule was, swallow your words, chew on your sorrow. Opal had told Lucy many times: Mommy won't mix her grief with yours.

And what did it matter? Neither words nor storage would change the blackness of the holes in their world.

"You poor kid," Dustin said when she told him about her mother's death at thirty-three from Bright's disease. She knew he didn't know what that was, but she let him chew on it a little while before she explained. She let him look at her, cow-eyed with pity, while she wondered when she would be too old for men to react like this. "Her kidneys failed. It was a long time coming. She had been in bed for a year. My grandmother was there, taking care of her." He shook his head, disbelieving. His mother had had nine children and was in vigorous good health. Good Catholic that he was, he said, "When I say a prayer for my mama, now I'll say one for yours, too."

Irritably, Lucy said, "She doesn't really need that."

He asked about her daddy. Bile rose in her throat. "I went to live with my grandmother. My little sister went with my Aunt Opal. And Daddy went with a redheaded legal secretary with very big breasts." She liked seeing Dustin's shock. The grotesquerie of her expression shoved aside the pain, now eight years old. "Besides, he isn't my daddy." She didn't say that she hadn't known that until her mother was buried and everyone began to sort out the children. She didn't say a lot of things, because she didn't know him well enough, and she wasn't used to talking about it. No one in the family had ever mentioned it to her—the "unrealness" of Charlie, let alone who might be "real"—although once she knew, it was obvious that everyone was relieved to have her know. Now they wouldn't have to pretend he meant anything, was anybody. He wouldn't have to be mentioned.

They didn't stand a chance, Lucy and Charlie.

The redhead—she still didn't think of her as Charlie's wife—had said, "I don't know what everybody expects of Charles. It's not like he's your father." In that moment, years and years of innuendo had turned to understanding. *Of course*, she had thought, over and over.

What about her sister? Dustin wanted to know. She was getting tired of the conversation. "She was in college in Lubbock. She quit and became a stewardess. I haven't seen her in a couple of years." Faith was part of childhood, and childhood was so far away.

He shook his head. Looseness of connection was strange to him. He said, "I miss everybody in my family. Except for me, and one brother who's a policeman in Fort Smith, all the kids live close enough to see the folks every week. My sister Joella lives next door." He grinned. "When we have a potluck, it's a hell of a feast."

"That's all very nice, Dustin," she said. They were in the house, with the paper open. "Are we going to go to a movie or not?"

He wasn't stupid. On the way to the car he stopped and took her by the shoulders. "I don't know anything about that kind of hurting, Lucy, but I know you can have a family of your own, and little ones make you look forward instead of backward."

"Thanks," she said, trying to be nice. He was nice, that was for sure. He was nice, he was good looking, and he sure was around a lot.

She took the papers out of the envelope her grandmother had put on her bed. First she looked at the one from the hospital. She ran her fingers around the tiny footprints. Then she put it behind the other paper, the birth certificate. There were her parents' names: EMMA LAURA CLAREHOPE. And HOLLIS ALBERT BERRY.

She took it into her grandmother's room.

Greta was propped up in bed, looking at a magazine. She saw what Lucy was holding. Before Lucy asked, she said, "She made up the name. She wore a ring, so she could say she was married, and later could say she was divorced. You have to understand, that was the way it was back then."

"Are you ever going to talk to me about this?"

Greta turned a page and slapped it into place. "Your mother went away, to California, and then she came home. I told her then she didn't have to tell me what went on. She was my child, and she had come home."

Lucy stood there for a minute. Greta stared at the page. Then she looked up and said, "You were ours, that's all I know, Lucy. Do you think you didn't get enough love?"

Lucy laid the papers on the end of Greta's bed. "You should put these with the other things."

"Put them with the photographs," Greta said. So Lucy did.

Soon after, she was talking to Gordon on the phone.

"Don't you wonder about my family?" she asked him. "I know a lot about yours."

"Whatever you want to tell me," he said. "It's you I love."

"Did you know I lived in a welfare housing development once? Actually, it was one of the nicer places I've lived."

"Do you think I care about that, Lucy? Do you really think I care?"

"I don't even know who my father is. What does that make my mother?" When he didn't speak, she said, more softly, "They could have been in love, couldn't they? Sometimes lovers are separated. *Casablanca. Intermezzo.*"

And he, softly too, said, "I don't see how we can talk about this on the phone. You're bringing up things too important to you to throw away like punch lines. Is this a test?"

"You're too smart for me," she said, really meaning it.

"Just tell me about now. What you're doing. How you are."

"We built a storage shed and cleaned house. Mommy's fighting with unemployment, because of her severance pay. I started working at the pharmacy. I give people prescriptions and take their money. It's called clerk."

"That's it, Lucy?"

"That's everything. My whole report."

"You got your paper in?"

"Yes."

"Maybe you'll get back in graduate school someplace else."

"Maybe."

"I'm flying out to California for interviews, then I'll know what's going to happen."

"And me?" She wasn't sure she cared what he would say anymore. It was like losing weight slowly. You wouldn't notice, day to day, and then one morning you'd wake up skinny. Or not in love.

"Then I'll tell you, and you'll know, too," he said.

Dustin called a little while after she hung up the phone. He wanted to know if she was free Saturday. He thought they could take a long drive and let her use her new sports-car-driving skills. "You have any ideas?" he wanted to know.

She knew exactly where she wanted to go, even though it wasn't something she had ever thought about. "We went there when I was a little girl," she said. "We had good times."

"This is your trip," he said.

She said, "Pack a bathing suit."

She went to visit Sister Boniface. They sat in a front parlor in which there was a beautiful grand piano. Sister told her about the assignment a new history teacher would have. A new teacher like her would have a lighter load than others, she said. And of course the students were very well behaved. She said she wasn't sure about the pay. "I assume it will be embarrassingly low," she said. "Sister Genevieve can explain it to you."

"I don't know, Bonnie. Honestly, I don't know what I'm going to do. I didn't really come to talk to you about that, although in a way it's all related. I wanted to talk to you about men." She was very embarrassed.

Sister Boniface laughed. "Now this ought to be interesting. Do you know, once I graduated from high school, the only boy I saw was Joe McMurtry, do you remember him? He was always in trouble for something, but he was so smart." The boys had only gone to Mary Immaculate through eighth grade; after that the school was for girls only. The boys had gone to public school. God save the souls of boys, the nuns used to say.

"He was your boyfriend?"

"Oh no. We only lived a few blocks away, I've known him all my life. So I'd made plans to go into the convent in August, and I pan-

172

icked all of a sudden. What if I was wrong? Never to be a mother? I'd never been with a boy, how did I know what I was giving up? All the usual doubts, but when you're having them, they're awful."

"They sound real enough to me."

"I tried to seduce Joe! Oh, I was awful. I got him all hot and bothered, and me, too." She stopped. "I'd die if anybody knew I was telling you this. But I haven't had a girlfriend talk in years. Your friendships in the convent—they're different. They don't really encourage friendship, you know."

"Are you going to tell me? About Joey?"

She blushed. "Well, we didn't. Leave it at that. In fact, we ended up laughing hysterically. I love it, you know, this life. I wake up happy. They tell us there will be dark nights, doubts, loneliness. I don't know when that will come, but it hasn't yet. I'm happy."

"That's what I came to talk to you about. Being happy. Only with a man, not without. I want to marry, Bonnie. I thought I wouldn't get used to calling you Bonnie, but it's easy. I want to have children." She started to cry. "I want to have a family."

Sister put her hand out, and when Lucy took it, Sister squeezed it just hard enough to stop the tears.

Lucy told her about Gordon, and Sister said he sounded like the sort of man a girl dreams of until she finds out he's too busy. "But that doesn't mean he won't come to his senses."

"But now there might be somebody else," she said. "Can we go outside? It feels so claustrophobic all of a sudden."

They went out onto the playground, and ended up strolling along the periphery of the grounds. The ground was dust, a few rocks. The few old trees were near the building. There was a cyclone fence, about waist high, between the yard and the sidewalk. It didn't seem tall enough to be worth anything.

Lucy stopped and put her hands on the fence, and leaned back, like a little girl. She stared straight up at the hot, clear blue sky. She turned around and leaned against the fence, and she tried to explain about Dustin. The easiest way was to tell all the nice things he had done for them, and the comfortable feeling her grandmother seemed to have with him. Like two Sundays ago, when they'd all gone to the farm and he had filled the water barrels from the outside tank, and then repaired the chicken coop. He'd shouted out conversation with old Daddy Pa, and then played 42 after supper. He was young; he would grow even more handsome.

"But it's not your grandmother who would marry him. What do you feel toward him? Are you in love with him?"

"I keep thinking, he's someone I know. I wouldn't spend my whole life guessing what he's thinking. Or trying to be something I'm not. And if I were nice, Bonnie, he would treasure me. That's the kind of family he comes from. He would cherish me."

Sister Boniface took her hand again, and they walked back to the building. "Let's see. He's Catholic. He's patriotic. He's sweet, and he has good manners. Your grandmother is crazy about him, and his best friend is a Negro. I ask you, Lucy. Why do I have the feeling the two of you have nothing at all in common?"

On the way up to the Wichita mountains, she read a short story aloud. She had seen copies of Mickey Spillane novels from the base library lying on the floor of Dustin's car, and she had looked through a lot of books, trying to choose something he would like.

The story she read was "Big Two-Hearted River," by Ernest Hemingway. She finished reading the first half, in which the protagonist, Nick, hikes in to the river carrying a heavy pack and sets up camp and goes to bed.

"That's a good feeling," Dustin said. "Walking long and hard to get to a place to fish. I don't know about trout, though. Mostly I've fished for bass."

"It's only the first half of the story," she said. She had closed the book. "I thought I'd rest a little from reading."

By then they were in Oklahoma. There was a sign saying that there was a buffalo preserve ahead. Soon they saw cars pulled off the road. "Look," she said.

And then, without thinking, she burst out, "I remember! I remember!" She was very excited. She could see them lined up at the fence, Laura, Charlie, Lucy, Faith. The massive animals in the pasture. Once they had seen two of them jousting. "Why are they butting heads, Daddy?" Faith asked. "Are they going to get a headache?" And Charlie, scooping her up, then reaching out to pull Lucy close, smiling over Lucy's head at Laura, saying, "They do it to prove how hard their heads are, punkin." And her mother's laughter.

It was just a moment, and then she was calm again, feeling a bit foolish. Dustin asked her if she minded if he smoked a cigarette. She nodded no, and he shook out his pack. He offered her one, but she didn't smoke. They sat on the bumper of the car. It was very hot and still and bright. She was wearing a scarf to hold her hair, and sunglasses, big like Jackie Kennedy's. Dustin's head was bare, and she thought he might burn, but he was already brown, and he hadn't complained of the sun. He was wearing jeans and a short-sleeved checked shirt. The muscles of his upper arms were well defined. She didn't think she had ever gone out with anyone stronger, or nicer. He had kissed her a few times, saying good night, but he had never put a hand on her to touch her. He wore Old Spice deodorant; she had begun to like the smell. She thought she had begun to love him. The trick was not to think so much, just to feel.

They went over to the fence with the other sightseers. They could see several buffalo on a slight rise, a hundred yards or so away. They heard a child's voice calling them to come closer, as if they were doggies. Dustin grinned and put his arm lightly over Lucy's shoulder. She reached up for his hand, and he edged closer. She felt something run along her flesh, almost a chill, but a nice feeling at the same time. They went back to the car. Lucy had brought some oranges. Dustin peeled one for each of them, and they ate standing up by the side of the car, licked their fingers, then got in.

She read the second part of the story.

First Nick makes all the morning preparations, coffee and buckwheat batter, and he gathers grasshoppers in a jar.

She glanced over at Dustin. He was grinning, enjoying the story. It goes on and on, the water and the trout and the incredibly male pleasure of it all. It was more fishing than she cared about, but, read aloud, the story had a droning, hypnotic rhythm. When she got to the end, she closed the book and laid it on the floor, and didn't say anything.

Maybe it wasn't fair, making him speak first, but she wanted to hear what he would say. He shook his head back and forth. "You wouldn't think you could see something so clearly, just from what a man puts on a page," he said. She smiled. He went on. "We never read that writer in high school. I'd remember if we did. We read a lot of dull stories. And Poe, that Cask of something, that was dumb, huh?"

"It was," she agreed.

"I remember a story about a bridge, though," he said. "It was in the Civil War. A man being hung."

"'Occurrence at Owl Creek Bridge,'" she said.

"That's it! I liked that one."

"And you liked this one?"

"I did. That was nice of you, Lucy. You want to read another one?"

She leaned back and tugged at the scarf to make a bit of shade over her eyes. "Not right now. I'll lend you the book, though."

"I'll read it," he said, with all the earnestness of a promise.

They swam in a mountain pool that was so cold she thought she must be turning blue. They had come here many times in her childhood, on trips they made to Chickasha to see Laura's relatives on her dead Papa's side. Today the other swimmers were all families. Plenty of shrieking children and mothers calling out directions. Don't get away from Daddy, now! Don't go underwater! Stop splashing your sister!

She and Dustin swam off from the edge of the pool away from the children to the other side, and pulled themselves up onto the bank. They were both pimply with cold bumps, shivering. She snuggled up close to him. "You wonder why somebody wants to do this," she said. Her teeth were chattering.

"It's a hundred degrees today," Dustin reminded her. "It feels real good."

"I'm hungry," she said.

"Want to swim fast or slow?" he asked, sliding back into the water. There wasn't anyone near them on the bank or in the water.

"Wait," she said. She slipped into the pool, too, and slid her body close against his, from above her waist all the way down along his legs. She felt his hip bones, and she felt the fleshiness of his crotch. They were standing on solid bottom. He started to take a step away. She caught him with her hands on his lower back. "Wait," she said again. She put her face up so he could kiss her. A long fish brushed her leg, and she jumped and shrieked once. They both laughed, and then swam in long strokes to the other side. They walked to the car and took their towels and clothes out of the trunk, then went to the little changing huts to get dry. Now they were awkward, confused, like teenagers. She kept stealing looks at him, and caught him stealing looks at her. They decided not to brave the slapped-together sandwiches at the snack bar. They would drive down the road, to where they had passed a real cafe, where they could get something hot.

By the car, in the parking lot, she reached for him. She put her arms around him and kissed him again. He caught his breath, as if he had just come up from that cold water. He reached around her, and put the key in the ignition. "We're going to starve," he said. "We've got to eat something."

She climbed into the car happily. They spent the time of the short drive to the cafe in silence. She leaned back, her eyes closed, and tried not to think anything. Her whole body was alive, hot again now in the afternoon sun. When they reached the cafe, she said, "We'll be late getting back. We could find a cabin, I bet. We could spend the night." He didn't say anything, and she added, speaking more rapidly, "Mommy's over at the farm, nobody will know. You want to, don't you? You want to spend the night with me?"

He pulled up in front of the cafe too fast, spinning his wheels in the gravel. His face was red from too much sun that day. "I have to be on base in the morning," he said.

She put her hands behind his head and made him look at her. She knew he was aroused; she could see the bulge in his jeans, so she tried not to let her eyes look down. "I'd like it," she said. It was thrilling, knowing that was true.

"Let's see how far back we get," he said.

They drove all the way home, of course. A good Catholic boy. Why couldn't he see that if he made love to her, she might love him? Did he have no experience at all? She fell asleep, lulled by the roar of the car. She woke and it was dark. She couldn't remember where he had put the top up. She hadn't driven at all. He had even thrown a sweatshirt over her, but it wasn't cold, it wasn't at all cold, and she had thrown it on the floor, on top of the book of Hemingway stories.

They were north of Burkburnett. "Please," she said. "Pull off somewhere. Please, Dustin. For a few minutes."

He found a rural road. Once he had parked, they were in deep darkness. Even the moon was hardly there in the huge black sky. "You don't have to go away from the side of the car," he said. "Nobody will see you." He thought she had to pee.

"It's not that," she said. Awkwardly in the silly little car, she maneuvered herself so that she could kiss him, and then she turned and jumped out of the car. "Come on!" she said. "Come on!" She went around to his side as he climbed out. She pressed her body against his, and now he kissed her deeply, hungrily, as a man kisses. She moaned, and she reached down to cup his genitals. He drew in toward her hands, as a man who might fall.

"No one will see us here," she said. "No one." Over his shoulder she could see a farmhouse, so far away it looked like a toy, with tiny lights at one end. There were night sounds, insects, someplace in the distance another car.

He clung to her and kissed her. She was wearing a blouse, and she reached up to unbutton it. He fumbled with her, and she pulled the blouse off and let it drop to the ground. He gasped. She wore no bra. She put his hands against her breasts. "Oh, oh," he moaned. She kept reaching for his crotch, and he pushed her hands away.

"We can't," he said. "No, Lucy."

"Why?" she said. She pulled his hand against her pubes.

"Not like this," he said.

"Come home with me, then. My grandmother's not there."

"No." He put his hands on her shoulders and pushed her so that he could look at her.

"I'm a virgin," he said.

She couldn't keep from laughing, just a short, barking laugh. She was mortified. "So this would be the first time," she said. "Not for me."

"I love you, Lucy," he said. "I love you a lot."

"Dustin."

"I don't want to fuck you. I want to marry you."

She was trying to undo his jeans, but she couldn't manage the fastening. She whispered, "At least, take care of it, Dustin." He groaned. She stepped around behind him, and put her arms around his waist. She pushed against his buttocks. Her hands were on his belly, up under his shirt. "See, I won't look. I won't touch. But I'm here. Go on, Dustin, I want you to. If you won't put it in me—"

He let out a long low groan, and then she felt him tugging frantically at his jeans, and then the sigh as he was released from their constriction. He rocked as he masturbated, and she rocked with him, thrilled, excited. After he came, he slumped against the top of the car, and threw his arms over it, and she fell against his back, her arms flung up over his shoulders. "I love you, too," she said.

She could. Now that she knew how much she could want him, she knew she could love him. She tugged at him, and he turned around and embraced her. He was sobbing. They stood on the edge of the dirt road, their clothes awry, and clung to one another. She felt safe. Oddly, she felt free.

As they neared the house, she said, "We'll talk tomorrow, Dustin. Sweet Dustin."

He said, "Yes." She thought he sounded happy.

They turned onto Grant Street and she saw that she had forgotten to turn on a light. The house, inside and out, was dark. There was a car in front. Dustin said, "Somebody's at your house."

It wasn't her grandmother's car. "I don't think so," she said. "There aren't any lights."

He pulled up behind the car. "Lock yourself in, and let me go see what's going on," he said. He reached behind his seat and took out some kind of tool. "Lock this door behind me, now."

She could barely see him make his way up to the stoop. That was when she saw that he was right, there was someone there, someone who stood up slowly. She heard their voices, soft, polite.

Dustin came back to the car. She unlocked it and he opened the door.

"He says he's come to see you," he said. "Unh," he grunted, as if he had lost the words. Then he leaned over and he said, "He says he's your fiancé."

They were married two weeks later in the vestry of Sacred Heart Church. The priest—now Monsignor—who performed the brief ceremony had baptized her, had buried her mother. He had not been happy, at first, to rush the marriage, to skip the banns, but Gordon had spent a long time in Father's study the morning after his arrival, and when they came out, both of them were smiling. Gordon returned to Austin, then to Wichita Falls. He bought flowers for every room of Greta's house.

Opal came from Monahans with her daughter Clancy. Clancy, who was eight, took Gordon's hand and said, "Now are you my cousin?" Gordon knelt down to her height and said indeed he was.

Roosevelt, solemn and handsome in his dress uniform, came to see her married. He said Dustin had not been able to leave the base. He had sent a gift, a white pearl rosary. Sister Boniface came. One of the Knights of Columbus came, at Father's request, to be a witness. Afterwards, Gordon offered to take everyone out for a steak dinner, though Sister could not go, and Roosevelt said he, too, had to be on base. Father did go, and ate heartily. He engaged Greta in a discussion of gardening, and she promised to bring him apricots from her trees.

Gordon was patient through the ordeal of a long leave-taking. Opal cried aloud, and Clancy cried because her mother did. Greta cried quietly, tightly, without a sound. There were so many embraces. From Wichita Falls, they would go to Austin for a few days. Gordon had already packed and shipped most of the things worth shipping, but Lucy had paperwork to do for her degree. Then they would drive to Santa Barbara, where Gordon would be in the history department that had been his first choice. His sister Bliss lived there. Her husband was on faculty, too, a philosopher.

Lucy felt as if she were moving to a new country.

She took her grandmother aside and tried to give her the six hundred dollars she had saved. Greta was insulted, but Lucy insisted. "I'm marrying money, Mommy," she said. The compromise was Greta's idea. They went together to the bank and opened a joint account. The money would be there if Greta needed it. Lucy said she was to draw on it whenever she wished. Greta said, "You don't need to worry about me." She had enrolled in a program at the college, to train vocational nurses. It would take a year, and she was receiving a small grant, and her unemployment, now translated into a sort of remodeling stipend. "I think I'll take care of old folks," she said. Lucy was hurt that she had not heard these plans before, but Greta said it had all come together just the other day.

Lucy packed the nude photographs of her mother, a packet of childhood photographs and Willie's photographs of her, the birth certificates, her clothes, a few books, including her mother's prayer book. "Is that all?" Gordon said twice, when he saw what they had put into his trunk.

"This is it," she said. She tried to make a joke. "Aren't I going to buy everything new?"

"I suppose you will," he said, perfectly serious.

Opal hugged him goodbye and said, "You take care of our baby." Greta allowed a reasonable approximation, like people in a French film. Lucy clung to both of them, then pulled free and got in the car. As they drove away, she turned onto her knees to look out the back until she could see no more the figures of her aunt and grandmother on the stoop, weeping, waving, waving.

In Austin, they lay down together on the one remaining bed and made love slowly and solemnly, until they could not hold themselves back anymore. Lucy felt herself filled with Gordon, and with the new person she had become. Afterwards, she rose up on her elbow and ran her hand over his chest in circles. "It was very romantic of you," she said. He had shown up that dark night with roses, a ring, and his University of California contract.

"I came as soon as I could."

"And did you tell your mother first?"

"I haven't told her yet." He didn't know that already there was that thorn.

She sat up and hugged her knees. She didn't feel like discussing his family. When and how they would hear about her. When and where they would meet.

She was thinking about her own family.

"Daddy took Faith and me camping one summer in Balmorhea."

"What's that?"

"Not what, where. It's a spring-fed pool way west of Odessa, out in the middle of a hot dry nowhere. It's only green right around the edges of the pool. The water is icy cold. You can camp nearby. There's a long roof with spaces like an oversized carport. You have to fill up your water bottles at a single spigot. It's hot and dusty. We slept in the car, and he slept on the ground."

"How old were you?"

"We went more than once. The last time was the summer before Mother died. So I was thirteen, going on fourteen in August. We cooked hot dogs and marshmallows. Oh, we had a wonderful time. You know what else he did? After Mama died? He took Faith and me to a motel. It was the first motel I'd ever been inside of. He went and got hamburgers and milkshakes for us, and he turned the TV on loud, and we sat on the beds and ate. Back at the house, there was weeping and wailing, but we were in that motel trying to stay together. Faith was crying, and Daddy blew his nose so much it was raw. I'd give anything to remember what was on TV."

"Lucy, look at me."

She was crying, of course. Married ten hours, and this was what he got.

He sat up in front of her. Their knees touched. "I'm your husband now, and we're going to make a good life. So you listen to me. I'm never going to abandon you. I'm always going to be there. I'll always tell you where I'm going and when I'll be back. I'll never leave you."

She cried a long time against his chest, enveloped in his arms. Then she washed her face and brushed her hair and got back in bed.

"Now you listen." She meant what she said. She had no experience, no way to know how hard it would be. She said, "I'll be your wife. I'll be everything you need me to be."

September 8, 1969

Dear Dustin,

I was surprised and relieved to hear from you. Ever since you called to say goodbye, right after Lucy left for California, I have had you in my prayers. We have lost so many of our boys in such a far-off land. My son Amos was in Korea. He fought on Pork Chop Hill, and I have always thought it ruined him in some ways. It hurt his hearing, that's for sure.

But you are home safe, what a blessing. Maybe your mother can sleep nights now. I am so sorry to hear about Roosevelt. I know you were his good friend. He was so strong and good, you would think he would have been protected, but he is one of many good boys to die for a war I do not understand.

And look at you, coming home with a wife! I cannot see her real good in the snapshot you sent, but I am sure she is a sweet girl and you will make each other happy. I hope this first child you are expecting will be healthy and smart and good to his parents. Aren't you glad he (or she!) will be born on American soil.

Lucy is in California and I guess she is fine. I have not seen her in 1969. Her husband is a professor, and she does college work of some kind. She says it changes with different projects. I will tell her I heard that you are well.

I will surprise you with news of my own. I was just married recently myself. I met Ben in a rest home where I work, when he was recovering from eye surgery. He has a nice piece of property down at Possum Kingdom, so we will do a lot of fishing. I have always been sorry that I did not get to take you there, like I suggested. Or Roosevelt, either.

God bless you and keep you safe. Yes, I think it is very smart of you to stay in the service. I always was sorry that my son left. He only had five years left till retirement, but he got mad and that was that. You didn't seem like you had a temper. It is best to keep it under control.

God bless you, Dustin. The storage shed is still just fine.

Yours,
Greta (Clarehope) Kitteridge

OREGON

1

In 1987, the autumn that Laurie Hambleton was in ninth grade, her English teacher, Mrs. Stevens, gave the class an assignment to write about a favorite family story. She encouraged the students to talk to their parents and ask about family history. She hoped the assignment would spark a closeness between child and parent—early adolescence could be such a difficult time—and of course she hoped it would result in good writing. What surprised her was how various the results were, and how obvious it was that the students had not talked to anyone at all. They had drawn from what they already knew, not so much retelling a story as spilling secrets.

I don't know very much about my dad's family. They've been Americans so long you'd think they predated the Indians. They have always lived in New York and Massachusetts until Aunt Bliss and my dad came to live "out West," as they say in his family. I think it made Grandmother Bell unhappy that they left. The

185

Hambletons don't tell many family stories. They like to talk about books and politics. They play tennis and they swim a lot. I always spend July with my grandmother and Aunt Lynnie's family in Nantucket, and August with Aunt Bliss and Uncle Ted in Santa Barbara.

One story I do remember, though it was my mother who actually told it to me. It's about Uncle Peter, who is Father Peter, a Jesuit priest. He was adopted. When he arrived (I don't know where he came from), and Bell's mother saw his thick dark hair and dark eyes, she said, "Oh, Bell, no one will ever believe he's yours, darling!" and Bell is supposed to have said, "He's not mine, Mother, he belongs to God. I'm just taking care of him until he grows up." So Uncle Peter always knew he would be a priest, because that is what Bell wanted him to be.

The other story is about Grandfather's death. He was much older than Grandmother. (He had known her since the day she was born!) He retired early from teaching and devoted about twenty years to the study of birds. Every other year he went somewhere to do the Christmas count, which is an annual census that bird people make. One year before I was even born, he went to Costa Rica, and just as he called out, "My God, it's a—!" he died of a heart attack. I have asked everyone what bird it was that he saw that excited him so much he died, but no one knows or at least no one remembers. When I asked Grandmother, she said, "That is an unseemly question, Laura. People of good breeding do not pry."

My mother's family is completely different. Most everybody is dead, but I know a lot of their stories. One is about how Grandfather Ira died. He was working for the railroad, I think. Anyway, a baby tornado picked him up and smashed him down on the ground, and left Mommy (that's what everybody called my mother's grandmother) and her three kids behind, very poor and desperate, because it was the Depression, and they didn't have welfare yet. I have heard my mother's Aunt Opal tell this story, too. The way she tells it, after the accident, Mommy went to work for the railroad herself, and took my mother's mother, Laura, with her, and left Opal and her little brother behind at somebody's farm. Opal must have minded a lot, because she brings it up every time I see her. I remember Mommy, who died a few years ago, pretty well, but I never felt close to her the way I do to Grandmother Bell. When she talked to Mother on the phone, I would have to say hello to her, and she would always say, "You be sweet to your mother, now. You won't always have her." Is that weird?

Another story is that my mother's mother, Laura, died when my mother was fifteen. I'm not sure what she died of, but I know that my mother was in the room with her, sitting in a chair with a high back. Her daddy, Charlie, crawled up on the bed and hit Laura's chest and yelled, "Don't do this!" but it wasn't like she could help it. If my mother was dying, I would want to be with her, but I wouldn't want to see it. I know this is a contradictory statement, but it is how I feel.

Since my mother's grandmother died, she doesn't talk about her family anymore, but I think she still thinks a lot about them. She has photographs of her mother and grandmother hanging in her study. Sometimes I think she thinks more about her mother than she thinks about me. She says the only way you keep the past alive is by remembering it. What would be the point of that? I am never going to spend time looking back. I would rather my family was happy now, instead of just polite. That's a Hambleton trait, being polite. I remember Grandmother Bell telling me, "Sometimes good manners are all you have." I have no idea why she said that.

On Laurie's paper, Mrs. Stevens wrote something very much like what she wrote on all the others: *Thank you for sharing this with me. This is so special, so real. Keep writing.* All in all, she felt it had been a wonderful assignment.

"What in the world could she have been thinking?" Gordon asked. He was looking at the photographs from Laurie's "shoot" at the end of her modeling course that next spring. He slid the photographs away from him on the table. "What were you thinking?"

"Her girlfriends were taking the course. What did it hurt?" Lucy said. It had seemed frivolous, but they could afford it. In fact, if Laurie hadn't wanted to stay in town during spring break, they would have gone to Cabo San Lucas for the week.

"This one's not so bad." He held up a rather pretty photograph of Laurie in a tennis dress and tennis shoes, holding a racket. It was taken on a city street, fuzzy and light-washed behind her. She had turned her head just before the shot, and her long blonde hair swung over one shoulder. She had on too much makeup, true, but her smile was radiant.

"But this—" Gordon slapped down a shot of Laurie in purple sunglasses and leather pants, straddling a huge motorcycle.

"It's pretty silly, I grant you. But it's not worth getting excited about."

"She left these here—" He meant the kitchen table. "She'll expect me to say something."

"Tell her she's pretty. Ask her if she had fun. It's not like she picked the wrong college, now, is it?" Why was he pretending she knew more about their daughter than he did?

188

He drank the last of his coffee and stood up. "If she brings it up I'll think of something to say. But we're not kidding her about this, are we? She can't have some notion she could be a model."

"She wants to be everything. Look, she just went off to practice piccolo with her group at seven-thirty in the morning. Anyway, she knows she can't go to New York or Japan at her age—"

"Japan?"

"They like the farm-fed Oregon look."

"Do not encourage this."

"You've been so busy, Gordon. Maybe she won't need these pictures if she's still her daddy's girl."

"We'll play tennis this weekend. She should be working on her serve." He put on his jacket and picked up his briefcase. "I have a decent schedule today. I'll be home for dinner." At the door, he gave her a long look. "You've got a project going, don't you?"

"More than one." She carried their cups to the sink so he wouldn't say anything more.

Originally, her study had been a breakfast room. It had a whole wall of windows and now it had built-in bookshelves and a long desk. Her mother-in-law, when she saw that they had converted the room, said, "But you've lost the morning light." She meant in the kitchen. There was another window on the other kitchen wall, and they were not a family to linger over breakfast anyway. What Bell minded was that the change violated her own idea of what the house should look like, even after all these years. She had had enough say. When Gordon took the job at the college, Laurie had just been born in Santa Barbara, and Lucy was in no shape to look for a house and manage a move. Bell had flown out and helped Gordon choose a house built in the twenties, a nice house on a tree-lined street above the boulevard, with fine features and an old kitchen that would have to be redone. She stayed in a bed and breakfast and supervised the remodeling while Gordon finished up one deanship and started another. She alerted the nearest neighbors: a new baby and a weak wife on the way. They promised quiet tidiness, a ready sympathy.

Lucy and the baby lived with Bliss for four months. Once, Lucy had wanted a baby more than anything, but her passions were gutted by an early miscarriage and ten years of a hobbyist's life. There had been Gordon, ambitious and aloof, and the shadow of her sister-in-law (whom she loved), there had been too many nights of ragged dreams. She had gone from eager faculty wife to someone shaken by a slammed door or a cryptic glance. What she had in reserve she had already spent on an unsteady lover. (He had been just what she deserved.) How had it gone by so quickly? How had she become this Lucy? She couldn't shake the memories of her mother, secretive and pining, buried in her bedroom, a burden to everyone. Nearly a decade's marriage, reviewed like sin on the conscience, weighed on her mind in the last week of waiting. She pledged herself to yet another new country, motherhood. She came back from delivery and found a roommate, hearty as an Olympian, running her own household on the phone. Lucy sucked the very air the woman breathed, but in her heart, she would have gladly sent tiny Laurie home with her. The baby terrified her. She refused her mother's breast, to Lucy's secret relief. She screamed in the middle of the night; only Bliss could soothe her. Lucy begged Greta to come out to California, but Greta was old. She wanted to be alone with her anger; the blind husband had abandoned her to return to his ex-wife. Stooped and slow, rounded with belly fat, she was working in a nursing home and labeling all her possessions for inevitable dispersal.

Lucy saw a counselor. The counselor said most young mothers are scared at first. Lucy pointed out that she was thirty years old, nearly as old as her mother when she died. The counselor, who knew they didn't have much time, said maybe that was the underlying problem. Lucy didn't know how to be older than her mother. Maybe she didn't believe she would ever *be* older than Laura, and she would leave a little baby, worse than what happened to her. Could anything be worse? she asked, and Lucy wept. She had named her daughter for her mother, and now the name would kill her. She called the baby Laurie instead of Laura; she insisted everyone do the same.

The counselor was infinitely patient. Lucy could tell the littlest details. She could tell the same story twice. Suddenly time and the demands of a baby seemed to be robbing her of Laura. The photographs in her head were losing their contrast; soon her mother would fade to milky gray, then blankness. She tried to remember everything about the end: her mother outside the bathroom, leaning against the wall, her eyes rolling. "Call a priest," Laura said; later, Greta swore she said, "Call the police." Already, it was mostly gone. Lucy could remember the discomfort of the wing-backed chair where she sat to wait. She couldn't remember if Laura made a sound at the end. She couldn't remember who said, *It's over.* Or was it, *She's gone?* Everything slammed against the sounds of Greta screaming and the thick snuffling of Charlie at the edge of the family circle. Every day, more was lost in the baby's wails.

It was a shock when they left California and Lucy had to do so much alone. The counselor had told Lucy she would need some help in a new place. Gordon said she would have all the help she needed, but help wasn't that easy to find in a small town. Neither of them mentioned counseling. Neither wanted that to be the first information about the new dean's wife, that she needed a therapist. They had great faith in a change of venue. They thought a nanny would be just the thing, but all she got was someone to do the cleaning. Laurie was Lucy's full-time job. When Gordon, coming and going, saw her anguish, he said, "There is no perfect mother. Just keep her safe." He thought a child needed only the mother's cautionary attention. He forgot his mother had had help and the help had had help, too. The most help Lucy ever managed was a high school girl a few times a week while she shopped. There were no books then, except Dr. Spock for fevers and swallowed beans, commonsense things she wouldn't have hesitated to call their pediatrician to ask, anyway. She wrote her Aunt Opal: *I don't remember how you did it, only that you were so much there.* Aunt Opal sent her a photograph of the family on a picnic on the Oklahoma river near the farm, Big Red. They were all lined up, twenty of them, all ages, holding pies and pots of food. The picture triggered memory like a mist, a sense of the easiness of her childhood, when she drifted among adults, never needing much. It was a sudden, piercing, sweet revelation: she hadn't suffered until the move to Odessa, the isolation, her mother's last illness. She had been plenty loved. The children had been protected, had been precious. *Her mother hadn't had to do all that much.*

They shouldn't have left Bliss and Ted in Santa Barbara. Or they should have moved to Massachusetts. Lucy should never have had to do this alone. She had thought having a child would be the same as making a family, but now she knew family was something larger, something you constructed, and she didn't know how. Gordon, who still spoke to Bell every week—at least—had work. He thought family was the conduit to independence. He thought Lucy, product of a truncated youth, had thereby grown up early. Or had once thought it.

She did all the things she saw other mothers doing. They lived near the park. They spent part of every pleasant day there, where Laurie had the company of other toddlers, and Lucy found comfort in the familiarity of faces. Something about her forbade too close an approach; none of the mothers suggested friendship. Lucy didn't mind, didn't even notice. She talked to Laurie as a person talks to herself. She told her about her family and whatever she knew about Gordon's family. She read her books a child couldn't possibly follow. It was better than simple child chatter, and no friends. First the baby was her reason for no public life, and later, there was some unspoken understanding about her temperament. Not feeling well. That was the template that excused her; she had a reputation as a fragile woman (all the way back to Bell!), no help to Gordon, though he was never heard to utter a word of criticism. He was promoted without her help. Her health was fine, though. She had one of her mother's migraines three or four times a year, that was all. She never got colds.

Even when Laurie started school, the days were never much more than filler; Lucy divided her time between sleep and reading and long aimless walks, whatever the weather. She drank coffee at a kiosk and surveyed the street like a tourist. She drove Laurie and an allotment of her classmates wherever it was time to go: roller-skating, a hike at Table Rock, visits to tortilla factories and a model pioneer farm. Gordon took more interest, gave more weekend time, when Laurie was old enough to start learning athletics. Lucy, as spectator, was more and more content. Hadn't she learned from Bliss the true secret of parenthood—a certain distance, close enough for supervision, far enough to foster independence? The photograph of her own family at Big Red was put away, forgotten. She remembered a certain chaos, blowups with cars screeching out of driveways, phones slammed, tears, tears, none of it a model now that she was in charge. In her own clumsy way, maybe she had given Laurie a Hambleton childhood. The summers away helped. Lucy went to Texas, Laurie to the Hambletons, both of them special people to their hosts. Then one September day nearly four years earlier, Laurie, a miracle of confidence, got on a school bus and went off to middle school across town, and Lucy realized she didn't know who in the world she had become. She didn't see where the years had gone. She was middle-aged. She used a rinse to cover the shoots of gray at her part. The only work she had ever done was research assistantships on the university campus in California, a long time ago. This wasn't a university, and besides, the provost's wife couldn't go begging for dribbles of funds. She had no training for teaching or social work, and both fields were oversubscribed here anyway. She would have looked for a clerk's job—perhaps in the library, or in the medical center in the city fifteen miles away—but Gordon would have been embarrassed. So she turned the breakfast room into a study and got to work at the only thing she could think to do, which was write. The idea—what to write—came when Laurie worked on a library assignment and said, "There's nothing there!" Lucy knew there was, but the information required her mediation. Laurie's little report became Lucy's first book proposal. It was some place to begin. It was something.

Her desk was under the windows, so when she sat at it, she looked out on the garden bed that was tucked into the shade along the corner of the bedroom. It was a lovely time of year for the colors there—deep apricot, pink and white, and her favorite, the yellow-eyed black violas. She remembered the years that she and Gordon bent over gardening manuals and seed catalogs, conferred with landscapers, and set out dozens of flowering shrubs and perennials themselves, then the bulbs and the annuals. They had a big foldout blueprint of the yard, marked for sun and shade. Laurie ran around shrieking with delight in the overturned dirt. There were days of contentment then, making a new place beautiful, weren't they? Starting over. They didn't talk about it being a new beginning, they just lived it. When Laurie was born, Gordon said to her in the hospital, "We'll forget, Lucy. A child makes life new." She had humiliated him with her indiscretion—Richard was a hotshot in Gordon's own old department—but they had vows between them. Now they were a real family. It helped that the baby was so fair, with a Hambleton nose. And then Gordon took the job in southern Oregon, such a surprising shift in his career plans, but a big help to forgetting.

Now the yard was kept by a gardening service, hardy young college students supervised by the husband or wife who owned the business, all of them always in shorts and knee pads whatever the weather.

She handled index cards and bits of paper idly, as if touch, more than sight, were her day's entry to her work. She had done a series of work-for-hire books for young readers, following someone else's outline, books about the Oregon Trail and the Gold Rush and several biographies of Western women. Now she had a contract to write her own series of books for middle grade readers, about accomplished women at a significant early point in their lives. The editor who liked her ideas thought she should start with someone well known and American. Lucy thought of Georgia O'Keeffe as a young art teacher in Amarillo, Texas. Everyone connected O'Keeffe to New Mexico, but Lucy would show how she found her subject, and therefore in a sense her style, on the high plains of Texas.

She opened her file folder. Second-hand. Third-hand. All the information was someone else's work. This wasn't scholarship, she reminded herself, though it wasn't easy. She had to tell a story in scenes, so that the subject lived on the page and in the mind of the reader.

She wrote the date of O'Keeffe's journey to Amarillo on a lined blue note pad. August 1912. What a bold thing it was for Georgia to come to that brawny young town. They were the same age, the girl and the town. She had opened with that scene, of Georgia stepping down off the train into a dusty wind. She planned to tell about the exercise the young art teacher wanted to do with the students, a study of positive and negative space, with a leaf on a piece of paper. Only she could not find a leaf.

She drew posies in a line across the top of the page.

She gazed out the window. Near the garage, the plum tree was in full bloom. At the foot of that tree, their cat lay down one balmy day last winter and died of old age. There would be so many kittens at the pound now. She should take Laurie to choose one.

She picked up her notes from an interview in the *New Yorker*. O'Keeffe had said, *Oh, the sun was hot, and the wind was hard . . . I was just crazy about all of it.*

She had read somewhere that the land was so flat and the country still so wild in those days, you could see cattle drives two days away. You could see a change of weather coming toward you.

For lunch, she cut some cheese and washed a handful of strawberries. She sat at the table and looked again at Laurie's photographs. In them, Laurie looked at ease, as if the camera were an old friend. She was beautiful, and Lucy could hardly think that she knew her. The makeup, her hair pulled up, it had to be those things. She seemed to be saying to the photographer, *I'm better at this than you are. I'm doing you a favor.* Laurie wasn't old enough to think such things, yet Lucy thought: There, I've done my job. Never mind that she had never known what she was doing. Somehow, Laurie had turned out all right.

Lucy put her plate in the sink. She changed from her slacks into a navy blue knit dress, and pulled her long hair into a ponytail. She tidied Laurie's pictures into a pile and slid them into the manila envelope and went outside. From the driveway she saw Zoe next door on the deck working on her laptop. She waved, and for good measure, blew Zoe a kiss.

"Off to see Andy?" Zoe called. In the six months she had been housesitting for the Pattersons, she had become Lucy's closest friend. Her only friend, if honesty and intimacy were criteria.

She nodded.

"I can always tell," Zoe said. She pointed at her computer and made a face. "The living dead." She meant her current script.

"Call me if you need pointers," Lucy said. They both laughed.

Andy was always at the restaurant by early afternoon. She put her nose to the front window and peered in to see if he was at the bar. There he was, with papers spread along the bar in front of him, bent over so that she could see the top of his head, where he was starting to lose hair. She liked seeing him before he saw her. He wasn't handsome, exactly, but he was sexy, like the fifties singer Bobby Darin. A little taller, darker, brought up to date for the eighties in baggy olive khakis and a pale blue shirt, almost his uniform. He didn't sing. He was a chef who hardly ever cooked, an amateur photographer who had sold photos to regional magazines, a businessman with great instincts. And he had other talents.

She tapped on the window loudly. He looked up, smiled, and came to let her in. As she stepped inside, he kissed her cheek.

"I just said to myself, if Lucy came by I could take a break."

"How long have you been here?"

He smiled. "About forty-five minutes."

She walked past him to a booth and slid in. "Take five minutes. I want to show you something." He slid in beside her. She laid the photographs on the table. "This is my daughter. She took a modeling course, one of those mall ripoffs. The pictures were part of the package."

He bit his lower lip, a habit when he was musing. "Amateur photography, beautiful daughter," he said. She had never showed him a photograph of Laurie before. She thought of her affair as King's X, time out from her life.

He touched Laurie's forehead in the smiling closeup. "She has your mother's widow's peak."

"It's the only way I see she's mine," Lucy said. She pulled the photographs toward her and put them back in the envelope.

"Do you have a little time? I could get away."

"I have to go to the bank."

"There's ten minutes."

"Why don't I go to the bank, then meet you." She didn't see how they could still be a secret, but she had promised herself, if not Gordon, that she would never again be indiscreet.

"I need to pick up a lens that arrived. I'll do that, and see you there." *There,* of course, was his apartment.

He walked her to the door. She said, "You should marry, Andy. Somebody needs you." It was too late for her.

"Is that a proposal?"

"I'm too old for you. You'd be a good father."

"It hasn't happened," he said. "It hasn't even come close."

She walked toward the library, then turned to the bank. The intersection was as frantic as ever, with cars speeding, and too many entries into the street right at that corner. There was the bank, the turn from the library, the turn into another bank across the way, and the cross street. She stepped into the intersection and waited for a car to bother to stop, then carefully made her way, watching for the other lane. When would they ever get a light?

The first person she saw in the bank was Mrs. Mason from the college admissions office. Mrs. Mason was one of those officious busybody types who had managed, over twenty-five years, to bloat her clerk's job to quasi-administrative status. She was the kind of woman who felt entitled. Seeing her was a cold reminder to Lucy that she was a kind of public property. She nodded in the woman's general direction and stood at the counter, pretending she had slips to put in order before approaching a teller. All she really needed was a single withdrawal slip, but she made entries onto the calculator. She tapped in twenty-three, the number of years she had been married, and fourteen, the age of her daughter, and she wondered what the sum meant. Had she loved for thirty-seven years? Been loved that long? Had she given, or received, all she was entitled to?

Should she subtract her child from her marriage? Or add her to her life? And what should she make of a year with Andy? Or the year with Richard in California?

"Hello, Lucy," Mrs. Mason said, scooting alongside her at the counter. "We missed you at the opening."

"Mrs. Mason," Lucy said. She had to think, what opening? Ah, the art building for which Gordon had campaigned for years. There would have been no benefit to Lucy standing beside him as he cut a ribbon. She hadn't attended an official function in years. She remembered the last occasion, a keynote address by a lesbian poet, the kickoff of Women's History Month. The poet's inflammatory remarks provoked several young men to catcalls and fist-thrusts from the back of the room. Gordon himself ushered them out of the room, his arms draped over their shoulders paternally.

Mrs. Mason was holding a pink receipt in her hand, indicating that her own transaction was completed. Seeing this, Lucy instantly felt bolder. "There's bound to be another, isn't there?" she said. She smiled and moved past Mrs. Mason to stand in line. Mrs. Mason would make the most of Lucy's airy terseness back in Admissions, but Lucy had been civil, the extent of her official duties. Gordon had long ago settled for her self-sufficiency, in lieu of social partnership.

She laid her envelope down and gave the teller her withdrawal slip. She stuck her cash carelessly into her purse, tucked it over her shoulder, and picked up the envelope. It was ripping along one side.

At the door she blinked in the bright spring sunshine. If she turned right, she had three blocks to walk to Andy's, but then she would have the five blocks back to her car to walk. She decided she would retrace her steps to the restaurant, get the car, and park near the apartment. She never got away as quickly as she meant to do. She stepped into the crosswalk. A couple of cars whizzed by and then there was, amazingly, an empty street. She started across. She heard her name called—"Lucy! Over here!" and looked across to see Andy coming out of the camera shop. She heard someone call out, "Mother!" and thought it was Laurie. Pausing, she looked around just in time to see the car upon her. The driver, a young woman, was touching up her lipstick. Her neck was craned so she could look in the rearview mirror. She was driving too fast. Lucy froze, not that it mattered.

Don't! Lucy cries. She is catapulted straight up into the bright light. Her purse pops open and bills fly above her, and Laurie's photographs fly, too, first up, then down, like leaflets from the sky, falling toward her, a beautiful shower of color and dazzling smile and wheat-white hair.

Downstairs, Laurie was distraught. She didn't want Aunt Bliss to leave. "I can't do it," she cried. They were sitting at the kitchen table. Bliss cupped her hands over Laurie's. "All you have to do is take lunch up to her," she said. "Let her lean on you if she wants to go to the bathroom. Mostly she sleeps, you know. You're a big girl. Your mother needs you."

"She's ruined my summer," Laurie said.

"Shh, I know you don't mean that," Bliss said. It was true, of course. Lucy had been as helpless as a torn bag for weeks. Slowly her violent purple bruises were fading to yellow, and whole panes of scabs were shed, but she was thin, her eyes were sunken, and she barely managed to hobble from the room on her crutches. She had not been downstairs except the few times she had had to be taken to the doctor and, most recently, to the physical therapist. She was humiliated by the spectacle. Although Gordon said carrying her was nothing— she was the weight of a child—she balked. At first a hired nurse came to bathe her and check her vital signs, then she was left to her family. Bliss left Ted and Bell behind in Santa Barbara and came to help. Gordon and Laurie were thrilled. With Bliss there, everything was livelier. Downstairs, they told Lucy, was their company, but she cared nothing for it. Dutifully, she thanked Bliss for coming, then turned

200

away. She spoke not at all, except in monosyllabic responses, more like grunts of acquiescence or refusal. Bell had had delivered a television with a huge screen, but the few times someone had loaded a movie for Lucy, she had turned her head and feigned sleep. Day or night, tears trickled out of the corners of her eyes. The doctor prescribed an antidepressant, but the first pills gave her nightmares and she wouldn't take more. Even awake she relived the accident as a scene projected on her own private screen, day in, day out.

She had flown into the air all akimbo, then landed on the hood of the car. Her left foot struck the edge. At the ankle, it cracked open like an egg. She knew these things as a child knows a terrifying tale, something she has been told and cannot forget. "Thank God they had the sense to take you straight to the bigger hospital," everyone said. "Thank God they could reattach the foot," they said. "Thank God you're alive."

She hadn't thought to thank God for any of it. A stupid woman in her stupid car, hard upon her in the crosswalk. She had been maimed. She would probably never walk steadily again, she had been in great pain for weeks. Why would she be thankful? She had no gift for suffering, no stoicism. She was broken, and worst of all, the accident had severed her from her own life. No one knew her. She knew no one.

In the ambulance, she had seen Andy. His camera was swinging from his neck; she looked straight into the uncapped lens. "It's my fault," she remembered hearing him say.

The pain had not been like any pain she had ever known. It covered her like a blanket. It seared her like an iron. It ran through her with the pin-thin quickness of shock. It was not yet specific to her foot, where there was a certain busy attention. Andy had insisted they take her to the larger medical center; they had thought he was her husband. She didn't remember when he had gone, when he had metamorphosed into Gordon beside her. By then she had been to surgery. She had been cleaned up, stitched, bandaged, groomed. Gordon had never seen her as she was hot off the stretcher. He had neither seen her flying nor coming down hard.

She remembered how, at times of important change in her life, she had told herself *I have entered a new country*. Now she was exiled. She might never come home again.

She lay in bed and let memories float through her like feathers on air. The bank book Opal had found in Greta's house after the funeral, showing nine hundred dollars in a joint account with Lucy. Lucy cried desperately when she received it. Why hadn't Greta spent it? Why hadn't she stayed with Opal, instead of in her own house? Why hadn't she fled when the rains came so hard? Why had she died, when she was the only one who truly loved Lucy? Loved her best. The table-flat city of Wichita Falls had turned to a rising lake with the driving, incessant rain, and Greta, perched on a table, had yielded to her bursting heart. *I'm not ready!* Lucy thought when Opal called her. She was furious with her grandmother, who had not taken enough care. Just like Mama! Lucy thought. She did not travel to the funeral. All her images of Greta dead were dream pictures in which she floated and burst in a falling rain of Lucy's pleas. Sometimes she saw her on the table in her flooding kitchen, but she had Laura's face. Don't go! she cried, but they left her—her mother and her grandmother—again and again.

She remembered the first, lost baby. She had been at a faculty wives' luncheon, smug and happy with her secret pregnancy, still too early to be surmised. Then a terrible dread had filled her. She had thought she was like a cat, sensing an impending earthquake. She cried out and fell to the floor, crouched as in the old Russian bomb drills of her childhood. She didn't know she was clutching her belly and moaning. The women gathered around her like cooing birds. They were wonderful. But when it was over, no one spoke of it. Gordon had a special Mass said. He promised her other babies. Only her body remembered, cramped in grief. She did not conceive again for seven years, like the cycle of a drought, broken by rain.

There was no one to tell these things. She called Opal but there was too much distance between them. Opal had never been to Oregon. She listened with half-attention; in the background a baby was crying. Someone came to her door; Lucy could hear the doorbell ring from

Texas to Oregon. She hung up angry, though she thought she didn't show it. *Me! Me!* she wanted to scream, like the colicky baby. She wanted Opal to hear it, because Opal was the only one left, the last of her mothers. She never thought of Laurie as anyone but a Hambleton. She never thought of her sister at all. Her cousins didn't count. She needed her mother.

Richard came to her in dreams. She had loved him for his brashness, his selfishness, the freedom from obligations. She had thought that if he wanted her and there was no giving in it, then she must truly be the thing he coveted. Loved. His desire was as pure and undemanding as high wind. She only had to lean into it. Now, in her daydreams, he mocked her. *How like you*, he said, to stand in the way of a foolish driver. She was in line behind him, waiting for a movie. They sold him the last ticket and shut the doors. Let me in! she cried, but the doors were locked tight. Inside, a young Laura was the star, bigger than life, imagine such a notion!

Self-pity held Lucy up like those special cushions that prevent bedsores. She turned in it and felt embraced. At first everyone felt sorry for her, then they lost patience. No one would say aloud how boring she was. Instead, they praised the fine June weather, Lucy's surgeon, the promises of therapy and time. They brought visitors up to lay magazines on her bed and they all turned and tiptoed to the stairs.

Downstairs, Bliss put her bag by the front door. "We've all been so concerned about Lucy," she told Laurie. "We forget you almost lost your mother." Laurie, bored with her own whining, had turned sullen. "It's not fair," she muttered.

Gordon came home rushed. It was difficult for him to take time in the middle of the day. "This is silly, Bliss," he said. "Of course I should drive you."

Bliss, still advising, pointed skyward. "Spend the time with her," she said.

Laurie burst out crying. "I wanted to see you off."

Bliss, naturally, suggested a solution. Laurie would go with her in the cab, then come home in another. Later, Laurie would meet everyone in Santa Barbara for a week, Lynnie and her brood, too. Bell, grown frail, had moved in with Bliss. Bliss was so whole, the mother of Laurie's dreams. She had even taught Laurie to ride a horse, something Lucy had ever refused to do. Bliss, who had been a good mother to her own children, but aloof, as Bell had been, now had everything to give her niece. Bliss would never be caught in a crosswalk by an errant driver. She was too sensible, too lucky, too loving and wise.

Upstairs, Gordon settled himself in the comfortable club chair they had moved into the bedroom. "You've had your lunch?" he asked, to be polite. Bliss would never have left Lucy hungry. Lucy opened her eyes long enough to give Gordon a nod, then shut them again. Gordon, uneasy with the strain of silence and his wife's battered face, talked on. "It seems certain Svoboda will go to Higher Ed," he said. Although he had mentioned the matter to Lucy last week—the college president was in line to direct the system at the state level—Lucy gave him no clue that she remembered. He explained it all again. The good part, of course, was that as provost, he was sure to be named president in Svoboda's stead. He told her this, not with excitement, not with relief, but with some emotional tone that captured both. Once he had eyed the upper reaches of a grand university system, and his position was of course much less— this was only a college, for one thing—but goals have a way of shifting in reality, especially if you are a sensible man. "Eberhardt, at Higher Ed, has already told me he's open to some discussion about our name." He didn't say what Svoboda thought. He was ambitious, now for the college as for himself; the first assault would be toward approval of "university" in their name. A shuffling of colleges, perhaps, to fit the larger vision. Gordon had held himself back as provost, as befitted his secondary status, but also to keep his pack uncut in his pocket until the right time.

"Of course nothing formal has been said," Gordon went on, as if Lucy were alight with questions. "I expect the announcement of

Svoboda's move will come out in the next week or two. Then I'll be acting president for the while. It's just as well the official change is a way off, with you sick and needing attention—"

"Not sick—" she said weakly. "I'm not sick, I'm maimed. It's not the same."

"Injured, then," he said, his voice liquid with diplomacy.

"Nothing wrong with me except a car too fast," she added.

"Of course, Lucy," he said, unable to keep his impatience hidden. What was the point of a semantic squabble?

She closed her eyes. Who had told him he would head the college? Svoboda? And did he have the authority? Despite her lack of interest, some hazy thought worried at her rest. What if he was wrong? What if they brought in someone over him? How would he put up with that? She was in no shape to offer succor, not even the basest sort.

"It's all fate," she said. She meant all of it, his career as much as her own, but of course he thought she meant the accident. He nodded solemnly.

He went to the bed and took her hand carefully. Her fingers were long and thin and pale. The nails had grown long these weeks. She felt him stroking her palm with his cool fingers. "I almost lost you, darling Lucy," he said. "Such a wakeup call for all of us it was."

She let herself drift away from him. Who had been asleep? she might have asked. Where had his attentions gone? But she found she didn't want to ask, didn't care to know. The stroke of his fingers on her palm sedated her. Downstairs, doors closed, a car pulled away from the curb. Bliss was gone.

Zoe came by in the afternoon and made her laugh. She read to her from her new script, called only "Living Dead" now to wait for a better title at the end. Who knew what would suit, in translation? It was a script commissioned by a Japanese producer, to be shot on a lavish soundstage north of Tokyo. Zoe was going next week. There was no need for it, she said, but why not? The plane tickets were first class. The director was going, too, an old friend from film school, Billy Darmon, who had learned enough Japanese to patch together cast and crew, with some help. He seemed to be the real appeal of the paid-for trip.

What she had really come to say was that she was moving. The Pattersons were due back before Zoe's return from Japan. "Alas, *alors*," Zoe sighed, "we're to be neighbors no more."

Lucy tried to laugh. Her chest felt pinched at the news. "Where will you go?" she asked, fearing the answer was L.A. or Mexico, or someplace farther still. Zoe was, had always been, peripatetic. She could pack everything she owned in an hour. Here, she had never settled into a place of her own, moving from housesit to housesit, the darling of the L.A. emigré and college sets. In between, sometimes she lived in a motel on the boulevard where the owner, who had written many screenplays and sold none, gave her a spectacular break on rent.

"East for a few weeks," Zoe said. Her mother lived summers in Maine, and Long Beach all the rest of the year. "The Carsons—he's the photographer in Art—are going to be in China spring semester, so I'm looking for something until Christmas. Things always turn up."

"You can always stay here," Lucy said. There was the spare bed in the room next to Laurie, downstairs. She had made the offer as soon as she heard that Zoe's housesit had an end in sight.

"Me live with Gordon?" Zoe made a face. She knew how Lucy loved it. No one ever mocked Gordon. He didn't give you anything to use against him. She got up and gave Lucy a kiss on the forehead. "I saw your sister-in-law leaving. That's good, Lucy. You should let Laurie help you for a while." It wasn't like Zoe to be full of advice. "If she doesn't, she'll feel guilty, and take it out on you. And look at you, there's nothing left to beat up."

Lucy wanted to talk about Laurie, but she couldn't find anything to say. Zoe spoke first.

"So I've got to go. I'll see you tomorrow, promise. I'll bring you Charlie Chaplin videos, you could sit up for that."

"Don't go," Lucy said, but Zoe was already on the stairs. Lucy had forgotten to ask, who would translate Zoe's script? Why were there no Japanese writers? Who in Japan knew to ask her? It was a strange business. Money moved all over the place, and hardly anything ever got done. Zoe had written twenty-two scripts and never had a credit. She said it didn't matter as long as she got paid. In her heart of hearts, she was really a poet. Living dead, indeed.

She had to ask Laurie to help her get to the bathroom. Both of them hated it. Lucy didn't have the hang of her crutches yet, and the foot, swathed in bandages and encased in a canvas sling, swung clumsily and upset her balance. Laurie managed to get her to the toilet, where Lucy leaned against her while she pulled up her shift, threw her crutches forward, and sat down hard.

"Okay?" Laurie asked, unable to keep disgust from her tone.

"Two minutes," Lucy said. She cried as soon as Laurie shut the door. She was going to have to tell Gordon to get someone to come for a few hours in the middle of the day. This was too much for Laurie; it was too much for her. Her helplessness was one more failing, something she had brought on herself, and everyone else had to bear up.

She wanted to get up by herself, but one of the crutches was lying crookedly, and when she tried to lean over and scoot it toward her, she fell forward. The fall wrenched her leg and bumped her injured foot and made her cry out sharply with the pain. Laurie came in quick enough to see her sprawled on the floor. Lucy heard her breathing like someone hauling debris. Oh sigh, oh sigh, it went. They managed to get Lucy upright and onto her crutches. Humiliated and exhausted, she hobbled to the bed and flung herself on it. "Go on, I'm all right!" she said sharply, and Laurie turned on a dime and stomped away.

Lucy lay there hating the world and her daughter in it, until she dozed. In her dream her mother, wearing a gauzy white gown, was floating above a staircase, her pale feet peeking out from under the skirt. Lucy wanted to call out to her, but she couldn't make a sound. She knew her mother was out of reach, unattainable as an angel, ephemeral as love, a wraith conjured by longing.

*　　*　　*

Downstairs, Gordon had made spaghetti and Laurie made garlic bread. The garlicky smells, faint trills of laughter, the sounds of clattering cutlery on dishes went up the stairs. Lucy didn't mind. She liked the idea that life went on without her. It was only right. Life going on—that relieved her of her role in it. She could lie in bed forever. From the bed, she thought, she might move to a wheelchair, and from there to a chair in the kitchen where she would read all day. It wasn't so bad. She didn't think of herself working anymore. Someday soon she would have to call her agent and give her the news. It was a relief, actually. The sight of Georgia on the long wooden sidewalk was evaporating. The whole idea bored her.

The phone rang several times. She heard the TV switched on downstairs, and the sound of someone at the door, in and out in a short while. At some point Gordon came up and looked in on her, but she lay looking away from the door, and when he called her name softly, she held herself still as stone. Then, without willing it, she fell asleep truly.

When she woke, it was dusk. She thought, *Now I'll be awake all night*, but she had pills for that. The room was in shadows, its pieces indistinct. As she became accustomed to the dark, she saw that there was someone at the end of the bed. Laurie, her head on the foot of the bed, her pale hair spilling on the covers. She had pulled the chair close, to lay her head there. Her hair, so light, was a shock of contrast in the dark. Lucy felt her heart tugged, remembered the feel of her daughter in her arms so many years ago, the Laurie who today had moaned in disdain at the sight of, the burden of, her mother.

Laurie stirred. Slowly she pulled her head up, then sat back in the chair, in the shadows. Lucy couldn't see her face. She put her hands down beside her waist and pushed hard against the bed, to raise herself higher on the pillows. She grunted as her leg pulled up. She reached over and switched on her bedside lamp. Its soft glow spilled over the bed and the rug and the edge of the place where Laurie sat.

Lucy settled against her pillows. Higher, in a new position, she worked different muscles; her back twinged. Her shoulders ached, strained by the simple movements she had just made. She felt the throbbing of her poor patched foot. She stopped fidgeting and let her gaze go to her daughter.

Laurie, sitting forward again, was watching her with wide, sad eyes. The corners of her mouth drooped. Her hands clutched the bedcovers. Oh my darling! Lucy thought, stricken with her child's anguish, as visible as a wash of paint. She recognized Laurie's countenance as something familiar, seen before, no, something known viscerally, in the flesh of her own face. It was the look she had had sitting in the wing-backed chair at the foot of her own mother's bed, thirty years ago. It was her own waiting face, staring back at her.

"I'm not going to die, sweetheart," she whispered. Her voice, so constricted, sounded hoarse.

Laurie burst into sobs and ran from the room.

In a few moments Gordon appeared at the door. "Are you all right?" he asked urgently. "Laurie is so upset."

"Gordon, she's a child. This is too much." She spoke so gently, he looked at her in surprise. She went on. "Take her out, honey. A piece of cake, some ice cream? Really. Go out for a while."

"You're sure you'll be all right?"

She reached for the remote control on her stand and clicked on her TV. "I'm fine. I'm going to watch some news."

He looked at her with a faint disbelief, then came over to kiss her lightly. "We won't be too long."

"I'm not going to answer the phone, though," she said, and she laughed. She actually laughed, and so did Gordon, halfway down the steps.

She heard them leave. What she did then took many minutes. She had to work her way sideways on the bed, easing her foot inch by inch. She had moved it, when she had help, more easily than this, but there was the feeling of defiance, colored by trepidation, that confused her at first. In a while she was sitting on the edge of the bed. Her crutches were propped against the wall, just on the other side of the nightstand. She could reach one but not the other. After several vain and scary tries, she thought to hook the second crutch with the first and pull it to her. Then she was able to stand and hobble to the door.

She made her way into the bathroom, where she ran a brush through her hair and put on lipstick. Her hand shakily drew a crooked bottom lip, but she dabbed at it with her little finger and let it go.

At the top of the stairs, she got against the wall and, pushing her crutches in front of her on the steps, slid to a sitting position. It was a ridiculous position; she could see months and months of twisted postures, unintentional comedies, pitiful movement. Fuck! she cried, and then a long string of curse words, all she could remember and some she invented. Her chest loosened. She lifted the crutches and threw them to the bottom of the stairs. They made a terrible racket. Well, everyone would have to get used to it. She wasn't going to try to negotiate the steep stairs on crutches. Her butt would be much safer.

She made her way, step to step, by pushing off with her hands and her good leg and thumping with her bony bottom onto the middle of the stair. It was mildly painful, but there was something rousing, too, something bold and glad and crazy, that made her laugh and call out as if she were her own private rodeo.

By the time she got to the bottom, she was so exhausted, she turned and laid her head on a step and rested. After that, she set about retrieving her crutches, but she just did not have the strength to pull herself onto them, even though she scooted to the wall and tried to use it to brace herself.

When Gordon and Laurie returned, bearing a small white box, she was still sitting on the bottom step, her crutches neatly stretched out beside her.

"Lucy!" Gordon gasped.

"I was wondering if someone could help me to my feet. Foot," she said. She pointed at the box. "I hope that's for me. I've worked up a hell of an appetite."

Laurie said, "It's carrot cake. I picked it out."

"My favorite," Lucy said. Gordon helped her up. Her crutches back in place, she was able to make her way to a kitchen chair. Her foot was aching with a throb so strong, she thought it ought to be making a sound.

Laurie set the cake on the table and fetched a fork for Lucy. She pulled out a chair and sat down. Gordon sat on the other side. Lucy looked from her husband to her daughter. Laurie's eyes were brimming with tears.

"Mommy," she said. Her mouth trembled.

"Shh," Lucy said. "Let me eat my cake. I need my strength." She put her hand on Laurie's cheek. "I'm going to get well, darling. I'm still your mother, for a long long time."

She ate the first bite of cake and discovered that she was indeed hungry. She felt self-conscious, eating while they watched, but she went on anyway. She wondered how long it would take, how much it would hurt, and if she was strong enough. She wondered if she would ever tell anyone how much she had thought she would die, and how little she had minded. Already the memory of her despair frightened her. She would never give up again.

OREGON

2

It was the first of the month and a line of customers was awaiting tellers at the bank. Lucy saw Andy Lincoln ahead of her, a couple of people between them. She leaned forward to touch his arm, and he moved back beside her. They squeezed hands and chatted like old friends—weren't they so?—about the weather, which changed day to day this time of year, about the students in Beijing, how brave and hopeless their plight, about a movie neither of them had seen but thought they should have. Small talk, but they were so pleased and surprised at their encounter—imagine, at this very bank—as if it might never have happened.

"It's funny, you know," he said. "I don't have my account here, I hardly ever come in.

"You look great," he said. "I love your hair." She had cut her hair short for the first time in her life, in one of those close wedges at the neck, long in the front so that it swept her cheeks when she walked. She thought she looked like a hybrid of athlete and catalog model. He touched her hair lightly, brushing the bottom of her ear. His fin-

212

gers were hot. He stepped up to the teller. She heard him say he had a check from a debtor drawn on an account here; he didn't want to wait on his bank to clear the funds. Then a teller was free for her.

He waited for her. She stepped away and put her money and a deposit slip into her wallet. He said, "Just great. You were really lucky."

The bank was crowded. Someone behind her bent over at the counter to write, and their hips bumped. A little boy shoved past her and dived into the wooden toys in the corner of the room where there was a sign that said WE TOW UNATTENDED CHILDREN. Two pretty women nearby embraced and kissed, continental style, on their cheeks; they were both dressed in shorts and tight Lycra tank tops, and you could see right away that they had not suffered for their looks.

Lucy was rigid with sudden anger. She spoke slowly. Her jaw felt stiff. "Whatever are you thinking?" she asked, maybe too loudly. "Lucky is when you win the lottery or sell your novel or find an Old Master's drawing in a garage sale. Lucky isn't getting struck by a car driven by an idiot checking her lipstick." By the last words she was definitely shrill.

The two women in shorts looked at one another, then back at Lucy. Another woman stepped between Lucy and the boy with the toys.

"God, Lucy, all I meant—" Andy tugged her arm and urged her toward the door, but she just could not stop.

"You think I'm lucky because I'm not dead. How lucky would you feel if you had spent the last eleven months hobbling around, learning to walk on a butchered foot?" Even as she said it, she knew "butchered" was the wrong word, implying knives and malice, when in fact her foot had snapped away from her leg precisely, efficiently, as if that had been the driver's intention all along.

They were still inside the bank, at the door. Customers had turned to stare, then turned away again. Someone who had just entered asked, "What's going on?" Lucy's hands flew up to her face, and she shook her head. She was flushed, embarrassed. It was seeing Andy again, she knew. A moment out of her control. She tried to laugh. She wanted everyone who was watching to see it was a misunderstanding. She said, "You can't imagine what it's been like. The only thing going on in my life for nearly a year has been my foot." She knew she made it sound worse than it was. Her obsession should have receded as the injury healed; she had recovered amazingly well. Her doctor told her over and over again to slow down, to let time do some of the work. Only her physical therapist, Tom, had understood. He had told her in the beginning, "Not many people fully recover from an injury like this." She asked him why not, and he said, looking at her so directly, so *personally*, as if she mattered to him, "They don't work hard enough." She decided right then that she would be one of the workers, one of the healed. Day after day, it took all her attention, but what mattered more? She worked with weights. She walked on the treadmill, and rode a stationary bike. She swam. She went for massage, for acupuncture. When she stopped, she fell asleep, too tired to talk or cook or care about anything. But she walked with only the slightest limp. There were things she couldn't do, but she wasn't a sore sight on the street. She deserved some respect. Some time ago Laurie said, "You know, Mother, you ought to stop exercising and eat something. You look like a stick." But she had surprised everybody. Luck had nothing to do with it. "It's not about luck!" she said now, in a last spurt of protest.

Andy put his arm over her shoulders and nudged her out the door. In the parking lot, he still had the one arm around her, and then he put the other. He stood in front of her and leaned his forehead against hers, as if the whole world wasn't driving by on the main street, yards away. "I've missed you like crazy," he said. "I didn't know how much until I saw you in there. I didn't let myself think about it. I thought, after something like that, they'll be like all new people in her house. So grateful. I thought, this will have changed all the equations." He pulled back and grinned. "They'll feel so lucky."

She said nothing, but the tension had drained away at his touch. She felt the warmth of his arms over her, the hardness of his bone on her bone where their heads touched. He had hardly crossed her mind. She hadn't thought of anyone but herself, and had had good reason, for once.

"I'm sure you've kept yourself busy," she said. She had extricated herself from his embrace by then. They were standing on the curb of the flower garden at the edge of the parking lot. Dozens of tulips and daffodils were in bloom, postcard bright.

The boy and his mother came out of the bank and walked past them. The mother pushed her son to the other side of her, away from Lucy. Anger flushed up into the roots of Lucy's hair. To have called attention to herself—it was the worst sort of indiscretion. It was Andy's fault, and she meant to leave him in that instant, but the warmth of his gaze, and his tiny gold crucifix dangling on a chain at his neck, and the crisp crease of his ironed shirt—these things made him irresistible. She touched his sleeve, then drew her hand away. "Hasn't there been anyone?" she asked quietly.

"I tried being serious about someone, actually," he said. "A real estate agent with a seven-year-old son." He sighed. "The kid did us in. I gave him a big bag of candy right before Halloween. For his class, I said. He said, 'We aren't allowed to bring refined sugars to school,' prim as some old maid. His mother thought it was darling. She drives him out of their neighborhood to go to that school because it's so—so unrefined."

She laughed lightly. "I've got to go."

"Can I see you? Can you make it up my stairs? You can't just walk off from me now, Lucy." His gaiety changed to urgency. "Please, Lucy. Tell me I'll see you."

She thought of his keys. They were in her sock drawer, under the pale-colored nylons she would probably never wear again. "You haven't changed the lock?"

"Nope."

"You're on the same schedule?"

"More or less. I don't get up any earlier, that's for sure."

"We'll see."

He walked her to the car. He opened the door for her and she sat down clumsily, careful of the way she put weight on her foot. Before she had pulled her left leg in, he dropped to his knees and touched her shoe where it came up around her ankle. "Does it hurt?" he asked.

"It hurts." She settled on the seat and shut the door. The window was down. She put her hand on the edge of it. "I heard you were going to open a Texas grill. What happened?" Zoe told her all the town gossip, convinced she cared, deep down. She never required any response, though. She required nothing, really. Like Lucy, she was a person with few expectations.

"It's back in the works, but with a Miami theme. I've hired a Cubano chef. What do you think?"

"I think the tourists will love it," she said.

Her hand lay on the edge of the window. He tapped her knuckles with his fingertips lightly. "I'd like it just the way it was."

She started the car and put it in reverse. She would never admit out loud how many times she had told herself how lucky she was that it was her left foot that was injured; she was able to drive six weeks after the accident.

He was still standing there. "Don't worry, Andy," she said. "Even a near-death experience doesn't alter my character." She hadn't known that until just then. "It'll be like no time has passed. Like the wink of an eye." She wondered if he ever really thought it was up to him.

She drove over to see Zoe. She thought she wanted to talk about Andy, but by the time she pulled in the driveway, she knew she wouldn't so much as mention his name. There wasn't anything to tell. Nothing had happened.

She let herself in the kitchen door. Zoe was bound religiously to her work schedule, eleven to four, but it was almost four. Lucy made herself a cup of strong black tea and stirred in honey from the crock on the counter. She sat down by the window. The sun fell across her hands and the cup and was reflected in the polished oak of the table. She sipped her tea and tried, for a few moments, to think of nothing at all.

She was startled from her reverie by the sound of the doorbell. She went to answer it, and met Zoe, who had emerged from her cubby to do the same. It was a UPS delivery, two large boxes marked FRAGILE and written on in Chinese characters as well. Zoe asked the delivery man to set them in the living room under the front windows.

"They're acquiring, you see," she said of her hosts, the art professor and his wife. There were numerous boxes stacked against the wall. "You couldn't go to China and not bring back things, could you?" Lucy heard both wonder and disapproval in Zoe's voice, at the character of people who own so many things. Zoe still thought of herself as a stripped-down woman. She didn't count her collection of poetry books, forty-odd.

Back in the kitchen, she made herself her special, wickedly dark coffee, then lightened it with milk. She warmed Lucy's tea in the microwave, and they settled down to talk.

"The Germans came through with full payment," Zoe said, "and I've got another all-American rewrite." She had lately negotiated credit for the rewrite of a *film noir* being produced by a second-string star, but a household name, nonetheless. It would mean more work, more money. "I'm looking for a house."

"I admit I'm amazed," Lucy said. "And pleased, of course."

"Country, I told the agent. Maybe on the other side of the mountain."

"You'll have to have four-wheel drive."

"When the snow covers the windows, I'm bound to write more poems." Zoe readily laughed at herself, but she wasn't kidding. "How are things at your house?"

Lucy shrugged. "On and on we go. I don't think Gordon's ever going to get over Jim Comer's appointment as president. He's totally stalled, and he can't swallow it."

"He always looks so perfectly poised. And I know he's respected."

"He's respected, but he isn't president. It was a bad blow."

"For you, too?"

"Me?" Lucy was surprised Zoe would ask. "Why would I care—

except for him, of course. I suggested he look at nonprofits, something out of education, and he looked at me as if I'd gone mad. He's furious."

"You mean he raves? He blows steam?"

"Never. Not Gordon. Anger makes him stiff. Even when Laurie came home with a card full of C's, he was calm. I could see her looking at him, daring him to yell at her, but he just asked if she needed a tutor, if she needed to cut back on other activities. She said she didn't know, all sullen and adolescent and brimming with defiance. He didn't push her at all. Later he said to me she isn't going to be able to bring her grades up the last quarter of the year, so he'll make some arrangements for the summer. It's only her sophomore year, there's still time to make a showing before college applications. I could see his mind working. Knock them dead in trig next year, chemistry, third-year French. I don't think she gives a damn."

"What did you say?"

"I told him she needs her summer. We all need summer. She goes off to the aunts."

"You, too, off to the aunt?"

"Not this year. I'm trying to get her to come up for a week. She says she's afraid of flying, something about her heart. But I don't think I'll go anywhere. I have this idea I better stay around Gordon. What if he does blow? What if he has his limit?"

"What if he does, Lucy? What will you do?"

"I'll get him to go to the gym with me," Lucy said. She put her cup in the dishwasher. "This has been a wonderful year. I've learned you can work everything out on a treadmill. It's better than the painkillers ever were."

She started for the grocery store, then changed her mind and drove all the way out to the farmer's market. She was standing by a pyramid of baby crooknecks when she heard her name. She turned to see Mary Chapman, her doctor's wife.

"You're simply stunning, Lucy," Mary said. "You look like Mary Decker before she fell."

"How apt," Lucy said. She didn't mean to be rude, though, and she quickly added, "I'd have to say you look just the same, which is to say, wonderful."

"I asked Bill about you. He said your recovery was amazing. He gave you all the credit."

"I've worked at it."

"Well." Mary picked up an avocado. "I love this time of year. One wonderful crop after another, for the next three months."

"Me too." Lucy shifted more of her weight onto her good foot. (She was going to start thinking of it as her "perfect foot." The other one was pretty good, too.) "Nice to see you, Mary." She put squash in her basket.

"Let me ask you something, Lucy. I wonder—would you ever be interested in tutoring?" Mary ran the language center, for migrant workers and their wives, mostly.

Lucy was surprised. "I don't speak any Spanish," she said.

"All the better. You'd be teaching English."

"I don't know. I don't think so. Sorry."

"Well, I just thought I'd ask. I thought—it would be nice to see you sometime, Lucy. You could call me. Maybe lunch?"

"Sure," Lucy said, now anxious to get away. What did Mary Chapman think they would talk about?

"We think it's terrible that Gordon was passed over," Mary said. "And for someone from Oklahoma!"

"My family came from Oklahoma," Lucy said. She could see she had embarrassed Mary, who murmured goodbye and walked away. Too bad, Lucy thought. Mary should have known better, in Spanish or English either one.

The house was quiet. She emptied the bag of vegetables in the sink. She had shopped for color: the yellow of the squash, the red of tomatoes, an expensive purple hothouse pepper, a peeled white onion, pale green celery. She hadn't stopped to consider what she would cook with the vegetables. Gordon would eat anything. Laurie was in a vegetarian phase. They could have rice, but how would she make a protein? She couldn't remember the rules Laurie had spouted at her.

Laurie's books were stacked neatly on the end of the kitchen table. Beside them was a book bag. Lucy looked at the monogram: TH. Tim Heidegger. She wished he weren't around so much. She was afraid he was depressing Laurie. His mother had died of breast cancer last year, between Thanksgiving and Christmas. The poor kid. He was Laurie's pet project, and what could Lucy possibly say?

Maybe he would stay for supper.

In the hall she could hear music from Laurie's room. Gordon had told her he didn't approve of her being in her room with a boy with the door closed, but she had rolled her eyes and said, "He's not a boy, Dad, he's Tim." It was true they had been friends almost their whole lives. It was true his mother was dead.

Lucy tapped on Laurie's door. Laurie opened it a crack. "What?" she said rudely.

"I'm home."

"Okay."

"Laurie—"

"We're studying."

"I saw your books on the table."

"He's explaining something. Mom."

"Okay. I wondered if he'd like to stay for supper."

"Wait." Laurie shut the door, then opened it again. "We're not hungry." She shut the door again.

Lucy sighed, then went back to the kitchen to clean vegetables. She cut them up, ready to stir-fry or steam. The phone rang. She stood there and let it. After three rings, Laurie opened her door and screamed, "Mother!" After the fourth, the machine picked up. Laurie's voice said, *You have reached the Hambletons. We can't take your call just now. Please leave us a message after the tone.*

It was Gordon. "I've got a meeting that will run late. I'll grab a sandwich, don't hold supper."

She put plastic wrap over the vegetables and set them in the refrigerator. They could eat pizza later. In or out, Laurie's choice, and Tim was still invited.

She went down the hall, and outside Laurie's door, she yelled out that information. She felt idiotic. Laurie didn't answer.

She lay down on the couch, pulled the throw over her aching legs, and fell almost instantly asleep.

When she woke, it was nearly seven. The house was quiet. She went down to Laurie's room and tapped on the door. There was no answer, so she opened the door gently and leaned in, careful not to step inside uninvited.

"Laurie, are you hungry yet?"

Laurie was propped up on her bed. She was wearing a huge T-shirt from Maui, dating back to Christmas of her eighth-grade year. She had covered her legs with a blue cashmere scarf, last year's Christmas gift from Grandmother Bell. She was leaning against half a dozen pillows, wearing earphones, and turning the page of a fashion magazine. Her face was drawn and tear-streaked, but when she looked up and saw Lucy, she tried out a wan smile. "Hi," she said, shifting the earphones to one ear. "I had a nap."

"Dad's hung up on campus. I thought we could go for pizza."

Laurie plucked at her baggy shirt. "I don't want to get dressed."

"I could pick it up."

"I'm not hungry. I don't want anything. I'll eat an apple later or some cereal or something."

Lucy shrugged. "Say when, and I'll heat up some soup."

"Such a mom," Laurie said, with an edge of sarcasm. She replaced the earphones and looked back to her magazine.

"How's Tim doing?" Lucy asked, but Laurie didn't hear, or pretended not to. The conversation, if you could call it that, was over. It seemed to Lucy that there had been at least two climate zones in those few minutes.

She arranged herself a plate of pickles, olives, and feta cheese, and went to look for a tape from her collection of old movies. She chose *Mogambo*, with Clark Gable, Ava Gardner, and Grace Kelly. She had watched it so many times she could recite the dialogue along with the actors. That was one of the reasons she liked it. There was no suspense.

* * *

Grace Kelly had decided she was a lot better class of woman than Ava, who minded but acted as if she didn't. Clark, the dashing safari leader, had decided he wanted Grace. She was the blonde. That was when Laurie wandered down from her room. She was now wearing her fleece robe with the black and white kitties on it. She curled up on the couch and leaned against Lucy. She, too, knew the movie. Everyone was loaded into boats to go upriver, where they could climb a mountain and find gorillas.

"I don't like it when they throw spears at Clark Gable," Laurie said. It was a test of his courage, to bring good luck to the bearers.

Lucy reached for the remote control. "I can turn it off. It doesn't matter."

"Fast-forward," Laurie said. "There." The plot thickened at the gorilla camp. Laurie, uncharacteristically, snuggled against Lucy, who scooted about slightly to accommodate her, to let her know she was making room for her.

Grace had shot Clark in the arm, which meant the movie was almost over, when Gordon came in the back door. He leaned over the couch to give Lucy and Laurie each a kiss, then poured himself a little Scotch and settled down on the other side of Laurie. He looked especially tired. Lucy turned off the TV.

Laurie had shifted her weight toward her father. She was leaning against him, tucked under his arm. He felt her forehead. "Are you sick?"

"I don't think so." In her most pitiful voice, she added, "I'm hungry, though. We never had supper."

Gordon glanced at Lucy, who was instantly furious.

"I tried," she said, and got up to put away the video.

After a few moments of consultation, Laurie agreed that Gordon could make milk toast for her. Milk toast was a soothing, sweet, mushy dish both Lucy and Gordon remembered from childhood, almost the only thing, Lucy had often reflected, that was common to their upbringing. Of course Gordon always cut off the crusts.

"I hope you're not coming down with a flu," Lucy said. She was standing around while Gordon fussed with the toast and warmed the milk. Moments like these were awkward. She felt she should offer comfort. Laurie didn't bother to answer. Gordon set her dish on the table. He sat down and skimmed the newspaper. Lucy felt like someone skulking in the background. Where is the mother in this picture? she would write under the frame. She could think of nothing to say or do. Laurie ate a few bites and moved the rest of her soggy toast around in the bowl. Lucy offered to run a bath for her. Laurie sighed and agreed she ought to do so.

In the bathroom, Lucy ran the water very hot, leaning over the flow to feel the steam on her face.

"She doesn't look good," Gordon said to Lucy when Laurie was in the tub and they were back in the kitchen out of her hearing. He had poured himself another, larger drink.

"I don't think she's sick," Lucy said. "Probably it's something at school. Some friend who looked at her the wrong way."

"That doesn't sound like her," he said. He looked at her, his eyebrows knitted, and asked, in that maddeningly neutral tone of his, "You didn't ask?"

"I did not. If she wanted to confide in me, she would. When does she ever?" Which, Lucy did not add, she didn't mind not hearing. Her daughter's confidences had always been pleas for advice that she was likely as not to resent, so Lucy never had much in mind.

"She doesn't want to, does she?" Gordon said. Exactly. "I'm not criticizing you," he said. "I'm talking about her. She's been so remote lately, don't you think?" He was used to an easy confidence with Laurie. He took pride in that. Maybe, Lucy thought, there were surprises in store for him. Maybe he should read a book on adolescent psychology. He probably didn't learn much of that, studying the Civil War. Not that she knew much, either. She had not had the luxury of adolescent angst.

She shrugged. "She's fifteen. It's not so bad." Laurie, she thought but did not say, had everything, including considerable poise and beauty. One day soon she would undoubtedly feel utterly superior to her mother, and in some way, she was bound to be right.

"I said—" Gordon said, a little loudly. He had lost her attention. "It's a difficult age."

"Every age has its difficulty. Laurie has plenty of support. She has both her parents."

"And you, of course, did not," Gordon said.

"I was thinking of Tim Heidegger."

Gordon, caught in his small *faux pas*, blushed. "Sorry, Lucy. That was uncalled for."

"It's not something I recall mentioning in a very long time," she said stiffly.

"'You're forgiven' would be a welcome phrase," he said.

Lucy jumped up, but where was she to go? She poured herself a glass of grape juice and sat back down. "Is this about Laurie? Or is there something else?"

Gordon touched her hand, then drew back again. "If you wanted to confide in me, you know you could, don't you?"

"But you already know everything about me, Gordon."

"I don't believe that. I don't think even you know everything about you."

She got up. "This is turning into a strange conversation."

"At least it's a conversation." He yawned. "We need to talk."

"There's all the time in the world. For heaven's sake, go to bed. You look exhausted."

She chose *Rear Window* from her tapes. She heard Laurie go into her bedroom and shut the door. She heard Gordon moving around upstairs, and the sound of the shower. She turned on the movie. She liked the pace of it, the time Hitchcock took to build the story. Jimmy Stewart's slow turn in his wheelchair as he heard footsteps on the stairs.

Later she went to bed in her room. She didn't look in to see if Gordon was awake. They could talk some other time. Later would be soon enough.

There had been a time when they should have talked. There had been a time when she could have loved him again as she had loved him in the beginning. A time when they could have started over. Not when Gordon thought. Not when the baby was born, and he said, *We'll forget.* Before that. When the baby came, it was already too late. Too many things had to happen. There was never a time again.

Richard had been beautiful and vain and careless, but he had loved old movies. That was where they had begun, with Gene Tierney and Margaret Sullavan and Rita Hayworth and Susan Hayward. Both of them haunted the revival houses. They saw one another around Santa Barbara whenever an old film was shown. They talked about them at faculty parties. Then one weekend she drove to Santa Monica, to walk on the beach and go to a Bette Davis festival on Second Avenue. Richard was in line for the first show. She already had a motel room; he had been planning to drive back. "Mizzus Doctor Hambleton," he called her when she said hello in the line. "Lucia Lucia," he called her in the motel room.

Sometimes they made plans and he did not appear. Sometimes he called her at home. She accused him of being cruel and thoughtless. He said their lives were separate, how could they keep from errors now and then? He didn't care who knew he was sleeping with the wife of Gordon Hambleton, once his chairman, now his dean. Everyone knew.

Gordon spoke to her with steely control. "You have to stop seeing him," he said. "Him?" she said. "Him?" She wanted him to name Richard. She wanted him to yell at her. She wanted him to want her more than Richard did, more than she wanted Richard, but Gordon was Gordon. He was polite, firm, diplomatic. "He's eligible for a sabbatical," he said. "His chairman is going to suggest next semester would be a very good time for it."

"And what about me?" she demanded. "Where are you going to send me?" They were in their bedroom—they had one bedroom then, with a king-sized bed—and if he had thrown her on the bed, she would have resisted for the briefest time. They were in the middle of the obligatory scene; here the music would come up. But this was Gordon and there was no scene. "You'll be my wife again." They slept with a desert between them.

The next day she moved to Richard's apartment. It was in a pleasant building with a small private courtyard and a sunny kitchen. She had a job on a soft-money research project in psychology. It was all paperwork by the time it got to her. When she came home in the afternoon she walked around Richard's apartment naked, the shades drawn. He laughed when he came in and found her, but the first thing they did, every afternoon, was make love.

She had been there six weeks when she discovered she was pregnant, the end of the first trimester. They talked about it for maybe ten minutes. She didn't know whose baby it was. He said it didn't matter, one way or the other, it couldn't be his. She thought he meant he didn't want it. Days later she thought maybe he meant he was sterile, but she never asked. She preferred the suspense, like a crazed Frenchman in an old black-and-white movie, driving without brakes. Richard packed his things and moved in with his ex-wife across town. He took his sabbatical and went to Italy.

She stayed in his apartment. He had left his parakeet and all sorts of good books. Here and there were snapshots of Lucy, stuck up on handy surfaces. She always looked breathless and self-conscious. Silly. He set her up for foolishness, with his remarks before the shots, like: *Give me a jiggle, Marilyn. Don't lie to me, Marlene.* Or once, *Portrait of a Woman as Mistress.* He liked to say, as the shutter clicked, "Hah." She liked the photographs, though, because she knew Gordon had never seen those Lucys, and Richard had already forgotten. They were as secret as a diary. She took them all down and hid them in her clothes.

She quit the job in psychology. She walked, and read, and talked to the parakeet. She slept a lot. She was waiting for Gordon. At first, when he called, she was polite, but she said she didn't want to see him. There was something slightly thrilling about the undertone of pained bafflement in his voice. She had begun to show.

Gordon wrote to her and assured her she could come home. She wrote checks on their account. Bliss called and spoke with her cheerily, as if they were all characters in a sprightly New York play. Everyone was winding down very tight. Things could not go on forever.

She was six months pregnant when she woke up in the night and found blood in her bed. Not again! she screamed. Dear God, not again. She called Bliss, and in no time an ambulance was there. She hadn't lost the baby. She had to stay in bed, the doctor said. Someone had to care for her.

Gordon came to the emergency room and then back again two days later to pick her up. He took her to Bliss's house. She was furious with him for his calm. She was living in another man's house (never mind that the man was gone), she was in danger of losing another child, *she didn't even know whose child it was!* and he was as calm as a man at a board meeting.

Like his mother said, Sometimes good manners are all you've got.

She thought she would live alone when she had the baby. She knew Bliss would know what to do when the time came. She tried to think of herself as someone in a movie; she couldn't think who would play her role.

She was mad, in her quietly desperate way.

Then Gordon began to woo her. He came as she lay in bed in his sister's guest room. Her belly was a mound between them. He brought her flowers and a book of photographs of stars from the forties movies. She was quite touched. He spoke to her of inconsequential things. He spoke kindly. "We'll have to talk soon," he said. She pulled herself up against her pillows, all ready. "Later," he said. "When you're better." As if she were an invalid like her mother.

She realized that she wanted to talk. She wanted to tell him about the dreams that came to her every night, dreams of Laura, in which she floated down a staircase in a white gown, her skin as pale as the gauzy fabric of the gown, her hair around her head, lifted by the air. She thought her mother came to comfort her. Her mother knew what lay ahead. Her mother had been there.

She wanted to talk about the baby. She had been in Bliss's house when Bliss's children were young, but those terrible days of infant dependency had already been over. What did she know about having a baby? What would she become? What would she have to become?

She wanted to talk to Gordon. About her awe of him. Her regret and shame at what she had done, and her pride and amazement that that old Lucy, the Lucy he had first known, was still inside her, passionate and reckless and desirable. *Alive.*

She wanted to fall in love with him again.

She wanted to tell him about her exiled daddy's rented room, two blocks away from the house where her mother lay dying. It was a neat, crowded bedroom in the home of a woman whose husband had been killed in an oil field fire a long time ago. On the afternoon of the day her mother died, she had gone to that room to escape the weeping of her grandmother and the emptiness of her mother's bed. She had crawled under the covers of her daddy's bed and slept deeply, freed of waiting for it to end. She hadn't dreamed she would lose him, too. She hadn't known it would get worse.

Those thoughts crowded her head the way the baby pushed against her bladder. She was too full. She was sick with things to say. That was when she called her grandmother and begged her to come, but her grandmother said she was old. Lucy had another family now. Let them come.

Gordon came with a new look on his face. He, too, was full of things to say. He sat on the bed and took her hand. "Yes?" she said. He would speak first, and then she would open her heart to him. Something in her lightened.

"I'm selling the house," he said. "There's to be no career climb in California." He spoke quietly, kindly, as if it were all a minor matter. "I've taken a position for the new year, at a state college in southern Oregon. We'll make a fresh start, you and I and the child." He hardly paused for breath. "Mother will come out and help me find a house. Bliss will take care of you and the baby. It's all arranged, Lucy. We'll be a family, in a new place."

They didn't know whose baby it was, or whether it was a boy or a girl. That was the kind of man Gordon was, the kind of responsibility he was willing to shoulder. How could she not be grateful? How could she not be full of fresh resolve? He was her governor, with a pardon.

"I've made an appointment for you to see someone," he said. "Someone Bliss knows. She's highly recommended. Someone for you to talk to." At last, he took a long deep breath. It was her turn, only what was left for her to say?

She remembered how she had wept beneath him, the first time he made love to her, and she cried again, but it was a still and silent crying, and he did not touch her.

He did say, *We need never mention any of this again.*

In the morning, she heard her daughter in the bathroom, retching. Gordon was already up. The smell of coffee wafted down the hallway. Reluctantly, leadenly, she pulled on her robe. Her foot always ached first thing, then lessened as she got going, then hurt worst at the end of the day. Carefully, she maneuvered the steps to the first floor.

She made her way to the bathroom door and tapped on it lightly. Laurie hadn't pulled it all the way shut. "Laurie, honey, can I help?"

There was only the sound of her daughter's dry gags.

Lucy pushed the door open.

"Sweetheart—" she began, but Laurie turned, ugly with fury.

"Go away," she said. She was sitting on the floor by the toilet. She leaned against the tub. "Just please leave me alone." Her hair was damp and matted against her skull. She looked like one of those punk singers who scream and wear black crucifix earrings. Like she was waiting for her costume.

"Should I call a doctor?"

"*Go away!*"

Lucy wanted to go back to bed, but not at the price of climbing the stairs again. Gordon called to her from the kitchen. "Do you want coffee?" She answered no, and lay down on the couch. In a while she heard Laurie go to her own bedroom, and a few minutes after that,

Gordon quietly enter her room. She heard their voices, low, muffled, and calm. No screams to go away.

She put her face straight down in a pillow and went back to sleep.

When she woke, Gordon, of course, was gone, and Laurie, too, was gone, her books off the table. She ate a bowl of cold cereal and dressed for the gym in well-washed black leggings, a black cotton polo shirt, and for the hell of it, a pair of red socks Laurie had given her last fall to celebrate the day she started walking without crutches.

She drove down the boulevard, all the way past Safeway on her way to the gym, before she turned around and drove back to Andy's. He lived in a roomy apartment over the first floor, which he rented to a naturopath and a spiritual counselor. She parked a block away, by the bakery, and walked back to the building, swinging her keys with her thumb.

She took plenty of time to climb his stairs up the back. At the top, out of breath, she sat for a few moments and surveyed the yards of the neighbors and what she could see of the street. No one was likely to notice her, one more middle-aged woman in gym clothes, probably waiting to counsel her spirit. It was a quiet neighborhood. Kids were in school. As if to defy her observation, a large black bird in a tree hardly more than an arm's reach away squawked. She laughed, rose, and went inside.

She loved turning the key. Entering his apartment because she wanted to. Once, some months after she began seeing him, they sat out on the little porch at the top of the steps, and she showed him the nude photographs of Laura. She told him about Laura, near the end of her life, in love with her doctor. How she waited in her bedroom for the end of the day, for the doctor to come, and how when he was late she would take out a double-edged razor blade to snip at her cuticles. Once, he missed two nights in a row entirely (he did call), and she cut so deeply, her fingernails were rimmed with blood, then scabs, and on several fingers a smear of infection rose. The doctor, when he came, held her fingers and dabbed them with disinfectant, then an antibiotic ointment. He called to Lucy for a glass of water, then shut the door. After he left, Lucy checked on her mother. Laura was limp and dreamy-eyed. "His wife has gone to Pecos," she said, before falling into her sedated sleep.

Lucy told these things to Andy while he held the photographs on his knees. He picked them up carefully, by the edges, and helped her slide them back in the envelope. "There was that much life left," he said. "And she wasn't going to let it go." Later, before Lucy went home, he gave her his key on a sterling silver chain with a tiny horse attached to it. He kissed her fingers, every single one.

Andy was still in bed.

He had decorated his apartment as if it were a city loft, with most of the walls down, replaced by screens and half-walls. To Lucy, after nearly a year away, it was a sight of deeply pleasurable familiarity. Its whiteness, sparseness, the sense of modest artistry seemed impossibly cosmopolitan. One wall was hung with small handsome metal ladders and on them Andy had attached photographs. Lucy remembered that he changed them often. One corner of the apartment was closed in like a closet, with a red light above the door—his darkroom.

She laid her keys and her small purse on a table near the door, and went to examine the pictures. She recognized one as her own naked back; she didn't think anyone else would know. The picture was a study of light and shadow, more a technical exercise than a portrait. Seeing it, though, Lucy anticipated Andy's fingers down the ridge of her spine. His breath on her collarbone. His mouth on her breast.

There were photos of rocks up close, and of the back of someone's house where a clothesline was strung. There were several photos of a pretty young woman in a white sundress. In one she was posing exaggeratedly, her mouth pouty, her eyes half-closed.

Andy's bed was on the other side of a rice-paper screen. Before she went to him she stripped, except for her red socks, and dropped her clothes on the floor. He was lying with his face toward the wall. She didn't think he was asleep, but she didn't speak. She crawled in beside him. The crisp white sheets were freshly laundered, or perhaps even new. She moved close to him. Still he didn't speak. She pressed herself against the back of his body. She buried her face in his shoulder and pushed her groin against his buttocks. She slipped one arm beneath him and wrapped herself around him.

He turned around and wrapped his arms around her. "Welcome back," he said.

He had taken photographs of her often. Somewhere there was a drawer of negatives: Lucy on his steps, on his bed. Lucy standing at his window. Lucy in jeans, in a long batik skirt. But mostly, Lucy naked. She remembered thinking, before the accident, that he was documenting the almost imperceptible disintegration of her youth. Her beauty, whatever it was. She remembered thinking: *There will be a "before" and an "after," and you will see me change in those pictures, if we are lovers long enough.*

Now he changed the lens on his camera and adjusted the shutters on the window to let in more light.

She protested. "I really am getting too old for this."

"You look incredible," he said. "Your body has changed so much since the accident. You look like a long-distance runner." He looked at her over the camera, then through its eye. "I see you a different way through the lens." They had talked about that, back when she had second thoughts. A provost's wife, naked in Andy Lincoln's apartment. She had always been a fool for a man with a camera in his hand.

"I want one of the old photos, from the first year," she said.

"I'll print one for you."

"And one of these."

"They're for you?"

"Of course. For the bottom of my desk drawer. For when I am old and fallen and shrunken."

"My my, are we practicing our melancholy today?"

"Every day, Andy, or have you forgotten?"

"I remember everything," he said. "Sit there." He pointed to a pile of folded rugs in the corner.

Bathed in his attention, she relaxed. She trusted him.

He handed her a silk kimono. It had always been here; she thought of it as hers.

He warmed up a dish of polenta with a sauce of chanterelle mushrooms. With it they drank a rosé wine.

He wanted to talk about her foot. The red socks were lying in a mound at the foot of the bed. He told her about the day of the accident, how she was launched into the air and he thought he would never take another breath. In the ambulance, he blacked out; they had to remind him to breathe. He couldn't believe she hadn't been killed.

"I had my camera with me," he said. "In the emergency room, I took a shot of your foot."

"A photograph of my foot?"

"I wanted to give it to you, but I didn't know how to manage. Come up to your door and hand you an envelope? Hi, Lucy, remember me? I was there?"

"You should have come to see me in the hospital."

"It wouldn't have been right. I asked Zoe so often about you, she said I was driving her crazy."

"Where is it? I want to see it."

He pulled a picture out of a long shallow drawer. When he turned, he grinned and patted the drawer behind him. "My Lucy bin," he said.

He handed her an eight-by-ten photo of her foot, exposed in a stainless steel trough on a table at the end of the gurney where she was lying. Between the foot and her ankle the broken ganglia were white, like worms.

She turned it over. "I guess it's silly, but I can't look." When he reached for the picture, though, she asked him to put it in an envelope for her.

He sat on the end of the bed and lifted her foot into his lap. He ran his finger over the dark scar.

"I can't run," she said.

He kissed the tops of her toes. She didn't have the heart to tell him he had chosen the very place where she had no feeling at all.

"They tell me I never will."

He scattered his kisses up her leg.

She parked at the top of their long sloping driveway, in front of the garage. There were three stone steps up to the back yard walk, leading to the deck off her studio. Gordon had installed an iron railing for her. Climbing the steps wasn't really difficult, but it was slow. She put her good right foot down, then followed with her injured foot beside it, then on to the second step. In physical therapy, she was working on the flexibility in her ankle. At the gym, she was spiking her treadmill workout with five-minute segments at five percent slope. She could go up a set of stairs in a normal way, with care—Andy's steps, though steep, weren't as difficult as these. The stone steps were uneven, and especially high and deep. And coming down them was something else entirely. If she stood sideways on her injured foot, and put the good foot down, with a long reach of the leg she could almost—almost—make it. She could do it if the therapist was standing below her. But if she stood facing forward, and put her good foot out into space over the lower step, nothing happened with the other foot. It simply would not bend at the ankle. The knee started to go out, pulled at the lower leg, and—nothing. Nothing except frustration, pain, her tears. A fall or two when she pushed her body weight forward over the lower foot and lost balance. Tom said he didn't know if she would ever be able to step normally. "It's not so bad," he told her. "You can compensate." She could lead, on each step, with her injured foot, gingerly placing all her weight on it and following with the foot that bent. It did the job. It only slowed her down.

She spent ten minutes exercising on the steps before she went in. By then her ankle hurt like hell, and her eyes were full of tears. Still, she felt happy.

She put her photograph in her desk drawer and went into the kitchen, where the answering machine light was blinking. She sat down at the table and pulled off her shoe and sock. The release of her foot from the snug fit was both painful and relieving. Cautiously, she twisted her foot back and forth in a small arc, then she bent to massage her toes, the ball of her foot, and her calf. She stood on the other foot and shook her leg. Then she touched the answering machine for the message.

"Where the hell are you!" Gordon barked. She was so shocked, she called him immediately.

"What's going on?"

"Stay right there," he said. "I'm coming home."

"Wait. You have to tell me what this is about. Is it Laurie?"

"She's all right. I'll be there in a few minutes."

"Where is she, Gordon?"

"She's at school. Just wait for me."

She limped hurriedly to the shower, pulled on a loose cotton dress, and was brushing her hair as Gordon came up the driveway.

She met him at the bottom of the stairs. On the step above him, she said, "Just tell me what's going on, and tell me now."

"She's pregnant."

She sat down on the stair step. "Oh shit," she said.

"She came to my office this morning. I tried to get you at the gym, but they said I'd missed you."

"She's sure?"

"She had one of those dipstick tests. The morning sickness. Come on, I need a cup of coffee."

She busied herself with that while he talked. He pulled out a pad of paper to make notes.

"She called the clinic from my office. Look, you've got to take her to see Dr. Jason, and they want her to talk to the social worker at the clinic. I suggested a counselor, but she said she knew what she wanted. She was adamant. Do you know she has the right to do all this without our permission?"

"You didn't tell her she couldn't!"

He shook his head. "I'd talk her out of it if I thought I could, but her mind is made up. I don't know what to think, Lucy. I'm stunned, to tell you the truth."

"Poor Laurie. Where is she?"

"I sent her back to school. She doesn't need to be lying around getting more upset."

"Poor Gordon," she said. "Poor darling." He was so Catholic. He laid the pen across his list. He looked burdened and baffled. He laid his head down on the table, his forehead pressed against the pen, and with no sound at all, he began to cry. His shoulders heaved slightly. She thought there must be something she ought to do, but it seemed such a private moment.

It's not even a baby yet, she thought. She wondered if anyone would want supper.

She went to his room and crawled in beside him. He asked her if she knew anything about Laurie. She knew he wondered who the father was. "Don't keep it from me." The funny thing was, she wasn't particularly curious. If there had been trauma—a rape, too horrible to think—they would have known. But all Laurie's friends were nice kids. Smart kids. With one of them, she had tried out her young womanhood. It didn't seem like something her parents needed to know.

"If anything, I'm more surprised than you are. For one thing, I thought she had more sense. Birth control. Kids aren't stupid these days. Not here." Not Laurie, she thought, but who would have told her anything? She hadn't.

He said, "I didn't think she had a boyfriend."

"Mostly they go around in a herd, as far as I know. I've never had a hint that someone was special. She's been with Tim a lot since last winter—"

"Tim?"

Tim wore braces and had pimples on his neck. He was shorter than Laurie.

"I don't think so," Lucy said. "Tim's her friend. I think she feels sorry for him."

"She's a good kid."

"Good kids try sex."

"I know."

"Sex—" she said, but she didn't know what the rest of the thought was. Something about nature and time and the wonder of it. "I'll take her to her appointments. I'll try to talk to her, get her to talk to me—" She was doubtful, but Gordon needed to hear that.

She put her hand flat on his chest. His nipple, beneath her palm, was cool and erect. "Gordon," she whispered, stretching out.

He lifted her hand off of him and laid it on the bed between them like an object.

"Gordon?"

He was staring at the ceiling. He looked lonely.

"Gordon, don't you think this is as good a reason as any for us to pull together? You and me, I mean? Don't you think we need one another?"

He turned his back to her.

"I can't run," she said in a little while. "What am I supposed to do, if I can't run?" She lay on her back, staring up at the ceiling. "This isn't my fault, you know. She's not a toddler. I can't walk her back and forth everywhere she goes. It's not my fault."

"Shut up, Lucy," Gordon said. She was as shocked as if he had slapped her.

Laurie was lying on a cot in a cubicle at the clinic, divided from her neighbors—there were three of them, all waiting for "the procedure"—by white curtains. Like boarding school. She was floating on the pleasant vapors of Demerol. She reached out for her father's hand, then went slack and didn't want even that. When they came for her, she said, "You'll be here when I get back?" but it was to neither of them, or both.

That morning, the gynecologist had put a little ring of dried seaweed in her, and since then, as Lucy understood it, the ring had softened and swollen, stretching the cervix. The doctor told Laurie it wouldn't hurt at all. She would be happy on Valium. "Forget all that stuff you've heard," she said. "I won't be doing the procedure myself, but I'll be there, and I'll hold your hand."

"Not her," Laurie had said, with the slightest nod toward Lucy.

Lucy couldn't tell if she meant anything by it. She couldn't tell if it was a question or a command.

Now, while they waited, Gordon and Lucy took a walk around the grounds. It was a pleasant, sunny day.

Back inside, they waited on a couch outside the recovery area. There was a table with coffee and hot water, packets of cocoa and tea. There were piles of magazines. They both took tea. They stirred and stirred, then sipped, then set their cups on the table between them, and didn't pick them up again.

"I've been so proud of you this past year," he said. He was looking straight out ahead of him. There were double doors and tall windows. They could see grass and, beyond that, the street between the clinic and the hospital. "When you came home from the hospital, you looked impossibly injured. I thought you would be crippled. I thought it was the cruelest blow, and you would never recover. I cried myself to sleep the first night you were home. Those first weeks, I told myself, she'll get better. I meant, you would sit up, you would eat, look around. You'd start getting well. I had a modest idea of what that meant. Really, you scared me. And then, when Bliss went home, and Laurie and I came back from the restaurant and found you on the stairs—you never gave in again. Every day you got stronger."

"I cried a lot. It just took time to get my courage up. To recover a little from the trauma. Gordon, why are we talking about this now?"

"Everything you did was, I don't know, ahead of schedule after that. I asked the doctor what to expect, and you were always better than what he said. You were like a champion skier, injured on a long jump, getting back to training. You were quite amazing, you know."

"Gordon?"

"I wrote my mother. I said, 'You should see her. You would be so proud of her.'"

"I didn't want to be grotesque. And I was afraid for Laurie, you know. For what it looked like to her."

He kept on talking, not quite looking at her. After a while she wanted to shake him, or brush his gaze off her shoulder.

"All these years, we've made so many accommodations for you.

For our marriage." He did look at her. "I never wanted to ask too much, Lucy."

"So you didn't," she said, feeling the heat of anger flushing through her. She knew this was going somewhere. She wanted him to get on with it.

"You are much stronger than I ever thought you were. Maybe stronger than you knew."

"You are what you need to be, I guess," she said, and she meant to barb him. "I wanted to walk. There was finally something I wanted badly enough to work at it."

He reached across the little table and squeezed her hand. Then he let go and leaned back on the couch and closed his eyes. He put his hand up across his forehead, a parody of those old silent movies, where the heroine can't pay the rent.

"You tell me what this is about, you sonofabitch," she said. A nurse, walking by, glanced at her. "Spit it out."

"I'm taking a leave next year."

"A sabbatical?"

"No. A leave without pay. I'm going to Fletcher for the year." She knew he meant Fletcher College in New Hampshire, the tiny, elite, expensive college where he had earned his B.A., where his mother had earned hers. "I'm going there as interim president."

"I don't believe it. Once again you've made a huge decision for this family *all by yourself*. Once again, I've been left out of my own life."

He said, "It's not about your life, Lucy. Only my own."

For a moment she forgot to breathe. Then she pulled in air through her nostrils noisily. She said, "Do you mean—you're going alone? You're going to leave me?"

He opened his eyes and turned toward her. He spoke very quietly. A young man had just sat down in a nearby chair and was reading a book by a popular horror writer. He glanced up, caught Lucy's eye, and looked back at his book guiltily.

Gordon said, "I'm fifty-two years old, and my life—I am talking about my work—has never gone the way I once thought it would. It has never gone the way of my dreams."

"Oh, Gordon, honestly. Why now? Do we have to talk about this now? Our daughter is lying on a hospital bed—"

"I'm not sure we need to talk about it at all. I'm just going to do this. It's the first thing I've really wanted to do since I realized you were sleeping with Richard Passero in Santa Barbara."

She gasped. "You've been walking around, holding that against me, for sixteen years? That's your idea of good manners?"

"Maybe they'll want me to stay. Maybe I'll move to a different college. If I have to, I can come back here, but I don't expect I will." He added, sadly, "I'm sorry."

"And if Laurie wants to go?"

"I think that should be up to her, don't you?"

"You bastard."

The young man looked up at them again, now openly curious. Gordon walked away to the door. "I'm going to wait outside," he said. "Call me when she's out, please."

Lucy trembled, but she didn't cry.

They were in bed: Gordon upstairs, Laurie down. The house was dark. Lucy had watched two movies, both with Katharine Hepburn and Spencer Tracy. She didn't look at the clock, but it had to be after midnight.

She called Zoe, who was sleeping, but who said it didn't matter.

Huddled in the kitchen in the dark, rocking back and forth, one hand clasping the knee of her banged-up leg, Lucy told Zoe about Laurie.

"Listen, it'll all go away, you'll see," Zoe said. "That's the great thing about an abortion. It goes away, by definition. You don't make a big thing of it, and neither will she. I had two before I was twenty, and look at me. A picture of mental health."

"It was that poor boy, Tim Heidegger."

"Who?"

"The boy whose mother died of breast cancer last year. I told you."

"Oh, I remember."

"She told us when we brought her home. She said Tim doesn't

know anything about it, and she doesn't want him to know. She said he has enough problems. I asked her how could it be? How could it be Tim? I thought they were like brother and sister. You know what she said to me?" She was crying now. "She said it was because of his mother. I said, 'Well, of course, darling. You were trying to comfort him.' I thought, oh, now it all falls into place. Only she glares at me— and her father sitting right there—and she says, 'You do not have any idea what I think. You have never cared. I let him do it with me because I understood exactly what he feels.'"

"I don't get it," Zoe said.

"Like I'm the one who died," Lucy said, and wept. "Like I didn't just spend a year getting strong *so she would have a mother*. I told her that, and she said, 'I hadn't really noticed what you were doing, Mother. I just knew you weren't anywhere I needed you to be.'"

"Oh, Lucy. Kids. What can I say?"

Lucy sniffed. "Nothing, I guess. But I feel better telling you."

"You probably need a good night's sleep the most."

"That's not all."

"It's not?"

"No. Gordon, too. I'm too tired to talk about it, though."

"Oh, him," Zoe said. "Tell me tomorrow. He's not going anywhere, is he?"

Lucy started to laugh, then cry again.

"You want me to come over? You want to come over here?"

"There's something else. I saw Andy."

"Christ," Zoe said. There was such a sudden chill in her voice, Lucy didn't tell the rest, not even when Zoe said, "Well? Well?"

"Nothing."

"Did he mention Annie?"

"I don't know any Annie."

"You know who she is. That really tiny waitress who's worked at the Bistro since forever. I think it was her first job."

"I'm not going to like this, am I, Zoe?"

"I just thought maybe he would mention that she's pregnant. She says, 'We're having a baby.' *We're*, in case you didn't get it, means

Annie and Andy. She says *we're* looking for an apartment with more room."

"Zoe, this is the wrong script. I was looking for comfort."

"Better not to be a fool."

"I've had a lot of bad days in my life, but this one goes right up on the A list."

"Come over here in the morning. I'll take the day off. We'll pick all the bones clean."

Lucy put the phone in the cradle and poured herself a glass of wine, then sat on the floor with her back against the cabinet, her legs stretched out. She dialed Andy's number. He answered on the second ring.

"Andy."

"Lucy, hey, is that you?"

"Andy, hey, why didn't you tell me? How could you?"

"Lucy, Lucy."

"No, it's Annie, Annie. She's the girl in the white dress, isn't she? The girl on your wall. She's pretty."

"I couldn't tell you that first thing. I wanted to see you."

"All those photographs you took today. How could you?"

"I love you."

"Stuff it."

"I don't know if I'm going to marry her. Nothing is decided."

"Some things are. More than you know. You listen to me. Children need their parents. You better grow up right now."

"You don't know everything. She isn't living here, you know. You've got my key."

"When I hang up, Andy? Listen carefully in that first moment. Hear the sound of your silver chain hitting the bottom of my trash barrel."

"Wait, Lucy."

Gently, she put the phone down. Then she pulled herself up and went outside.

Holding onto the iron railing, she put her good foot out over the next step down, and willed her left ankle to bend. She stood there, bound to the metal rod of the railing, one foot dangling, the other stubborn and refusing, and she fought tears and exhaustion and the huge black cloak of despair.

Gordon would never come back.

Laurie would never stay with her.

She sat down.

She thought of the photographs Andy had taken that day. How she had looked at him over her shoulder like the girl in Vermeer's *Portrait of a Girl,* so that you couldn't tell if she was turning away, or toward you.

She was happy he had taken the photographs. That one, especially. She liked to think that he would put them in one of those wide, shallow artist's drawers of his, put them away and forget all about them. One day, when she would be old, and ugly, or dead, someone would find the photograph, and see her the way she was that day.

They'll say, What a pretty woman, in her own way.

ACT OF ACCEPTANCE OF DEATH

To the faithful who at any time in their life, with a sincere love for God, and at least with a contrite heart, form the resolution of receiving from the hand of God, readily and willingly, any kind of death which God wills, with all its anxieties, pains, and sorrows, is given: An indulgence of seven years.

A plenary indulgence to be gained under the usual conditions only at the moment of death if they should have devoutly made this act at least once in their life.

O Lord my God, I now, at this moment, readily and willingly accept at Thy hand whatever kind of death it may please Thee to send me, with all its pains, penalties, and sorrows. Amen.

From Laura's prayer book, *Moments with God*

Oregon
Texas
New Mexico
California

The Hambleton manners prevailed. Gordon and Lucy spoke politely. They went over the projected finances for the year. Except for minor bills, Gordon had always managed their expenses. Now, he explained, the taxes, the insurance premiums, the investment reports, would all be handled by their accountant. She only had to pay the utilities and her own expenses. The mortgage came out of their account automatically. He had arranged for a monthly transfer of funds into checking. There was nothing to worry about. She yawned, then opened her eyes extra wide, trying to appear diligent and attentive, as she had once done in church as a child.

Laurie came and went with her friends. Tim was around, too, but seldom by himself. Lucy assumed he knew nothing of the abortion. As if it had never happened, Gordon and Lucy never mentioned it—not to Laurie, not to each other.

Gordon did manage to get Laurie to see a therapist, however. In the weeks before they left for the East Coast—they were going to Nantucket in mid-June—she saw the woman half a dozen times. The office was within walking distance. She kept her own appointments. Lucy was reminded of them only by Laurie's return, which was inevitably remarked by slammed doors and hours of silence. Gordon, of course, was tied up at the college late every day, six days a week. Lucy, left to herself—there was nothing new about that—continued her exercise regimen with particular vigor, saw every movie that came to town (occasionally Laurie accompanied her), and spent part of almost every evening with Zoe.

She begged Zoe to live with her. Zoe had no plans after the art teacher and his wife returned from China. She was going to spend some time in L.A.—things had heated up with the director Billy—and there was talk of a trip to London for some research, but where would she stack her books of poetry? Where would she pile her winter coat? Lucy argued for practicality. And she wanted Zoe's company in the house, as a transition. She did not expect Laurie to return until time for school to start. She had stretched her plans out at either end of the summer, going early to Nantucket, and from there, after Independence Day, to Bliss's in Santa Barbara. Finally, Zoe agreed that after Gordon and Laurie left, she would move in—temporarily, she stressed. She would take Lucy's room, and Lucy would take Gordon's. Zoe was making an offer on a house she hoped to move into by August. A stay with Lucy made good sense for both of them.

Lucy tried to help Laurie with her packing, but Laurie said, "No thanks," and went about it by herself. The night before they left—the plane was at 6:30 A.M., and they were being picked up by a taxi—they went out to eat Chinese food. It was a good choice—noisy and cheery, full of families. One of the nicer restaurants would have put all the burden on them for diversion, and Lucy didn't think they would have been up to it.

Later she sat in the chair in Gordon's room while he put the last items into his suitcase. He had already made arrangements for more things to be shipped; he hadn't asked Lucy to do any of it. He told her he had put a roll of printed labels on the desk for her to use if she forwarded mail to him. He was so polite she wanted to scream, but she sat there, somewhat slumped—he hated poor posture—and watched him until he was done. He was already dressed for bed, in pajamas and his silk robe.

"We'll talk on the phone," he said.

"How else?"

"I mean, I'm not going to the moon."

"Mmm."

"But I am going to bed. Laurie and I have to get up before five."

"I'll make coffee. Laurie won't want to eat that early."

"We've got time to eat some breakfast in San Francisco. Don't bother, Lucy, it's too early. You needn't even wake up. Tell Laurie good night tonight. You know what she's like in the morning. She can call you when we get there tomorrow night."

"Are you going all the way to Nantucket tomorrow?"

"No. We'll stay overnight in Boston, with my cousin. I put his number on the pad by the phone. Laurie will be fine. You'll be fine, Lucy."

"Will I?"

He untied his robe, slipped it off and folded it and put it in a drawer.

"You won't need a robe in New Hampshire?"

"Not that one," he said. He was doing a bad job of suppressing his impatience. He put his hand out to help her out of the chair. "How's your foot tonight?"

"There's no particular difference, night to night. Is that all we can think to say?"

"This is awkward. I've loved you for a quarter century, Lucy. It's very strange to put myself first. I'm not sure I'm happy about it, but I've made a commitment now."

"Don't turn hypocrite on me," she said sharply. He still had her hand. He stepped closer and put his arm around her briefly. "If there's anything—"

She pulled free. At the door, she said, "I just want my family,

Gordon. I want my life. It started when I was maimed, didn't it? More than my foot got cut off. It would have been so much easier for you if it had been my head."

"Sometimes, Lucy, you are a very raw person."

"Sometimes, Gordon, you are a jackass."

He switched off the bed lamp and she closed the door.

She changed into a nightgown and robe and made her way slowly down the stairs to Laurie's room. Her door was partway open. Music was playing softly, something old, from the sixties. A woman singing. Lucy couldn't quite place it.

"I've come to say good night," she said.

Laurie's two bags sat ready by the door. She was standing at her mirror, brushing her long hair. She put the brush over by her back-pack, on a stool by the other bags, and got into bed.

"Did you hear me?"

"Say it, then," Laurie said.

"I wish you wouldn't leave like this. With a chip on your shoulder."

Laurie smirked. "I love those old-timey expressions. 'Swell' and 'keen' and 'chip on your shoulder.'"

Lucy sat down on the bed. "I don't understand why you are angry with me. I didn't know what was going on with you—was there something I should have done? Did we not help you in the way you asked for help? Was there something more you expected?"

"Why would I expect anything? Isn't the rule around here, you take care of yourself?"

"You're fifteen. I respect your privacy."

"No, Mother, you respect *your* privacy. Even when you're nearly killed, it's all *your* business. Even then, you had no use for us."

"Wait a minute. You're angry because I'm not an invalid?"

"The first day Aunt Bliss leaves, you get up! God forbid you should need any help from me! I'm just the child, you can do it all yourself. Do you know—you have never once shown me your scar? I have never looked at your stupid foot?"

"All you had to do was ask, Laurie. I didn't dream you would want to see it. It's quite ugly. And at that, it's not as bad as it was at first." She lifted her foot to the bed. As always, she was wearing thick socks. She rolled the sock down on her ankle.

Laurie turned her head.

"Why don't you look?" Lucy said, but she rolled the sock up again. "Laurie, honey, you're hurting me. You're really hurting me."

Laurie whipped her head around again. "So what! I'm not supposed to take care of your feelings. You're the mother. You're supposed to take care of me."

"And you don't see that you've contradicted yourself entirely in the past two minutes?"

"Navarre says you're the kind of mother who doesn't understand your job."

"*Navarre?*"

"My therapist."

"She knows what I'm doing wrong, does she?"

"She knows that my adolescence is supposed to be about me, Mother, not about you."

"And it's not?"

"Not."

Lucy got up. "Either you've taken a quirky turn on what your therapist said, or she's an opinionated woman who needs a dose of reality," she said. "Either way, I hope it's all been a whole lot of help to you, because I am thoroughly confused."

"It doesn't matter."

"You're not going to have your father around next year, Laurie. I'm very sorry about that, it wasn't something I had any say in, but you and I better pull together, because we're what we've got."

"He's leaving because of you." Laurie began crying. Lucy saw that she was fighting not to cry harder.

"Do you want to go with him?"

"I'd rather do that than stay here with you! He doesn't want me to. He says he'll be busy all the time, and I won't have my friends."

"He's probably right. His important new life sounds lonely."

"He doesn't want me, and you don't want me—"

"That is not true."

"And I don't want you, either!" Laurie turned and flung herself down on her bed. "Go away."

"I couldn't bear for you to go like this if I didn't know you would be having a wonderful time on Nantucket with Lynnie and all the clan. So I'll settle for a phone call confirming your safe arrival. And there's something else. If I do things wrong, or if you hate me, or if we're apart, I'm still your mother. And if I die and you remember telling me how awful I am, be sure you remember that I said that, and that I love you."

Laurie rolled over again. "Oh, Mommy," she said. "You're hopeless. Do you think I didn't see that old movie? Do you think you're Debra Winger?"

Lucy bent and kissed her daughter quickly, before she could protest. "Call me," she said, before she shut the door.

She knew she couldn't sleep. She ate a bowl of cereal, and then sat down at her desk. From her bottom drawer she took out the manila envelope with the nude photographs of her mother, and another of the photos Willie had done of her so long ago. In the bottom of the drawer there was an old green stationery box. Inside were more photos of her mother, and some of her own girlhood pictures. She sat for a long time going through them. She wasn't thinking. She was looking.

The light didn't suit her. In the kitchen she turned on the lamps that hung over the table, and spread the photographs out into a patchwork of images. At the top she put herself, a little girl with her bottom bare, coy and self-aware; another, dressed for First Communion in crisp ruffles; at play in weedy yards. There was a pretty one of her standing by a kneeling Laura, both of them wearing cheap fur coats. Laura's hand was at her chin, her head held high, she both proud and wistful. Had she already seen what was coming? Or was she merely posing?

Closer to her, she spread out the nude photographs of her mother. She left Willie's pictures in a pile at the side.

She was trying to read the pictures of Laura. She had always thought there was a message in them for her, something her mother had wanted to say. Something plain as day. She had never wanted to understand more than now. What she wanted was her mother's voice. She couldn't remember the sound of it. She couldn't remember anything particular she had ever said. The realization of this was like being stabbed. There were sharp painful points of entry.

There were a few photos of Laura on the bed, dressed in a nightgown—Lucy remembered it as yellow—pulled down over her shoulder. Lucy could see the thin stiff texture of her hair, which she had bleached and curled, and the line of pencil on her naked brows. In others, she was looking away through the window. She had pulled back the drapes, leaving a filmy white scrim through which the light flooded in. In the most striking photograph—Lucy remembered this image when she thought of the photographs—Laura was standing full front, one leg slightly bent, one hand behind her as if reaching for the curtain. Lucy tried to find the word to describe the look on her face. Not so much "proud" as "direct." She had lost the beauty of the earlier photographs, but her skin in the light from the window was luminous and unblemished. Her smooth, undimpled hips and buttocks curved into her firm thighs. She was dying, and she was beautiful, though not so beautiful as she had been, and she wasn't pitiful. She looked peaceful. Lucy hadn't seen that in the photographs before. *See how I have moved on*, her mother said.

She didn't hear Gordon come up behind her.

"That poor woman," he said.

Invaded, she stretched out her arms and swept the pictures together in a messy pile. "I think she was ready," she said.

Gordon touched her shoulder. "You'll never get over your mother, Lucy."

Lucy whirled and struck him in the gut. Although she wanted to hurt him, she didn't. He caught her hands.

"I don't want to hear what you have to say about her!" she said.

He let her go and sat down at the corner of the table. He reached into the pile and took out one of the photographs. Laura was on the bed, in her gown. He looked at it, then set it down again.

"Why now?" he asked.

"Why not? What else have I got?"

"Why not photos of Laurie? Of us, of our lives?"

"What, those?" she scoffed. "So organized, in albums, stacked neatly in the living room cupboard. I remember every one of those pictures. I don't even have to look at them to remember. Don't you understand, Gordon? All those pictures are *after the fact*. These, *these* are all I have left from the most important event of my life. And I was hardly there! I was like Laurie, all caught up with myself, furious with my mother half the time, and I don't even know why now. Did she understand? Did she forgive me? I don't trust my memory. All I have are these photographs."

"But they aren't real, Lucy. They're just images of a distant past. You pick one or two, you frame them and hang them—those are your tokens. My dog, the summer house. Your studio portrait of four generations. Those things honor our memories. But this—when does it end? I wonder if you're not still there—" He pointed back at the photograph of Laura. "With her, instead of us."

She rummaged in the photographs, moving them aside. "You've never seen these." She slapped down the Willie pictures furiously.

He put his fist up to his mouth.

"That bad?" she said hatefully. "That disgusting?"

"They're beautiful," he whispered. "You're just a girl."

"Willie took them the summer before I met you."

"Yes, I see." He picked one up and studied it. She picked up another, and laid it beside one of her mother. Laura, Lucy, turned to the light. It didn't seem fair; she was so much younger, and healthy. She pushed the table back, and stood in front of Gordon. She shook her robe off. It slid to the floor.

"Lucy, I don't think—"

"That's right. Don't think." She lifted her gown and sat on his lap, straddling him. She could feel him recoil. "My mother's photographs disgust you, don't they? 'That poor woman.' And my photos. And me.

Weeping and fucking and lying and needing. That's why you married me, isn't it? I was your thrilling forbidden Lucy, a slap in the face to the Hambletons. I was the orphan who needed you. Then you were stuck with me. Until the accident. Did it make me too ugly for you? I'm not ugly now, Gordon. I'm stronger than I've ever been. Look at me. Damn you, look."

She pulled her gown over her head. His hands were raised in the air, up near his ears, like someone at gunpoint. "No."

She reached for his hands and pulled them to her breasts. He resisted, then yielded. His fingers dug into the flesh. She felt his thighs grow rigid.

"We don't have a camera," she said. "You'll have to remember what I look like in your mind."

His hands slid to her hips. He bent his head. His lips brushed her neck. "Lucy."

She tugged at his pajama bottoms. He was erect. She raised herself to take him inside. Her ankle was hurting. She was angry, and exultant, and aroused.

"It's been a long time," she said.

"I wish we were upstairs," he said, but there wasn't any way they were going to move just then.

Later she left her clothes and the photographs and her husband and went upstairs to bed. He sat at the table with his pajama bottoms gaping and his head in his hands.

She heard the honk of the taxi in the drive. She grabbed her terry robe and hurried to the stairs. Her hands splayed against the wall as she went down the stairs sideways. She heard noise on the porch, the creak and click of the door as they shut it, their voices. "Wait!" she called. "Wait!"

By the time she reached the porch they were in the taxi. She called their names. Both of them were in the back seat. As the taxi pulled away, Laurie turned and saw her through the back window. Lucy stood as if frozen; in the confusion of the moment, she couldn't remember how to get down the steps. She sat down hard and bumped down the steps. Laurie held up her hand but didn't wave. The taxi moved away down the steep street.

Lucy, at the bottom of the steps, tried to stand up and tumbled over onto the walk. She cried out in pain. Her neighbor from two doors up was passing with his dog. He ran to help her up. Lucy waved away his hands. She had made it up onto her knees; now she bent forward, her hands at her mouth.

"Are you all right, Lucy?" her neighbor asked. "Should I get an ambulance?"

Lucy let him help her stand. "I went too fast, and fell, that's all," she said. The taxi, at the bottom of the street, was turning left. "Sometimes I still forget I'm lame."

Inside, she found Gordon had moved the photographs out onto her desk, in tidy stacks, covered by the envelopes and held down by a book. Her nightclothes were folded neatly beside them. She walked through the house, crying. Everything looked so clean and neat, as if the house were for sale. Laurie had even made her bed.

"The only cure," Zoe said, "is distraction."

"The only cure for what?" Lucy said.

"Anything that hurts," Zoe said.

When Lucy was a girl, she loved to go to her Aunt Opal's. As the oldest of the kids—the next in age were Opal's Joy and Lucy's sister Faith, both four years younger—she was never quite a child. Opal took her with her everywhere. They shopped for groceries and picked up the cleaning. They stopped to see friends, to leave a casserole or a recipe, to gossip and complain. From the time she was eleven, Lucy went with her aunt to work at the hospital in Monahans; she spent the afternoons in the lab, reading. Opal kept up a running commentary on her life—on life in general—and Lucy took it all in. The way men ran the world but couldn't be depended on. The way doctors told dirty jokes in surgery and depended on nurses to catch their errors and save their patients and never say. Hemlines rising, but those beautiful old tulle dresses were worth saving for parties. And sometimes she would say, with a little huff, "Your poor mama." Laura was sick so much. Lucy and Faith went to Opal every summer except one, and gave Laura breathing space. The one time she didn't send them out to West

256

Texas (the towns changed, and sometimes weren't towns at all, but oil field camps) it was because she was so angry with Greta, she sent the kids to the Clarehopes in Chickasha. They spent the summer with strangers, which wasn't so bad—there were kids there to play with, and a library so she could read—but ten-year-old Lucy was lonesome. Nobody in Chickasha knew she was grown up, so they didn't talk to her in a grown-up way. For lack of conversation, she went to the priest who said the nine-thirty Mass on Sunday and said she was going through a dark night of the soul. He did his best not to laugh and asked her what she knew of such things. "My mother told me," she said. "She read Saint John on retreat at Subiaco Abbey last year. She says the dark night is a gift from God that marks you as special, but it doesn't feel that way. It hurts." He wasn't an unkind or ignorant man. He put his thumb gently on her heart and pressed her loneliness. "God doesn't scourge His children," he assured her. She was away from her mother; it was to be expected that she should be sad. He said sometimes it helps to pray the rosary, and to read. He lent her *Lives of the Saints,* full of shocking details of martyrdom; she met with him two or three times a week, for fifteen or twenty minutes at a time, to talk. Eventually she poured out her longings: to be pure, holy, and smart. Her only other wish was to have breasts, but she assumed that would come in time. He told her to say the Hail Mary once each waking hour, and to put her holiness in her Holy Mother's hands. He said he was confident she was smart already.

"Remember the summer we had to stay with Aunt Rowena?" she asked Opal all these years later. She felt closer to Opal, since Greta died, at least when they were together. And Opal, whose husband Russell was working on a pipeline in Colombia, was happy to have her in Lubbock.

"Remember? It nearly broke my heart." Opal was putting a lemon pie together and her hands were busy, but she sighed with all the force of a woman with her hands at her breasts. "Your mother was mad at Mommy over what they'd done in that hospital the year before."

"What had they done?"

"Oh, sweetie, I don't know, really. I was in Kermit with babies. But those years, if you were depressed—" She shrugged. "They didn't have drugs for it yet. And with Laura's migraines to complicate things—"

"What did they do?" She already knew.

"I expect they gave her shock treatments."

"That's horrible."

"They sent her to a Catholic hospital, you know, in Dallas. It was all on the recommendation of your mother's priest. What did Mommy know? She was afraid Laura would kill herself. You know, I don't think there was a thing in the world wrong with your mama except she was so frustrated. Nobody ever made us feel we could do anything in those days. She was so pretty and smart, and she'd always had big dreams, and there she was—" Opal shook her head. "She was proud being your mother, though. Don't think she wasn't. I always thought that was why she became Catholic, so she could give you better opportunities. Those nuns, they took a lot of the burden off her."

Lucy said she needed to wash her hair, and went off to the shower.

When Lucy came back, Opal handed her some snapshots of her grandson, Clancy's baby Murphy. "He's cute," Lucy said. Clancy was living in Wichita Falls with her daddy's mother, Elizabeth, who was frail and didn't want to live alone.

"I sent them to Russell in Colombia. He thinks Murphy's so darling. Murphy calls him 'Dadoo,' isn't that cute? Whoever's going down from the company will take packets with them. You're not supposed to send dollars, but I do. It's easier for him."

"I don't understand why he'd want to be in Colombia. Isn't he afraid of all the thugs? The drug wars? Isn't he afraid he'll be killed? Aren't you?"

"Boy, aren't you full of questions. I was mad as hell when he said he wanted to go. I was so lonesome when he was in Africa. And then Clancy taking Murphy off to Wichita and all. But honey, the money is real good, and he has a million-dollar insurance policy." She looked at Lucy slyly, to see if she was paying attention.

"I know you are trying to get me going, Opal." Lucy laughed. "I've got a quarter-million-dollar policy on Gordon, but the most danger he's going to be in in New Hampshire is frostbite, if he bothers to go outdoors."

"The company takes good care of the men. Their housing is in a compound surrounded by a high fence with dozens of security guards. They build another fence around the segment of pipeline they're working on, and when it's done, they move the fence. And if Russell has to go out in a truck, he sits in the middle between two guards."

"Still, it leaves you high and dry."

Opal swept her arm to remind Lucy about the kitchen. "I paid cash for this remodel. Remember how dark and miserable it was?" Now the kitchen was white and white—floor, cabinets, walls—with little touches of tangerine. "And it gave me time to visit in Wichita without hurrying back. Besides, now I'm working." She slathered the last of the meringue on her pies and slid them in the oven. "And you're here."

"Are we supposed to eat two pies?" Lucy asked.

"Got to eat something," Opal said. "This will be ready in a jiffy. Let's go to the mall and look around."

"I don't need a thing in the world."

"Shoot, you don't know what you need till you see it. That's what shopping is about." She winked. "It's what credit cards were invented for."

"I can't remember the last time I shopped."

"See? It's what you need. We'll eat at Furr's and then tonight we'll just have pie."

It was like that day after day. Opal had a million errands. She had friends to see. One was a retired drug salesman who lived with his wife out on the edge of Lubbock in the breaks, on an old ranching homestead. Cows came right up in the yard. Opal took Lucy to work with her one night, too, and had her counting spools of ribbon and stocking thread. Opal worked three night shifts a week at a Wal-Mart, in crafts and fabrics. At home she had projects all over the place; she was paid to prepare samples for display. On her days off she went over to the houses of her co-workers, some her age, one no older than thirty. They had coffee and pie and complained about management, but jovially. They all liked crafts and fabrics. Lucy thought Opal was happier than she had seen her in a long while, even with Russell missing and Joy and Clancy moved away.

Lucy got out the vacuum cleaner and did all the rugs. She liked the roar of the machine. Russell's house was big—four bedrooms—but Opal had most of it closed off. Lucy's bedroom and bath were all the way across the house from Opal's. She told her aunt, "It's like I'm living down the block," because she knew it tickled her. She slept late, and read all of Opal's back issues of women's magazines. They were piled in a huge basket behind the couch, with at least a hundred catalogs. To her surprise, Opal had a little stationary bicycle in one of the spare bedrooms, so Lucy could still get plenty of exercise without going out onto Lubbock's insane streets to walk. Opal wanted to move the bike into the living room so Lucy could watch TV, but Lucy explained that she liked to pedal away like someone drugged, not paying attention to anything.

Right at the end of June, she talked to Gordon and Laurie in Nantucket. Gordon said everyone sent love. He was going up to the college the day after the July Fourth festivities. He sounded just like he had sounded every time he had gone east without her, except this trip was going to last a little longer; you wouldn't know, listening to him, that he'd just split up his family. Lucy said, "That's nice," and "Goodbye, Gordon," as civilly as she could manage. Then Laurie got on the phone and said hello, and she was fine, and her favorite cousin Stephen was there, and goodbye, all as woodenly as if she was a bad actress reading a script.

Lucy got off the phone and started crying. "They act like they don't know me. Like I'm some distant relative they talk to as an act of charity."

Opal said, "Let's get out of here."

"I don't know what everybody's so mad at me about," Lucy said. She had fallen into Opal's rhythms; she was even picking up the

Texas accent again. It always happened if she spent more than a few days in Lubbock.

"We could go over to Farmington and see Joy and Otis next week."

"I should go home."

"Why's that?"

"Hell, I don't know," Lucy said.

They went to one of the new wineries and tried three kinds of blushes. Lucy took little sips, because she had learned a long time ago that wine was a sure way to get a headache. Opal said she couldn't tell the difference, but she liked the winery. People fussed over them and gave them crackers to clear their palates. When they were back out in the car, Opal said, "I love that expression, 'clear the palate.' It always makes me think of picking up bedding off the floor."

Lucy laughed. "Once Lynnie's kids came with her for a visit and it turned hot. I mentioned that when we were kids we lay down on the floor on pallets in the hot part of the day, under the air conditioner. The kids were wide-eyed. 'All together?' they wanted to know. Lynnie sniffed and said they had never had air-conditioning in her summers on 'Sconset. I never liked her the way I like Bliss. Lynnie's more like Bell, skinny and superior and blonde."

"Bliss," Opal said. "I wish I'd thought of that when I named Joy. It's such a classy name."

"It's snooty is what it is," Lucy said. "All the Hambletons are born with their noses in the air."

Opal mentioned that she had a box of things for Lucy from Greta's house. "We didn't get much out," she said. Partly, it was the flood. Then what was left got sold in an auction at the house. The house, too. Lucy got three thousand dollars, eventually.

"What's in it?" she asked Opal.

"Mommy's Bible, you might as well have it, my kids wouldn't care. And there's an old album I think Laura put together with pictures from the family. Some of them go way back. There's only one of Papa as a boy."

"And you don't want it?"

"Shoot, Lucy, you're going to come down here one year soon and discover I'm an old lady. I don't want to hoard everything the way Mommy did. Take the pictures. Take it all."

"I don't know if I can look at it right now."

"Let's ship the box up to your house and you can look at it whenever you feel like it."

"Okay."

Tears were welling in Opal's eyes. "I still can't stand it. I miss her so much."

"I know, me too."

Opal jumped up. "I'm going to put some beans on. We've got that ham left over."

While Opal did that, Lucy looked at the paper. She couldn't find much to interest her; the Lubbock news was a mix of religion, sports, conservative politics, and pages of high society pictures, like luncheons and charity auctions and engagements of girls with big hairdos.

"This sounds interesting," she said. She had come across an announcement of an exhibit at the university museum. "It's photos from the Depression years. People are treating 1989 like the fiftieth anniversary. You see all kinds of books out."

"We were poor a whole lot earlier than 1939," Opal said.

"It's because of Steinbeck's book, I think. *Grapes of Wrath*?"

Opal sniffed. "Never read it, but I saw the movie. I thought it was tacky."

"Anyway, this exhibit is photography taken right around here. Maybe there would be something you'd recognize."

"We were only in Aileen a little over a year," Opal said. "But why not? If you want to."

"I like photographs from that time," Lucy said. "Maybe there'll be some Dorothea Lange. I like those skinny mothers with their children. I like the way they're still holding on."

There were no famous photographers represented. The exhibit was called "Plain Seeing." All the work came from studio photographers and amateurs who had lived in the region. There was a whole wall of pictures of dust storms, big black boiling clouds that blocked the sky. Most of the photographs were of people on farms or at big gatherings, like church and school and fairs. They worked their way down the line of photos. Once in a while one of them said something to call attention to an interesting feature: an old tractor or car, the clothes, a table laden with cakes. Lucy liked a cluster of pictures done in a small town—storefronts and folks gossiping. The studio portraits were of better quality, but stiffer and less appealing. Opal moved along more quickly, satisfied with less analyzing.

They had been separated for five minutes or so when Lucy heard her aunt cry out. Her first thought was that Opal had had a heart attack; Lucy's own heart seemed to skip, then thud. She turned so fast, looking for Opal, she put a strain on her bad foot and sent a terrific pain up her leg. Opal, a few yards away, was staring at the wall, her hand clamped across her mouth, her eyes wide. She didn't appear to be sick or hurt, only shocked.

"What in the world?" Lucy asked, rushing to her. Opal turned and clamped onto Lucy's arm so hard it hurt.

"I just wasn't expecting it," she said. "You don't go in a museum and think you'll see your own mama—" She pointed to the photograph on the wall in front of her. Lucy stepped closer to take a look.

It was a picture of the Clarehopes in Sunday dress. Ira, Greta, Laura at twelve or thirteen, then Opal and little Amos. It looked so familiar.

"What an odd picture," she said. Ira was reaching for something in the wind. Laura had her skirt pulled up across her face, peeking over the hem. "Where have I seen it?"

"It was the same as the other one—" Opal eased her hold on Lucy's arm. "The one in my hall."

"Of course," Lucy said. She saw immediately what had happened. The photographer had taken both pictures close on one another, and kept this one, as you'd think he might. It was almost a comic picture, everyone a little lost in the wind.

Lucy took Opal through the museum and found someone to ask

about the exhibit. She learned that they could request a photo for six dollars. "But I want to know who took it," she said.

"But I know that," Opal said. "I was there."

Lucy laughed at herself. "I never wondered even once before. Now it's suddenly the big question. Well, you'll have to tell me about it."

Opal was about to cry. "This one looks so much more real. All of us scrambling. I'd forgotten all about the wind that day." She sniffled. "Like the wind that killed my Papa."

"I know," Lucy said. She took Opal by the elbow and led her out. There was a bench in the lobby. "Sit down a minute. I've got to run back and get the number of the photo. We'll check at the archives tomorrow, and see what else they might have by this photographer."

"He only took the two pictures," Opal said shakily. Then she blinked. "That day, I mean. But he took a lot of photos after that. Maybe dozens. Do you mean—they might have them?"

"I don't know. We'll find out."

She wrote down the number of the photograph. They had labeled it "Sunday Portrait, 1938. Perkins Studio."

When they got home, Lucy made coffee for them. "I've looked at that picture hanging in your hall now hundreds of times through my life and never given it a thought. Now I see this one and I can't believe how much I want to know about it." She stirred sugar in her coffee. "You're pretty little in it. Do you remember anything about the photographer?"

"He was just a boy," Opal said. "It was his mother's studio."

"What a pretty little girl you were," Lucy told her.

Opal twisted her mouth. "You should meet him."

"Oh, sure, I'd like that!" Lucy laughed.

"You should have met him years ago. I feel so bad."

"What are you talking about?"

"He should meet you." Opal patted the table nervously. "And I know where to find him."

They flew to Albuquerque and rented a car.

"How do you know he's still there?" Lucy asked.

"I called him last night. We had a good long talk."

"You're full of surprises."

"I was through here a while back, maybe ten, eleven years ago. I called him then, too, but he wasn't in, and I thought, Well, that's the way God wants it."

"You make it sound like a big deal." Lucy, who was driving, glanced over at Opal. "Did he remember you?"

"I just told him I was your mother's sister. He remembered. He was in love with her."

"She was a little girl!"

"Later. We were in Gallup, and then we discovered he was, too. Lord, Lucy, it's such a complicated story. To tell you the truth, it's hard to remember just what happened. But I know he was crazy about your mother, and you might as well meet him."

"I wanted to talk to him about his photographs. I don't know if I'm up for *This Is Your Life*."

Opal leaned her head back on the seat. "All of a sudden I'm so sleepy. Do you mind if I take a little nap?"

"How do I know where I'm going?"

"You can't miss Gallup." Opal pointed. "Straight ahead. Wake me when we get there."

They checked into a motel and ate lunch in a cafe. Lucy said, "Only you would take me all the way to someplace I never heard of to meet somebody you haven't seen in nearly fifty years."

Opal looked pleased. "Neither one of us has anything else to do, do we?"

Wesley Perkins looked pleased, too. He was waiting out at the top of the long dirt driveway that curved up to his house. As the car bumped into the alley, he waved his arms big, as if flagging down a rescue truck.

"I can't believe he still lives over here," Opal said when she got the directions. "This is where we lived back then." That was only partly true. The street they had lived on was long ago destroyed for a free-way. But the Perkins place was a little higher up the side of the hill, taking up two big lots. The house was exceptionally wide, with a high stone fence in front. Stretched across the roof were long solar panels, six of them, one broken out. Cars were pulled into a wide paved space between the end of the house and a small outbuilding. Back of that there was another large building with a tin roof. Wesley walked them around and gave them a history. There had been two stucco houses. He had bought them both more than forty years ago, when he got married after the war. He had put his mother in one, and his bride in the other. Then, as his family grew—he had three sons and two daughters—he connected them and added on, too. "I paid cash and did all the work myself. So when I wanted to build a store, I borrowed on my property." The property looked to Lucy a little like an old motel. There was a nice walled-in patio, though, and it turned out that was a blessing, because his wife needed the space to walk safely, or, more accurately, to be walked about.

"Here we are in better times," Wesley said as soon as he had escorted them into the house. They were in an anteroom with a stone floor. Although it was at least eighty degrees outside, it was cool enough in here that Lucy wished she had a sweater. She rubbed her arms as they looked at the wall display of family photographs. The one Wesley pointed to must have been at least fifteen years old. The children were all grown, some of them with spouses and babies. A couple of the spouses were out and new ones in, Wesley said, with a shrug that said, What can you do with kids? In the photograph, he was dressed in a snappy suit, and his wife, Lila, was wearing red. They had changed a lot in the interim.

Wesley, a short, wiry man with heavy eyebrows and deep-set dark eyes, was now wearing a tan polyester jumpsuit and brown leather bedroom slippers with elastic at the sides. He had a thick mane of hair, worn a little long, but it was silvery now, with none of the color he'd still had when the photograph was taken. Lila, a decade into Alzheimer's, by Wesley's explanation, wore sweatpants and a heavy cotton cardigan. Her hair, though not coiffed elegantly as in the pictures, was nonetheless nicely done in a shorter style. She was hardly recognizable as the woman in the family portrait. She grimaced and worked her mouth, and mumbled and gargled constantly the whole time they were there. None of her sounds were intelligible. A dark plump woman was walking her in the courtyard, around and around, talking sweetly to her about the weather.

Lucy and Opal followed Wesley into the house. He directed them to sit at the round kitchen table, where there were glasses and a pitcher of apple juice set out for them. He reached for the pitcher clumsily, and Opal said, "Let me do that, Wes," as if they'd been sitting at this table once a week for forty years. It made Lucy smile.

"Opal said you have questions about a photograph I took," Wesley said to her. "I think I remember it. It was kind of a big day for me."

"I was able to get a photocopy of it from the archives," Lucy said. She pulled the folded paper from her bag and smoothed it out, then passed it to Wesley.

He studied the paper. "My, we were all so young then," he said. He folded it and handed it back to Lucy.

"How did the Southwest Collection get the photograph, do you think?" she asked. "They had a file with at least fifty pictures, but no more of our family. The file was 'Perkins Studio.'"

"My dad had been living away from us. He was a cameraman for the movies. He wanted us to come out to L.A. My mother closed everything up and we went. Five, six years later we came here. My dad left again and went back to L.A. He died out there a few years later. My mother said she wasn't going anywhere else. We could stay here or we could go back to Aileen."

"I guess we were gone by then," Opal said.

"Just like that," Wesley said. He snapped his fingers. "I went off somewhere on business for the station, and when I came back, you were gone." His eyes were red and moist. "I went all over, asked everyone I could, that old Greek at the cafe, people at the Harvey House. Anybody know about the Clarehopes? It was like you fell in one of them sinkholes. I never understood. Nobody told me." His nostrils glistened. "And your mother dead so young, it's not right. I never thought of her dead."

Opal looked sorry as she could be.

Wesley got up and excused himself. They heard him in another room, blowing his nose. Opal looked at Lucy and shrugged. "He can tell you some things, Lucy."

"Why don't you do it?" she asked. Something was going on here.

"I think it's up to him." The two women from the patio came in and walked past them into another room, the one babbling, the other crooning softly. "You had a good walk, didn't you, Lila?" the one woman said.

Wesley came back carrying a clean folded handkerchief, excused himself, and sat back down. He had a photograph in a silver frame. He showed it to them. It was a picture taken of him with Lila before they were married. They were a good-looking couple. Lila was a little taller than Wesley; she looked strong and vital. Wesley laid the picture down. "I'm not having the old age I was looking forward to," he said. He smiled. "We liked to travel."

"Course not," Opal said. Lucy couldn't think of anything that would be right to say, and she didn't want to comment on his sick wife. The whole situation was too personal too fast for her.

Wesley went on. "I just want to say, talking to you both—it's not something I ever thought about. Not something I'd have thought to look for, though I always wondered. And it doesn't take anything away from Lila, from our forty-two years together."

"Course not," Opal said.

That said, Wesley seemed more collected. They could still hear Lila in the other room, babbling. Wesley said, "Mother and I went back to Aileen and we saw right away there wasn't anything there for us. She put the house up for sale, and the studio. There was a lot of stuff in the studio. I mean a lot. Tintypes, plates, negatives. My grandfather had been a photographer, too, and a collector of old photos. I'll show you some of the prints I've got up in my office. Cowboys. He was crazy for cowboys. Real good stuff. I sell postcards made from those old daguerreotypes. But we left a lot, too. We couldn't take it all. I expect it changed hands, or who knows, got sold broken up, and some of the negatives got picked up by the archives." He folded his hands and took a long, deep breath. "Never crossed my mind, you know? Photos nowadays—they're so easy. It used to take a week or ten days to get the film developed. We'd have to send it to Albuquerque. We got it down to four days, and then Lila said to me, Why don't we do it ourselves? People want their pictures fast."

"I was telling Lucy about all the pictures you took out at our place," Opal said. "I was thinking you might have some of them."

He thought about that. "Let me show you something," he said, getting up. They followed him to the far end of the house, into a room that smelled dusty and was cold. It was piled haphazardly with boxes, deer and elk antlers, a dressmaker's form, and many other items. Wesley gestured toward the boxes. "I've got to go through all this. I bet I have a thousand snapshots of the family. And postcards. Lila and me, we traveled a lot. We've been to Europe and the Caribbean, to Africa and New Zealand. Everywhere I go, I take pictures. But I don't know which box has what. I'll tell you this, though. When Lila started getting sick, she was funny about me. About everything I'd ever done. She went through a lot of my photos and threw them out. I used to have one of your mother, Lucy. My mother took it in Aileen. A formal portrait in a long green dress. I looked for it once, maybe five, six years ago. I don't know what got into me. But I couldn't find it. I think maybe Lila got to it."

"But there might be something?" Lucy asked.

Wesley was walking around, patting the boxes as if they were patient animals. "Maybe. I've got to go through it all one day."

"I'd like to have anything that has to do with my mother," Lucy said. She wished she knew how to hurry this along.

Wesley reached out quickly and took her hands, both of them, in his. He moved so fast, and held onto her so hard, she flinched. He was about to cry again. "This doesn't have anything to do with Lila, now. But I never forgot your mother. She was—she was special to me."

Opal, behind Lucy, said cheerily, "So special he asked me out on a date and when he came to pick me up he took Laura out instead." She had broken the tense mood. Wesley laughed with her and they left the room.

"Come on," he said. "Let me show you around."

For the next two hours, he drove them around Gallup. He owned two large drugstores and two fast-finishing photo shops. "I've got twelve of them around New Mexico," he said. "My son John manages them. Eddie manages the drugstores. My daughter Susie is a CPA. Jim and his wife run the portrait studio. We sell cameras and equipment, too. My mother worked there when we first came here. We got the chance to buy it when the owner retired, and we got everything. It turned out he had a cache of negatives from the twenties and thirties, Indian stuff. Good as Curtis. We sell prints, real good ones." By then they were in a cafe, pausing for coffee. "We can go over there next."

"I'm getting a headache," Lucy said.

"My ladies leave me supper all made up," he said. "One goes home at four, the other at six, and then I take care of Lila for the night. Amelia's making her enchiladas, they're real good. I told her you'd be having supper with me. You will, won't you?"

"I don't know," Lucy began, but Opal interrupted. "Why don't we leave the car up at your place for now, and go to the motel and rest. You can pick us up at five-thirty. This is awfully nice, Wesley. It's tiring, though, isn't it? Getting old and looking back."

"It's hell," Wesley said. He paid the bill and went out of the cafe with Opal's hand in his. "Where'd it go, Opal? How much is left?"

Lucy tried to beg off from supper, but Opal wasn't going to agree to that. "He's a nice man," she said several times. "Where are your manners?"

"I honestly don't know what we came for. I don't know what I was thinking, what I wanted."

"I know what we came for, and we haven't got it yet."

"The pictures? He's never going to find any pictures in that dump he calls a storeroom. If he's got old plates, and those Indian pictures—they ought to be in archives where they can be taken care of. He's too sentimental to think about it. He's got piles of history, and he's worrying about his postcards."

"Never mind the pictures. He's got something to tell you about your mother. I want him to tell it."

"I'm going to learn something about my mother from that old man?"

She went. And learned nothing. Lila sat in a recliner in the living room in front of the TV while they ate—the enchiladas were delicious—and then Lucy and Opal sat in the living room while Wesley got Lila into bed. She slept in a hospital bed in a little room just off the kitchen, maybe once the pantry. One of "the ladies" had already bathed and dressed her. They heard bits of Wesley's chatting to her, and her cruelly meaningless sounds.

He joined them. They were sitting on facing couches. He sat in a second recliner and pointed to a table by its side. "I'd go crazy if it wasn't for puzzles," he said. There was a half-done jigsaw of a ship at sea. Opal got up to look at it and made approving sounds. "I have the hardest time with those darned things," she said.

"I'm thinking I'll go to one of those navy reunions," he said. "I've kept up all these years. They have newsletters. My daughters say I ought to get away."

"Do you good," Opal said.

Lucy felt sick to her stomach and excused herself. She spent a long time in the bathroom. When she came back, Opal and Wesley were working the puzzle together.

"I need to go," Lucy said. "I don't feel good."

"Altitude," Wesley said.

"Beg your pardon?"

"High here. Gets to lots of people."

"Maybe," Lucy said, aware that she was being childish and sullen, and that she was desperate to escape.

At the door, Wes hugged Opal and reached for Lucy, who managed to turn his effort into a handshake. He said, "It's hard to know how much you look like her, 'cause of course she was so young when I saw her last. Eighteen, was she, Opal?"

"Let's see. I was fifteen when we left here. So she was seventeen."

"Seventeen, you say? She seemed older."

Good night, they said. As Lucy put the key in the ignition, Opal leaned out the window and yelled to Wesley, "See you in the morning."

"I can't," Lucy said back at the motel. She stripped and fell into bed in her underwear. "I can't talk to him. I can't listen to any more."

"Honey, don't be rude. He's important to you."

"He's not. I don't want his pictures. I don't care. I'm so sad from pictures I could drown in crying. I just want to go home and sleep in my own bed and think what to do." She turned and put her face down in her pillow.

"He's still cute," Opal said. "But oh, he was a handsome devil then. He was a killer."

"If you say so," Lucy said. She absolutely did not believe it.

Lucy slept well enough to get her manners back. Wesley met them at the cafe near the motel and treated them to breakfast. Opal said she had to go back to the room and get something, and disappeared before Lucy could follow.

"I couldn't sleep all night," Wesley said. "Thinking about your family. I knew your mother's parents, too, of course. I was there, taking pictures, the day they came and said Mr. Clarehope was dead."

"Really?"

"I am going to look for those pictures, I promise you, Lucy. They ought to go to you and Opal."

"If you find them—" she said weakly.

"But I want to tell you something else." He patted her hand. She waited a moment, then put her hands in her lap.

"I don't know how to tell you. I mean, I don't know what words to use. It's been a long time. But I wanted you to know—well, your mother was more than a little special to me. She was—you could say, she was my first love. I loved her."

Lucy clamped her mouth shut.

"I thought she loved me, too. We went around quite a lot. Maybe Opal told you."

"She didn't."

"But she wanted to go to California. There was someone else we knew. Hardly knew, but still, he encouraged her. I always thought, seduced her, pardon the expression. Maybe she was in love with him, or maybe it was California. I thought that was where she went. With him."

"I don't know," Lucy said.

"I just thought I ought to tell you, because if you want to know about your mother, he might know more than me. I don't know. When the family left, I was heartbroken. I kicked around here a while, and I went to Aileen with my mother to close up the house and studio there, and then I came back and joined the navy. I thought, If she doesn't want me, for sure my country does. I was in the Pacific, on carriers, for three years. Came back, put it all behind me, met Lila."

Lucy smiled. "Had a big family."

"Built my business."

"Took a lot of pictures." They both laughed, but he was near tearful again, and she was uneasy.

"There's no knowing if he's dead or alive. He was a little older than me. Had family in Albuquerque. I thought about writing him, asking if that's where she was, but I was too proud. What would I have said? What would he have said?"

"So you're going to tell me who he was? Is that what you wanted to tell me?"

"I thought I'd go in the navy, we were at war, and when I got back, we'd get married, Emma and me."

"Emma?"

"Your mother."

"Oh. Her first name. Emma Laura." Lucy had never heard her called Emma before.

"But it didn't work out. So I wondered, did she marry him?"

"She married Charlie Widemar," Lucy said, as if that were the whole truth.

"Oh. Hmm." He took a noisy breath and sat back in the booth. "Not him, then."

"Him, who?" Lucy said.

"Why, that writer, Hollis Berry," Wesley said. He leaned forward. "I guess it doesn't matter. Guess she didn't go out there after all."

Lucy felt her ears buzzing. "She did, though," she said. "But then she came home and married my daddy." She scooted out of the booth. "Let's see if we can find Opal. We've got a long drive."

At the motel he had them pose by a bush. He took their picture with an Instamatic camera, then he posed with each of them in turn. She couldn't stop him from hugging her goodbye. He was crying openly by then. Opal promised to stay in touch.

She waited until they were half an hour out of town before she said what she'd been sitting on all along. Forty-five years of sitting.

"He didn't tell you, did he? I guess he's scared of what his kids would say. I thought sure, when he saw you, he'd tell you. Oh I should have told you myself, a long time ago."

"Tell me what, Opal?"

"I just couldn't. I mean, all those years, it would have killed Mommy if I'd told. And then I was busy with my own life, I couldn't be jumping into yours."

"For God's sake, Opal, just spit it out!"

"Wesley Perkins is your father, Lucy. Didn't you look at his nose? His dark eyes?"

"I don't think so. He said there was someone else, Hollis Berry."

"Hollis was only here one night, for heaven's sake," Opal said.

"She went out there, to California. I know that. You've told me that story a jillion times, about her coming home. You always said nobody knew what happened out there. Well, now I know somebody knew. It was Hollis Berry. What was he like? What kind of nose did he have? His name is on my birth certificate, only Mommy always said she made it up."

"I only saw him for a minute, that one night. I guess he was a smooth operator, living in Hollywood. I don't know if she was in love with him, but he didn't marry her. She did make it up. She said she was married to him, and pretended she needed a divorce. She made up his being your daddy. She told Mommy if she told you, she'd take you away forever. It was an ax over Mommy's head, the truth about you. Mommy talked about it before she died, and even then she said, 'We mustn't talk.' I don't know why she didn't want Wesley, but that's who it was. You tell him your birthday and it'll be clear as day. He and your mother were together every day for weeks. The two of you should have looked in a mirror, side by side. Look at his nose, look at yours. He's your father. I'm sure of it."

"I'm not looking for a father. I got over that a long time ago."

"That poor Lila," Opal said. She sighed. "He's sure good to her. That shows you what sort of man he is. He'd be good to you, too. We ought to turn around and go back. Oh, he was handsome back then."

"I ordered us each an Aileen picture from the museum," Lucy said. "It's a wonderful photograph. You're sure cute in it."

"Never as pretty as your mother," Opal said.

"Your box got here yesterday," Zoe said when she met Lucy at the airport. "What's in it?"

"Stuff from my grandmother's house. Albums, a Bible."

"I was hoping it was pecans."

Lucy laughed. "Too early in the year."

"My house is going through."

"That's great. What about Billy?"

"He's got a house in Spain, and his apartment in L.A. We can do seasons, if we get to that."

"I need your help. I'm looking for somebody who used to be a writer in the movies. I mean, a long time ago. The forties. How do I find him?"

"Did you try Information?"

"No listings. Would he be a member of something?"

"I'm going down there the end of the week. Let me see what I can find out."

"It might be important. He knew my mother."

"In that case, I'll try hard," Zoe promised.

When she called from L.A., she said it hadn't turned out to be all that hard.

"He's still alive?"

"He's still a member of the Guild. On pension, I expect. And he guest lectures sometimes at the film school. Highly thought of. You know, I bet I've heard him. Hollis Berry. The school has some of his scripts in their archives. Did you know he was nominated for an Oscar in the early fifties? I asked around, but most of those old movies aren't on tapes. Some of them aren't even extant."

"I don't care about the movies. I just want to find him. Where is he?"

"Santa Monica. Lots of rent control out there. Lots of old movie geezers. I've got an address and phone number. You want to call him?"

For the first time she thought that he might have known about her all along, and not wanted her. She didn't know if she was ready to see him. "I don't know if I want to come right away. I'm going to the physical therapist for a few days."

"Why don't you fly down while I'm here? I'll be here another week or so."

"Okay." She might as well take the plunge. "Tuesday. Find me a motel out there. I want to be close to the beach."

"There's a big range," Zoe said.

"You pick it. Clean, safe, not ritzy. I want to feel really anonymous."

"You're coming to the right place," Zoe said.

"That would be a first," Lucy said.

He lived on Ocean Avenue, not far from the pier. His well-kept brick building sat between an almost identical one and a glitzy high-rise retirement complex. Lucy paced back and forth in front, then went on down Ocean and found a place to sit on a strip of grass on the promenade above the beach. She was going over what to say, trying to hear her own voice, to imagine his.

On a nearby bench she saw a girl sitting on the lap of a large Asian man. The girl was tiny, hunched over, a sweater draped over her shoulders. On the arm of the bench, another man, smaller, was speaking earnestly, with intermittent agitation. Lucy couldn't help being drawn into the drama. Now and then the Asian man said something curt, and the smaller man's voice got louder, then quieted. The girl never spoke. At some point she stood up, and the men traded places. Now she was on the smaller man's lap. The big man sat on the bench, squeezed in, his thigh covering her feet. The girl looked up and saw Lucy watching them. She smiled shyly, then giggled and pressed her head into the neck of the small man. There was a story Lucy couldn't even guess.

She found a pay phone. It was early afternoon, fairly hot, but with a faint breeze off the ocean. She was wearing a sleeveless dress and her ankle-high athletic shoes. At first she had felt self-conscious, but this was California. Nobody cared what she wore.

She rang the number Zoe had given her.

"Mr. Berry? My name is Lucy Hambleton. I'm calling because I'm doing some family history work, and I believe you may have known my mother, Emma Laura Clarehope, in the forties." A loud truck passed. She pressed the phone against her ear and put her finger in the other ear. Still she didn't hear him. "Mr. Berry, are you there?"

"Yes, but you've taken me by surprise. You say you're Emma's daughter? Where are you calling from?"

"I live in Oregon, but I'm here in Santa Monica. I'm trying to fill in gaps in the information I have about her early life. We know she came out to California in early 1943, but we don't know anything about what she did here."

"What does she say?"

"She's dead, sir. She died in 1959. Sir? Mr. Berry?"

"Who sent you my way?"

"Wesley Perkins, in Gallup, New Mexico. He thought she had come out here to see you. A screenwriter friend got your number at the film school. I hope you don't mind."

"I'm sorry. It's so much information all at once. And your mother, dead so young. I'm so saddened. You've caught me as I—I usually lie down this time of day."

"I'm sorry. I can call anytime you say. I hoped you would see me."

"I could see you later in the day."

"Would you like to have dinner with me? I'd be delighted to take you anywhere you say. I don't have a car, though. There seem to be many places to walk. Or I could pick you up in a cab."

"I eat so early—"

"Whatever you say."

Finally, he agreed, and named a place he said both of them could find nearby. She hung up, went back to her motel, and massaged her foot for a long time.

They ate jerked chicken and black beans at a Jamaican cafe on the boulevard. Hollis was a tall, distinguished man, dressed in well-cut trousers and shirt with a linen sports jacket. He was polite, soft-spoken, and attentive. He wanted to hear about Emma, as he called her.

"There's so little to tell," Lucy said. She gave him a brief summary of her own life, because it was the only way she knew to tell Laura's. "I was fifteen when she died. I lived with my grandmother, but really, I was almost grown. A little more than two years later, I was in college. I have a sister four years younger. I think it was worse for her. She hardly knew Mother. She was mostly raised by my aunt."

"I saw her once more. In the summer of 1950. I remember because it was after I was nominated for an Academy Award for Best Original Screenplay. It was for *Angel Time*. She had read my name in the paper."

"I confess I've never seen it. I'm quite a fan of old movies, though. I'd like to see it."

He shrugged. "They've never put it on video. I haven't seen it myself in twenty-five years."

"I remember that my mother came out when I was seven. It caused quite a ruckus in the family. She took my dad's paycheck and left a note. She worried everyone sick. They were afraid she wasn't coming back. Then she did, a week later on the plane—the first in the family to fly—and she was wearing a beautiful hat with a purple voile flower. I remember being taken out to meet her, and I remember the hat. Years later, after she was dead, we found a towel from a Beverly Hills hotel in her things."

"She told me she was married. She had pictures of her children. She said she was very happy."

"What had she come for? Do you know, Mr. Berry?"

"I think it was what you call a sentimental journey. She had had a lot of life compressed into half a year or so here. She wanted to see it again. I bought her the hat, as a gift. She had checked into a Hollywood hotel. I moved her to Beverly Hills. I wanted her to have a memorable visit."

"So you knew her all the while she was here? You know what she was doing?"

He ordered coffee for them, and plates of custard. She saw immediately that she would need to be patient and give him whatever time he needed. She found she didn't mind. At first he had made her think of Gordon—his height and poise, perhaps—but he was a Westerner, where Gordon would never be. For all his elegance, Hollis Berry was a warm, relaxed man. Already, Lucy liked him.

"I met her in Gallup and invited her to come out. She was an extraordinary beauty, ambitious and very bright. She found work right away."

She took a long, deep breath. "So you would know—" She hesitated. "You would know why she left?"

Hollis asked for the check.

"I invited you, Mr. Berry."

"You must let me be the gentleman, at my age. Please."

"Thank you."

They left the cafe together. Outside, he asked her where she was staying. She named the motel.

"Then you have a few blocks that way—" he motioned. "And I that way. Let me walk with you."

"It's not necessary. I'm certainly safe on a busy avenue like this."

"But I like to walk after dinner."

"Very well." She didn't know what to say as they walked. Was he brushing her off? He had answered none of her questions, yet he seemed kind. As she mulled these things over, evidently he was noting her stride.

"I can't help noticing you have a very slight limp," he said.

"I was in an accident last year. I'm mended, but there are residual problems. They're inconsequential."

"I hope I didn't offend you. I've always been observant and overly curious. I used to excuse it because I was a writer, but of course I'm the same person since I retired."

"You certainly didn't offend me. But you have worried me. Will I see you again? Will you tell me about my mother?"

"I would like to know a little about you first, Lucy. May I call you Lucy?"

"Of course."

"And you call me Hollis. We will be friends."

"I'm relieved to hear you say that."

"Do you have time to spread this out, Lucy? It tires me to remember the past. I am working on my files just now. My mornings are filled with memories. Your mother has been on my mind lately. Not that I have ever forgotten her."

"I have all the time in the world, Hollis."

In her room, she kneaded her foot and talked aloud to herself. "He has to work up to it." She realized she was excited. "He will tell me himself, if I don't push it." She had an urge to call Gordon and tell him what she had been learning, but it was midnight in New Hampshire, and she didn't suppose he would want to hear from her. What could he say? Hadn't he supplanted her need for a father?

The idea startled her.

She met Hollis for coffee at mid-morning, and he talked for a little while. He was a good storyteller, with a patience for details. He told her about taking her mother and a friend dancing, and watching them do a sort of Lindy hop. Then he went back to work. His apartment was cheerful and sunny and well furnished. A cherrywood desk was neatly covered with stacks of files and papers. There were numerous photographs on the wall, many of them of people who seemed vaguely familiar, taken with Hollis. Several were of Hollis with a much younger man, taken on the beach or on a verandah. They looked happy.

"I'm writing what I suppose you would call a memoir. It's about the people I've known in the business, going all the way back to nineteen-forty. Only it's not about the famous people who waved to me on sets or confided to me in a single lapse of judgment. It's about the people I knew and liked and admired who disappeared from the business. There are a lot of them. Writers and costumers and directors and actors and makeup artists. You name it. In the mid-fifties I went to Paris for two years to get away from the blacklisting. I hadn't been targeted, but I knew that sooner or later they'd call me. Some of my friends were lost to that. Others just never made it. Some remain a mystery."

"What an interesting notion. Will you try to publish it?" She was embarrassed at her question as soon as it was out. Why else would he be writing?

He said, though, that he thought he would probably donate it to the film school archives. "I understand there are young people who care about this sort of thing. For me, it's an act of ordering, that's all," he said. "I seem to need it."

"As do I," she said. "I feel this terribly deep need to know about my mother. Her whole life seems like a mystery to me, even the parts that include me."

"We'll start at the beginning," he said.

She met him again at the end of the morning for a sandwich or a bowl of soup, and then they separated to rest. Later in the afternoon they strolled down by the beach and found a bench. He told her about meeting Emma Laura at the railroad station. He remembered what she wore. He told her about her part in *Jane Eyre*. He invited her to come back in the evening and watch it in his apartment. They stopped the tape and started over ten times. Lucy was gulping. Then she got the hiccups. She looked at the tiny image on the stopped screen—Hollis said it was her mother—and she asked, expecting no reply, "Why didn't she tell me?" Hollis insisted on sending her home in a taxi.

The next day he told her about the screen test, and the early parts.

"What happened?" she asked. She didn't want to make him leave anything out, but she wanted to know how her mother had been sent, pregnant and unmarried, away from her California promise.

"I had to go east in the spring. I went to work for the Office of War Information. She left while I was gone. She left no word. For a long time, I waited to hear from her. By the time I did—seven years!—she was a different person. She called me from a small hotel in Hollywood. She said she only had a few days. That's why I moved her to Beverly Hills. I wanted her to feel special. I put her on her plane to go home. I knew I'd never see her again. She wouldn't even give me her address. She said there was only Hollywood and not-Hollywood."

"I see. I was thinking more of the early part, when she first came."

They were suddenly awkward with one another. Lucy excused herself, but Hollis said, as he let her out of the apartment, "Tomorrow, come and stay the morning. I'll tell you the rest of it. But I'm too tired now. Forgive me." He shook her hand, as he did every night. "Sleep well, Lucy."

He let her in with a wave of the hand. He was on the phone. She studied the photographs of him with the young man. He had to be his son. There was such an easiness between them, and a certain similarity in looks—the long slim bodies, the elegant features.

He had laid out rolls and cheese to eat with their coffee.

"You've been generous with your time," she said. "I appreciate it."

He set his cup down. "I loved your mother."

"Someone told me that she loved you."

"Yes," he said.

Lucy looked up at the photographs. "Is his mother dead?"

"What do you mean?"

She got up and touched the frame of the photograph. "You must have loved his mother more," she said. She knew she was being horrible, but the words came of their own accord. "Not to have sent her away."

"Lucy, you don't understand."

Her voice trembled. "I didn't know that Charlie Widemar wasn't my father until Mother died. Afterwards, I told myself I didn't care who the real person was. I loved Charlie, and I didn't want to know. As I got older, sometimes it crossed my mind, like a leaf in a breeze—"

"Lucy, you don't understand, dear."

"I know, I know. I don't understand what the times were like. I don't understand the war. Or the forties. Or was it religion? You didn't want her, did you? It just would help if you could tell me why. You seem like a good person, I'll believe what you tell me. It's not fair for you to know something about her that I don't know. It's not right for you to keep anything from me. Even if it's something bad, I want to know. I want to know my mother."

She didn't realize that she was pushing against the photograph so hard. Suddenly her finger slipped and the frame twisted away hard, in an arc, and settled again, crooked. "Oh, I'm sorry!" she said.

Hollis stepped over beside her and gently straightened the photograph. "You really do misunderstand."

"He's very handsome, your son," she said. "Does he live here? In California?"

"He's dead, Lucy."

"Oh my God, I'm so sorry."

He reached for her hands. "My dear, Dominic wasn't my son. He was my beloved companion of many years. I lost him five years ago. He drowned. He was only forty." He glanced at the photograph again, then back at Lucy. "Of course, the photograph was taken years ago, when we were young and happy."

She felt she might swoon. "I'm so sorry. Oh, I've made a fool of myself."

"Here, dear, sit down." He led her to the couch, then sat beside her. "The only woman I ever loved was your mother, but it was never what you were thinking. I wasn't capable of that kind of passion. When she told me she was pregnant, I said I would help her do anything she wanted, but I also said I thought we should marry. I would have married her, but she said no. And of course she was right to refuse me. I would have cheated her of a full love, which she went on to find."

In a tiny voice, Lucy said, "You aren't my father?"

He pulled her against him as she began crying. "I'm not your father, child, but I would be very happy to be your friend."

Laurie had a beautiful pale gold tan and an all-suffering air. Lucy and Zoe had driven up from L.A. and Bliss had made lunch—she had enlisted Laurie in its preparation—and they were sitting on the patio under an awning. Bliss had set the table with lovely Italian pottery and flowers from her cutting garden. In spite of her initial nervousness, Lucy felt relaxed. She was seated out of Laurie's direct line of vision. Her daughter picked at her food delicately while the women talked lightly of nothing. Once, Zoe shared a bit of gossip about an actor in a new film, and Laurie said, "I read a review that sounds like you'd like it, Mother," and they all looked at her, as surprised as if she had cried out. Finally, Bliss sent Laurie off to get the dessert fruit. She looked at Zoe, then back to Lucy, awkwardly, and Lucy said, "Zoe's my best friend, Bliss."

"Gordon won't talk to me," Bliss said. "Not about his defection. I confess astonishment and dismay and all my sympathy for you. Whatever was going on with his professional life—or with you— I would never have expected him to go away like this."

"Thank you, Bliss. It's not as bad as it looks."

"It isn't?" Zoe asked wryly, one brow raised.

"I've had almost two months to get used to it," Lucy said. Bliss, apparently disbelieving, smiled sympathetically. "I'm serious, Bliss," Lucy said. "For the first time in nearly twenty-five years, what I choose to do doesn't really matter to Gordon. It's very freeing."

"What is it you are doing?" Bliss asked.

"Ah, but that's the good part. I don't know yet. First I have to mend things with Laurie. She's been angry with me for a long while."

"I don't think she's angry now," Bliss said. She was fiddling with her cutlery. "I'm sure it was Gordon leaving. Girls always blame their mothers for everything."

"I hope she's not," Lucy said.

"She does need to talk to you," Bliss said.

"Of course."

Just then Laurie appeared with a beautiful platter of fruit.

"How do people live without wonderful lunches?" Zoe asked brightly, helping herself. "How will I go back to yogurt!"

"We ate so many berries at the summer house, I thought my skin would turn blue," Laurie said. She scooped up a spoonful of raspberries and put them on her mother's plate.

"Why, thank you," Lucy said.

Bliss said, "I'll make coffee."

Zoe said, "Let me help."

Lucy and Laurie were alone. Lucy said, "I hope you aren't angry with me now."

Laurie, on the spot, shrugged and didn't quite look at her mother. "I'm okay," she said. Lucy thought she was struggling to say something else, so she waited in patient silence. Finally, Laurie said, "I'm all over—what happened—you know."

"I'm glad you feel that way."

Laurie held her hand up as if to examine her nails. Enough said, Lucy took that to mean. To change the subject, she said, "I've met some people who knew my mother when she was young."

"That's nice," Laurie said. She seemed unimpressed.

"One of them wrote for the movies in the forties. He's a very interesting person."

"That's nice."

"She had some little parts in movies herself, isn't that amazing?" When Laurie didn't answer, Lucy asked, "Do you have something on your mind? Did you have fun at the beach?"

"I heard Lynnie tell Daddy that there has never been a divorce in the family. Are you and Daddy getting divorced?"

"There's been no discussion of it. I expect he's very busy with school right now. I don't think either of us knows. There's no hurry, Laurie. And I can promise you, we'll never put you through anything nasty and awful. We have had too much, and we love you too much." She smiled. "And aren't we Hambletons?"

"Bliss says you are brave and strong. She says she admires you."

Lucy, surprised, said, "That's nice of her. I would say I am neither of those things, but I am stubborn."

"Everybody's upset with Daddy."

"It's really not anyone's business but ours."

"Oh, Mother, you know what the family's like. Everything is everybody's business."

"I'll be going home in a few days. Zoe's staying with me, but she'll be out before you get back."

"I need to talk to you about that."

"You do?" It hadn't crossed Lucy's mind that Laurie might mind Zoe. "She's not in your room. Nobody goes in your room, sweetheart."

"Mommy?"

Uh-oh, Lucy thought.

"I'm not going to go home, okay? I'm going to stay here with Aunt Bliss and Uncle Ted. They want me to. There's a Catholic high school here. I could go to that."

"Have you talked to your father about this?"

"I don't see why he has any say."

She is still angry, Lucy thought. "He'll like the Catholic high school part," she conceded.

"You don't mind?" Laurie's gaze was wide and surprised.

Lucy wanted to say the right thing. "I want you to be happy," she said. Truthfully, it was her only ambition for her.

Bliss and Zoe came back with coffee. By the time it was poured, Bliss's younger daughter, Caroline, had driven up with her kids. Laurie excused herself and ran to greet them.

"She told me," Lucy said to Bliss.

Zoe said, "I'd really like to look over your garden, Bliss," and left the table.

The kids ran past the table. There were three of them, two boys and a girl in the middle. Caroline came after them, a bit breathless, followed by Laurie. The two young women looked like sisters, with their long blonde hair and beautiful bony bodies.

Lucy and Caroline embraced and Caroline took a cup of coffee. Laurie said she was going to look after the kids.

"I guess you'll have a willing babysitter this year," Lucy said. Caroline and Bliss exchanged glances.

"It's all right," Lucy said. "To tell you the truth, I don't mind at all. I grew up in other people's houses. Even convents. This has always been Laurie's second home." She was eager to leave. Seeing their expressions, she said, "Should I make a fuss? She wants to stay here. She's happy here."

"Only if it's okay with you," Bliss said. "I do love her. I feel involved with her in a way I wasn't with my own—" She looked at Caroline wistfully, Lucy thought. Or was it regretfully?

"You know I don't want to interfere," Bliss said.

"Well, you are looking after my child," Lucy said. Realizing she might be misunderstood, she hastened to add, "for which I am eternally grateful."

Caroline excused herself to look for her children.

"I can hardly remember not knowing you," Bliss said. "My sister is much stranger to me than you. I don't relate to her life at all anymore, though it might have been my life, if we had simply stayed in the East. You have jumbled my heart from the beginning, kept me astir with affection and concern, and envy, too."

"Envy!"

"At your freedom. Your sense of selfhood. All of us kids had been bent to Bell's will. We girls married men who could have been our brothers. Only Gordon chose new blood. I don't think he understood what he had done. I used to think: He'll never make her conform. He'll never change her."

"That certainly turned out to be true, didn't it?" Lucy said ruefully, but she discovered that she did feel a small pinch of pride.

"Someday Laurie will appreciate those things about you."

"The things that ran off her father?"

"It was his idea."

Lucy said they ought to go. She stood and waved at Zoe across the yard. "The only thing is," she said to Bliss as they said their good-byes, "I'm wondering if all these changes aren't irreversible. All of a sudden I can't imagine any of us living in that house in Oregon again. I can't imagine the pieces going back together." They all looked at one another awkwardly. Zoe arrived, keys out.

Bliss said, "Come again, Zoe." To Lucy, "Bell will be sorry she didn't see you." The old woman had been asleep through lunch. At ninety, she lived on her own schedule.

"Next time," Lucy said.

"Any time, you know that," Bliss said.

"We should never have left you," Lucy said, and kissed Bliss goodbye. Bliss didn't reply.

In the car, Zoe said, "That went okay, did it?"

Lucy switched on the radio. Puccini. "The Hambleton maw has swallowed my daughter."

"Did you put up a fight?"

"Not for a minute." *The only way to be free,* she thought, *is to give up love.* Maybe her mother had known that, withdrawing, year after year, until she disappeared into her own death.

She reached down and undid her shoe.

She knew she would have to find work. There would be enough money, but also too much time. She thought perhaps on one of the university campuses she could qualify for one of the kinds of posts she had once mocked: administrative assistants who went over candidacy forms. Financial aid officers. Library aides. One day, walking, she came across a thrift shop. The clothes were all donated; the proceeds went to help women in all sorts of trouble. She bought two well-washed cotton knit dresses—three dollars each!—and gave the clerk a twenty-dollar bill, no change, thank you. Maybe she could do something like that, she thought. She remembered the doctor's wife, asking her to volunteer at the language center. She was ashamed, remembering her brusqueness. Maybe she could teach. She saw ads for a center that trained people to teach English as a foreign language. There were so many immigrants. They wouldn't ask what she had been doing for a quarter century. They wouldn't judge.

What did it matter, so long as her days were filled? For now, her life was busy. She kept a calendar again. She rented an apartment below the avenue, just across from the beach. She could walk to Hollis's apartment in ten minutes. She had two rooms and a tiny kitchenette in a shabby clapboard building on a side street near the pier. She had to climb stone steps to reach it, but there was a solid

290

wooden railing, and she thought of it as physical therapy. Her legs had grown stronger.

The windows swung out. Over the roof of the house below her she could see the sea. A haphazard rock garden of cactus, roses, and climbing flowers below her window delighted her; none of it was her responsibility.

The bedroom was tiny. A double bed almost filled the room, but she squeezed in a narrow table. On it she put her notes and photographs, and the contents of the box Opal had sent her. A family album. Lucy's baby book, with her mother's careful annotations. The Bible, in which her grandmother had pasted announcements of family deaths, and had copied sentimental poems. Ira's letters from Arizona, the faded pencil scrawls barely legible. Laura's prayer book, marked with underlined and starred passages. On one of the first pages, she had written out "St. Teresa's Bookmark": *Let naught disturb thee,/Naught fright thee ever* ... Lucy didn't spend time with these things. She glanced over them, put them into new manuscript boxes, and made brief entries into a notebook she had bought for that purpose. Mostly, she wrote questions as they occurred to her. Were the prayers and readings a comfort to Laura? Did she ever stop believing? Why had she stopped going to the Catholic church in Odessa? Had she thought she was sinning when she fell in love with her doctor? Was their love physical? Had she loved Charlie? Why had she told Hollis she was "very happy"? Had she ever been very happy?

Had she hastened her imminent death with too many pills? Had she thought of Lucy at the end?

She tried not to concern herself with the impossibility of ever knowing the answers to her questions. It helped to write them down; it took them out of her. She merely wished to separate the artifacts from the enigma. She thought—was it her old lessons in historiography?—that if she knew what could be known (facts!), she could let the unknown go. She intended, later in the year, to write for birth, marriage, and death certificates; to go out to Aileen with Opal, though it would surely be changed; to visit Laura's grave in Wichita Falls. She did not think, yet, of interpretation. She compiled.

One night, after studying the photograph from the museum in Lubbock, she tried to write about it: where it was taken, when. The way it seemed to bleed off the page. One thought led to another, until she had filled half a dozen notebook pages. Then she was too sleepy to continue; she set it aside for another time.

Everything that Hollis told her she entered in her notebook.

He took her to see Pilar Andreatta, the former Mrs. Parrish. A widow in her late seventies, she lived in an elegant condominium in Pacific Palisades. She was thin; she reminded Lucy of photographs of the Duchess of Windsor. Hollis went for a stroll in the garden. Mrs. Andreatta took Lucy out onto a large balcony. A maid served them tea. Mrs. Andreatta told Lucy that she remembered her mother well. She had been a beautiful girl; they had wanted to adopt her baby, and had taken her into their home. She spoke graciously, but Lucy detected an undertone of bitterness. Of course Laura had disappointed them. Emma Laura.

"Was there anything in particular that happened?" Lucy asked. "To make her go?"

Mrs. Andreatta said she had seen it coming as Emma grew larger with child. "We were very close friends," she said, "but I didn't know how to ask her what she wanted. I felt she had to say. We used to pray the rosary together, and take long drives. I was with her almost constantly. One night she said she wanted to go home to her mother. She never told you about this?"

"No, ma'am. I knew nothing about her time in California. Of course, I am fascinated. A whole new side of her has come to light for me."

"My husband would have made her a movie star, but I think she didn't trust him," Mrs. Andreatta said. "Although by the fifties, there wasn't much call for her type. Tiny, pale, ethereal." She smiled. "She was no Marilyn, was she?"

"I don't know about that," Lucy said stiffly. "I think of them both as vulnerable women."

"Of course I didn't know her as a real grown-up," Mrs. Andreatta said. "When she left my house, she was still only a girl."

Lucy set her cup down. "I should be going."

"She wouldn't let me take her to the train station. I had to put her in a taxi. It was quite upsetting."

"I'm sure," Lucy said.

On their way out, Mrs. Andreatta showed Lucy her display of photographs. "Mr. Parrish and I divorced shortly after the war was over. I married my doctor and had four children. Funny, isn't it? Did Emma have other children?"

"I have a sister."

"She was much blonder than you."

"She was seventeen," Lucy said, and offered her hand. Mrs. Andreatta took it very briefly.

"I didn't much like her," Lucy told Hollis. "There's residual feeling there. I guess Mother hurt her."

"Or the other way around," Hollis said. "I wish I had been here."

"Me, too," Lucy said.

"Maybe you should call Wesley Perkins," Hollis said.

"Don't you start," Lucy said, but there was something nice in the easiness with which she could speak to him.

He smiled. "You may not have all day, you know," he said.

Soon after, Hollis took her to the station. They sat in the waiting room, then walked down the long gates. "I should have thought to bring you here before," he said. "It's the same as then."

They sat at small tables and drank coffee. She told him the story about Laura's arrival in Wichita Falls. She tried to remember it exactly the way Opal always told it.

He said, "She couldn't give you up. It's actually quite simple, and beautiful."

"I guess it is," she said. "Do you think it's true that she could have been in movies?"

"She already had been."

"In bigger roles?"

"I think so. How can we know? I'll tell you this, though, Lucy. When she decided to go home to have her baby—to have you, and raise you—*she* thought she could have been a movie star instead. She decided the price was too high. She chose you."

"I'll never understand her, will I?" Lucy said. "I'll go through everything I have, and there will be more questions than when I began. For years I thought she was a weak, pathetic woman, maybe an adulteress, and on top of that I thought she didn't fight hard enough to live. Maybe I even thought I was just like her, because I couldn't help being so. Now you're telling me she was a sweet vulnerable girl in the world's oldest trouble, and she decided not to wriggle out of it. Maybe that's all I really need to know about her, that she wanted me enough to keep me when she could have done well to give me away. That she was brave enough to live her life and give me mine." Of course she was crying then.

Hollis clasped her hands in his. "I wrote over a hundred screenplays, not counting hundreds more false starts. If I learned anything, it's that character is too deep to catch in a single storyline. What really moves us—what makes the great stories, and there aren't so many of them—is the inevitability of character. The destiny. All we see is the arc. We'll never penetrate the secrets of the living, let alone the dead. I've spent my whole life trying to understand people, and all I've learned is that the deeper we look, the greater the mystery. At the core, each person is unknowable. Maybe that's the soul? I have to respect that. The mystery, in fact, is what I've loved the most, in people and in stories as well.

"Now you, you've got to decide what you want to do with your questions. You can fall into Emma Laura's mystery and be lost, as in a void; or you can explore it for the wonder it is, knowing that, in the end, it will elude you. Or you can shut it away and let it go."

"I don't want to let her go, ever. If I do that, she's really dead."

"She is dead," he said gently.

"Not to me. Never to me. I just have to listen to her in a different way. I need her. I need her voice. I need my mother. Recently, I saw a woman with Alzheimer's. Wesley's wife. I'd never met anyone like that before. It wasn't just forgetfulness, it was a woman living in that void you talked about. All knowing was gone, as if she had never had a life. And her with five children! I haven't been able to get her out of my mind. The memory goes, and then who are you? It's the worst thing. Worse than dying. I won't let my mother be lost unless that happens to me. I won't let it happen because it might be easier for me. And it wouldn't. It would be terrible to live without her. Don't you understand, Hollis? I still need my mother."

"But life is more than our memories, Lucy! You need her, but in such a way that she doesn't hold you back from your life. She wouldn't have wanted to stall you. She loved life." He sighed. "Listen to me advising you, I with my own losses. When Dominic died, I thought I would die, too. All I knew to do was to get busy. Now what have I done? I've immersed myself in the past! Of course, I'm much older than you, Lucy. It seems somehow more suitable."

"I've been thinking about your project," she said. "I think you're underestimating the worth of it. I have something to propose."

She found a housesitter for the Oregon house and spent a week putting it in order. She moved a lot of personal things into Laurie's room and shut it off. She drove her car back to Santa Monica. She waited until she was back in her little apartment to tell Gordon what she had done, and that the house would be free during the Christmas holidays. They needn't decide what to do about it until later.

"Should we meet there for the holidays?" he asked. "You and I and Laurie? Don't you think she'll want that?"

"No. You're expected in Santa Barbara on the twenty-second."

"You'll be there?"

"No. I'm flying to Spain Christmas Day to spend a couple of weeks with Zoe and her friend. I'll see Laurie before I go. Before the twenty-second."

"I think we should talk about that," Gordon said.

"I'm sorry, Gordon, but I don't agree. In fact, I'd prefer not talking at all. Write me if you wish. Tell me whatever you like. God knows I've spent enough years wondering what was on your mind. I don't know if I will answer or not. If ever I don't want to read any more of your letters, I'll mark them *Return to Sender* and send them back."

*   *   *

In late October, Opal brought Murphy out for a visit. They took him to Disneyland. A little older than two years, he knew enough to be overexcited and intolerant of waiting in lines, but they managed to entertain him long enough to convince Opal it had been worth the ordeal. On the drive back to Santa Monica, Opal told Lucy that she had been talking to Wesley every now and then. "He's waiting to hear from you."

"I have no plans to call him," Lucy said.

"I told him the date of your birth. He desperately wants to talk to you, to see you again. He wants to be your father, Lucy."

"I don't know what I want, but I know I can't take on another complicated relationship anytime soon." She supposed they would have blood tests. There were his other children. It was funny to think, but she was as related to them as to Faith, if all you counted was blood.

"He's a nice man. And look how successful he is."

"I've had a successful man, Opal."

"He's a sweet man, he was a sweet boy, you'll see. It'll be a good thing for both of you." Her children had given her no end of heartbreak, she wanted somebody's story to have a happy ending.

"Not right now, Opal. I can't. I don't want to."

"What about Hollis Berry?"

"He's a friend and now a colleague. I'm comfortable with him. We're interested in the same things. By the way, I told him you were coming. He said he would be happy to meet you."

"I met him once already, thank you very much."

"There's no reason not to like him."

"There's no reason to see him."

"He's not in competition with Wesley Perkins. Nobody is. Well, maybe Charlie."

"Charlie!"

"I've been thinking of him so much lately. Faith says he lives in New Mexico, too. Small world, isn't it?" She laughed. They had gone on the "It's a Small World" ride twice at Disneyland. "I don't know how we'd get past all the blank years, though, even if we both wanted to." Thinking of Charlie made her sad.

"I swear, you're as complicated as your mother ever was," Opal said. "But I loved her, and I love you."

"I love you, too," Lucy said. Murphy screeched that he had to poop, and Lucy pulled over to look for an exit.

Laurie came down the first weekend in November. She liked Lucy's apartment. "I would never have imagined you would live in something like this," she said. She stood at the window looking out at the sea. In the sunlight, her hair and her skin and her pale dress were all one shade of whiteness.

They met Hollis for a late breakfast, and Lucy explained to Laurie that he was writing a book about people in the movie business. "And I am assisting him," she said. "With great pleasure."

"Collaborating," Hollis corrected her. "With mutual pleasure. Your mother is doing a lot of research. She's thought of so many things I hadn't." He was more excited about the project than he had ever been. Lucy was digging up material in the film school archives, and in the county libraries. She had found half a dozen of the people on Hollis's list, too, scattered around Southern California, and they had interviewed one makeup artist and a stuntman so far.

"I work all morning with Hollis," Lucy explained, "and then I swim." She had joined a gym with a pool. Once in a while she accompanied Hollis when he visited old colleagues who still lived in the area. One screenwriter was in a rest home in Venice. Hollis had had to introduce Lucy anew each time, but once he described her as his goddaughter, the old friend remembered her at subsequent visits. His memory for the old days was excellent, and entertaining. Lucy mentioned him and then an old cameraman who had been a favorite of Rita Hayworth, but she could see that Laurie wasn't especially interested. She said they ought to go. They had plans. She dreaded the idea that Laurie would show her boredom to Hollis, but Laurie clicked into her Hambleton manners instead. Hollis shook Laurie's hand gravely, and Lucy noted, with a rueful sort of pride, that her daughter had considerable poise. She actually leaned forward and gave Hollis a peck on the cheek.

After they left Hollis, Lucy told Laurie how much she appreciated her poise with him, but Laurie said nothing. Lucy said, finally, "I've learned a lot from him. There are things I want to tell you, sweetheart."

Laurie sighed. "More old stories?" she asked, with the disdain of superior youth. Where were her good manners now? "I know, Mother. Everybody died young and the rest all suffered."

Lucy made herself smile. "I do have an idea of something for us to do. Would you like to visit a studio backlot with me? They're whole little town streets, where they shoot movies."

Laurie said, "Whatever you say, but Mother, you need some lipstick. You look gray on the lips."

Tears sprang to Lucy's eyes. She went into the bathroom and dabbed at them, then put on her brightest color. When she came out, Laurie rewarded her with a big grin.

They drove out to Burbank to tour the Warner Brothers backlot. "Many movies are made like this, rather than on location," Lucy explained. "I thought you'd enjoy seeing the sets. They look so real, but they're made up of some version of styrofoam and plywood and plaster and every kind of fakery." They walked around in a small congenial group. At first Laurie seemed reluctant and bored, but they had a good tour leader, an old, spry woman who said she had retired from working in costumes, and who was full of interesting anecdotes and explanations. They came to a false-front old New York, and the tour guide gave them a few minutes to look around.

Lucy told Laurie about the film her mother had made with Gene Tierney. "It would have been on a set like this, with a bench where she sat in a long dress with a parasol—"

"Your *mother* was in a *movie*?"

"Laurie, I've been telling you that for weeks."

Laurie looked up at the high false buildings. "Can I see it?"

"Remember, it's only a few seconds. There's another one I can get, too. I'll rent the videos and we can look at them over at Hollis's apartment."

The tour guide called them all back together and they walked on into the Wild West. The sun was brilliant and hot. Lucy took off her jacket and carried it, and Laurie's sweater, over her arm. She shifted her burden and pulled a camera out of her bag. In front of a saloon set, she asked Laurie to pose.

"Give me one of those ravishing model looks," she said.

Laurie held her hand up to her eyes. "I can't believe I forgot my sunglasses." Nearby, the guide was telling some of the group about a TV movie that had recently wrapped on this very set.

Laurie said, "I'd rather wait and watch your mother sometime when you're up in Santa Barbara. I don't want to go over to Hollis's again today."

"Why not?"

"Oh, Mother. It's all sort of creepy. All this ancient history. Couldn't we just see a *new* movie and go out to eat? Could I get sunglasses? Could we go to Universal Studios, where they have rides?"

"You'll hate it there," Lucy said. "You will really really hate it."

"Could we?"

Lucy didn't hesitate. "Yes, and yes, and yes," she said.

She felt the sun hot on her face, and the ache in her foot that reminded her she was strong enough to keep going when other people would have quit. She looked at her beautiful, strange child. She wondered if they would ever know one another, if any mother and daughter ever could. At least they had time. Someday Laurie would be grown, and Lucy would be old, and in between there was a whole canvas of possibility. They had time. For now, Lucy could only try to see the plain truth and live a real life, her own life, a present life, something she felt she was only now beginning.

She put the camera up to her eye. "Now, smile," she said. "Look right at me, darling, and give me a great big smile for posterity." She snapped the picture, and another. "Great!" she said. "Great!"

"It's just a picture," Laurie said, but she gave her mother a dazzling smile, and cocked her hip for good measure.

Lucy put the camera away and brushed her hair back with her hand. Over her daughter's shoulder, the buildings looked blurred.

Laurie looked at her closely. "You're crying," she said. "Why are you crying, Mommy? Why are you sad?"

December 7, 1989
Gallup, New Mexico

Dear Lucy,

Your Aunt Opal gave me your address so that I could send you the
enclosed pictures. I have found a considerable number of negatives,
and I am working to organize them and label them. I developed these
for you. They were taken of your mother in Aileen in the spring of 1938.
My mother had just bought a camera from a German man, and I was
learning to use it. It was the first time we had had a camera so easy to
use. That probably sounds funny now, when cameras are simple enough
for children.

I can tell you I shed some tears, looking at these photographs. Isn't
she a pretty girl? Your aunt sent me a photograph of you around that
age, and I can see your mother's expression on you. That same way of
looking right past a person, as if she was seeing something that wasn't
even there.

I am writing to you on Pearl Harbor Day. I expect everyone who was
old enough remembers just where they were on that day in 1941. We
couldn't believe we were so vulnerable. Well, that's the way I feel about
the day I went to your mother's house and nobody was there. It didn't just
happen to me once, it happened to me twice, though the second one hurt
worse. Of course I went on and had a good life with my beloved wife Lila,
but that doesn't mean I didn't love Emma. It breaks my heart to think of
all the years you were growing up and I could have helped you and
helped your mother and she never gave me the chance. I don't know
what she was thinking, and we'll never know, but I would like to make it
up to you in some ways if you would let me, for her sake, and yours, and
mine. I will not push you on this matter, but if you could see your way
clear to it, I would like to invite you to come to Gallup any day you want
for a visit. My daughters, in whom I confide, say they would welcome a
sister in the family, to even things out. I have not talked to the boys as of

yet. I put your picture next to the girls, and I can see it, plain as anything, in the noses. If you want to have a blood test some time for confirmation, I will pay for it, because I have checked and it is an expensive procedure, but if you don't want to, it is entirely unnecessary in my mind. I know when I was with your mother, and I now know when you were born. It's simple arithmetic.

I leave it to you, Lucy. I know I would love you because you are your mother's child, but I would love you for you, too. I am not the smartest man in the state, or the handsomest, that's for sure, but I know I have a heart big enough for one more daughter.

I wait for your reply, when you feel ready. I am sure I am your daddy.

Yours truly,
Wesley Perkins